I0564534

The Ghosts of Anatolia
An Epic Journey to Forgiveness

The Ghosts of Anatolia

An Epic Journey to Forgiveness

STEVEN E. WILSON

H-G BOOKS

The Ghosts of Anatolia: An Epic Journey to Forgiveness
Copyright © 2011 by Steven E. Wilson
All rights reserved under International and
Pan-American Copyright Conventions.
Published in the United States by Hailey-Grey Books
Website: Hailey-Grey-Books.com   SAN: 255-2434

First H-G Books Edition: 2011
Library of Congress Control Number: 2010920945
ISBN 9781732915121

Cover photo from George Grantham Bain Collection.
Library of Congress Prints and Photographs Division
Washington, D.C. 20540
Book design: Janice Phelps Williams, www.janicephelps.com

MANUFACTURED IN THE UNITED STATES OF AMERICA

The Ghosts of Anatolia is a work of fiction.
Any resemblance to actual persons, living or dead, is coincidental.
Historical references and figures are used fictitiously.

Wilson, Steven E. (Steven Eugene), 1951–

The ghosts of Anatolia : an epic journey to forgiveness / Steven E. Wilson. --
Cleveland, Ohio : H-G Books, c2011.

   p. ; cm.

   1. Turkey--History--20th century--Fiction. 2. World War, 1914-1918--
Turkey--Fiction. 3. Turkey--Ethnic relations--History--Fiction. 4.
Forgiveness--Fiction. I. Title.

This book is dedicated to my father, Gilford Eugene Wilson, who fought as a quartermaster on the battleship USS *Mississippi* during World War II at the Marshall Islands and the Battles of Leyte Gulf, where he lost his best friend to a *Kamikaze* attack, and witnessed the signing of the Surrender of Japan while at anchor in Tokyo Harbor near the battleship USS *Missouri*. He taught me to always strive to be the best at everything I do.

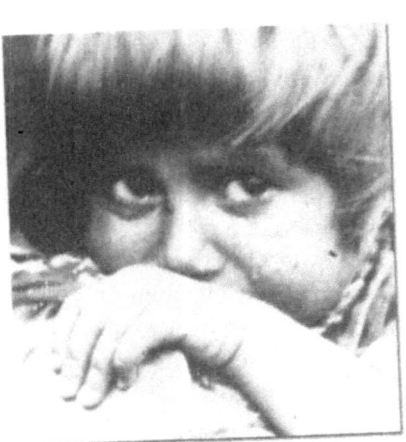

PART ONE

Turkey to Jerusalem

CHAPTER 1

April 1996
Richmond Heights, Ohio

Stooped by rheumatism, Sirak Kazerian bore all the corporal lines and creases expected of a man his age. Yet he retained a sparkle in his heavy-lidded eyes that belied the internal wounds and scars wrought by nine decades of anguish and sorrow. He still had his wits about him, too, unlike many friends who'd long since faded into the murky senile years of loneliness that often precede the grave.

Sirak gripped a wooden cane with his gnarled fingers and rose from the table. He stepped tentatively across the dimly lit kitchen to the stove, and, lifting an old percolator, poured his cup half-full with coffee. Steadying his tremor, he inadvertently banged the pot down on the burner.

He took a drink of the hours-old brew, and grimacing, spit it into the sink. He opened the cupboard, grabbed a coffee bag and shook it. Only a few grounds rattled at the bottom of the bag. "Damn!" he barked. He tossed the bag into a cardboard box in the corner, and re-gripping his cane, shuffled to the window.

Sirak pushed apart the blinds and peered down the street at the mailman walking up the driveway of the fifties-vintage tract home a few doors down. He steadied himself with his cane and wobbled through the living room to the front door. Unlocking the deadbolt, he stepped outside, fished his keys out of his pocket and locked the door behind him.

"Good morning, Doctor Kazerian," a cheerful voice called out.

Sirak turned on the steps. "Hello, Samuel," he replied to the mailman. "You got anything for me besides junk?"

Samuel fingered through a stack of letters. "An electric bill," he offered, smiling through glasses that magnified his eyes to nearly twice their natural size.

"Junk mail and bills....That's all I ever get anymore."

"Now, now, Doc... I know that's not true. I brought you a card from your great-grandsons just last week."

"Yeah, I suppose you did."

Samuel turned and headed up the walk. "Have a blessed day, sir," he called back over his shoulder

"Thanks, Sam," Sirak called after him. "See you tomorrow." He turned back to the door and stuffed the envelopes into the mail slot. Zipping his jacket, he hobbled down the sidewalk and across the street—his cane click-clicking with each step.

Despite the chill in the air and painful stiffness in his knees, Sirak made his way slowly up the street to the corner and turned onto Richmond Road. Automobile traffic was light, even for a Saturday morning. He stopped in front of a large home where several workers were busy with spring cleanup.

One of the workmen waved and walked toward him across the grass. "Hey, Doctor Kazerian, how'ya been?"

"Much better, thank you. How about you, Rudy?"

"We're busier than two-peckered billy goats, Doc. What a winter, huh? Any damage to your place?"

"I lost those saplings you planted in the backyard. The blizzard split the trunks nearly to the ground."

"That was one hell of a storm. Shaker Heights lost most of the new trees they planted down Shaker Boulevard. What about yours—want me to replace 'em?"

"Why bother? Just remove the trunks when you get around to it."

"How 'bout the end of next week?"

"Whenever—I don't get outside much anymore."

"Will do. Where ya headed, Doc?"

"Over to the coffee shop."

"D'ya wanna a ride? Martin can take you over in the truck."

"No thanks, Rudy," Sirak replied. "I'm supposed to walk a block or two every day—doctor's orders."

"Well, take care of yourself. I'll see you next week."

Sirak nodded and limped up the street for another half-block, before heading diagonally across a parking lot toward a line of shops. He scooted through the parked cars and, taking a step onto the sidewalk, stopped dead in his tracks. He stared for several moments at two middle-aged men sitting on a bench outside a coffee shop. They were engaged in an animated conversation peppered with laughter.

Sirak clenched his teeth with rage and charged up the walk. He lifted his cane over his head and brought it down with a resounding crack on the nearest man's head.

"Son-of-a-bitch!" the man howled. He dropped his coffee cup on the sidewalk, leaped to his feet and turned to face his attacker. Short and stout, with a swarthy complexion, his head was hairless, except for small patches above his ears. A trickle of blood streamed down his forehead.

The other man jumped up from the bench and grabbed the cane. "Papa!" he shouted incredulously. "What are you doing?"

Several other people stopped to watch. A deliveryman with a crate of milk gawked in disbelief.

"I warned him!" Sirak bellowed vehemently. "I warned him to stay away from you. For God's sake, Keri, he killed your brother!"

"He did not, Papa. George had nothing..."

"Yes, he did!" Sirak yelled breathlessly, his face red as a beet. "This bastard killed Ara, just as if he pulled the trigger himself."

Sirak shuffled to a bench. Gasping for air, he sat down.

The coffee shop door opened and a young man in an apron rushed outside. "Here, sir," he said, handing a stack of paper towels to the bloody man. "I called the police."

"You idiot!" the bleeding man snarled. He pressed the towels against the top of his head. "Call them back and tell them not to come. Tell them it was an accident."

"But, sir," the young man protested, "he busted your head..."

"Call them back, damn it! I'm alright."

The young man shook his head, and stepped back inside the coffee shop.

"Let me drive you to the hospital," Keri said. He glanced sternly at his father.

The man checked his bleeding with a fresh towel. "No, I'm okay."

Keri reached out apologetically. "George, I'm sorry."

"It's okay," he replied. Holding the towel against his head, he walked to a car in the parking lot and opened the door. "Get him to a shrink," he yelled, before ducking into the car. He revved the engine, backed the car up and squealed out of the lot.

Keri turned back to his father and pulled him up from the bench. "Come on, Papa. I'll drive you home."

"I told you to stay away from Liralian," Sirak muttered unabashedly.

Keri held his tongue. He led his father through the gawking spectators to the passenger's side of his blue Toyota.

The two men rode back to Sirak's house in tortured silence. Keri helped his father into the house and set him in a chair in the living room.

"Papa, listen to me. I went to the coffee shop and George happened to be there. Before today, I hadn't seen him in years."

"I don't want you anywhere near that degenerate. How can you speak to him? Ara's blood is on his hands. And, besides that, he's a Marxist."

"No, he's not. George assured me he didn't know what happened to Ara in Beirut. It's been thirteen years, Papa. It's time to let it go."

"He was there," Sirak said pointedly.

"Papa, a lot of people were in Beirut back then."

Sirak took a deep breath and sighed. "George Liralian knows what Ara got mixed up in. If he wanted to, he could tell us what happened. I'll never forgive him until he tells me what he knows about the death of my son, and *your* brother. I expect you to respect my feelings."

"What does it matter, Papa? Ara is dead, and he'll still be dead even if we somehow figure out who killed him."

"It matters to me," Sirak whispered. "Look at the photograph on the wall." He pointed at a yellowed image of two teenagers beaming with joy. Each boy was standing with one foot on the pedal of a bicycle. "Have you forgotten your brother?"

Keri turned and peered across the room at the photo. "No, Papa, I haven't forgotten."

"I remember like it was yesterday. You two were all I had left, and Ara was taken from us in the blink of an eye. I want to know why. George knows, but he's not telling. Until he does, nobody in this family will speak to him."

Keri sat in a chair across from his father. Staring introspectively at the floor for several moments, he finally looked up and peered into his father's deeply furrowed eyes. "Papa, I could hold you to that same standard."

Sirak's eyes narrowed warily. "What are you saying?"

"I'm fifty-nine years old. *Fifty-nine.* What's the big secret? Why do you never talk about our family? Ara and I grew up knowing next to nothing about our mother, our aunts and uncles, or our grandparents. How many times have I asked you? A hundred? Five hundred?"

Sirak stared back in agonizing silence, and finally looked away, muttering to himself.

"What, Papa?" Keri persisted.

"I said, it's too painful."

"What's too painful?"

Sirak cupped his forehead with his hand and stared down at his feet. "Everything," he muttered. He looked up at his son, and tears were pooling in his sorrowful eyes. "The things that happened to our family... to your grandmother."

"I want to know, Papa. Your grandchildren want to know, too. There's no reason to shelter us anymore."

"It's not you, Keri. I haven't spoken a word about what happened to anyone, except Ara, in seventy years...and telling your brother was the worst mistake I ever made."

"Why, Papa? Why was that a mistake?"

"Because it killed him!" Sirak snapped. "Telling your brother killed him, and now I'll have to live with that for the rest of my life."

"Information about our family didn't kill Ara, Papa. Evil killed Ara."

"But if I hadn't told..."

"No, it was not your fault," Keri interrupted. "And now it's time you told me, too. Neither one of us is getting any younger; I deserve to know about our family."

"Son, I love you *so* much," Sirak whispered. "You and your children are all I have left."

"We love you, too, Papa, but you've endured this burden in silence for too long. Please, tell me—what happened?"

Sirak inhaled deeply and exhaled through pursed lips. "God help me," he muttered, wiping a sleeve across his eyes. He took another deep breath. "We lived on a small farm just outside of the village of Seghir, a few miles east of the great walled city, Diyarbekir, in southern Anatolia."

"In present-day Turkey, right?"

"That's right. We were poor cotton farmers eking out an existence on the land your great grandfather, Misak Kazerian, left to your grandfather, Mourad, and your great uncle, Bedros. Let's see, in 1914 I was six years old. I know Papa was forty-six when I was born, so he and Mama would have been fifty-two and thirty-eight then."

"What was your mother's name?"

"Kristina. Her maiden name was Malekian. She was a beautiful, loving woman. I had three older brothers. Alek was twenty. I remember that because he had to report to the army that year. Stepannos was a year or two younger, and Mikael must have been about twelve. I also had two sisters. Flora would've been fifteen. She looked just like our mother. My younger sister, your aunt Izabella, was only four or five at that time."

"So there were six children in the family?"

"Yes." A hint of a smile came to Sirak's lips, as long-suppressed memories came flooding back. "What a great family it was, too. We were poor, but so happy—at least until the war destroyed everything." He shook his head pensively. "Where do I begin?"

"Begin where you can, Papa. I want to hear what happened."

CHAPTER 2

September 8, 1914
Ten kilometers east of Diyarbekir, the Ottoman Empire

Mourad, his trousers caked with mud, turned at the whinny of a horse. He leaned his shovel against an old stump and wiped a muddy sleeve across his brow. As he peered through the dazzling afternoon sunlight, a lone rider trotted up the path from the main road. The horse scattered a bevy of squawking chickens into the adjoining field.

Suddenly, a broad grin broke across Mourad's face. "Bedros!" he called out, jogging up the path. "What a surprise! It's so good to see you. I wish we'd known you were coming."

"Mourad, my brother," Bedros sighed wearily as he dismounted his horse and hugged his younger sibling. "My letter didn't reach you? I sent it three months ago."

"We never got it. You've lost so much weight. Are you sick?"

"I had a nasty bout of the grippe last winter. It took me months to regain my strength, but I'm much better now. How's Mother?"

"She's a lot worse. Her joints are so stiff she rarely gets out of bed. Then, last spring, she began losing a lot of weight. It's her heart. The doctor said she might not make it to winter."

— 8 —

"Thank God I came. I wish I'd brought the family, but the roads are too hazardous. The political situation is deteriorating."

"How is Liza?"

"Liza is well, but she's fretted day and night since Garo and Aren reported for the mobilization. We haven't heard anything from them since they left home in August."

"God bless you both," Mourad replied understandingly. "There's nothing worse than not knowing what's happening. We haven't heard from Alek, either."

"Alek?" Bedros queried, his heavy black eyebrows shooting up with surprise. "He's only nineteen."

"No, Brother, Alek turned twenty this summer."

"God help us," Bedros sighed. He shook his head. "I pray our country will stay out of this insane war, but I fear the worst."

"How are Alis and Mairan?"

"They're just fine. Alis finished her nursing apprenticeship, and Mairan recently expressed an interest in becoming a teacher."

"Uncle Bedros!" a curly-headed young boy shrieked. He ran headlong from the house and jumped for joy.

"Sirak, my spirited bear cub!" Bedros lifted the boy, twirled him into the air and set him on his shoulders. "You've gotten so big. How's my favorite nephew?"

"I'm fine, Uncle. You know what?"

Bedros chuckled. "What?"

"Papa taught me to ride the plow horse this summer. Then, last week, he let me ride my colt for the first time."

Bedros grinned at Mourad. "My, you really are getting big. Soon you'll be old enough to help your papa plow the field. How old are you now?"

"I'm six and a half. Papa, can we show Uncle Bedros how I ride?" the boy pleaded excitedly. His dark eyes sparkled with excitement.

"Not today. Uncle Bedros has ridden a long way and he's very tired. We can all take a ride together tomorrow. Can you stay, Bedros?"

"Yes, of course; I'd hoped to stay a few days while I take care of business here in Diyarbekir. Would Kristina mind?"

"What do you mean, would she mind?" Mourad scoffed. He took his brother's reins. His horse, its flanks glistening with sweat, at first resisted his tug, but finally yielded. "Papa left this farm to both of us."

The two men walked across the farmyard to a ramshackle barn with its roof bowed at one end. Mourad lifted his brother's bags down from the horse's back and led the old mare into an empty stall. He poured water into the trough and carried feed from stores on the opposite side of the barn.

Sirak pulled Bedros out the rear door of the barn. He led him to the corral, where two yearling colts were running free.

The shorter of the two colts, a chestnut with white accents on his nose and legs, kicked up his heels. He bolted past his brother, and whirled around to face the visitors. Tossing his head back, he whinnied, trotted to the fence, stuck his head through the rails, and gently nuzzled Sirak's arm.

Sirak climbed up on the fence and stroked the horse's neck. "Isn't he beautiful, Uncle?"

"He's magnificent," Bedros uttered admiringly. He shaded his eyes from the bright sunlight and watched the colt bolt away to the back of the enclosure.

"Papa gave him to me for my very own."

"He's a fine horse. What's his name?"

"Tiran, and his brother over there is Alexander."

Bedros leaned against the fence and watched the colt gallop toward the barn. "Tiran's destined to be a fine riding horse, Sirak. He reminds me of the horse your grandfather gave me when I was a boy. I named him Tartus. To this day, he's the best horse I ever owned."

Mourad walked from the barn carrying Bedros' bags. "I watered and fed your horse. Let's go inside, and I'll ask Kristina to prepare you something to eat."

"Thank you, Brother. Where are Stepannos and Mikael?"

"A new American missionary school opened in Chunkoush last year. I let them go whenever I can. They attend full time, now that we've picked the cotton. They'll be home later this afternoon. Come on, let's go inside."

Bedros took his bags and the two men walked to the house.

Mourad opened the front door. He stepped inside the cramped front room. The kitchen was tucked in one corner and a hall in the back led to the bedrooms.

Kristina, a slender, fair-skinned woman, her dark-brown hair covered with a scarf, turned from the stove at the sound of the door. "Bedros!" she exclaimed. She brushed past her daughter and kissed him on the cheek. "You look so tired. Is everything okay?"

"Everything's fine. I just need a little rest and a bit of your wonderful cooking."

She smiled. Tonight I'll prepare a special dinner just for you. Where's Liza?"

"She decided to stay in Istanbul with the children." Bedros squatted and smiled at a slight, dark-haired young girl sitting on the floor playing with a tattered doll. "Izabella, my little princess, are you ready to give your Uncle Bedros a hug?"

The dark-haired cherub looked up and shook her head.

"No hug? Have you forgotten who gave you that doll? Then, I guess you're not interested in the new doll I brought for you." Bedros set his bag down, and crouching to the floor, fished through the bottom. He pulled out a small red ball and held it out to Sirak. "This is for you, Nephew."

Sirak beamed with joy. He took the ball and turned it over in his hands.

Izabella got up from the floor and shuffled shyly toward her uncle.

Smiling broadly, Bedros pulled out a baby doll dressed in pink night-clothes, and held it up. "Do you like it? Your Aunt Liza made the clothes herself."

Izabella, her eyes sparkling, glanced at her mother. Kristina smiled reassuringly and nodded. Finally, Izabella reached for the doll, but Bedros jerked it back.

"Oh, no! First, I want a hug."

Izabella frowned, and glanced at her mother.

"Your uncle Bedros traveled a long way to see you, Izabella," Kristina reassured. "Go ahead, give him a hug."

Izabella peeked out from beneath her long bangs. Finally, she warily hugged her uncle's arm and Bedros pressed the doll into her tiny hands.

Smiling with heartfelt glee, Izabella clutched it to her chest. Bedros, Mourad and Kristina erupted into laughter.

"And these are for you, Flora," Bedros said. He held out a small red box.

"Thank you, Uncle," Flora replied politely. She took the small box, and with a gleeful smile, opened it. Two ruby earrings were fastened to white silk in the bottom. Flora beamed with delight. She handed them to her mother and Kristina helped her put them on.

Bedros handed three wooden boxes to his brother. "I bought these ivory-handled knives from an African trader in Istanbul. They're for the older boys. Make sure Alek gets one when he comes home to visit."

"Thank you for your generosity," Kristina said appreciatively. "You're always so thoughtful."

Bedros smiled. "We all miss you so much and look forward to the day when we can return to Anatolia. We long to celebrate birthdays and Christmas together as a family."

"There is nothing we pray for more than this," Kristina said. "Since you moved to Istanbul, there is an emptiness in this home that can only be filled when you and Liza and the children return. Especially now, with all the uncertainty..."

"But we appreciate the sacrifices you've made for the Armenian people," Mourad interrupted. His eyes shot daggers to silence Kristina. "Representation in the central government has never been more important. There will be plenty more birthdays and Christmases after you've completed your term."

Bedros tugged at his beard with his fingertips. "I'd like to see Mama now."

Mourad took his brother's arm. "She stays in the back bedroom."

The two men walked down a short hall past two rooms. They stopped at a closed door.

Mourad tapped lightly on the door. "Mama, Bedros is home. Can we come in?"

There was no reply. Mourad pulled the door open and stepped into the small room.

Muted light filtered through the faded-blue curtains. A frail-looking, gray-haired woman, covered with blankets up to her neck, was lying in a bed that nearly occupied the entire room.

Mourad squatted beside the bed. "Mama," he whispered. "Look who came to see you."

The feeble old woman opened her droopy eyes. After a few moments, a look of recognition swept across her face. "Bedros," she whispered. "My son, God has answered my prayer."

Bedros leaned over the bed and kissed his mother on the forehead. He sat on the edge of the bed. "I'm sorry I've been away so long, Mama. We wanted to come last spring, but Tania came down with the pox."

A worried frown furrowed her brow. "My Tania?"

"She's fine. We're all fine. Garo and Aren reported for army duty, but I'm sure they'll watch out for each other."

"Thank God," she whispered.

Bedros took his mother's hands and sat gazing at her for a long while. Falling into a contented sleep, she didn't stir as he lovingly massaged her twisted knuckles and fingers. Finally, he leaned over and kissed her on the cheek. "Rest well, Mama. I'll come back later."

Bedros stepped into the front room and brushed a curl of wet hair back from his face. He lifted his nose into the air and took in a whiff of the spiced aroma wafting through the room. "You've prepared something wonderful, Kristina? Lamb stew?"

"It's my mother's pilaf chicken with burghol. I hope you're still hungry."

Bedros didn't reply. His attention was fixed on a small painted statuette of the Madonna and Child on the counter. "I'm starving," he finally said. "I didn't carry enough bread to last the journey. I'd hoped to buy provisions at stops along the way, but as I traveled farther from Istanbul, I discovered that most of the inns—including the Bournouz Khan where we stopped with Father when we were boys—had been abandoned."

The front door opened and Mourad stepped inside with his older sons. "Welcome back to the living, Bedros. I take it you had no trouble resting. Your snoring nearly shook the walls down."

Bedros chuckled, and the laugh lines in his temples morphed into deep furrows. "You have said it! I haven't slept that well since I left Istanbul." Bedros stepped forward and wrapped a brawny arm around each of his nephews. "And what have you two boys been doing the past year? Up to no good, I suspect."

"We've been working with Papa on the farm most of the time, but we go to school in Chunkoush between the cotton harvests," Stepannos said.

"Promise me you'll study very hard. Farming is honorable work, but it is bad for the back, and even worse for the money belt."

"Dinner!" Kristina called out.

Flora set a loaf of bread on the unfinished wooden table set for four. Then, she placed two bowls of stew on a small crate on the floor. Mourad pulled out a chair for his brother. "Bedros, sit here next to me." The men and older boys sat at the table, while Izabella and Sirak knelt at the crate. They all bowed their heads.

"We thank Thee, Christ our God," Mourad began, "for Thou hast satisfied us with Thine earthly gifts. Thank you for guiding Bedros safely home. We pray you will watch over Garo, Aren and Alek while they serve in the army, and that there will be peace in the Empire. Forgive us for our sins. Glory to the Father, and to the Son, and to the Holy Spirit, now and ever and unto ages of ages, Amen."

Flora served pilaf chicken from a large dish. Mourad broke off a crust of bread from the loaf and passed it to Bedros. Flora smiled at Sirak as she filled his bowl. Putting down the pot, she ruffled his hair and kissed him on the cheek. "There's plenty more if you finish that," she whispered to her brother.

Mourad took a bite of bread. He chewed contentedly and swallowed. "Well, Bedros, what news have you from Istanbul?"

"Nothing good. The capital is in complete turmoil. There is the ongoing mobilization of the army throughout the Empire. The enlistment is a disorganized mess, with mass desertions in the southern and eastern provinces. Everyone is preoccupied with finding enough money to pay the *bedel* to keep husbands and sons at home. As far as the fighting between Russia and Germany—there is little information, but I heard from a friend that Ottoman troops have been skirmishing with British infantry near Damascus."

A look of concern gripped Mourad's face. "What's your best guess? Will the Ottoman Empire join the war?"

"Who knows? There are rumors. German military officials, including General Otto Liman Von Sanders, have been spotted in Istanbul, and talk is that the Triumvirate is solidly behind the Germans. We're all hoping cooler heads prevail."

"The Triumvirate," Mourad hissed. "I don't trust them one bit—especially Enver, he's too ambitious."

"If you ask me, anything's better than the Bloody Sultan. Have you forgotten what happened in Diyarbekir only two decades ago?"

"How is it better? For weeks we've been hearing reports about widespread looting in Diyarbekir...of stealing being carried out under the pretext of war collections. Hundreds of Armenian shops and warehouses were looted and burned only a week before Alek was conscripted. How is this better? Tell me."

"Old habits die hard. At least the Young Turks are trying. I understand Jemal Pasha provided great service to our people after the massacres in Adana Province in 1909. I also heard him speak in August, and I must say I was impressed with his grasp of the problems facing the Empire."

"I guess we'll see how things go," Mourad replied. His mouth was overflowing with chickpeas. "I still have grave concerns. How much was your *bedel?*"

"Three thousand one hundred *lire*. How much was yours?"

"Three thousand nine hundred. It was no easy task coming up with it, either. I used the rest of the money Papa left me, and still had to sell one of the workhorses and my two-year-old colt. Then I felt guilty about paying *bedel* to spare myself, rather than reporting for army duty with Alek."

"That's nonsense. Someone must care for the family and manage the farm. How's the harvest?"

"Ah, our best crop in years. Old man Tarik bin Sufyan died in June, but his son Kemal helped me with the first picking. We couldn't have done it without Kemal."

"Özker and I helped, too, Papa," Sirak called out from the smaller table.

Mourad gave him a devoted smile. "Yes, you did. You've both become excellent cotton pickers."

"So, old man Tarik finally died," Bedros said. "Somehow I thought the old ox might live forever. Did you know he taught me to harness a wagon when I was a boy?"

Mourad took a bite of stew. "He taught me, too. Papa must've told me fifty times how he would've lost this farm without Tarik's help. Tarik worked in the fields to the very end. Then the typhus swatted him down like a fly. One day he worked with me and the next he was flat on his back."

"It seems like only yesterday when he helped Father clear the corral. Kemal and I carted off all the rocks and dumped them in that gorge behind the pond. How is Kemal?"

"He's fine, although, as you might expect, he took Tarik's death very hard. I expect him to come by tomorrow for his share from the first picking. He'll be excited to see you. He's always telling me stories about you two hunting together when you were young."

"Is Özker coming, too, Papa?" Sirak called out from the side table.

"I don't know, Son. We'll just have to wait and see. Flora, bring Bedros another serving of chicken. We need to put some flesh on his bones before he goes back to Istanbul."

Kristina set about clearing the children's table, and brewed a pot of black tea. Beads of sweat gathered on her forehead while she worked. Even though it was September, and the worst of the summer heat had passed, the house was still stifling on hot days.

Bedros pushed himself back from the table. "That was the best meal I've had in a long time. I'm looking forward to finishing my term in the assembly, so we can move back and share a lot more family dinners."

Kristina smiled. "That would be wonderful." She poured tea for Bedros, Mourad and Stepannos.

"Have you decided once and for all not to stand for another term?" she asked her brother-in-law.

"No, I haven't, but I'm leaning toward making this my last term. We've made a lot of progress, but there is still so much to do. Someone else deserves a turn."

"What do you do in the assembly, Uncle Bedros?" Stepannos asked inquisitively.

"Well," Bedros sighed, "not much. I do my best to protect Armenian interests, but the Triumvirate is running the show. There's no doubt about that. How old are you now, Stepannos?"

"I turned eighteen in July, sir."

"That's good. You have almost two years before you report to the army."

"I'm plenty old enough to fight now. Two of my friends quit school to join Andranik's forces fighting with the Russians. The Russians are our true friends."

"Stepannos!" Mourad barked furiously.

Bedros' face flushed red with anger. "Where did you hear that shit?"

"From my friend at school," Stepannos whispered. He glanced regretfully at his father.

"You must never repeat this!" Bedros bellowed. He reached across the table and grabbed Stepannos' arm. "Never! Talk like that is all the provocation the Turks need to bring disaster upon us all. Do you hear me?"

Stepannos' head dropped with shame. "Yes, Uncle."

"Stepannos, go feed the horses," Mourad demanded brusquely. "Mikael, you go with him."

The two boys shot up from the table, hustled out the front door and shut it quietly behind them. An awkward silence descended over the table and hung unbroken for several minutes.

"He didn't mean anything by it," Kristina finally said. "It's just the idle chatter of boys."

"It's dangerous talk," Bedros said. "You must not allow it in this home. This past August, the Young Turks asked the Dashnak Convention to stir up an uprising among the Armenians in the Caucasus to occupy the Russians. The Dashnagtzoutune refused their request, but gave their assurance that in the event of war between Russia and the Ottoman Empire, they'd support the Empire as loyal citizens. Any other position is tantamount to suicide for all Armenians. We must not tolerate such talk."

"I'm sorry, Bedros," Mourad replied ruefully. He patted his brother on the forearm. "I'll speak to Stepannos. Rest assured, there will be no further mention of Andranik in this house."

"I'd appreciate it. But that can wait until tomorrow. It's pleasant enough outside, and I brought a bottle of Raki and a box of cigars from

Istanbul. Grab some glasses and let's take a walk down to the pond. Is Gourgen Papazian still living with his uncle?"

"Yes, of course; we had dinner at his house two weeks ago."

"I'd love to see him. Let's ride over and offer to share our Raki."

"Why not? He'll be delighted to see you."

CHAPTER 3

Sirak jammed his heals into his colt's flanks. "Papa, look!" he yelled. The chestnut and white horse bolted from a standstill and streaked across the enclosure. Gripping the reins, Sirak tipped to one side and nearly tumbled to the ground.

Mourad laughed. "Slow down, Sirak! You'll fall off."

"Turn, Sirak, turn!" Bedros yelled, as the horse skirted the far end of the enclosure and galloped along the fence. "That boy knows no fear, brother."

"That's what worries me."

"Okay, Son!" he shouted, "that's enough for now. Walk him back this way." Mourad climbed over the fence and grabbed the reins. He lifted Sirak off the horse and set him on the ground.

Sirak ducked through the fence and ran to his uncle's side. "Did you see, Uncle? I ride fast, just like Mikael and Stepannos."

"I'm very impressed," Bedros said, with a wink at Mourad. "Someday you'll be the greatest horseman in Diyarbekir."

"Papa says Tiran will be the most famous show horse in the province. I'm going to ride him in all the big competitions—maybe even in Istanbul! And Papa promised to teach me how to jump soon."

Bedros and Mourad turned toward the clatter of a horse-drawn cart driven by an old man wrapped in a heavy, tattered coat. Several teenage boys were crowded into the rear.

"Good morning, Vache," Mourad called out cheerfully. "Hurry, Stepannos; the wagon is here!"

"Sorry I'm late, Mourad," the old man said. "I had to wait for an army convoy on the old river bridge."

"Don't worry about it, Vache. Let me introduce my brother. Bedros is a member of the Ottoman Assembly in Istanbul."

"I'm honored to meet you, sir," Vache said respectfully, removing his fez. "I hope you plan to stay for a while."

"Unfortunately, I can only stay a few days. It's a busy time in the capital."

The old man grunted and nodded. "I expect so."

The door opened and Stepannos and Mikael bounded from the house wearing baggy cotton trousers and white shirts. Each boy had a knapsack slung over his shoulder.

"Stepannos!" Bedros called out. "Come here for a moment."

Stepannos exchanged anxious glances with Mikael before turning and walking to his uncle.

Bedros placed his hands on the teen's shoulders. "Stepannos, I'm sorry I got so angry with you last night. What we talked about is a very sensitive subject now that there's a real possibility of war with Russia—especially in Istanbul. Do you understand?"

"Yes, Uncle," Stepannos replied contritely.

"Good. I want you to study hard at school today. You're a bright young man and learning to read and write should be your first priority."

"Yes, sir."

"Very well, then," Bedros said. He patted the top of the boy's cap. "Be on your way. We'll all go for a ride out to the river when you get home. Maybe we'll catch some fish for dinner."

Stepannos turned, and running to the back of the cart, climbed into the bed with the other boys. Old man Vache grunted, and flicking the reins, turned the wagon in the barnyard. It bumped along the pebble-strewn incline down to the road. Mourad waved after them and stood watching until the wagon crested the embankment at the edge of the property.

Bedros turned and sighed. "Perhaps I was too harsh."

"It was a good lesson for Stepannos. He'll think twice before he mentions Andranik again."

"Andranik," Bedros muttered with a sigh. "Sometimes I don't know whether to praise him or curse him."

"Are they really training with Russian troops in the Caucasus? I heard a rumor in Chunkoush."

"I've heard those rumors, too, but who knows what they're really up to. I do know they've gotten the attention of the Ottoman leaders. Armenians in the Empire must not cast their lot with the Andraniks or any other resistance group, or they risk disaster. A Muslim assemblyman gave a blistering speech in support of the Germans two weeks ago. At one point, he held up the front page of a Hunchak newspaper published in Paris last summer. The headline was an appeal for Armenians to take up arms against the Ottoman Empire."

"Dear God," Mourad muttered. "Surely the leaders in Istanbul realize how many of our young Armenian men have loyally reported for duty."

"I keep telling them, my brother—every chance I get."

"Maybe we will learn something more at church on Sunday. Are you planning to go?"

"Yes, of course, but I must return to Istanbul Monday morning."

Mourad heard the whinny of an approaching horse, and setting his hammer down, walked out of the barn. A man wearing a turban and worn worker's clothing trotted his horse to the barnyard. A young boy sat astride the horse in front of him.

"Good afternoon, Kemal," Mourad said, waving.

"Mourad!" Kemal replied cheerfully. "Are my eyes playing tricks, or is that your long-lost brother returned to mingle with the peasants?"

"It's wonderful to see you again, my friend," Bedros said. He grabbed the reins to steady the horse, and Mourad pulled the boy down to the ground.

Kemal dismounted and, grinning broadly, embraced Bedros. "Don't they feed you in Istanbul, my friend? You're skinny as a fencepost."

"The grippe had its way with me last winter, and I still haven't gained back what I lost."

"Thanks be to God, you were spared. What you need is a few weeks of Kristina's cooking to put some flesh back on your bones."

"Unfortunately, I can only stay a few days," Bedros said. "I was deeply saddened to hear of your father's passing. He was a loyal servant of God."

"It was a great shock to our family, but God is merciful. His time had come and his suffering was short. Bedros, you remember Özker, my youngest son from my second wife, Nahid?"

"Yes, of course. Hello, Özker. You've grown like a weed. I hear you're quite a cotton picker."

The young boy didn't reply. He peered warily up at Bedros and scooted behind his father, then tugged at Kemal's pants. "Where's Sirak, Papa?"

"He's behind the barn feeding the horses," Mourad replied. "You boys can play, but don't stray too far from the house."

"Can I, Papa?" the dark-skinned boy asked eagerly. His unruly black hair fluttered in the gusting breeze.

"For just a while. I'll come get you when it's time to go."

Özker sprinted headlong across the barnyard. "Sirak! Where are you?"

The three men watched until the boy disappeared around the side of the barn.

"Where does the time go?" Kemal lamented. "It seems like only yesterday he was suckling at Nahid's breast. Well, Mourad, how'd we do?"

"Not as well as I'd hoped, but better than last year—four thousand two hundred *lire*."

"Forty-two hundred *lire*," Kemal repeated. "It could've been worse. I took my wives to Diyarbekir yesterday, and we ran into a friend of mine with a larger harvest who managed only four thousand *liras* from an army buyer. God willing, we'll get more for the second picking."

"I hope you're right. We must pray the heavy rains stay away and there's no war."

"Oh, that reminds me," Kemal said. He reached into his pocket and pulled out a small strip of paper. "I picked up a copy of the *Agence* in Diyarbekir. I'm afraid it's bad news." He handed it to Mourad.

Mourad took the paper and read for a moment. "Oh, my God! The government ended the protections."

"What?" Bedros exclaimed in horror. "Let me see that." He took the news bulletin and read the feature story. "I can't believe it," he muttered. "As of October 1, all the treaty rights of foreigners are to be ended. This is a disaster. Enver Pasha has turned against us."

Sirak picked up a smooth flat stone and hurled it across the pond. "Four skips!" he shouted. "Özker, did you see that? Four!"

Özker selected a stone from the bank and tossed it across the pond. It dove directly into the water with a loud kerplunk. Frustrated, he picked up another stone and threw it twice as hard, but still managed only two skips. "Come on, Sirak, we better go back now. Papa may be looking for me."

"No he's not. He'll call for us when it's time." Sirak heaved another rock, and running along the edge of the pond, jumped over a knee-high rock.

"Ahh!" he screamed. Tumbling to the ground, he splashed onto his side in the shallow water.

Özker sprinted to his friend. "Are you hurt?" he yelled, before stopping dead in his tracks. A meter-long, olive-colored snake, with a brown zigzag band down its back, slithered away into the nearby brush. "Viper," he gasped.

Sirak struggled to stand up in the ankle-deep water. He took two steps and dropped face first into the murky pond.

"Sirak!" Özker screamed. He splashed into the water and rolled him over. Grabbing Sirak's ankles, he dragged him into the grass along the shallow bank. "Sirak, open your eyes!"

Sirak was pale as bleached cotton. He convulsed involuntarily and water gushed from his mouth and nostrils. He coughed weakly and half-opened his eyes. Then his eyes rolled up into his head.

Özker stared down in shock. "I'll get your papa," he cried out. He stumbled to his feet and dashed headlong through the adjacent field. Running along the corral fence, with his hair whipping in the breeze, he sprinted into the barnyard toward Kemal, Mourad and Bedros. "Sirak!" Özker exclaimed breathlessly. He grabbed his father's jacket sleeve. "Sirak!"

"Calm down, Özker," Kemal said. "Sirak what?"

"He got bit!" the boy cried out.

Mourad's face twisted with alarm. "Bit by what?"

"A viper! He's at the pond!"

Kemal picked up Özker and followed Mourad to the end of the corral. Dashing down a row of belt-high cotton, they emerged from the field at the dry end of the pond.

"Where is he?" Mourad shouted, glancing around the perimeter of the pond.

"Behind those rocks," Özker sobbed.

Mourad bounded along the shoreline to the cluster of boulders. He caught sight of Sirak lying on the ground. "Merciful God, no!" he cried out. He knelt next to his son and grasped his hand. "Sirak, open your eyes!"

Bedros knelt beside Mourad. "Dear God. Look at his foot."

The foot was grotesquely swollen and discolored a mottled purplish-red. Telltale puncture wounds dotted the center of the engorgement.

"He's still alive," Mourad muttered anxiously. He gathered his son's limp body into his arms and rushed back through the cotton field. Jogging around the end of the corral and through the rear barn door, he set Sirak in the bed of an old wagon littered with wisps of cotton. "We must find a doctor," Mourad exclaimed. "Bedros, tell Kristina to bring water and blankets." He jerked a rope down from a hook and crawled up into the wagon. Ripping the leg on Sirak's trousers, he tied the rope tightly around his calf.

Kemal heaved a sack of feed into the wagon. "Prop up his head on this. I'll harness the horse." Kemal rushed to the back of the barn and led a powerfully built draft horse from his stall. He harnessed the beast and rushed to the rear of the wagon. "How's he doing?"

"His breaths are very shallow," Mourad whispered frantically. He brushed a strand of Sirak's hair back from his eyes. "Dear God, save my boy."

Kemal jumped up into the driver's seat. "You stay with him, and I'll drive to the hospital."

Kristina rushed through the barn door carrying a basket and several folded blankets. "Is he conscious?" she gasped.

"No, but he's breathing," Mourad replied. He jumped down from the wagon and helped her into the bed. Climbing back up, he knelt beside his son's motionless body.

Kemal pulled Özker up to the driver's seat, and taking the reins, clattered into the barnyard.

"I'll stay with the children," Bedros shouted as the wagon rumbled past. "Where are you taking him?"

"The military hospital in Diyarbekir," Kemal bellowed.

"No," Mourad yelled, "the American Missionary Hospital in Chunkoush."

Bedros nodded. "Kemal, I'll get word to your wife," he called after them. He watched the wagon crest the rise and disappear down the road headed east. He glanced down at wide-eyed Izabella. The little girl was clutching her doll to her chest.

Suddenly, she burst into tears. "Is Sirak hurt?" she sobbed.

Bedros picked up the tearful little girl. "Yes, my little angel. Your brother is very sick, and now we must pray very hard for God's mercy." He drew Flora to his side and they walked solemnly to the house.

After an hour and a half of bone-jarring travel along a rutted dirt road, the wagon climbed into the barren hills below Chunkoush. As they rumbled through the arid countryside, they passed several groups of travelers journeying along the narrow road through the rock-strewn landscape. Most of the people were on foot. Some were headed toward the Armenian village, but most were headed away.

"Emergency! Clear the road!" Kemal shouted each time the wagon slowed for another group.

The wagon crested a steep switchback and rounded a long sweeping turn. "Whoa!" Kemal shouted. He pulled up on the reins and slowed the wagon to a crawl.

Mourad braced himself against the sidewall and lifted his hand to shelter his eyes from the bright afternoon sun. A motley unit of soldiers was scattered across the road. A lieutenant on horseback rode at the front of the unit. The rest of the foot soldiers were dressed in cotton shirts and trousers. Most wore the fez popular with the Turks. Only a handful had weapons.

"Please, sir, let us pass," Kemal called out to nobody in particular. "My boy was bitten by a viper."

The leader dug his heels into his horse's flanks and trotted to the wagon. A rather young man, with handsome features, he pulled up at the rear of the wagon. "I'm Lieutenant Gashia of the Ottoman Third Army." He peered into the wagon at the lifeless boy lying in his mother's arms. "Did you say a viper?"

Mourad stood in the wagon bed. "Yes, a viper. My son's barely alive. Please, sir, let us pass. We need a doctor."

The lieutenant spun his horse around and shouted at the unit of men. The soldiers scattered into the rock-strewn trenches on both sides of the road. "Follow me!" the sergeant barked. "The hospital is very close."

Lieutenant Gashia galloped up the hill and the wagon rumbled after him trailing a cloud of dust. Winding through a set of steep switchbacks, the road suddenly flattened onto a plateau, and the scattered rock and earthen buildings of Chunkoush came into view. The village contrasted sharply with the barren wasteland they'd just crossed and the bare hills in the distance, although there were only scattered pockets of olive green where the determined roots of small trees and shrubs eked out enough water to survive.

Lieutenant Gashia galloped through the gate of a rock-walled compound of single-story buildings. Leaping from his horse, he ran inside the largest structure.

Kemal eased the wagon to a stop beside the front entrance. "Stay here with the horses, Özker." He tied the reins to a post and rushed to the rear of the wagon. "Is he alive?"

"I don't know," Mourad whispered. He handed Sirak down to his neighbor.

Kemal clutched the young boy to his chest. "*Allahu Akbar,*" he mumbled.

Mourad jumped down from the wagon and took the boy's limp body in his arms. He ran to the front door.

A tall, fair-skinned man in a white doctor's coat hurried outside behind Lieutenant Gashia. The gaunt physician pressed his fingertips to the boy's neck. "His pulse is very weak," he muttered worriedly. He pulled Sirak from his father's arms, and pushing past the lieutenant, rushed into the hospital. "Elizabeth," he shouted, "bring the emergency cart to treatment room one. Hurry!"

Dr. Charles grabbed the last cloth from a basin. "Get me more," he muttered.

The countertop in the cramped treatment room was crowded with bottles and jars filled with every sort of bandage and suture. The strong smell of alcohol wafted through the air.

In the muted light of a kerosene lantern, Nurse Barton watched the missionary-physician cleanse Sirak's foot and ankle. The dark purple skin over the lower appendage was stretched taut and a large weeping gash extended vertically from the top of his foot to well above his ankle. The grotesquely swollen digits only vaguely resembled human toes.

Charles dropped the cloth into a basket and loosely wrapped the limb with a stretch of white cloth. "Let's hope that the alcohol will cleanse the wound." He gazed down at the unconscious little boy. "Well, Elizabeth," he said, with a forlorn sigh, "the rest is up to our great and merciful God."

"It's a miracle he's still alive. God *must* be looking out for him."

Dr. Charles reached into his trousers for a pocket watch and held it up to the flickering lantern. "Already three in the morning," he uttered tiredly. "I'll update his parents and bring them in to stay with him. I must check on the other patients. We have a busy clinic in the morning. Get some rest."

"I'm fine, Dr. Charles. Julie was asking for you. You should tend to her. Don't worry, I'll come get you if the boy takes a turn for the worse."

"What did we ever do without you?" He rested his lanky arms on her delicate shoulders and smiled appreciatively, then left the room.

Elizabeth looked thoughtfully after Dr. Charles. Then she cleared the unused supplies from the bed.

Mourad, bleary-eyed, with deep furrows in his forehead, bolted up from his chair when Dr. Charles entered the cramped waiting room. He reached down and gently squeezed his wife's arm. "Kristina, the doctor's here."

Kristina bolted up. She clutched her hands over her heart. "Doctor, tell me my son's still alive."

"His pulse has strengthened. It's truly a miracle. I suppose the snake's bite was dry. Otherwise, a small boy couldn't have survived the venom. I'm worried he'll lose his foot, but I'm confident the worst is over."

"God bless you, Doctor," Mourad whispered. He wrapped his arm around his wife's shoulders. "Can we see him?"

"Yes, yes, of course. Please come with me."

They walked down a shadowy corridor past several darkened rooms and stepped into the treatment room. Nurse Barton was sitting on the edge of the bed sponging Sirak's forehead. She glanced up and smiled. "He's asking for you, Mrs. Kazerian."

Kristina sat on the edge of the bed and took Sirak's hand. She tearfully kissed his forehead, and his sunken eyes fluttered open. His tongue darted across his parched lips.

"Can I have some water, Mama?" he pleaded weakly.

Kristina glanced up at Dr. Charles and he nodded.

"Of course you can, my little mouse." Fighting to maintain her composure, she brushed tears from her eyes.

The nurse handed Kristina a cup of water, and the latter held the cup to her son's lips. Sirak took several sips and dropped his head back down on the pillow.

"I love you, Mama," he whispered.

"I love you too, my little mouse." Kristina sniffled. She leaned down and gave him a tender hug. "Now you need to sleep so you can get well."

Sirak didn't respond. He took a deep breath and, closing his eyes, exhaled contentedly.

Dr. Charles stepped across to the bedside. "Mr. and Mrs. Kazerian, I'm sorry, but I must examine the other patients. I'd appreciate it if you'd talk Nurse Barton into getting some rest. We have a busy day tomorrow, but, as usual, she won't listen to me." He glanced with amusement toward Elizabeth. "I'll be in my quarters. Don't hesitate to send for me."

Mourad pulled himself up from the floor and grasped Dr. Charles' hand. "Doctor, my wife and I thank you from the bottom of our hearts. We'll stay with him. Nurse Barton, I insist you go get some rest."

"Okay," she chuckled. She grabbed the pitcher off the bedstand. "But he needs lots of water. I'll be back in a minute."

Mourad knelt beside the bed and wrapped his arm around Kristina's back. Leaning her head against his shoulder, she clutched Sirak's tiny hand.

The nurse returned with the pitcher of water and placed it on top of the instrument cabinet. "Try to get him to drink as much as he can," Elizabeth whispered. "If you need anything, you'll find me in the exam room across the hall. I'll be back in two hours."

"Thank you for your kindness," Kristina whispered. "May God bless you."

"Oh, I've done nothing. It's Dr. Charles who deserves your thanks and prayers. He's the most devoted physician I've ever known—dutifully giving his heart, mind, and soul to every man, woman, or child who comes here for help."

"How does he keep up such long hours?"

"He's always worked hard—often sixteen hours or more a day. Then, last week, an Ottoman official ordered him to admit several dozen soldiers to the hospital. Most of them are burning up with typhus, and several have already died. He's had little sleep since the soldiers arrived. The man's a saint."

"May God bless him," Mourad whispered. "I heard about the American Missionary Hospital from a cotton farmer who lives near Diyarbekir. He told me this was the place to come if anyone in my family ever got sick."

"It's good to hear the hospital's reputation is growing among the people of Anatolia. It was a chaotic mess before Dr. Charles arrived from Mus two years ago. In fact, I'd given my notice—I was fed up with the incompetence and turmoil. I accepted a new job in Van. Then Dr. Charles arrived and everything changed. Within two weeks, he totally revamped the system. Most importantly, he instilled a new spirit of cooperation and hope into everyone who works here. I agreed to stay for another year because I saw great things ahead for this hospital. I wouldn't leave now for the world, and neither would anyone else on the staff."

Mourad smiled admiringly. "Thanks be to God for leading us here," he whispered. "Nurse Barton, please, go get some rest."

"Okay. You know where to find me. I'll be back in two hours for medication rounds."

Dr. Charles left the hospital and trudged across the courtyard along a short cobbled path. He opened the front door of the darkened cottage and stepped into a room that was adorned with worn, second-hand furnishings. He eased the door shut behind him and shuffled through the shadowy room toward a flickering light that shone through the half-opened bedroom door.

"David, is it you?" a feeble voice called out from the bedroom.

"Yes, darling," Charles replied. He stepped through the doorway. Pulling off his long white coat, he hung it on the bedpost, then went to the empty side of the bed. He leaned across it and brushed an errant strand of hair from his wife's sunken eyes. "Can I get you anything?"

She smiled tiredly. "No, thank you, darling," she whispered. She reached to grasp his hand and grimaced with pain. "Natalie brought me food and water."

Charles looked at the tray of dried apricots and cheese that sat, untouched, on the bedside table. "But you haven't eaten any of it." He picked up an apricot and pressed it to her chapped lips. "You've got to eat."

She turned away. "I'm too sick now. Maybe later. Get some rest before they call you back."

"Okay," he whispered. He leaned over and kissed her tenderly on the forehead. Lifting her head, he readjusted the pillow and peered into her blue eyes. "I love you."

"I love you, too."

Charles kicked off his shoes and extinguished the oil lamp. He rolled onto his back next to his wife. Lacking the energy to remove his shirt and trousers, he lay awake listening to his wife's shallow breaths for a few minutes. Finally, his light snore reverberated through the darkness.

Nurse Barton bolted up out of a deep sleep. Loud shouts echoed from the front of the hospital. She hopped out of bed, and smoothing down her dress, scurried from the room and up the corridor. "Just a moment! I'm coming!"

The foyer echoed with resounding knocks. She hurried to the door, and pushing back the bolt, opened it wide.

A gaunt, middle-aged soldier, in the uniform of an Ottoman Army lieutenant, stood before her. Behind him, the road in front of the hospital teemed with horse-drawn wagons that were overflowing with sick and wounded soldiers. Some of them wore ragged and soiled military uniforms, but most were dressed in tattered civilian clothes. Some men were clad in little more than bandages and dressings. Nurse Barton flinched in horror at the stench of gangrene wafting through the air.

"Who's in charge here?" the lieutenant demanded. He was lean and erect, with a bushy mustache.

"Dr. Charles," Elizabeth replied. She glanced past the lieutenant. A team of soldiers was already unloading stretchers from the nearest wagon.

"I must speak to him at once. Get him for me."

"But he just went to rest after more than twenty hours without a break."

"I'm sorry, but I've got orders from the governor-general. I must deliver them to him immediately. Take me to his quarters."

"Right this way." Elizabeth stepped outside and led the officer down the dirt path and around the side of the hospital. "Dr. Charles," she called out, knocking lightly on the front door of the darkened cottage.

The lieutenant reached past her and pounded on the door. "Dr. Charles!" he shouted.

"Who is it?" a weary voice muttered inside.

"Lieutenant Mehmet of the Ottoman Army; I must speak with you straightaway, sir."

The door creaked open. The bleary-eyed physician still wore his wrinkled slacks and shirt. "Yes, what is it?"

The lieutenant forced several papers into his hand. "By order of the governor-general, the American Missionary Hospital must care for the soldiers I've brought from the Russian front."

Charles glanced down at the papers and then looked up. "Okay. How many do you have?"

"Three hundred twenty, sir."

"*Three hundred twenty?*" Dr. Charles gasped incredulously.

"Yes, at least when we left Bitlis. Some of them died along the way. Half the men have the typhus. The military hospitals in Diyarbekir and Bitlis are already overflowing with sick and wounded."

Dr. Charles glanced at Nurse Barton, then back at the lieutenant. "We don't have room or supplies to care for that many men."

"You must make room, Doctor; they have nowhere else to go. All non-military patients are to be discharged immediately. Those who need further medical care are to proceed to the military hospital in Diyarbekir."

"That's impossible! Many of my patients are too ill to be moved, and you just told me the hospital in Diyarbekir is overflowing with sick soldiers."

"Those are my orders. I intend to carry them out."

"Then you'll have to see to it yourself. I'll not be a party to this madness."

"As you wish," the lieutenant barked, his pitch-black eyes coldly indifferent. He spun on his heels and marched off toward the front of the hospital.

"Lieutenant!" Charles shouted before Mehmet rounded the corner of the building.

Lieutenant Mehmet stopped, turned in place and stamped his foot. "Yes, Doctor, what is it now?"

"The hospital won't be much good without physicians to treat the sick and wounded. If you want us to care for your soldiers, then you must work with us."

"My orders are inflexible," the lieutenant called out. He took a few steps back toward the cottage. "All of the non-military patients must go to Diyarbekir."

"Will the army provide transportation?"

"Once the soldiers are unloaded from the wagons, they can be used to transport anyone who's too sick to walk or ride."

"Do I have your word on that, Lieutenant?"

"Yes, Doctor, you have my word."

"Okay, just give me a minute to change my clothes."

There was a firm knock on the door, and Mourad and Kristina awakened with a start.

A surly soldier opened the door and leaned into the room. "This hospital is being evacuated," he barked. "You have five minutes to gather your things."

The man disappeared down the hall before Mourad or Kristina could respond. They glanced at each other in bewildered silence. Mourad pushed himself up from the floor and opened the door. The corridor was in chaos. He watched two soldiers carry a stretcher from a room.

A young doctor followed behind shaking his head. "This woman has a high fever! She can't be moved!"

His admonishment went unheeded. The two soldiers continued down the hall toward the front of the hospital. The young doctor whirled in place and threw up his hands in frustration.

Mourad caught sight of Elizabeth helping an unsteady patient walk. "Nurse Barton! What's happening?"

"I'll be right back, Mr. Kazerian. Let me help this woman outside."

Mourad watched with growing angst, as another patient was carried out on a stretcher. Several other patients walked out with an orderly.

The soldier who'd poked his head in their room headed their way. "Are you ready?" he demanded.

Mourad stepped out of the room. "My son is too sick to move."

"All civilian patients must leave this ward immediately," the soldier replied. "Anyone who's too sick to go home is being transferred to the Diyarbekir Military Hospital."

"Diyarbekir?" Mourad gasped. "My son is too sick to travel that far. He'll die."

"He must go. Get your belongings together, or you'll be forced to leave them behind."

"We will not go!" Mourad barked angrily. He stepped in front of the soldier. "Not until my son is stable enough to travel."

"We have our orders!" the soldier shouted. He grabbed Mourad's arm. "Step aside or I'll arrest you."

At that moment, Nurse Barton and Dr. Charles appeared out of the vestibule—followed by Lieutenant Khan. "Hold it!" Dr. Charles shouted.

"Let him go," Lieutenant Mehmet ordered.

"I need to examine your son, Mr. Kazerian," Dr. Charles said reassuringly. He patted Mourad on the shoulder and stepped past him into the room.

Kristina was sitting with the boy's head cradled in her lap.

Dr. Charles knelt at the side of the bed and pressed his fingertips to Sirak's neck. Then, he unwrapped the bandage on Sirak's swollen foot and examined the angry-looking wound. He got up from the bed. "He's a little better, but his pulse is still weak. He's still too sick to move. We must debride that necrotic tissue from the side of his foot to prevent gangrene."

"He can get the treatment he needs in Diyarbekir," the lieutenant insisted with growing impatience.

"Damn it!" Dr. Charles bellowed. He stepped in front of the bed to block the way of the soldiers. "He'll never survive that long trip."

"Doctor," the lieutenant sighed, "you're challenging the limits of my patience. Our orders are to remove all civilians from this hospital and that's what we're going to do. My men will use force, if they must."

Kristina rose from the bed to confront the lieutenant. "What kind of animal are you?" she screamed. "My son will die! Have you no measure of decency, sir?"

Mourad gathered his wife into his arms, and she began to sob uncontrollably. The lieutenant was unmoved by the tirade. He pushed past them and motioned to the men carrying the stretcher.

Dr. Charles regained his composure. "Lieutenant, your orders are to remove all of the patients from the hospital. Correct?"

"That's right, Doctor."

"But you expect my staff and me to stay and treat the soldiers."

"As you say. The governor-general himself signed the orders."

"Well," Charles said defiantly, "if you want me to stay and care for these soldiers, I must insist on moving this boy into our personal quarters behind the hospital until he's well enough to travel."

Mourad glanced up with surprise.

The lieutenant stood for a moment pondering Dr. Charles' request. "Okay," he said finally, "that's acceptable, but move him out of the hospital immediately."

Charles grabbed the stretcher from the soldiers and passed an end to Mourad. "Nurse Barton, please gather the supplies we'll need to treat the boy's foot."

Kristina transferred Sirak off the bed. The soldiers stood clear and the two men carried the stretcher into the corridor.

"Excuse me, Lieutenant," Mourad said. "How were these soldiers wounded? Has war broken out with the Russians?"

"No, sir, three days ago one of our army convoys was ambushed by Andranik's forces near Kars. Dozens of soldiers were killed, and even more were wounded."

"Andranik?"

"Yes, Andranik," the lieutenant said pointedly. "His forces have swelled with hundreds of volunteers—including many of your fellow Armenians from Anatolia."

Mourad made no effort to conceal his irritation. "Lieutenant," he said with a huff, "my eldest son is serving in the Ottoman Army."

"I'm pleased to hear that you take the defense of the Empire seriously, sir."

Mourad did not respond. Re-gripping the stretcher, he followed Dr. Charles.

CHAPTER 4

Ten days later

Dr. Charles finished rewrapping Sirak's leg with fresh dressing and got up from the couch where the boy was lying. The doctor's eyes were bloodshot and darkly ringed from the nonstop care of the soldiers transported to the hospital from the Caucasus the previous week.

Sirak stared up at his mother standing beside him, while Mourad stood watching from across the room.

"Sirak, your foot is healing up nicely," the doctor said. "We won't remove any more tissue, and within a few weeks, I expect you'll be running and playing with your brothers. You're ready to go home now— as long as your mother changes the dressings twice a day. She'll need to keep that up until the skin heals. If it hasn't healed completely in two weeks, your father will bring you back to see me." He motioned toward a box of supplies next to the couch. "Mrs. Kazerian, take these dressings with you."

Mourad smiled thankfully. "How can we ever repay your kindness?"

"I've done nothing. The only explanation for Sirak's rapid recovery is intervention by our merciful loving God. I'm sure He must have a plan for him and I'm pleased I could contribute—at least in small part."

"You're too modest, Dr. Charles," Kristina said appreciatively. "Only a true man of God would've taken us into his home—especially considering Mrs. Charles' condition. In our eyes, you'll always be Sirak's guardian angel."

"Any true Christian would've done the same. Well, I must return to the wards. My wagon and driver are at your disposal. I wish you the best."

The doctor turned and stepped toward the door.

"Thank you, Dr. Charles!" Sirak piped up from the couch, his voice brimming with childhood exuberance. His dark, mischievous eyes darted from the doctor to his mother and back again.

"You're welcome, Sirak. You're a very brave little boy. Please come back and see me sometime. Okay?"

Sirak glanced at his father, and Mourad nodded approvingly. "Sure, Dr. Charles," he finally replied, "I'll bring my horse, Tiran. He needs a check-up, too."

Dr. Charles and the Kazerians burst out laughing.

"I'll look forward to that," Dr. Charles replied, with a wink at Mourad.

Kristina followed the lanky doctor to the door. "I want to thank Nurse Barton, too. Where can I find her?"

The doctor glanced at his timepiece. "Right now she's working in the surgery ward. I'm sure she'll be disappointed if she doesn't see you before you leave."

"If you happen to see her, please tell her I'll come find her before we leave."

"I'll be happy to. I wish you a safe journey."

Elizabeth Barton glanced up from her notes and beamed when she caught sight of Kristina stepping through the door. Kristina returned her warm smile.

"Good morning, Kristina. Dr. Charles told me you're leaving today."

Kristina kissed Nurse Barton on the cheek. "God bless you for helping him save my son's life."

"I didn't do anything. Even Dr. Charles only played a bit part in this miracle. Sirak has extraordinary inner strength, especially for such a young boy. I pray God blesses me with two or three sons just like him someday—and perhaps a couple of daughters, too."

"God will reward you for the kindness you give, without measure, to the people of Anatolia. I know in my heart, you'll have a wonderful family of your own someday. It would be a shame for someone who's so wonderful with other people's children not to have her own."

"If God does bless me with children, I pray I become half the mother you are. Thank you for all your help this past week."

"There's no need to thank me. Most of these soldiers are little more than boys, and it gave me great comfort to provide what little assistance I could to ease their suffering. I couldn't help thinking of my own son, Alek. If he's suffering somewhere, I pray one of these boys' mothers helps him."

"I will pray for Alek's safe return. Well, it's been wonderful getting to know you. I only wish things weren't so hectic right now, so we had more time to sit and talk. I feel we could become good friends."

"We *are* good friends, Elizabeth. I'll return to Chunkoush with Sirak for checkups, and I'll be disappointed if we don't get a chance to see you. I think you need a friend."

Nurse Barton smiled awkwardly. "You are a perceptive woman."

"Anyone can see that you work too hard. You're still a young woman, and you take no time for life outside this hospital. I admire your dedication to patients, but you need to work someplace where you have a chance to meet people. You know, someone to love—someone to marry."

Elizabeth's expression melted into somber melancholy. She looked down at her hands. "I'm only planning to work here in Chunkoush for another year or two, Kristina; but it provided an escape when my life came crashing down around me."

"I'm sorry, Elizabeth, I didn't mean to..."

"No, it's okay," Elizabeth interrupted. "My fiancé, Gordon, was killed in a train accident in New York City a month before our wedding. After nearly a year in a fog of mourning and depression, I answered an ad in the newspaper and ended up here—doing missionary-nursing work in Anatolia. It gave me an opportunity to redirect my sorrow into helping even less fortunate people than I. I don't have time here for my mind to drift to those agonizing memories and what-ifs that haunted me back home in the States. Gordon's spirit still haunts me sometimes, especially late at night when my work is done, but those memories have faded..."

"I'm so sorry, Elizabeth."

"It's fine. I'm learning to put it behind me. You know, this is the first time I've mentioned Gordon to anyone since I arrived in Anatolia. I can finally say his name without falling apart. That represents real progress," she said, with an awkward smile.

Kristina let out a long sigh. "Elizabeth, there's something I want to say to you. This is very difficult, but I must speak my mind. I've noticed how attracted you are to Dr. Charles."

"Kristina!" Elizabeth blurted out with surprise.

"You're in love with him."

"No, I'm not. I respect and admire him, but that's it."

"If you really believe that, you're not being honest with yourself. Any fool could see it. But as wonderful as Dr. Charles is, he's not the man for you."

"Of course he's not the man for me. He's married."

"But Julie is very ill, and the poor woman will not be here much longer. I've spent a lot of time with her this past week. You know what she told me last night?"

"What?"

"She confided in me that her husband has always been married to his work. What she regrets most, she said, is that they never had children or a life away from the hospital, and now it's too late. I know Dr. Charles is fond of you, Elizabeth, and I'm afraid that once Julie passes, he'll turn to you in his sorrow and loneliness. That's not a life that will make you happy. I know it in my heart."

Elizabeth bit down on her lower lip and stared in silence at Kristina. "I'm sorry," she finally said, "but I can't talk about this. I've got to get back to work. Please take care, and I hope we can talk again when you return for Sirak's checkup."

"Goodbye, my new friend. Please think about what I said. I only want you to find the happiness you deserve."

"Thank you," Elizabeth whispered. She kissed Kristina's cheek. "Thank you for your friendship. That's what I need most right now."

Sirak opened his eyes and smiled up lovingly at his mother. Kristina absentmindedly stroked his head and listened to Mourad's bantering conversation with the wagon driver. A staccato of rapid jolts flung everyone to one side, as the wagon rumbled through a succession of deep ruts in the sun-baked dirt road.

Just before noon, the wagon reached the crest of a particularly steep incline. "Whoa!" the driver yelled. He pulled the wagon onto the shoulder to make way for the advance unit of a column of Ottoman troops strewn haphazardly along the road.

A few of the men were dressed in Ottoman infantry uniforms—including an officer on horseback, who was clad in a gray uniform, accented with a red fez, collar, and cuffs and knee-high boots. But most of the soldiers wore tattered civilian clothes.

One by one, Mourad scanned the sorrowful faces of the ill-equipped, dispirited soldiers as they streamed past. Suddenly, he bolted upright. "Alek!" he called out to a young man carrying a stretcher.

Kristina rolled to her knees and peered out across the multitude. "Where is he?"

The young man turned his head and glanced at the wagon.

"It's not him," Mourad whispered sadly.

Kristina also scrutinized the faces marching past. Finally, the last few stragglers slogged by—including many men carrying stretchers that bore the sick and wounded.

Once the last vestiges of the column passed, the driver pulled the wagon back onto the road and continued on to the east of Diyarbekir.

Finally, as the last rays of the late summer sun dipped beneath a nearby hill, the wagon turned onto the short trail that led to the Kazerian farm. The driver slowed to a stop at the front of the farmhouse. Bedros rushed outside carrying Izabella. Stepannos, Mikael and Flora tailed close behind.

Bedros jogged to the wagon and peered down at the bed where the sleeping youth lay. "Brother, tell us Sirak lives."

"We nearly lost him. He surely would've died if not for the skill of the doctor at the American Missionary Hospital. He lost a bit of his foot, but it could've been much worse."

Mourad passed Sirak down to Stepannos, and Izabella giggled with delight at the sight of her young brother.

"See, Izabella," Flora exclaimed excitedly, "I told you Sirak would be home soon."

She reached out and patted Sirak's head and kissed him on the forehead. "I love you, little mouse. We prayed for you night and day."

Mourad helped Kristina down from the wagon and gathered Sirak into his arms. "Thank you, Sergeant," he called out.

The driver turned the horses and drove the clattering wagon in a circle around the barnyard. The man nodded and touched his hand to his fez before rumbling away to the main road.

Mourad made his way into the darkened front bedroom. He set Sirak on the small blanket-covered bed, and Kristina stuffed a pillow beneath his head. His uncle and brothers crowded into the room.

Mourad sat on the edge of the bed and patted Sirak's leg. "How are you feeling, Son?"

"I'm sleepy—even more sleepy than when we picked the cotton."

"Ha," Mourad chuckled. "Then you are very tired, indeed. A big boy like you needs a lot of rest after a long trip. You sleep now and your mama will bring you some dinner a little later. I promise you'll feel better soon."

"Papa, when can I ride Tiran?"

"Dr. Charles told me he expects you to be able to do everything you want to do in a few months. That includes riding, but you need to be patient."

Mikael scooted past his father to the side of the bed. "I'll water and feed Tiran, Sirak, but he won't let me ride him."

Sirak struggled to keep his eyes open. "Tell him I'll come see him when I feel better," he murmured.

"Let's let him sleep," Mourad whispered to Mikael and Stepannos as he shepherded them out the door. "You boys go tend to the horses. Flora, feed the chickens, and take Izabella with you."

Mourad slumped into a chair at the table.

Bedros sat down beside Mourad. "Sirak looks better than I expected. That's a special little boy in there. His single-mindeness reminds me of Papa."

"He's got a temper like Papa, too," Mourad sighed.

"He got some of that from his own Papa," Bedros chuckled. He poured a cup of tea from a pot. "Well, Mourad, I'm glad I could help, but I must be on my way first thing in the morning. I'm sure Liza is worried sick."

Mourad gripped Bedros' forearm. "Thank you, Brother. I'm sorry we didn't get to spend much time together, but thank you for taking care of the children."

"I'm glad I was here. Gourgen Papazian and several other people from church brought food to the house while you were gone. Gourgen wanted me to be sure and tell you the whole church was praying for Sirak."

"I'll ride over and thank him tomorrow. He is a wonderful friend."

"He asked me to bring Liza and the children back next spring. He suggested we all plant our crops together."

"It'll be just like old times, and something wonderful to look forward to."

"How did you find the situation in Chunkoush?"

"It's total chaos. The authorities took over the hospital and threw out all of the civilian patients because so many soldiers need care—mostly from typhus, but some from wounds suffered in attacks by Andranik's forces."

"The Andraniks are fighting the army?"

"Yes, I heard they're very active in the northeast. Men were dying there by the hundreds. I was afraid the whole time I was there that Garo, Aren or Alek would arrive in the next infirmary wagon. We passed thousands of soldiers on the road today and they all looked terrible. Most of them didn't even have uniforms."

"God help us," Bedros muttered, with a sigh. He sipped from his teacup. "I wish there were some way to come up with the money to send the boys to America when they come home on leave."

"I've thought about that every day since Alek left. If there were a way, I would've done it last summer, when war began to look inevitable; but even if we sold all the horses and used the money from the cotton harvest, there still wouldn't be enough."

Bedros tapped his finger on the side of his teacup. "We could sell this land."

Mourad recoiled in horror. "Sell the land? You must be delirious."

"Who knows what the future holds here in Anatolia? If the Empire blunders into this war, anything could happen. Remember when we were boys and tens of thousands of Armenians were slaughtered in Diyarbekir and villages throughout the province? I remember when Papa took us through the village down the river, where everything had been obliterated—even the church. If war comes, horrible atrocities like those could happen again. You and your family would be much safer in Istanbul."

"No, Bedros," Mourad said, shaking his head, "Papa fought to keep this land, and I'd rather die than sell it."

"Look, I know how you feel. I feel the same way, but there are some things even more important than land."

The two brothers stared at each other for several moments.

Finally, Mourad shook his head. "No, my brother; remember the last words Papa whispered to us before he died? I will never sell this land."

"Things have changed. Think about it. Anyway, the Turk, Abdul Pasha, came by while you were in Chunkoush. He renewed his offer to buy the farm."

"So that's what planted these dreadful thoughts in your mind. That scum is worse than his father. Remember when his father tried to get Papa to sell the rest of the land after the Armenian massacres in Diyarbekir? He even threatened us. That must've been sometime in 1895 or 1896. Remember how Papa told Pasha to get off the farm? You should've done the same with Abdul. What's it been, three years since the last time he came here? Damned vulture. I told him never to come back."

"He was pleasant enough. He offered one hundred thousand *lire* for the farm and all the livestock."

"*One hundred thousand!* That's half what he offered three years ago!"

"He said he'd offered you more, but he pointed out that the situation has changed since then, and he would be taking considerable risk in expanding his farm now. I told him he'd have to discuss it with you. He said he'd come back in a few days."

"I'll never sell this land to him. Besides, where would we go?"

"You could move to Istanbul and share our house. Kristina, Liza and the children would love being together again."

"That will happen when you finish with the assembly and move back here. This is where our family belongs. I am not leaving here—no matter what. "

Bedros stood up from the table. "Okay, I can see you're determined. But don't close the door just yet. Tell Abdul you'll think about it."

"I won't do it. Once the Turk senses weakness, he'll never leave me alone."

Bedros sighed frustratedly. "You are a stubborn mule—just like Papa. I must get an early start in the morning. I'll see to my horse and pack my bags before dinner."

"Thank you for everything you've done."

"That's what brothers are for. Besides, I got a chance to spend time with Mama and visit with the children. I took them to mass and we all got to see Father Murphy again. It was the first time I'd seen him since we left."

"It must've been a thrill for him. He never fails to ask about you."

"Did you know he's retiring next month? He's returning to Ireland."

"Really? He's talked about that for years, but somehow I doubted it would ever happen. He'll be sorely missed, I can tell you that. Sirak served as his altar boy last summer."

"He told me. I took Stepannos and Mikael fishing down by the bend in the river after mass...to that same place we used to go as boys. We had a long talk about the Empire and the Armenian contribution to peace between the different ethnic groups in Anatolia. They've both grown up to be fine young men. You should be very proud."

"God has truly blessed us, as he has you and Liza."

Bedros turned and stepped toward the door. "Send the boys to fetch me when dinner is ready."

"I will."

Bedros stepped outside and shut the door behind him.

Mourad stared at the closed door until long after his brother's footsteps faded into silence. "God, grant me wisdom," he whispered, with a long, apprehensive sigh.

CHAPTER 5

Bedros checked to make sure his bags were secure and patted his chestnut mare on the neck.

Mourad gave Bedros a bear hug. "Take care, my brother," he said solemnly. He smiled and handed him the reins. "Send us letters. I want to know when you hear from Garo and Aren."

"You do the same. We will pray for Alek. Remember what we talked about. No land is worth more than your family. You're all welcome in Istanbul—anytime." He handed Mourad a folded paper. "Take this just in case."

Mourad unfolded the paper and scanned down the page. "What is it?"

"It's a list of code words to use in letters. With these ciphers, each of us can let the other know what's really happening."

Mourad nodded and slipped the paper into his pocket.

The brothers walked out of the barn. Kristina and all the children, except Sirak, were waiting in the barnyard. The early morning rays of the sun shone across the rows of cotton plants heavy with ripening bolls.

Kristina handed Bedros a cloth sack. "Be careful, Bedros. Hopefully, this is enough bread and cheese to last until you reach Istanbul. Give Liza and the children our love."

"Thank you, Kristina. Goodbye," he shouted to the children.

"Goodbye, Uncle Bedros," they called back in unison.

Bedros mounted his horse and waved one last time before trotting up the path to the road.

Mourad wrapped his arm around Kristina's shoulders as they watched. Just before he crested the knoll at the edge of the farm, Kemal and his son, Özker, appeared on horseback. They paused for a few moments before Bedros trotted his horse toward the road.

"Good morning, Kemal," Mourad called out.

"Good morning, Mourad, Kristina. How's Sirak?"

Kristina smiled warmly. "He's feeling better," she replied. "He still can't walk very well, but the swelling in his leg has gone down."

Kemal patted his son on the shoulder. "Did you hear that, Özker? That's very good news."

"Can I see Sirak?" Özker asked.

"He's sleeping now," Kristina replied. "Come up to the house at lunch time. I know he wants to see you."

"Are you ready for the second picking, my friend?" Kemal asked.

Mourad glanced at the field. "Those bolls aren't picking themselves."

Kemal swung Özker down to the ground and dismounted. He led his horse to the barn and helped Mourad hitch the workhorse to the wagon.

Stepannos and Özker headed out to the field. They began picking cotton and stuffing it into worn cloth sacks slung over their shoulders. Lines of sweat streaked down Mourad's face and torso, as his hands darted from boll to boll picking the fluffy white cotton.

The men and boys finished one row and began another before Kemal tapped Mourad on the back and motioned toward the barn.

Mourad glanced over his shoulder and caught sight of three men on horseback conversing with his daughter, Flora. "Abdul Pasha," he hissed. He threw his sack of cotton to the ground and walked down the row.

"Don't give him the pleasure of seeing your anger, my friend," Kemal called after him.

Mourad walked away without reply. He rounded the end of the row and walked directly to Pasha. The Turk was cajoling Flora as his older son looked on amusedly. The girl glanced uneasily at her father and clutched a basket of eggs to her chest.

"Flora, your mother needs those eggs in the house," Mourad called out to her. He wiped the perspiration from his brow and tucked his hand-cloth beneath his waistband.

"Yes, Papa," Flora said, then scurried away to the house.

Pasha smirked and stared after her, before turning his menacing, deep-set eyes on Mourad. "Greetings, Kazerian," he wheezed. He erupted into a rattling cough. "Your daughter grows more beautiful every year." He swung his leg over the horse's back and lowered himself to the ground. "How old is she now?"

"How can I help you, Pasha?" Mourad asked pointedly.

The Turk's eyes hardened beneath his bushy brows before a forced smile emerged below his unruly mustache. "You remember my elder son, Timurhan, born of my first wife, Sabriye," he said, motioning toward the older of the two boys. He was a muscular youth with his father's bushy brows, prominent nose and dark complexion. He looked to be in his late teens.

Mourad acknowledged the young man with a nod. "Timurhan," he said.

Pasha nodded toward the younger rider—a frail, light-complexioned boy. "And my son, Erol, born of my second wife, Jasmine."

"Erol," Mourad muttered, glancing at the youngster.

The boy nodded shyly and looked away toward the field.

"Is there something I can do for you, Abdul?" Mourad asked. "I have work to do."

"Bedros told me your son got bitten by a viper. I've come to see if there's anything we can do to help."

"Thank you for your concern, but Sirak's doing fine now. Fortunately, it was a dry bite."

"*Allahu Akbar*," Pasha uttered. He wiped sweat from his brow with the back of his arm and glanced at the blistering sun. "Cursed serpents. I lost my best farmhand to a viper during the peak of harvest last year. He was dead in fifteen minutes, and there wasn't a damned thing anyone could do about it."

"I'm sorry to hear this," Mourad said. He glanced toward the field where Kemal and the boys were hard at work. "Well, thank you for your courtesy, but I must get back to work. I want to finish the picking before we lose the sunlight."

Pasha turned and gazed across the field. "It looks like you've been blessed with an abundant crop. Is that Kemal Sufyan?"

"Yes, it is."

"Kemal's a hard worker—at times overly blunt, but capable. I sought him out to direct my harvest, but the idiot refused my offer of two thousand *liras*. Well, I may as well get to the point. I've come to make another offer for your land."

"I've told you, Abdul, it's not for sale. I discussed it again with my brother and we are in agreement."

"You've yet to hear my best offer."

"It doesn't matter how much you offer. I'm not selling the farm."

"Your family would be much safer in Istanbul, Kazerian. You know, where your brother enjoys certain influence and..."

"We're not leaving Diyarbekir," Mourad growled impatiently.

"Anything could happen here if war..."

"You're wasting your time. If we do decide to sell, it won't be to you. That's a promise I made my father on his deathbed, and I intend to keep it. Isn't it enough that your father managed to pilfer the other two thirds of our land?"

"That stubborn old goat never did have a bit of sense," Pasha retorted. "I thought you might have more, but clearly I was mistaken."

"You're the last one to be talking about common sense," Mourad bristled, his face flushing red with anger. "If you hadn't cheated Todori out of a good portion of his wages, you wouldn't need Kemal Sufyan's help bringing in your harvest. And on top of that, you spread lies to try to convince the other farmers not to hire Kemal after he declined your job offer. We're not selling, and that's the end of it."

"We'll see," Pasha growled menacingly. He pulled himself up onto his horse and jerked the reins. "Let's get the hell away from these infidels," he muttered beneath his breath. He slapped the reins against his horse's flank and galloped off toward the road. The horses kicked up a cloud of dust and disappeared over the ridge.

Mourad turned, and shaking his head with disgust, marched back toward the field.

Several weeks later

Sirak walked gingerly across the barnyard under the watchful eye of his father. He stepped across a rut and headed for the corral. On the horizon, the last rays of the late-afternoon sun danced across the underside of a distant bank of purple and scarlet clouds. Sirak reached the fence ahead of his father and peered excitedly across the pasture. Tiran was standing a short distance from his mother on the opposite side of the corral.

"Tiran!" Sirak yelled out elatedly.

The chestnut and white colt's head shot up, but he stood his ground, staring passively across the enclosure.

"Tiran!" Sirak called out once again. "Why won't he come, Papa?"

"Give him time, Son. I'm sure it's been hard for him not to see you for such a long time. Let's get a little closer."

Sirak and his father ducked between the rails of the fence and took a few steps into the enclosure. Tiran trotted toward them, but stopped. Turning, he stared at Sirak from a distance.

"He hasn't been ridden since you got hurt, Sirak. Give him a few moments."

"Tiran, please," Sirak pleaded, holding out his arms.

Suddenly, the colt bolted forward, and, pushing his nose into Sirak's chest, nearly knocked him down. Sirak broke into a big smile. He brushed his fingertips through Tiran's mane. The horse whinnied happily and nuzzled against the boy's side.

"That's my Tiran!" Sirak exclaimed gleefully. "I missed you so much, boy!"

"Always treat him with great love and respect, my son, and he will be your loyal friend and companion for many years to come."

"How long *do* horses live, Papa?"

"Well, that depends. If you take good care of him, he may live for thirty more years."

"*Thirty years?* That's really a long time—isn't it?"

"Yes, that's a very long time. Tiran is a lucky horse to have such a loving master. And you know what?"

"What?"

Mourad smiled. "I think he knows that."

Sirak returned his father's smile and brushed his hand down Tiran's muscular chest.

Mourad slipped a bit into the stallion's mouth and pulled the reins across his back. "I'll lift you up on his back, but I'm not letting you ride on your own yet. Just let me lead him. Do you understand?"

"Yes, Papa."

Mourad lifted Sirak up onto Tiran's back. The boy grasped the horse's mane with one hand and the reins with the other. Mourad walked the horse slowly along the fence. The colt didn't make the slightest effort to gallop off with the boy—as he had many times in the past.

"I think he wants to run, Papa,"

"No, he doesn't. Horses are very intelligent and instinctive animals. I'm sure Tiran saw your limp, and he understands there's a reason you haven't been here to feed him and ride for these past few weeks."

Mourad led Tiran past his mother at the back of the corral. Continuing at a deliberate pace, he walked the colt three full circles around the enclosure before finally pulling up at the main gate. Tiran whinnied contentedly.

"Okay, Son, it's getting dark. That's enough for today."

Mourad lifted Sirak off Tiran and pulled the bit out of the horse's mouth.

Sirak wrapped his arms around the colt's front leg and gave him a hug. He turned and took his father's outstretched hand. "I'll be back tomorrow, Tiran," he called out.

Mourad stepped inside the house and Sirak limped slowly after him. Stepannos and Mikael looked up from the game of chess they were playing at the table.

Kristina stepped out of the kitchen. "There's plenty for Kemal and Özker."

"I invited them, but Kemal wanted to get home. He's helping the Tarkanians with their crop tomorrow."

Kristina cupped the back of her son's head. "How did things go with Tiran?" she asked lovingly.

Sirak smiled tiredly. "Papa let me ride him around the corral. I missed him so much, and I think he missed me, too."

"Of course he did. After all, you fed and played with him every single day from the day he was born right up until the day you got hurt. Horses get very attached to their masters."

"Did you ever have your own horse, Mama?"

Kristina stirred a pot with a wooden spoon and carried it to the table. "Yes," she said, with a nostalgic smile. "Her name was Nera. Papa gave her to me for my ninth birthday, and she was my closest friend."

Sirak frowned. "What happened to her?"

"She had a long healthy life and we had lots of fun together, but now she's in heaven."

"Do you want another horse? I think Papa would give you a foal, too."

"No, my little mouse," Kristina chuckled. She knelt down and hugged Sirak. "I don't want another horse. I've got you now, and there will never be another horse for me like Nera, just like there will never be another horse for you like Tiran."

Mourad smiled and walked into the kitchen. Pouring water from a pitcher into a ceramic basin, he washed his hands and face and dried them with a towel. He sat down in his chair at the head of the table, and Stepannos and Mikael took their places opposite Sirak.

"Flora told me Abdul Pasha came to speak to you this morning," Kristina said, without looking up from the loaf of bread she was breaking.

"Yes, the scum was here. He came to make another offer for our land. I told him we weren't interested."

Kristina returned to the kitchen. Picking up the stewpot with hot pads, she carried it to the table. "Was it a good offer?" she asked demurely. She turned to take a bowl of vegetables from Flora.

"I have no idea," Mourad replied impatiently. "We're not selling, so there was no reason to waste my time hearing him out."

Kristina glanced at Flora and took her spot at the opposite end of the table. Finally, with a nearly imperceptible shrug of her shoulders, she bowed her head.

Mourad stared with wide-eyed surprise across the table. "Do you disagree with this course, Kristina?"

"You are my husband," she whispered. "If it's your decision that we stay, then we will stay."

Mourad continued to stare across the table in silence. "We thank Thee, Christ our God," he finally began, bowing his head, "for Thou hast satisfied us with Thine earthly gifts. We thank thee for Sirak's continued improvement. We beg thy protection for Bedros on his journey back to Istanbul, and for Alek, Garo and Aren, wherever they may be. We pray for wisdom for our leaders and for peace for the Empire. Glory to the Father, and to the Son, and to the Holy Spirit, now and ever and unto ages of ages, Amen."

Mourad ladled stew onto Sirak's plate. He let out a heavy sigh. "Next time he comes, I will hear him out."

Kristina didn't reply. Looking up, she smiled approvingly.

CHAPTER 6

Early November 1914

Mourad led his mule into the barnyard and set about harnessing the old black to the wagon. He looked up upon hearing a shout.

"Good morning, Kemal," he called out cheerfully. "When did you get back from Bitlis?"

"Yesterday afternoon," the young Turk replied. He climbed down to the ground and lifted off Özker. "We're on our way into Diyarbekir to buy supplies. I thought you might like to travel together."

"You have perfect timing. We're just leaving for the city ourselves. We learned from our priest that Dr. Charles is working at the Missionary Hospital in Diyarbekir. We're taking Sirak for a check-up and then I'll purchase stores for the winter."

Kemal glanced at the gaunt mule harnessed to the wagon. "What happened to your workhorse?"

"Nothing, he's in the barn. The army is seizing horses, mules and donkeys throughout Anatolia, so I decided to take the old mule into town."

"That's very wise, my friend. They seized every work animal they could find in Bitlis to haul supplies and grain to the Russian front. My uncle lost both of his mules. I wish I'd ridden my old mare."

"Why don't you ride in the wagon with us?"

"That's very kind of you."

"What's the situation in Bitlis?"

"It's worse than I ever imagined. There were soldiers everywhere and a growing tension between the Turks, Jews and Christians. Several resistance groups are causing trouble in the north. And the navy bombarded Russia's Black Sea coast just before I left."

Mourad's face twisted in disbelief. "*What? When?*"

"On the twenty-ninth of October. I thought you already knew."

"This is the first I've heard of it. We've stayed here on the farm the past two weeks to stay clear of trouble."

"So you haven't heard the worst news of all. Russia declared war on the Ottoman Empire."

Mourad's expression melted into dismay. "Dear God," he muttered. "Our worst fears have come to pass. How did the people in Bitlis react to this news?"

"Some people were jubilant, but everyone else seemed stunned. Then alarming rumors began to sweep the city."

"What kind of rumors?"

"Rumors that some Armenians left to join the Russian forces in the east or that those who stayed were spying for the Russians. It felt as if the city would erupt into chaos at any moment."

Mourad shook his head and let out a long sigh. "Did you see any Armenian soldiers among the Ottoman forces you passed on the road?"

"There were hundreds on the road to Bitlis. Many of them didn't have uniforms or even a gun, but that's also true of many of the Turks. I kept an eye out for Alek, but, unfortunately, I didn't see him. You still haven't heard from him?"

"No, nothing, and Kristina gets more frantic with every passing day. Please don't mention the news about Russia. Let me break it to her gently."

"I won't say a word."

The farmhouse door opened and Kristina herded the younger children outside.

Özker broke free from his father's grasp and ran headlong across the barnyard. "Sirak, you're walking!" he called out gleefully. "It's wonderful to see you."

"I'm so happy to see you, too. Papa promised to take me to visit you soon."

"I've been so worried about you. Can you ride?"

"I can't ride fast like I did before, but I can ride with Papa's help."

"Allah is great. My mama and I prayed for you every day."

Sirak smiled. "Thank you. My mama says I'm a living miracle."

"Guess what? We're going to Diyarbekir, too. Can I ride in your wagon?"

"Can he, Papa?" Sirak pleaded.

"Of course. We've decided to travel together." Mourad lifted the boys into the wagon. Then he helped Kristina and his daughters.

Kemal led his horse to the barn and reappeared a moment later. "Are Stepannos and Mikael coming?"

"They're at school in Chunkoush," Mourad replied. "It's their first day back since Sirak got bitten."

Kemal's eyes widened with surprise. "The schools in Chunkoush are still open?"

"The American School is—at least for now. According to Vache, the others closed. We're taking things one day at a time."

"We're all taking things one day at a time," Kemal said solemnly. He climbed up on the wagon.

Mourad jumped into the driver's seat, and flicking the reins, gave the mule a shout. The wagon eased away from the barn and rattled slowly down the narrow trail to the main road.

The wagon bumped along a dirt road through the arid countryside, and traveled for nearly an hour before crossing a Roman bridge spanning a tributary of the Tigris River. They rounded a sweeping turn and the ominous basalt ramparts of the ancient city Diyarbekir sprang into view. The black stone walls and intimidating watchtowers soared above the surrounding countryside and lent the city a forbidding, medieval air.

Sirak's eyes were drawn to the detailed inscriptions and strange, animal-like statuettes on the façade of the nearest tower. Spotting an armed sentry atop the nearest watchtower, he squeezed Özker's hand. The two boys locked eyes for a moment before peering back up at the soaring gate.

Kristina wrapped her arm around Izabella and steadied herself against a sudden jolt when the wagon bumped through a muddy gully.

Falling in line behind a caravan of donkeys, Mourad headed for the open eastern gate. Armed soldiers were posted on either side. They took no more than fleeting notice of the scores of travelers entering the ancient city.

The wagon passed through the gate and Sirak's senses were assaulted by clatter and stench. The noise rose from the babble and shouts of every sort of person—young and old—civilian and military—Turk, Arab, Armenian and Kurd—wandering through a hodgepodge of bazaars and shops just inside the gate. The odor came from the overpowering mélange of rot, perspiration and feces.

Sirak's eyes scanned across the frenzied scene and locked onto the brooding eyes of a uniformed gendarme who caught sight of the wagon from his post near the gate.

The man stepped in front of the mule and held up his hand. "Halt! What's your purpose in Diyarbekir?"

"We're taking my son to see his doctor at the Missionary Hospital," Mourad replied calmly.

"Aren't you aware of the governor-general's orders for all transportation and work animals to be surrendered to the army?"

"No sir, we live on a farm an hour from the city. This is the first we've heard of this order."

Another older gendarme stepped outside of an adjacent guard shack and approached the wagon. "What's the problem here, Yusuf?" the portly, middle-aged man called out to his associate. Rolls of fat beneath his chin quivered as he spoke.

"This Armenian claims he hasn't heard about the military requisition orders, sir."

The ponderous gendarme grumbled something beneath his breath, and grabbing the mule's bridle, inspected his flanks and legs. "This old flea bag is worthless. Do you have other work animals back at your farm?"

"No sir, we had to sell our other horse to buy seed this past spring."

The gendarme stared up at Mourad for a moment. "You people are all the same," he finally said. "You can go now, but if you *are* hiding healthy animals, I advise you to immediately comply with the order and deliver them to the procurement center to the south of the city. Otherwise, you and your family members risk arrest and imprisonment."

"I understand, sir," Mourad deadpanned, "but, regrettably, this is our only mule. Thank you for your generosity."

Mourad coaxed the mule forward, and pulling away from the gendarmes, wove carefully through a throng of people in the center of the road. After crawling along the main road toward the center of the city for over an hour, they turned onto a narrow side street. They bumped slowly past several diminutive homes and a small mosque built from monotonous black basalt. The basalt was quarried from the plateau on which the city was founded nearly five thousand years earlier.

Mourad pulled the wagon to a stop just outside the main entrance to the Missionary Hospital. The reek of human excrement hung in the air. Sirak and Özker grimaced at each other, and shielded their noses and mouths with their hands.

A motley band of soldiers loitered in the yard outside the hospital. Several men holding eating utensils were huddled around a large pot—apparently waiting for lunch. They turned en masse to stare at the new arrivals. One of the soldiers stood up and, shouting unintelligibly, made an obscene gesture toward Flora. The others erupted into boisterous laughter. Flora ducked her head, and frowned apprehensively at Kristina.

"Kemal," Mourad muttered beneath his breath, "you and Özker stay here with Flora and Izabella. Keep an eye on the wagon."

"Of course, my friend; I'll park down the road by the mosque to get the children away from these roving eyes."

Mourad jumped to the ground and helped Kristina down from the wagon. "We shouldn't be gone long." He gathered Sirak into his arms and walked to the main entrance of the two-story hospital. They scooted past a stack of boxes just outside the door and stepped into a cramped reception area. A young, fair-haired woman, dressed in a white nurse's cap and dress, was seated behind a small wooden desk.

"Good morning," she greeted. "May I help you?"

"Yes, thank you. My name is Mourad Kazerian and we've brought my son Sirak to see Dr. Charles. The doctor treated him for a viper bite at his hospital in Chunkoush."

"I see. Well, unfortunately, Dr. Charles doesn't have clinic today. This is his surgery day. But if you'll wait here, I'll find out if he's available to see you later."

The woman turned and disappeared into the hall behind the desk.

Sirak swiveled in his father's arms. "Papa?"

"Yes, what is it, Son?"

"Why does it smell so bad outside the hospital?"

Mourad glanced at Kristina and brushed his free hand through Sirak's hair. "The soldiers relieved themselves on the grounds outside. I guess there's no place else for them to go."

"Dr. Charles told me he didn't allow that at his hospital," Sirak replied thoughtfully. "He said it spreads diseases."

"Well, he probably hasn't been here long enough to..."

The door flew open and Nurse Barton rushed into the foyer. "Kristina!" she called out cheerfully. "How are you?" Stepping around the desk, she hugged Kristina warmly. "I missed you so much. How wonderful to see you again."

"Oh, I missed you, too," Kristina exclaimed happily. She kissed the nurse on the cheek. "You've lost weight. Have you been sick?"

"I've lost a pound or two, but I'm fine. We've been too busy to eat regular meals."

"How long have you been in Diyarbekir?"

"It'll be two weeks tomorrow. The military doctors took over our hospital in Chunkoush and Bishop Chlghadian asked Dr. Charles to come help out here. It was either that or head home. I decided to come with him."

"Hello, Nurse Barton," Sirak said shyly. He still clung to Mourad's chest.

"Hello, Sirak!" Nurse Barton exclaimed. She kissed his cheek. "How's our little mouse?"

"I'm good. Papa let me ride my horse yesterday."

"He did?" she asked delightedly, smiling at Mourad. "You really are getting better. With such wonderful parents to look after you, I just knew you'd be fine.

Elizabeth greeted Mourad, then shared the news that Dr. Charles' wife, Julie, had passed away.

"How's Dr. Charles taking it?" Mourad asked.

"Not too well, I'm afraid. He only got a few hours to mourn her passing. He buried her in the Protestant Cemetery in Chunkoush the morning she died and was back to work early that same afternoon."

Mourad glanced at the growing line at the reception desk. "It looks to me like you're even busier here."

"Our wards are overflowing with patients. On top of that, staff members from the Military Hospital keep coming over to *borrow* supplies to treat soldiers—or at least that's what they say they're doing with the medicines and bandages they carry away. The clinic can't go on this way much longer."

Dr. Charles stepped out of the hall. "Now, now, Elizabeth, don't be telling stories about me behind my back."

"Dr. Charles!" Mourad exclaimed. He stared in disbelief, unable to conceal his shock at the doctor's obvious decline. He was pasty and frail, and had lost a great deal of weight. "Are you okay, sir?"

"I haven't been well the past few weeks, but I'm doing much better now, thank you. It's good to see you, too, Mrs. Kazerian." The doctor stepped around the desk and lifted Sirak's pant leg. "How's our boy here?"

"We kept him off of his feet for four weeks—just like you ordered, but we've been encouraging him to walk a little more each day."

"Excellent," Dr. Charles said. He palpated Sirak's foot and toes with his fingertips, carefully inspecting the skin on both the upper and lower surfaces. Then he pressed on the defect in the side of his foot. He checked the pulses and looked up with a twinkle in his eye. "You must be praying, like I told you, Sirak. Your foot's healed up very nicely. You should be able to ride that horse of yours now."

"I've already been riding—right, Papa?"

Charles frowned at Mourad. "He's been riding?"

"Only very carefully, with me leading him slowly around the corral," Mourad replied sheepishly. "We've been very cautious."

"I guess that's okay; but no hard riding. Do you understand me, Sirak? I don't want you to get a non-healing sore on this foot before the circulation is fully restored."

Sirak pouted and nodded his head up and down. Yes, sir," he replied disappointedly.

Charles patted him on the head. "Good boy. How have you been, Mrs. Kazerian?"

"I'm well, Dr. Charles. Please accept our entire family's sympathy for Julie's passing. She was a remarkable woman. Her faith and strength helped me through those darkest days when Sirak was so terribly ill. She's with our Lord now."

Dr. Charles sighed. "She was, indeed, a remarkable woman. I wish you'd met her before she got so sick. She was so energetic and spirited."

"I know she was. Even in sickness, her spirit was a comfort to us all."

Dr. Charles' smile faded and his jaw began to tremble. "Then you know why I miss her so much," he whispered. He brushed his sleeve across his eyes and stoically clenched his jaw.

"I'm sorry, too, Dr. Charles," Mourad said. "When should we bring Sirak back to see you?"

"Sirak's doing fine. He's much better than I expected this soon after a viper bite. You must not return to Diyarbekir until the unrest has past. I'm glad to see you, but I'm surprised you came today after the proclamation was publicized."

Mourad frowned. "What proclamation?"

"The Proclamation of Jihad against England, France and Russia."

"No!" Mourad replied. Taking a deep breath, he glanced at Kristina. The color had drained from her face. "This is the first we've heard of it. Dear God, what a calamity."

"It's the worst thing that could've happened. The tensions between the Turks and the Armenians, Greeks and other Christian minorities have increased dramatically since word of the proclamation reached Diyarbekir. I've treated dozens of Armenians and Syrians who were seriously beaten, and two men died. You must leave the city at once."

"Thank you for your concern. We'd best go now so we can make it home before dark."

"That would be wise."

"How long do you plan to stay here in Diyarbekir, Dr. Charles?" Kristina asked.

"I'm leaving Anatolia. As soon as I get my affairs in order, I'm returning to America to live with my sister and her husband on their farm in Oklahoma. I want to find a suitable replacement, so it will probably be next summer before I leave. Now that Julie is gone and the army has taken my hospital, there's no reason to stay."

"I'm sorry to hear this, Dr. Charles," Mourad said sorrowfully. "The Empire needs good men like you—now more than ever."

"There's something else I feel I must say, Mr. Kazerian. There are evil forces on the march here in Anatolia. I see them on the faces of people on the street, and I hear them in the conversations of the soldiers I'm treating in this hospital. I fear civility will vanish completely as the Empire stumbles into this godforsaken war. It already has in the eastern parts of the country near Bitlis and Van, and to the north into the Caucasus. You must take steps to safeguard yourself and your family. One of those steps is to stay away from Diyarbekir. Purchase the supplies you need for the winter and don't bring your family into this city again until the evil one has been vanquished. Now, more than ever, the devil's handiwork is visible all around us."

Mourad stared into Dr. Charles' sad eyes. His mouth grew dry as parchment.

"I'm sorry to be so plain-spoken," Charles continued, "but this is no time to mince words."

"Thank you for your candor," Mourad muttered. "Kristina and I will always be grateful for everything you've done for Sirak. God bless you."

"Thank you," Charles said. "Sirak, you take care of your family and your horse, okay?"

Sirak nodded soberly.

"That's my boy. Well, Elizabeth and I need to get back to surgery. Goodbye, Mr. Kazerian. Goodbye, Mrs. Kazerian."

Kristina took Nurse Barton's hand. "Goodbye, Elizabeth; I will pray for you."

"And I will pray for you and your family," she replied. She hugged Kristina one last time.

"Don't forget what we talked about back in Chunkoush," Kristina whispered. "I hope you return home soon, too."

"Don't worry, I'm scheduled to leave my post in January or February."

"God bless you."

"God bless you, too, Kristina."

Mourad carried Sirak to the hospital courtyard. Kristina tailed behind, clutching fearfully to her husband's coat. The number of soldiers had tripled and lunch was in full swing. The din of several hundred voices reverberated off the building and walls surrounding the yard.

Mourad headed down the street to the wagon. Kemal was perched in the driver's seat, conversing with a scruffy beggar dressed in a threadbare coat and tattered pants. Flora, Izabella and Özker were watching a crew of workers hoist large, pitch-black basalt slabs out of the bed of a horse-drawn wagon parked at a construction site across the street.

Kemal caught sight of the Kazerians walking toward him. "Mourad!" he called out.

The old beggar turned and abandoned Kemal. He limped awkwardly toward Mourad using a walking stick to support his weight and swiveling his hips to and fro in a rhythmic struggle to maintain his balance. The beggar's clothes were caked with dirt and a rank odor hung in the air surrounding him. "Sir, could you spare some *kurus* to feed my family?"

Sirak recoiled against his father's chest—mortified by the beggar's wall-eyed, broken-toothed appearance.

"Off with you!" Kemal bellowed. He jumped down from the wagon and rushed to grab the old man's arm.

"Let him be, Kemal," Mourad said. Fishing in his pocket, he pressed a few shiny coins into the man's outstretched palm. "May God be merciful to you and your family."

"God bless you, sir," the old man muttered deferentially, clutching the money to his chest. "Please accept my words of warning given in thanks. Steer clear of the eastern gate of the city. The gendarmes there take great delight in tormenting Christians who cross their path, and accuse them of every sort of offense. The worst is an evil soul named Osama Malek. He's stationed there in the late afternoons."

"Thank you for this warning, sir. We will heed your advice."

"May God repay your kindness tenfold," the old man said. He turned, and looking up the street, wandered away toward the hospital.

Mourad helped Kristina and the children back into the wagon. He climbed up into the driver's seat beside Kemal.

"I've seen this tramp near the Great Souk," Kemal said. "I would not trust his words."

"I'm not inclined to dismiss the beggar's warning so lightly, especially after our encounter at the gate this morning." Mourad glanced up the road. "The Bozikian Traders are just a kilometer shy of the northern gate. Once we've finished there, we'll lose less than an hour leaving by the north gate."

The wagon rumbled through narrow streets for nearly half an hour before crossing a small bridge and turning toward the open-air market where Mourad intended to purchase his winter stores. In marked contrast to their trip a few weeks earlier, the street leading to the souk was eerily hushed. Instead of bustling crowds, there were only a few stragglers milling about a pile of debris at the side of the road. Two old men in fezzes turned to gawk at the wagon rumbling past.

Mourad slowed the wagon to a crawl a short distance up the street. "Merciful God," he whispered, "they burned the church to the ground."

Sirak stared in horror at the empty churchyard where the centuries-old Armenian Orthodox Church had stood in all its glory only weeks earlier. All that remained were a few basalt blocks and piles of charred debris scattered haphazardly across the grounds. Several men were loading remnants into a horse-drawn cart.

Turning the corner in dumbfounded silence, the true magnitude of the calamity unfolded before them. Rather than the lively succession of shops and warehouses of old, the street was lined with abandoned stalls and buildings—most of which had been obliterated by fire. In the middle of the block, the doors of a large warehouse were standing open, and a huge sign reading "BOZIKIAN TRADERS" swung loose over the doorway.

Gawking in disbelief, Mourad pulled the wagon to a stop. His eyes wandered over the earthen warehouse floor that was littered with paper scraps, cloth sacks and other debris.

"This warehouse belonged to an old friend of my father's," Mourad muttered sadly.

"I'd heard there was trouble in some of the Armenian areas," Kemal offered consolingly, "but I never imagined this."

The wagon jerked forward and rolled slowly away from the scene of devastation. Mourad turned into an adjacent residential neighborhood. All of the homes on the street had been abandoned and ransacked. Several had been razed.

"Mother Mary full of grace," Mourad whispered. "What now?"

"I bought my winter stores at Berker's Warehouse in the Hakan Souk near the northern gate," Kemal said. "It's less than a kilometer from here. If we plan to leave through the Harput Gate, that'd be more convenient anyway."

Mourad glanced back at the horror-stricken expression on Kristina's face. "What other choice do we have? Let's try it."

Kemal guided Mourad through a residential neighborhood, and into a commercial district filled with fabric merchants, tailors and cobblers. A somber hush hung over the wagon as even the young children were silenced by the solemnity gripping their parents. Weaving through a busy intersection, Kemal directed Mourad into a lot overflowing with carts and wagons drawn by horses, mules and donkeys. Some wagons were filled with carpets, wares or grains intended for barter, but most were empty. In the back of the lot, dozens of men were milling around an expansive warehouse where teams of laborers rushed about like ants servicing the vehicles parked outside an enormous set of doors. "Berker Trading" was printed in Arabic script on the building facade.

A paunchy, middle-aged Turk hurried impatiently from wagon to wagon, barking orders in Arabic. His gruff, ill-tempered voice resounded across the souk. "Half *cheki* of flour!" he shouted to a waiting crew.

In the blink of an eye, the crew swarmed around the wagon in front of them. They stacked bags of flour high in the bed. When they finished loading, the driver secured the tailgate and led his horse away on foot.

Mourad edged the wagon forward until he was only a few meters from the open warehouse doors.

"Hold up there, idiot!" the acerbic Turk growled. He scrutinized Sirak and Özker standing in the bed. "You're too close to the cart ahead of you! What do you want?"

"Please, sir, forgive me," Mourad called down to the trader. "My mule has a mind of his own. I want a half *cheki* of flour, and one quarter *cheki* each of rice and beans."

The man stepped forward and peered into the bed of the wagon. Kristina and Flora lowered their eyes, but Izabella and the boys stared back in wide-eyed silence.

The man shielded his eyes from the blazing afternoon sun. "Do you have money?" he queried brusquely.

"Yes," Mourad replied evenly.

"Fifteen hundred *lire*," the Turk snarled.

"Fifteen hundred *lire*!" Mourad gasped incredulously. "That's outrageous!"

"Take it or leave it, infidel. You're fortunate to find anyone who'll sell to the likes of you."

Mourad took a deep breath, and biting his tongue, glanced at Kemal. "I'll pay you eight hundred," he offered evenly. "That's at least twenty percent above the market price."

"Fifteen hundred," the man repeated. He impatiently pulled at his beard. "That's my price."

Mourad scowled at the Turk for a moment, and then flicked the reins. "Thief!" he muttered beneath his breath.

The Turk followed along beside the wagon. "Fuck your God and sacred book, Armenian dog," he bellowed. "And take those whores and infidel-loving pigs with you."

Kemal clenched his fists in anger.

Mourad stretched his arm across Kemal's lap to calm him and fought a nearly irresistible urge to let loose a swift kick to the man's mouth. He wove the wagon through dozens of other carts and wagons and maneuvered it away from the warehouse. They barreled down the road through a fabric souk just inside the city walls. Seething with anger, he finally jerked the wagon to a stop on the side of the road and wearily dropped his face into his hands. "Dear God, help us. What should we do? We'll never make it through winter without provisions."

Kemal glanced up at the sun. "It's still three hours until sunset. Let's try the Hakan Souk. Then, if we hurry, we still have time to leave through the northern gate and make it home before dark."

Mourad pondered the suggestion for a moment. "Maybe we should forget about it and take Kristina and the children home now. I can try the Hakan Souk tomorrow."

"Do what's right for you and your family, my friend, but the situation in Diyarbekir grows more volatile by the hour. I think we should try the Hakan Souk today."

Mourad peered into Kemal's determined eyes. "You're right," he finally said. Waiting for a cart to pass, he pulled the wagon back onto the road and headed for the northern quarter.

Driving on for half an hour, they passed a steady stream of traffic headed in the opposite direction. Several times, the monotonous clatter of the wagon was pierced by the defaming shouts and threatening gestures of passing travelers, including a shrieked slur from a veiled old woman who shook her fist in frenzied anger from the back of a freight wagon.

Mourad stepped out from behind a stand of shrubs, and adjusting his trousers, glanced at the children playing with Kristina in the adjacent weedy lot. "I've decided what I'll do, Kemal. If our reception at Hakan Souk is hostile, I'll ride to Ergani tomorrow. I fear the food merchant was right."

"About what?" Kemal asked bemusedly.

"About us being fortunate to find anyone willing to sell goods to Armenians," Mourad replied.

Kemal shook his head with exasperation and wiped perspiration from his forehead with a handkerchief. He stuffed the rag into his pocket and climbed into the driver's seat. After a moment, he jumped down to the ground and hurried back to Mourad. "I have an idea. I'm sure it will work."

"What?" Mourad asked apprehensively.

"Do you trust me to do what's best for you, Mourad?"

"You know I do. What?"

"Before I saw it for myself, I didn't believe this hatred could reemerge so quickly. Now, I know differently. It's not that my people are evil. It's an irrational madness born of desperation and war. You were right; the price that scoundrel offered was at least twice the going rate. He knew you were desperate and thought he could cheat you. I'm afraid the same thing will happen at the next warehouse, and probably in Ergani, too."

"So where should we go?"

"To Hakan Souk."

"But you just said..."

"Not you, Mourad—me. I've bought provisions from Hakan Souk for years, and my father did the same for decades before me. So Özker and I will go on alone, while you wait here with your family." Kemal turned and motioned toward the foliage. "You should be safe hiding there in the brush. It'll take me at most an hour. Do you agree?"

Mourad took a deep breath. "You're the most loyal friend I've ever had," he whispered. He grasped Kemal's shoulders and gave him a bear hug. "How will I ever repay you?"

"You already have, Mourad—many times over."

Mourad slipped off the money belt concealed beneath his coat and handed it to Kemal.

"I'll negotiate the best possible price, my friend," the Turk said determinedly.

"I trust you, Kemal."

"I'll rush back here, and God willing, we'll make it through the north gate before it closes at sundown."

Mourad lifted Özker up to his father in the driver's seat. Kemal flicked the reins and the wagon eased away.

"Good luck, Özker!" Sirak called out.

"See you soon!" Özker shouted back.

Mourad led Kristina and the children into the half-dead scrub brush as far away from the busy road as possible. Their senses on knife's edge, they spread Izabella's blanket on the ground and joined hands in prayer. Mourad pleaded for God's solace for his family, and they huddled together on the ground to await Kemal's return.

For the hundredth time, Mourad peered at the waning sun through limbs of the shrubs shrouding the family. His stomach churned mercilessly, but he glanced back and gave Kristina a smile of false bravado.

"Don't torture yourself, darling," she whispered.

Mourad clenched his fists and peered out at the ebbing sun. "Damn it! They should be back by now. Why didn't I take you and the children home and try again tomorrow? How could I be so stupid?"

"You must have faith," Kristina whispered. She gathered the ends of her headscarf beneath her chin against the cold. "Kemal has never failed you. He will not fail you now."

"It's been too long. Something must have happened." He glanced once again toward the waning sun. "What will we do if he doesn't return?"

"He will return. You must be patient."

Mourad shook his head and peered out at the road once again. Soon he heard the clomping of hooves in the clearing. "Thank God!" Leaping from the shrubs, he ran to the wagon, relieved to see it laden with supplies. "Thank God, you're safe, Kemal."

"I'm sorry we took so long," the Turk replied remorsefully. "All of the traders at Hakan Souk were out of potatoes. We traveled nearly to the eastern gate to buy them."

"Potatoes?" Mourad laughed. "You put us through hell just to find potatoes?"

"I wasn't coming back here without potatoes, my friend. What's lamb stew without potatoes?"

"An excellent point," Mourad agreed, with a chuckle. "We'll have a feast on Saturday to celebrate."

"I also got a great deal on chickpeas." He held out Mourad's belt. "Here's the rest of your money."

Kristina herded the sleepy-eyed children out from the stand of shrubs. "Thank you, Kemal," she called out. "You're truly a saint."

"Hurry now," Mourad ordered. "We must rush to the gate before it closes for the night."

Kemal and Mourad restacked the supplies to create a sheltered cavity where Mourad, Kristina and the children could hide. Finally, he locked the tailgate, climbed into the driver's seat and thundered down the road toward the Harput Gate.

Abdul Pasha picked up a gleaming Mauser pistol from a wooden case the bespectacled, gray-haired arms merchant held out to him. "This is more like it! Try this pistol, Timurhan." He pressed the gun into his son's hand. "Can you feel the perfect balance compared to that Ottoman Army pistol?"

"Yes, I feel it, Father," Timurhan replied. He pointed the pistol at the wall.

"And look at the unusual handle. They call it the *Broomhandle*. You've got to hand it to the Germans; they really are the best gunsmiths in the world.

"How much?" Abdul asked the old man.

"These are the finest, handcrafted Mauser pistols I've ever had, sir." The merchant pushed his turban back on his head with his fingertips. "We can't get any more."

"How much?" Abdul growled.

"For you, Abdul, three hundred *lire*."

Abdul took another pistol from the box, and turning it over in his hand, jiggled it up and down to gauge the weight. He glanced up at the proprietor. "I'll give you two hundred," he said confidently.

"Two hundred seventy-five," the old man countered, "including four boxes of German-made ammunition."

Pasha looked down at the gun for several moments. "Two hundred fifty."

"Done."

Pasha broke into a grin. Wrapping his arm around Timurhan's shoulders, he hugged him tightly to his chest and pressed the pistol into his hand. "Happy birthday, Son. God willing, you will kill many Russian pigs with this pistol."

"Thank you, Father. The infidels will regret the day they dared challenge the Empire."

Pasha paid the shopkeeper and the man wrapped the pistol and bullets in a black cloth.

"Thank you," the shopkeeper said. He handed the package to Timurhan. "If you get your hands on a Russian officer's pistol, bring it to me. I'll pay you a handsome sum."

"I'll keep that in mind," Timurhan replied. He turned and stepped outside through the open door. Handing a scruffy attendant a coin, he took the reins of his horse and stuffed the package into his saddlebags. He pulled himself onto the horse and sat waiting for his father to finish his business with the shopkeeper.

Peering across the wide square, Timurhan scanned the procession of pedestrians, horses and wagons filing past guards at the Harput Gate. Suddenly, one wagon caught his eye. He watched as the driver turned and patted his son on the back. "Father!" he shouted, without diverting his gaze.

"I'll be done in a minute," Abdul called back.

"Isn't that Kemal Sufyan driving that wagon filled with provisions?"

Abdul stepped outside the gun shop and squinted across the square. "That backstabbing, infidel-loving, son-of-a-bitch," he muttered. "It's him—no doubt about it."

"Why is he leaving through the Harput Gate? He's added at least two hours to his trip."

"I'll tell you why. Don't you recognize that broken down piece of junk? That's ingrate Kazerian's wagon."

"Kazerian?" Timurhan muttered. "Are you sure?"

"I'm positive. Look at that scavenged white front wheel. I'd recognize that shit-hauler anywhere."

Timurhan glanced around to make sure the attendant wasn't listening. "In that case," he whispered, "it's a perfect opportunity to try out my new pistol."

"Not now. The roads are crowded with travelers arriving for the council. Our opportunity will come soon enough. Let's hurry before the gate closes."

CHAPTER 7

November 25, 1914

Timurhan Pasha, a duffle bag slung over his shoulder, stepped out of the farmhouse and glanced up at the threatening sky. Striding across the barnyard, he stopped and took his mother's hands.

Looking up at him, Sabriye sniffled quietly and dabbed tears from her cheeks with a natty handkerchief.

"Please don't cry, Mother," Timurhan whispered reassuringly. "I'll be fine." Wrapping his powerful arms around her tiny frame, he hugged her gently to his chest.

She clutched at his coat. "Write me every chance you get. Promise me."

"I promise, Mother. Don't worry, God willing, I'll be back before planting season."

"God's blessings be upon you, my son. We will all pray unendingly for your safe return."

One by one, Timurhan said his goodbyes to his younger sisters. Erol was standing at the end of the line holding his mother's hand. Towering above him like a giant, Timurhan squatted on the snow-covered ground and tenderly cupped his younger brother's head in his hand. "Don't forget what we talked about, Erol. Stick up for yourself. Father will respect you for it."

Erol squinted up at his brother. "I'll try," he muttered in a near-whisper. He wiped his tear-filled eyes with a sleeve. "I wish I could go, too."

"Someday you will."

Erol's mother smiled warmly and grasped Timurhan's arm. "I will pray for you."

Timurhan stood up and smiled with self-assurance. "I appreciate all your prayers, Jasmine. Thank you for baking bread for my trip."

"God bless you."

Timurhan turned and took a few steps to Hasan. Grasping his arm, he kissed him on both cheeks. "Goodbye, Uncle; I wish you good health."

The somber, dark-skinned Turk, his right arm hanging limply at his side, fought back tears of his own. He smiled sadly. "You must pray for your own health and well-being, Son. I will pray for you, too."

"Please, sir, while I'm away, I appeal for your encouragement and consideration for Erol. Father's much too hard on him, and without me here to..."

"I'll do what I can," Hasan interrupted. He glanced uncomfortably toward the barn where Abdul Pasha was waiting with his son's horse.

"Thank you."

Finally, the wiry Turk strode confidently to his father.

Abdul, his leathery face beaming, clutched the reins of a spirited black horse. Suddenly, the stallion reared up. Abdul jerked the reins down with both hands. "Steady, damn you," he growled. "Did you remember the extra boxes of ammunition, Son?"

"Yes, Father. They're here in my bag."

"Good. And the dagger Hasan bought you?"

"Yes, and the sharpening stone, too."

"Very good." Abdul's voice swelled with pride. Wrapping a brawny arm around Timurhan's back, he clutched him to his chest. "I only wish your grandfather were here to see the man you've become."

Timurhan glanced uncomfortably toward the other family members and caught Erol's stare. "Thank you, Father."

"Timurhan, my first-born, may you courageously serve the Empire and bring honor to the Pasha family. Allah has blessed you with the strength of an ox and the cunning of a lion. Now, in His name, go forth as a righteous sword of God and strike down the infidel who dares challenge this great empire and our way of life."

"I'll do my best, Father."

"I know you will. Go then, and may Allah be with you."

Timurhan lashed his bags behind the riding blankets, and taking the reins from his father, mounted his horse. Turning, he waved a last adieu to the family members. Finally, he nodded one last time to his father and trotted off across the dirt yard that fronted the Pasha family home.

Hasan waited until Timurhan disappeared over the crest before approaching Abdul. "The boy will do well, Effendi."

Abdul glared at Hasan. "Of course, he'll do well. The boy bears his grandfather's name—the hero of the Siege of Kars."

"Yes, Abdul, but the Russians won the Siege of Kars."

"Well, they won't win this one. For five long years I've promised to give Timurhan the Kazerian land. I'm determined to present that land to him when this war is over. Have you done what we talked about last week?"

"Not yet, Effendi."

"Well, do it!"

"I'll travel to Diyarbekir tomorrow and inform the authorities."

"Make it so, Hasan. We cannot let this opportunity pass."

Abdul, his arms filled with split logs, stepped into the house and walked across the room to the stove. He stacked the wood on the floor and glanced across the living room. Erol was sitting on the floor playing with his sisters.

"Erol!" he bellowed. "What are you doing?"

"Playing with Ayse and Fairuza," the boy replied deferentially. Fear filled his eyes.

"*With dolls?*" Abdul growled. Leaning down, he wrenched a figurine from the boy's hand. He flung the toy across the room and it broke to pieces against the fireplace mantel. "Even now your brother is rushing to meet the enemy. And what's Erol doing? He sits here, like a sissy, playing with dolls. You can't possibly be my son. That useless whore mother of yours must've fucked the farmhands."

Erol tried to duck away.

Abdul grabbed the boy by the collar and yanked him to his feet. "You're worthless! Do you hear me? Worthless!"

Erol's mother, Jasmine, rushed into the room. "Leave him alone, Abdul! He wasn't hurting anyone."

"Get out of my way, whore," the Turk bellowed. He slapped her with the back of his hand so hard she fell on the floor. "It's your fault this boy's so pathetically weak in mind and body." Abdul kicked the terrified boy in the backside and shoved him out the door. "Get your useless butt out to that barn and clean the horse stalls. All of them! Do you hear me?"

Too terrified to reply, Erol sprinted across the yard and disappeared through the barn door.

CHAPTER 8

Two weeks later

Mourad set his shovel down and gathered his coat against a biting gust of wind. "Stepannos!" he shouted above the howling blast, "clear that snow away from the barn door."

Stepannos was covered head to toe in heavy winter clothing. He nodded and thrust his shovel into the meter-high snow bank heaped against the door.

Mourad beat the snow off his woolen gloves. Exhaling a long stream of frosty breath, he clomped around the side of the barn. He found Sirak and Mikael struggling to clear snow away from the rear of the barn.

"Listen, boys!" he yelled, "it's very cold tonight. When you get done, make sure all the horses are covered with blankets. Come inside for dinner when you get done."

"Okay, Papa," Mikael called back. "We're almost finished."

Mourad smiled at Sirak. He brushed snow from his hair and trudged away through knee-high snow to the farmhouse that had wisps of smoke swirling out of the chimney pipe.

Suddenly, the pounding of hooves resounded above the wind. Looking down the road, Mourad saw a detachment of soldiers coming toward him.

"Ha!" the driver of a tailing wagon shouted. He flicked the reins and drove the wagon through a knee-high bank of snow.

The soldier riding the lead horse, a gruff-looking Turk with a scruffy beard, pulled up just short of Mourad. His fur hat and heavy winter coat were caked with snow. "Good afternoon," he puffed into the icy air. "I'm Sergeant Demurcu of the Turkish Eleventh Reserve Corp. By command of Governor-General Hamid, we're ordered to collect fifty percent of your winter foodstuffs." He held out a rolled paper.

Mourad took the paper and unrolled it. "For what purpose?" he bellowed.

"To support the Ottoman forces. All citizens of Diyarbekir Province are ordered to comply."

"But we don't have sufficient supplies to last the winter as it is. I've got five children, a wife and a sick mother to feed."

"I'm sorry, but I must carry out my orders. You're also required to surrender all worthy transportation animals—horses, mules, donkeys and camels."

"But if you take our horses, we can't plant our crops in the spring."

Sirak peeked at the soldiers through a crack in the barn door.

"I'm sorry, sir," the soldier persisted. "Let's begin with your animals. I need to check the barn."

Horrorstruck, Sirak glanced up at Mikael. He stumbled to his feet and ran to the stalls in the back of the barn. Slipping a bit into Tiran's mouth, he tore a heavy blanket off the horse's back and led him to the rear door.

"What are you doing, Sirak?" Mikael demanded.

"They're not taking my Tiran!"

"Are you crazy?" Mikael gasped incredulously. "Those soldiers have guns. They'll shoot you."

Someone yanked at the barn door, but only managed to open it a few inches. After a moment, the ring of a shovel resounded through the door.

"*They're coming!*" Sirak whispered. "Hurry, Mikael! Boost me up and push the rear door open."

"No, Sirak!" Mikael replied angrily. "You'll get shot."

Sirak glared at his older brother, and then glanced at the front door. The sound of men talking and shoveling snow echoed from the yard. Sirak led Tiran to one of the stalls, climbed up on a slat and jumped onto the horse's back. Spinning around at the front of the barn, he edged the spirited horse toward the door.

Mikael stepped in front of him. "What are you doing, Sirak?"

"If you won't help me, then I'll gallop past them as soon as they open the door. We'll be past them before they know what happened."

Mikael's eyes bulged in disbelief. "Listen to me, little brother. Those are real soldiers with real guns out there."

"Open the back door before they see my Tiran."

Mikael peered into Sirak's determined eyes. Sighing with exasperation, he jogged to the rear door and pushed one panel open. Suddenly, the bottom of the front door scraped across the icy snow.

"Halt!" the sergeant bellowed.

Sirak squeezed Tiran through the opening, and galloped headlong through the corral gate and across the enclosure. The powerful horse snorted loudly and, kicking up a cloud of snow, streaked across the pristine pasture.

Mourad bounded through the rear barn door with the sergeant and two of his men.

"Halt!" one soldier yelled. He raised his rifle to fire.

"No!" Mourad shouted. He deflected the rifle barrel just as it discharged with an ear-shattering blast.

Sirak flinched at the report of the rifle, but didn't stop. He jabbed his heels into Tiran's flanks and headed directly for the fence. Leaning forward, he prepared to jump.

Another rifle shot echoed across the pasture. Tiran whinnied, reeled away from the fence, and tumbled onto his side, sending Sirak head over heels into the snow.

Sirak remained face down in the snow for several seconds before rolling over and brushing the snow from his face. Tiran thrashed about in the waist-deep powder and struggled to right himself. Finally, he got to his feet and, whinnying loudly, with terror in his eyes, trotted aimlessly across the snow-covered pasture.

The soldier leveled his rifle at Sirak. "Don't move!" he ordered.

Stepannos squeezed past the man and knelt beside his brother. "Are you hurt?"

Sirak muttered unintelligibly, and rolling to his knees, craned his neck to find Tiran.

"Get your hands in the air!" the soldier shouted. He walked forward with his gun trained on Sirak. "You're under arrest."

"Hold your fire, Corporal!" the sergeant barked. "You idiot! Can't you see he's just a boy? Go get the horse and take him back to the barnyard."

"Yes, sir," the corporal replied. He jogged off after Tiran.

The sergeant stopped beside Stepannos and peered down at Sirak with a benevolent smile. "Are you hurt?"

Sirak, his face and body covered with snow, shook his head dejectedly.

"You've got the heart of a lion, Son. I wish I had a dozen soldiers like you under my command. You'll be a valiant cavalryman for the Empire someday."

"Please, sir, don't take my horse," Sirak pleaded. Tears welled in his eyes.

"I'm sorry, Son, but I must follow my orders or I'll find myself hanging from the gallows."

"What will you do with him?" Sirak asked angrily.

The sergeant turned his gaze on the corporal trying to corral Tiran. The man managed to grab the reins, but the belligerent horse reared back and galloped off to the back of the corral.

"Such a fine horse will likely be assigned to the cavalry. But first he'll go through training."

The snow whooshed behind them and the sergeant turned. The soldier who'd tried to shoot Sirak shoved Mourad across the pasture. Mourad's hands were bound behind his back and a trickle of blood was running from his nose.

"Untie him, Private," the sergeant ordered gruffly.

"But, sir," the soldier protested, "he interfered with me."

"As would any man with an *okka* of courage. You were shooting at his son. Untie him, damn it!"

The private, his jaw clenched with rage, untied Mourad's hands.

Mourad rushed past the sergeant and lifted Sirak to his feet. "Are you hurt, Sirak?"

"No, Papa," the boy sniffled. His voice crackled with emotion. "They're taking my Tiran." Bursting into tears, he pointed across the pasture.

Mourad turned to look. The corporal held Tiran's reins and was leading him to the barn.

"I'm sorry," Mourad whispered. He squatted and clutched Sirak to his chest. "I'm so sorry."

Sirak buried his face in his father's coat, and sobbing uncontrollably, peeked around to catch one last glimpse of Tiran before the proud horse walked into the barn.

Mourad stared blankly across the room and gently rubbed Sirak's neck. The crestfallen boy was lying on the sofa with his head in his father's lap. The room was lit only by dying embers in the fireplace.

Kristina crept silently into the room and scooted carefully around Stepannos and Mikael's pallet on the floor. "Is he sleeping?" she whispered.

Mourad nodded his head dejectedly. "He finally cried himself to sleep."

"Poor darling. I'll change him into his nightclothes."

"No, I'll carry him back to the bedroom in a few minutes."

"Did they take all of our horses?"

"They left the old mare."

"What about our food supply?"

"The sergeant apologized for taking so much, and he made a point of leaving more than half of the rice and beans. It could've been a lot worse."

"Do we have enough to last the winter?"

"Maybe, but we must carefully ration what's left."

"What will we do if it's not enough?"

"I don't know. We have the money I saved to buy seed in the spring."

"We'll need the seeds, Mourad. Let's sell the diamond necklace Mother left me."

Mourad smiled appreciatively and reached for Kristina's hand. "Thank you, darling. We'll see what happens. You know, it's funny, but I've been sitting here wondering whether God means for our horses and supplies to help Alek."

Kristina stared back in silence for a moment, before closing her eyes. "I just wish we'd hear something. A letter or short note...anything. It's the not knowing that drives me mad."

"I know, I know. If it weren't for Alek, I'd accept Abdul Pasha's offer and move to Istanbul or, if I could arrange it, even out of the Empire. But I keep thinking, what if Alek returns to the farm, injured or sick and needing our help?"

Kristina sat on the end of the couch, and leaning against Mourad's shoulder, stroked Sirak's arm. "I support you, whatever you decide, but I cannot leave Anatolia until Alek returns."

"You've changed your mind?"

"Yes, at least for now."

"Then we agree. We'll stay until Alek returns, no matter what."

"But if the opportunity arises to safely send the children to live with Bedros, I want to do it, even if we must sell everything. It's not safe here anymore."

Mourad glanced down at the boys on the pallet. He traced his fingers down Kristina's arm and grasped her hand. "I'll ride to Ergani to make inquiries once the storm passes."

CHAPTER 9

Kemal stopped at the crest of the hill overlooking Mourad Kazerian's farm and scanned the scene below. The barnyard was eerily silent. The roof of the house was cloaked in snow. A mound of fresh-fallen powder was heaped against the front door. Not even a wisp of smoke rose from the chimney and the small window at the front of the house was dark. It looked deserted.

Kemal walked his horse through a gully and headed down the snowy path to the farmhouse. "You stay with the horse and I'll check the house," he whispered to Özker. He slid to the ground, and walking toward the house, stopped a few paces from the front door. "Mourad!" he called out. He glanced over his shoulder at Özker. "Mourad, it's Kemal! I've brought flour!"

A moment later, the door creaked open. Mourad, looking gaunt and haggard, stepped across the mound of snow. He glanced anxiously up the path toward the main road. "Thank you for coming, Kemal. I'm so happy to see you."

"Is your family well?"

"As well as can be expected. We heard about the mass arrests and disappearances in Diyarbekir and the surrounding villages."

"You're right to be careful. This unrest is so terrible—unlike any before." Kemal motioned toward the chimney. "Do you need help chopping firewood?"

"No, my friend, we have plenty, but we only use the fireplace at night. We don't want to attract attention."

Kemal nodded glumly. "How's Kristina?"

"She's sick. She hardly eats since the soldiers confiscated our stores. I'm worried about Sirak, too. He's been inconsolable since they took his horse. I thought it would pass after a few weeks, but his depression has only deepened. The light's gone from his eyes."

"God is great, my friend. He'll forget with time. Maybe playing with Özker would help."

"I'll try anything at this point."

"And how's your mother?"

"A little better, thank God."

"I'm glad to hear it. Fadime sent two bags of flour. Can I bring them inside?"

"Of course. Forgive my bad manners. I can't begin to express our appreciation for your thoughtfulness and friendship. Kristina will brew a fresh pot of tea."

Kemal lifted Özker down off the horse and untied the rope holding two large bags of flour. "Now, Özker, don't forget what we talked about. Play with Sirak and try your best to cheer him up. Do you understand?"

"Yes, Papa."

"Did you bring the ball?"

"It's here in my pocket."

Kemal patted his son on the head. "Good boy."

Mourad stepped outside with his arm around Sirak. The boy's face was expressionless and pale, with dark rings around his eyes.

"Sirak!" Özker called out. He ran to his friend. "I missed you so much."

"I missed you, too, Özker," Sirak replied flatly. There was a vacant, far-away look in his eyes, and his face was devoid of emotion.

"Father told me about the soldiers. I'm sorry. I know how much you loved Tiran."

Sirak nodded glumly.

"Those bad men came to our farm, too. They took Father's best horses."

"I know God expects us to sacrifice to help my brother, but whenever I think of Tiran, all I..." Sirak bowed his head, and sniffling, buried his head in his father's coat sleeve.

Özker stepped to Sirak's side and gently patted his friend on the shoulder. He pulled a bright red ball from his coat pocket. "Sirak, would you like to play with my new ball?"

Sirak wiped his eyes on his sleeve and glanced up. "Yes."

Özker slipped his arm around Sirak's back and the two boys walked away toward the barn.

Mourad and Kemal stood watching them for several moments. Özker tossed Sirak the ball and took up a position a few meters away. Sirak dropped the ball on the snow-covered ground and gave it a glancing kick. The ball spun toward the barn and Özker ran after it.

"Thank you," Mourad muttered. "I'm grateful for anything to take his mind off the horse. A young boy should never endure so many heartaches. The tea should be ready by now. Let me take that bag."

"I should feed and water my horse before we go inside."

"Just tie him to that post. I'll send Stepannos to tend to him."

Kemal tied his horse to the post and, hoisting the second bag of flour onto his shoulder, followed Mourad to the front door. "You boys come inside if you get too cold!"

"We will, Father," Özker yelled.

Sirak kicked the ball against the side of the barn and Özker caught it. He heaved it back to Sirak and he kicked it high into the air. Diving to his right, Özker landed face first in a mound of snow. Rolling over, the young Turk struggled to his feet. He was covered head to toe in white powder.

Sirak brushed snow away from his friend's face with his fingertips and broke out in laughter. "You look like a winter fox that crawled into a hare hole."

"It's inside my coat!" Özker squealed. He opened his coat and brushed snow off his tunic. "Brrr, that's really cold. Hey, let's go see the ice on the pond!"

"No, I'm not allowed. Mikael fell through the ice and nearly drowned when he was a little boy. He would have, if Alek hadn't pulled him out. Besides, I'm too cold."

"Okay," Özker muttered disappointedly. "Hey, I know; let's play in the barn!"

"Sure! Do you ever feed chickens?"

"No, that's Verda and Lale's chore. I clean the horses' stall."

Sirak stopped dead in his tracks. He stared at Özker as though he'd been punched in the stomach. Turning away, he walked to the barn and kicked at the snow.

Özker ran after him. "What's wrong, Sirak?"

"Cleaning the horse stalls was my chore, too. Now they're all gone except for old Rock."

"I'm sorry, Sirak. I forgot."

Sirak glanced toward the snow-covered corral. "I wonder what Tiran's doing right now?"

"Maybe he found Alek."

"That's what Papa says. I hope he's not scared of the guns."

"Tiran wouldn't be afraid of the guns," Özker scoffed. "I'm sure he's very brave, just like you, Sirak,"

"Come on, let's go feed the chickens. I don't want to talk about him anymore."

The boys walked across the barnyard and Sirak opened the barn door. He led Özker to several pens stacked against one wall. Some of the chickens whistled and clucked at the sight of them. Sirak grabbed a pail of feed, and taking a handful, opened one of the doors to let a rooster eat out of his hand.

"Pepper here's my favorite. He's always happy to see me." Sirak held the pail out to Özker. "You feed those two. That's Natty and Tia."

Özker took a handful of the feed and reached inside. Both hens clucked contentedly and pecked at his hand. "It tickles!" he squealed.

Sirak grinned and tossed feed into another pen. "Özker, do you hate Christians?" he asked pensively.

Özker glanced over his shoulder with a puzzled expression. "No, I don't hate Christians. My mother told me not to hate anybody. Why?"

"I heard Mama tell Papa the Muslims in the walled city hate Christians. Many Christians have been killed there since the war started," Sirak said.

"You're a Christian."

"Yes, and everyone in my family's a Christian, too."

"Do you think I hate you, or my father hates you?" Özker asked.

"No, of course not. Papa says that your father is a kind and religious man, and if there were more men like him, the Empire would be a better place for everyone. But our neighbor, Abdul Pasha, hates us."

"Abdul Pasha hates everybody." Özker dropped the rest of the feed into the pen and locked the door. "Mother reads the Quran to me every night at bedtime and helps me memorize the important parts. I learned a passage that reminds me of you."

"Really? What does it say?"

"*Thou wilt find the nearest in friendship to the believers to be those who say, we are Christians. That is because there are priests and monks among them and because they are not proud.* Father said that passage reminds him of your papa, too."

"That's written in your holy book?" Sirak asked.

"Yes, it is. Mother says there's no harm in us being friends, no matter what other believers say. So we'll always be friends, Sirak, even when we're like the old men in town who only gossip and play chess. You must remember this."

Sirak smiled gratefully. "I will remember."

Özker thrust his hands into his coat pockets. "Brrr, I'm cold! Let's finish feeding these chickens and go see if your mother has something to eat."

Sirak set his bucket against the wall. "I'll feed them later. Mama baked sweet bread this morning. We'd better hurry before Stepannos and Mikael eat it all."

"Let's go!"

The boys dashed out of the barn, and matching stride for stride, sprinted to the front door. Sirak shoved the door open.

"Hello, Özker," Kristina called from the kitchen. "Are you hungry?"

Özker glanced at his father and Kemal nodded.

"Yes, Mrs. Kazerian. I'm starving."

"I've baked the Armenian sweet bread you love. Sit down by the fire and I'll bring you some."

The wood in the hearth crackled and smoked, and intermittently spewed hot embers onto the floor. Stepannos, Mikael and Flora—bundled in winter coats—sat cross-legged in front of the fireplace. Izabella was in Flora's lap.

Sirak and Özker held their hands out and playfully sparred for the heat.

Sirak scooted in beside Flora, and making room for Özker, smiled at his father.

Mourad smiled back and gratefully nodded at Kemal.

Kristina and the girls had gone to bed, and Mikael and Stepannos were slumbering by the fireplace. Sirak and Özker had fallen asleep on the floor near their fathers' feet.

Kemal peered through darkness lit only by dying embers in the fireplace. "It's late, Mourad," he whispered. "It's time to head home."

"You're welcome to stay until morning."

"No, I can't. Fadime and Nahid will worry. Can I have a private word with you before we leave?"

Mourad gathered himself to his feet. "Of course. I'll help you with your horse."

The two men stepped softly through the front room, and slipping outside into the crisp night air, headed to the barn. The scent of burning firewood wafted on the gentle breeze.

"Mourad, I've heard whispers the army suffered a devastating defeat on the Russian frontier."

Mourad frowned. "A defeat?"

"Yes, they say it was a rout. Shocking rumors are spreading about thousands of soldiers being lost—entire corps vanishing."

"God Almighty."

"Do you know where Alek is stationed?"

"No. We haven't heard a word since the day he left home."

"They say the Russian Army has driven deep inside Anatolia—nearly to the outskirts of Van. And there's something else you must know. There are reports of many Armenians joining the Russian volunteer regiments. Turks in Diyarbekir are calling for revenge."

Mourad stared back, unable to find his tongue.

Kemal grasped Mourad's shoulder. "Your family isn't safe here anymore. You must leave Anatolia now."

"But, where do we go?"

"Go join Bedros in Istanbul. He has perks and privileges there. The capital may be the only place in the Empire where Armenians are safe. And from Istanbul you could arrange safe passage out of the Empire."

Mourad stood contemplatively for several moments. "Who knows, maybe the situation isn't any better in the capital. I haven't heard a word from Bedros since his letter in October."

"It's got to be better than here."

"How can I move my mother to Istanbul? It's a long, hard trip, even for healthy people. How could she survive that in the dead of winter?"

"Mourad, you remember, of course, that my father and yours were good friends?"

"Yes, yes they were. We know that."

"Before Father died, he told me his biggest regret in life was not doing enough to save their common friend, Adom Tomassian. Did you know him?"

"Yes," Mourad replied solemnly. "We all knew Adom. He was a leader in our church."

"Well, then, you know what happened to him."

"My father spoke of it many times. He blamed his killing on the Bloody Sultan."

"Truly, Sultan Abdul Hamid must bear much of the blame, yet Father said we all bore responsibility because we didn't do enough to stop the killing. It haunted him until the day he died," Kemal explained. "Mourad, I don't want to bear this burden. You must act now, before the situation spins out of control."

Mourad stared into his friend's unwavering eyes. "Okay, I'll do it." He squeezed Kemal's hand. "It'll take a week or so to prepare for the journey, but then we'll go."

"You must stay at my farm until you leave. It'll be much safer. I'll return first thing in the morning to help you move your family."

"Are you sure?"

"I insist. Tell Kristina to pack only what you need to live for a week. We'll return later to gather belongings you plan to take with you to Istanbul."

"Okay, we'll be ready. I should've accepted Abdul Pasha's offer," he said with regret.

"To hell with Pasha," Kemal growled. "I'll watch the farm while you're away, and when everything settles, you'll return. Everything will be the same as it was before. You have my word on this."

Mourad embraced Kemal. "Thank you, my friend. You're a true man of God."

CHAPTER 10

Kemal lifted Sirak up to the driver's seat atop the wagon. He walked to his horse and, adjusting his saddlebags, untied the scruffy-looking mare from the barnyard post. Swinging up onto the horse's back, he reached down for his son. He positioned Özker in front of him astride the horse and pulled the boy's cap down on his head. "Okay, let's take it slow."

"Mourad, did you remember the note for Alek?" Kristina yelled from the rear of the wagon.

"Yes. It's in the spot we agreed on in case of emergency."

"What if he forgets?"

"Don't worry, he'll remember."

Circling around the barnyard, Kemal trotted up the snow-covered path. The wagon clattered after him.

Mourad peered up at the bright blue sky and glanced over his shoulder. Kristina and the children were huddled together behind three crates of clucking chickens and two chests of belongings. Izabella was asleep in her mother's lap, her beloved doll, a gift from Uncle Bedros, clutched in her small hands. Mourad's ailing mother, bundled from head to toe against the cold, stared back with a cheerless, vacant expression. He gave her a forlorn smile, but she quickly glanced away.

Mourad's eyes fell on the Khatchkar cross hanging on the front door of the house. He tapped out the sign of the cross. "Father, give us Thy protection," he whispered.

The rickety wagon crested the hill and Sirak turned in his seat to catch one last glimpse of the snow-cloaked farmhouse, the only home he'd ever known.

Sensing Sirak's apprehension, Mourad smiled and patted his son on the knee. "Don't concern yourself with the things of this world, Son. Put your faith in God."

The wagon turned west onto the main road, and Sirak's eyes wandered to three columns of smoke rising into the sky in the distance. He glanced at his father, but Mourad hadn't noticed. The latter's eyes were fixed on the bumpy road ahead, as his horse splashed through a puddle of melting snow.

Kemal, however, had noticed the smoke. Feeling a sense of foreboding, his thoughts drifted to another time and place. Taking a deep breath, he exhaled apprehensively. "*Allahu Akbar,*" he whispered.

Özker turned around. "What did you say, Papa?"

"Nothing, Son, nothing at all."

The wagon bumped slowly over the uneven country road for half an hour before Kemal turned onto a narrow trail that meandered through snow-draped spruce trees. Paralleling the bank of a frozen stream, the path opened onto a small clearing nestled between the river and a line of rocky cliffs. In the middle of the field, a small farmhouse, its chimney billowing smoke, stood a stone's throw from a dilapidated barn.

Kemal rode to the front door and the wagon clattered to a stop beside him. The door burst open and Fadime and Nahid, both wearing veils and long black dresses, stepped gingerly through the snow. Sabiha, Verda and Lale rushed past them, giddy with excitement.

"Flora!" Sabiha called out happily.

"Hello, everyone," Flora called out.

Özker jumped down from the horse and ran to the wagon. "Let's go, Sirak! I'll show you my river. Most of it's iced over, but we can throw rocks in the rapids."

Mourad lifted Sirak down to the ground and crouched beside him. "You can throw rocks, Son, but stay back from the water. Do you understand?"

"I know, Papa—the ice is dangerous."

"And the water is cold. Be very careful."

Sirak nodded. He turned and sprinted across the snowy pasture. "Özker, wait for me!"

Mourad watched the boys until they ran behind the barn.

Kemal walked up beside him. "They'll be fine."

"I know. This is a blessing for Sirak. He won't have to see our empty corral, or Tiran's tackle in the barn." He let out a long sigh and looked to the river. The boys were skipping along the bank hurling stones. "Thank you, Kemal."

"Please, my friend, thank me no more. We are brothers, and I know in my heart, you'd do the same for me."

Mourad nodded solemnly. Walking to the rear of the wagon, he picked up his mother and carried her to the house.

Kemal rushed ahead to open the front door. "This way, please. We've prepared a bed for her in Father's old room."

They stepped through a living room that was simply adorned with a pair of divans, a chest and a slew of hand-woven cushions and carpets. The Quran sat open on an ornate stand at the end of one divan.

Kemal led Mourad down a short hall and ducked through the last door. Mourad followed him into the tiny room and set his mother gently on the blanket-covered bed.

Nahid rushed in behind them and covered the old woman with a colorful woolen quilt. "It's always so cold in this room. I'll make her some warm soup."

Mourad leaned down and kissed his mother on the forehead, and her aged eyes fluttered open.

"Mourad, my son," she whispered, in a high-pitched, frail voice.

"Yes, Mother?"

"Don't let them take the land, Son." She clutched desperately at his arm. "Your father's grave...your grandfather's grave...you can't let them..."

"Don't worry, Mother, we're not leaving forever, just for a short while."

Catching her breath, she grimaced with pain. "Promise me."

Mourad glanced dolefully at Kemal. His friend stared solemnly back.

"I promise, Mother. We'll take you home soon."

"Thank you, Son." The old woman closed her eyes, and taking a deep breath, let out a relieved sigh.

Kristina fetched a box from the back of the wagon and handed it to Sabiha. "Here are Flora's clothes."

"Thank you, Mrs. Kazerian," Sabiha replied politely. "I'll put this in my bedroom. Flora and I will share the guest room in the back of the house, and you and your husband are in the large bedroom in the front."

"What about Verda and Lale?"

Fadime stepped from the house and smiled. "Don't worry. I moved the twins into the room in the back."

"Thank you. That's very kind."

"Unfortunately, the boys must sleep on the floor in the living room, but we've got plenty of pillows and blankets."

"That'll be fine. They love sleeping by the fire."

Kristina stooped down, and sitting on the end of the wagon, prepared to jump to the ground.

"Wait," Mourad called out. "Let me help you." He lowered Kristina to the ground and pushed an errant strand of hair beneath her headscarf. "You look exhausted, darling. You need a nap."

"No, Mourad. Fadime needs help with dinner."

"Flora can help her with dinner. You need to sleep, or you'll end up sick."

"You must listen to your husband," Fadime said. She took Kristina's arm. "There will be many more dinners. You must rest now."

Kristina smiled. "How can we ever begin to thank you?"

"No thanks are expected. We'll always remember it was your Mourad who offered my husband work when Abdul Pasha bullied the other farmers not to hire him. I don't know what we would've done, if he hadn't defied that evil brute."

They stepped into the house and headed to the bedrooms.

"Bedros and Mourad speak so highly of Kemal, and his father, Tarik. They both say Tarik was like a second father to them."

"You have said it," Fadime replied warmly. "Tarik counted them as the second and third sons his wives could never bear. He spoke of this many times."

Fadime led Kristina into a bedroom crowded with a small bed and chest. Pulling the blankets back, she fluffed the pillow. "There you go. Please get some sleep and I'll wake you for dinner."

Kristina took Fadime's hands. "You're such an angel. I know in my heart we'll be good friends."

Fadime squeezed Kristina's hands and smiled. "I feel this, too. May God give you rest and answer all your prayers." Fadime stepped out of the room and quietly closed the door behind her.

CHAPTER 11

January 23, 1915

Abdul Pasha stepped inside the house, and slipping off his heavy coat, hung it on a hook beside the door. Hasan was seated by the fireplace reading the Quran. Ignoring him, Abdul stepped around the divan and into the kitchen. He tore the end off a loaf of bread, stuffed it into his mouth and stepped back to the fireplace. Yawning, he glanced at the wood box beside the hearth and shook his head. "Damn it! brother-in-law, where's that worthless son of mine?"

"I'm not sure, Effendi," Hasan replied deferentially. He peered over his reading glasses, and stroked his beard. "He may be with his mother."

"Erol!" Abdul bellowed at the top of his lungs. "Get the hell out here!"

Erol came running from the back of the house and timidly stared at the floor. "Yes, Father."

"Did I not tell you to fill the box with wood?"

"Yes, Father, but..."Jasmine hurried from the rear of the house. "I asked him to help me make the bed and fold your clothes."

Abdul turned and glared at her. His eyes were filled with loathing. "And has he finished with the bed and clothes?"

"We just finished."

"Well, then, woman, I suggest you mind your own business and get on with preparing my breakfast."

Jasmine walked past Erol into the kitchen and filled the teapot with water.

"Now, boy," Abdul said, leaning his face close to Erol's, "you get that scrawny butt of yours outside and fetch more wood. If that fire goes out, I'll skin you alive."

Erol screwed up his courage to look at his father's wind-burned face. "There's no cut wood, Father—only a few scraps."

"Then get the hell out there and chop some more!" Abdul shoved Erol to the door. "Do I have to do everything around here? Tell me, woman, why did you burden me with this worthless runt?"

"He's just a boy, Abdul," Jasmine protested from the kitchen, her voice filled with contempt.

"He's eight. That's old enough for a boy to pull his weight in the household. Timurhan cut wood when he was even younger."

"Timurhan was always big for his age."

"As long as a boy can lift an axe, he can chop wood."

"But Erol doesn't know how. Timurhan cut the wood before he left, remember?"

"Come on," Abdul snarled at Erol. He jerked his coat down from the hook. "I'll show you. Then, from now on, it's your responsibility to keep the box filled with wood and the fire burning. Do you understand?"

"Yes, Father." Erol glanced fretfully at his mother and followed Abdul outside.

Abdul and Erol slogged through ankle-deep snow. They clomped around the side of the house to a clearing where several large logs were scattered on the ground.

"Damn it," Abdul grumbled. "There isn't enough here to last for more than a few days. We'll gather more wood tomorrow. Watch me carefully."

Abdul picked up the axe, and taking a powerful swing, knocked a patch of bark off one of the tree trunks. He swung again, and again, until he chopped completely through the log, splitting it in half. Straddling one of the pieces, he chopped a grove in the middle. "Okay, now it's your turn." He handed the axe to Erol.

Erol clutched the handle and clumsily lifted the axe off the ground, but stumbled and fell to his knees.

Abdul shook his head. "Worthless," he muttered. "Hold it farther from the end so you'll have better control."

Erol got up and took a feeble swing. The blade of the axe barely dented the wood.

"Again!" Abdul bellowed.

Erol swung the axe once more, but the result was the same.

Abdul moaned disgustedly. "We don't have all day." He jerked the axe from the boy's hand. "Today, you watch. Then, tomorrow, you will chop that smaller trunk. I don't care if it takes you all day. You will not stop until you are finished. Do you understand?"

"Yes, Father."

Wielding the axe with authority, Abdul chopped the trunk into several pieces, before splitting off several hearth-sized logs. Finally, he drove the axe into the nearby trunk and handed Erol one of the logs. "Carry this into the house."

The boy's arms drooped under the weight. Gathering several logs into his own arms, Pasha rounded the corner of the house with Erol trudging behind him, straining under the weight of his burden.

Abdul leaned his load against the door jam and pushed the door open. "Go on."

The boy staggered past him into the house and headed to the fireplace.

Abdul dropped his logs into the wood box. He grabbed the log from Erol and dropped it on the waning embers.

"Go get the rest of the logs. I'll make a man out of you yet."

Erol, head down, walked back to the door. At the threshold, he turned and glanced at his mother. Watching silently from the kitchen, she smiled sympathetically and nodded encouragement.

"Go on!" Pasha yelled. "Don't come back here without a log."

Erol cringed. Stepping outside, he pulled the door closed behind him.

Abdul slumped down on the divan. "Woman, where's my breakfast?"

Jasmine defiantly marched to the divan and handed Abdul a cup of tea. She turned to walk away, but he grabbed the belt of her dress.

"What? I'm getting your tray."

Abdul grabbed her wrist and pulled her close. He ran his hands across her breasts. "After I eat breakfast, we'll meet in your bedroom."

"I can't, Abdul. It's my time of the month."

"Bullshit!" he shot back. "Do you think I'm stupid enough to believe your menses come every week?"

"You believe what you want to believe, but it's the truth."

Abdul, his jaw clenched in anger, glared at his wife. She stared back, with equal measures of disdain and fear.

"Perhaps it's for the best," he finally huffed. "There's no sense taking the risk you'll get pregnant and bring another pathetic weakling into this family. I'll find something you can do for me," he glared, a wicked smile on his face.

The door opened behind them.

"I told you not to come back here without a log," Abdul growled at Erol, who was standing empty-handed in the open doorway.

"There are...there are soldiers, Father," he stuttered. "They want you."

"Soldiers?" Abdul repeated. Rising to his feet, he set his teacup on the end table and walked to the door.

Three soldiers on horseback were in the barnyard. Behind them was a wagon outfitted with a team of six horses. All the men were bundled in heavy winter coats, and the driver, an old man wearing a red fez, was wrapped in blankets.

One soldier dismounted and marched across the barnyard. "I'm Lieutenant Yasevi, sir," he said solemnly. "We're here to see Abdul Pasha bin Mohammad, father of Timurhan Pasha bin Abdul."

"I'm Abdul Pasha bin Mohammad. Is something wrong?"

"Sir, I regret to inform you that your son has been martyred in jihad."

"No," Abdul whispered, his expression melting into horror. He gaped at the wagon. "My God, no. You are mistaken, sir."

"No, sir. Unfortunately, I'm certain. We're returning your son's body for burial."

Abdul peered at the wagon through a suddenly heavy snowfall. Slowly, he sank to his knees. "No! No! No!" he cried out in anguish. "Not my son!"

Timurhan's mother rushed from the house. "What it is?"

"Our son is dead!"

Overcome with anguish, Sabriye sank to her knees and collapsed face down in the snow.

Hasan knelt by her side. "Come inside, sister," he whispered. Helping her to her feet, he led the sobbing woman to the house.

The other soldiers dismounted their horses. Walking to the back of the wagon, they opened the tailgate.

"Sir, let me help you inside," the lieutenant said. "My men will bring your son's body."

Abdul suddenly looked up at the lieutenant. His eyes were filled with rage. "How?"

"Sorry, sir?" the lieutenant replied.

"How did my son die?"

"He was guarding a supply convoy that was ambushed by Dashnak forces near Van. He was killed in the first volley of rifle fire."

Abdul's face contorted with fury. "My son was killed by Armenian dogs?"

"Yes, sir. Twenty-two men died in the attack, and seventeen more were wounded. Timurhan was one of my best men, a valiant soldier. I was with him when he died, and he told me to tell you he loved you. He also asked me to give you this." The lieutenant pulled the familiar Mauser pistol from beneath his coat and handed it to Abdul.

Abdul slowly turned the pistol over in both of his hands. "I gave this to him just before he left."

"I'm sorry, sir. He was a remarkable young man."

"Fucking Armenian infidels," Abdul muttered beneath his breath, as he rose to his feet. "The infidels will pay dearly for my son's death."

"Yes, sir. The general ordered all Christians in the Third Army to give up their weapons, and many were relieved of their duties. But, to be fair, some of our men who died in the ambush were themselves Armenians, including the lieutenant leading the supply convoy."

"Turncoat dogs," Abdul muttered, ignoring the lieutenant's comment. "Their bodies will rot on the ground." He walked to the rear of the wagon. There, in the bed, a body was bundled from head to toe in white cloth. Abdul placed his hand on his son's chest. It was frozen solid.

"Where would you like us to take him, sir?" the lieutenant asked.

Alone with his thoughts, Abdul did not reply. He stood staring into the distance toward the far-off mountains.

"Sir," the lieutenant repeated, "where would you like us to take your son?"

Abdul turned and stared vacantly at the lieutenant. "Help me take him inside," he finally whispered.

The soldiers hoisted Timurhan's body from the wagon and carried it to the house. Abdul, his shoulders slumped in despair, stepped past them to the threshold. Opening the front door, he let them pass and followed them inside.

Chapter 12

Sirak trudged across the snow-cloaked field after Özker. A few paces in front of them, Mikael tailed Stepannos, using his brother's body as a shield against a bitter westerly wind. Each boy had an armful of scrap firewood.

Snow gusted into Sirak's face, peppering his skin with icy needles. Too cold to speak, he struggled through a deep drift of snow next to the barn and clomped across the barnyard to the house. The wind waned for a moment, and a welcoming plume of smoke rose above the chimney.

Balancing the wood against his chest, Stepannos opened the front door and stepped inside the Sufyan home. Mikael, Sirak and Özker filed inside behind him.

Mourad was seated on the divan, and the girls from both families were crowded around the fire.

"Good work, boys," Mourad said cheerfully. He took Sirak and Özker's loads, and dropped them on the woodpile in the corner of the room.

Mikael dropped his wood on the pile. "It's getting worse. The wind is blowing harder than last night." He collapsed on the floor beside Flora and leaned his head against her shoulder.

"It's ten times worse," Stepannos muttered. "Listen to the wind whistling in the trees. Oh, by the way, a spruce fell across the trail down at the turn by the river. We'll need to clear it before we use the wagon."

"No problem," Mourad replied. "We won't be leaving anytime soon. We'll chop it up after the storm passes." He stepped over to the side of the room, and pulling the drapes aside, peered out at the snow whipping through the barnyard. "I hope Kemal gets back soon. It's a bad night to be out on the road."

No sooner had the words left his mouth, than the door burst open. Kemal, his face caked with snow, stepped inside and slammed the door behind him.

"Thank God you're home safely," Mourad said. "I was worried."

"God is great," Kemal puffed. Setting his bags down on the floor, he headed straight for the fire. "Old Brown almost didn't make it home. He definitely earned his feed tonight." Pulling off his coat, Kemal set it on the woodpile next to the fire. "Fadime, I'm starving. How about dinner?"

"In five minutes," she called back. "Please send the children to wash up."

"Okay, boys and girls, you heard her," he said, clapping his hands. "Off you go."

Kemal waited until all the children had gone before turning to Mourad. "I heard some more bad news in town," he whispered. "They hanged more men in Diyarbekir and a few in Ergani."

"In Ergani, too?"

"Yes, they were all charged with aiding the enemy. Many Armenians from the surrounding villages have fled. Even the priest of your church was arrested a couple of days ago."

"Father Adalian? Why?"

"The police accused him of hiding men who were wanted for recruiting resistance fighters. Apparently, Governor-General Hamid intervened personally on his behalf. They finally let him go."

"Merciful God," Mourad muttered. "You're right, Kemal. We must leave for Istanbul immediately."

"I'm afraid that's no longer possible, my friend—at least for now. I ran into Münir Mohammad at the souk. Do you remember him? He drives a wagon for the Aleppo Freight Company."

"Yes, I remember Münir. He transported Bedros' goods to Istanbul when he left to join the assembly. He's a good man."

"He just returned from Antioch, and he and six other drivers lost everything—seven wagons of goods and all of their horses. The bandits beat Münir and broke his arm. He's quit his job rather than risk another trip. They'd heard terrible stories of beatings, rapes and murders on their journey. Even Turks are hesitant to travel."

"Dear God," Mourad moaned. He buried his face in his hands. "What do we do now?"

"You must stay here with us. Perhaps the situation will improve in the spring."

"We've already burdened you enough. We're grateful for everything you've done, but we've got to find a way to get to Istanbul. It's either that or return to the farm."

"Nonsense, my friend. I insist you stay here. Your farm is too dangerous for Kristina and the children. Besides, the women and children are enjoying staying together. Oh, I asked the postmaster if you had any mail. I've known Talovic for years, so he gave me a letter he'd been holding for you." Kemal stepped across the room, and opening his pack, fished out a letter and handed it to Mourad.

"It's from Bedros," Mourad muttered. He tore the envelope open, and sliding out a single sheet of paper, held it up to the light. "It's dated December 5," he mumbled aloud. "He says the military leaders in Istanbul are giddy with anticipation for the coming war. They're expecting a great victory against the Russians."

Kemal shook his head. "What stupid morons. After the fiasco in Sarikamish, those fighting cocks got their spurs clipped once and for all. I also rode by your farm."

Mourad glanced up from the letter. "You did? Was everything okay?"

"Everything seemed fine. I even dug beneath the snow to find your message rock. Your letter to Alek was still there."

"Here come the children," Mourad whispered. He stuffed the letter into his pocket. "I'll read the rest later."

The younger children gathered in the kitchen. Nahid, dressed in a dark green dress and veil, handed each child a bowl before heading to the bedroom with a basket heaped with bread.

Fadime stepped out of the kitchen and silenced the room with a snap of her fingers. "Let's all wish Sirak a happy birthday. He's eight years old today."

The room erupted into loud cheers and applause.

"Happy birthday, Sirak!" Stepannos shouted. He patted his little brother on the head.

"Özker has a special gift for you," Kemal called out. He pulled an object from his bag, handed it to Özker, and pushed his son forward.

Özker beamed happily and stepped across the front room with a brown, multi-paneled ball. He tossed it to Sirak.

Sirak turned the odd-shaped orb in his hands. "What is it?"

Kemal laughed. "Shopkeeper Mohammed imported them from Istanbul. The British use these balls for a game they call football. It's a very strange game. You can kick the ball or even butt it with your head, but you can't use your hands. Both teams try to score by kicking the ball between two posts before their opponents can stop them." Kemal stuck his fingers through an aperture in the ball and pulled out a long stem. "You blow the ball up with this tube and then stick the tube back inside, like this."

Mikael ran his hand across the paneled leather surface. "What a funny game. Why would anyone want to play a game where you can't use your hands? It'll never last."

"I'm afraid the ball won't be much good until summer," Kemal lamented. "The shopkeeper told me not to get the leather wet. But you can play with it here in the house. Of course," he chuckled, "as long as Fadime approves."

"Don't kick the ball in the house," Fadime called out from the kitchen, "but you can roll it back and forth to each other in the hall."

Mourad stepped across the room to inspect the strange gift. "How many men play this game?"

"I don't know, but apparently it's become very popular in Istanbul. I thought Sirak might like it. It's easy to pack if you let all the air out of the ball."

"It's a wonderful gift, Sirak," Mourad said. "Tell Özker and his papa thank you."

"Thank you," Sirak said shyly, "I always wanted one of these."

Everyone erupted in laughter. Mourad shook his head with amusement and set the ball on the floor.

"Okay," Fadime called out, "all women and children into the back dining room while the food is still hot. Kristina and Nahid, I'll leave you to serve the men."

Mourad and Kemal sat at the table in the front room with Stepannos and Mikael. Kristina brought soup and bread, and filled their glasses. They mused about the snowstorm, the downed tree and the wind whistling outside the door.

Kristina gathered her shawl over her nightclothes, and stepping around the end of the bed, crouched beside a pallet on the floor. In the flickering light of an oil lamp, she rearranged the blanket over Izabella and Sirak. Izabella was sound asleep, but Sirak opened his eyes when she brushed a lock of hair back from his face.

"Goodnight, Mama," he muttered sleepily.

"Goodnight, little mouse. Did you have a nice birthday?"

"Yes, Mama."

She smiled. "I have something for you, too. I planned to give it to you tomorrow, but since you're awake, I'll give it to you now."

Kristina stepped around the end of the bed. She fetched a worn, leather-bound book from the chest where she stored her clothes, and kneeling on the pallet, pressed it into Sirak's tiny hands. "This Bible belonged to your grandpapa. It's very precious to me, but I want you to have it." She opened the book, and taking out a small photograph, held it up to her son's eyes. "This is a photograph of your papa and me with Alek and Stepannos. They were little boys when this was taken."

Sirak took the photograph in his tiny hand. The grainy image showed Mourad and Kristina standing on the stone steps at the church. They were proudly holding their toddler boys. "Thank you, Mama."

"You're very welcome." Kristina placed the photograph inside the Bible. "I'll set it here next to your pillow and you can look at it again in the morning. Grandpapa wrote some notes in the margin, so..." She stopped after realizing Sirak had drifted to sleep, smiled and ran her fingers across his forehead. "I love you."

CHAPTER 13

"Shit on you and your religion, Kazerian!" Abdul Pasha slurred heatedly. "I know you're in there, infidel!" The Turk whirled on his horse, and nearly tumbled off. "Come out, or I'll burn you out!" His red eyes bulged.

Abdul dismounted his horse and stood in the snowy barnyard outside the Armenian's farmhouse. The irate Turk tottered to and fro and waved Timurhan's handgun in the air. "You better come out, Kazerian, or I'll line up your family and shoot them all!"

Erol sat silently astride his horse a few paces behind the others taking in the scene. He shifted uneasily and fought a sudden urge to gallop off.

"Duman, go see if that dog is in there," Abdul scowled.

The scruffy-looking Turk limped through the ankle-deep snow to the front door. "It's open!"

"Search the barn!" Abdul bellowed to another farmhand standing with the horses. He turned and staggered to the front door. "Shoot them if they try to flee."

Abdul paused inside the doorway, and erupting into a hacking cough, glanced toward the kitchen. Several pots and a kettle were neatly arranged on the countertop next to the wood-burning stove. His eyes tracked across the front room to the fireplace and came to rest on a gold-framed painting of Jesus perched on the mantle beside a figurine of the Virgin Mary. He held out his hand "Give me your rifle."

"What for?" Duman asked reluctantly.

"Give me your fucking rifle!"

Duman passed his rifle to Abdul. The Turk stumbled across the room, and lifting the gun over his head, smashed the icons to pieces. "Infidels!" he growled. "Go check in the back."

Duman jogged down the hall to the bedrooms.

Abdul staggered across the room and thrust the rifle butt through the glass panel in the china cabinet, and a line of cups and plates shattered beneath the blow. Again and again, in frenzied rage, Pasha drove the rifle butt through the cabinet, until everything inside was smashed to bits. Then, he lashed out at the end table and snapped off a leg. "Fuck you, Kazerian!" he shouted. He stormed across the room, pulverizing everything in his path.

Rampaging into the kitchen, he resumed his crazed assault until every dish, utensil and pot lay in ruins on the floor. Bending over for a moment to catch his breath, he staggered back to the front room and determinedly pounded at remnants on the floor.

"Effendi!" Duman shouted.

Abdul whirled around and fell to one knee. Struggling to his feet, he tipped over the broken end table. "What?"

"There's no one here. The rooms are empty."

"Did you look beneath the beds?"

"Yes, Effendi. All of the beds are stripped and their clothes are gone."

"*Spineless coward*," Abdul hissed. "The bastard probably fled to Istanbul. Damn it! Now the Empire will claim his land."

Abdul stormed outside and caught a glimpse of one of his men walking through the corral beside the barn. "Any sign of them, Mohammad?" he called out.

"No, Abdul. The barn is empty, except for some old tackle."

Pasha clenched his fists and threw his head back. "Kazerian!" he screamed, at the top of his lungs. "Kazerian, if you can hear me, I promise you, one day you'll pay for my son's death." He staggered across the barnyard, grabbed the reins and re-mounted his horse. He sat gazing at the dwelling for a moment. "Burn the house and barn," he whispered calmly.

"Burn them?" Duman queried hesitantly.

"*Burn them*!" Abdul shouted. "Burn everything! God willing, we'll cleanse this land of any remnants of the cockroaches."

CHAPTER 14

February 22, 1915

"Here I come!" Sirak shouted. The exuberant boy ran away from the house. Jogging to the barnyard, he turned his face to the sun's rays and enjoyed the unseasonably warm weather. Rounding the corner of the house, he ran for the barn, but suddenly veered off to the back yard. He caught sight of his father crouching behind a pile of wood. "I found you!" he hollered gleefully.

"You found me," Mourad chuckled. He stepped out with an adoring smile. "You're running so much better." He ruffled the boy's curly dark-brown hair. "Okay, that's enough. It's time to clean the stalls in the barn."

Sirak jumped up and down with glee. "Please, one more time, Papa."

"No more, Sirak. I've got a lot of work to do before Kemal gets back from the city."

"Please, Papa, just one more time."

Mourad grinned and shook his head. "Okay, but just one more. I'm counting. Go!"

Sirak darted around the side of the house and sprinted toward the barn. "Özker," he shouted, "Papa's it. Where are you?"

The barn door creaked open and Özker, grinning excitedly, pressed his index finger to his lips.

Sirak ducked inside the barn. "Where should we hide?"

"Let's hide in the rock pile by the river. He'll never find us there."

The boys ducked out through the small door at the rear of the barn and jogged across the barren field. Sloshing through mud, they darted behind a great mound of rocks.

Mourad rounded the corner of the house and walked briskly to the barn. "Here I come!"

Sirak pulled Özker behind the rocks. "Stay down. Papa's got eyes like an eagle."

Mourad was nearly to the barn when the pounding of horses' hooves stopped him in his tracks. "Sorry, boys, that's it!" he shouted. "Özker's papa is back!"

Rounding the sweeping curve along the river bend, the wagon skirted a pair of towering snow-cloaked trees and rumbled for the barnyard.

"My friend," Kemal said to Mourad as he climbed down from the wagon, "I can't begin to describe what I found in Diyarbekir. The city is in total chaos. The closer I got to the gates, the more soldiers and refugees jammed the road. Hundreds of animal carcasses littered the sides of the road and the stench was unbearable. When I approached the city gates, I came upon dozens of corpses strewn on the ground beside the road. All of them had been mutilated and beheaded. Rather than continue on, I headed to Ergani, but even the village was in turmoil."

"God help us. The war must be going badly," Mourad said.

Kemal nodded. "Russian forces have advanced to within ten kilometers of Van and there's a desperate struggle going on between Russian-backed fighters and our forces in the city. Apparently, the chaos is spreading to the countryside surrounding Van and Bitlis. There are terrible stories of reprisal and retaliation all over Anatolia."

"Merciful God. I feared this would happen."

"Mourad," Kemal continued despondently, rubbing his tired red eyes, "there's more." He reached out and clutched Mourad's shoulder. "It's terrible."

"What is it?" Mourad asked apprehensively. "Is it Alek?"

"No, my friend, it's your farm."

"My farm?"

"I rode past it on my way back from the village. There was a fire."

"A fire?" Mourad gasped. His mouth was dry as parchment. "Where?"

Kemal reached out to steady Mourad. "Everywhere…the house, your furnishings, the barn…everything is gone."

"Oh, God, no! It can't be."

"I'm so sorry. I searched for belongings that survived the blaze, but unfortunately, I only found a few damaged pots and utensils and this." He pulled a charred silver crucifix from his pocket and handed it to Mourad.

Mourad stared at the artifact and clutched it to his chest. "It was my grandfather's." He leaned against the side of the barn and buried his head in his arms.

Kemal rested his hand on his friend's shoulder. "Mourad, when this war's over, you and I will rebuild your home. It'll be better than it was before. I promise."

Mourad nodded his head. He wiped his eyes on his sleeve, and turning around, took a deep breath. "I want to see it with my own eyes."

"No, Mourad, not now. It's too dangerous."

"I must see it for myself," Mourad replied determinedly.

"No!" Kemal whispered adamantly. "The corpses along the road—they were Armenians."

Mourad stared into Kemal's eyes. "Armenians? Are you sure?"

"I'm certain. A notice was posted nearby. It said they were traitors. Then, when I headed back, I saw an Armenian family attacked by a band of Kurds. They were merciless. You must not go."

Mourad stared at the ground. "What will we do now?"

"You will stay here with us until this madness ends," Kemal replied assertively. "We'll all be safer together."

Mourad turned and smiled gratefully. He embraced Kemal. "You are a true friend—the best I've ever had. Don't tell Kristina or the children about the farm. It's better they don't know."

"Don't worry. I won't say anything." Kemal reached into his pocket and pulled out a paper. "Unfortunately, I've got even more bad news. The government ordered all able-bodied men between eighteen and fifty-two, including all who previously paid *bedel*, to immediately report for army duty."

Mourad grabbed the notice. "Eighteen? Are you sure?" He read the notice and shook his head. "Well, they can have me, but they'll not have Stepannos. I'll not sacrifice another son for this Empire."

"No reasonable man could fault you, my friend. I've anguished about my own decision all the way home. Now that I've seen the bands of *chetes* wandering the countryside with my own eyes, I will not report either. I must take care of my family. If that makes me a traitor to the Empire, then so be it."

"Then it's decided. No matter what, we'll stay together and defend our families. Come, let's tell them the danger has passed."

CHAPTER 15

March 8, 1915

"No, damn it!" Abdul Pasha screamed. He jerked the axe from Erol's hands. "Hold the handle firmly—like this. Otherwise, you'll never even crack the bark. Do you understand?"

Erol cowered under the weight of his father's icy stare. The boy, his hair and brows caked with snow, trembled. "Yes, Father; I'm trying."

Abdul handed his son the axe. "Well, try it again!"

The boy lifted the axe over his head, and with a grunt, brought a glancing blow down on the log. This time a fragment of bark flew off the stump.

"That's better! Again!"

Abdul watched Erol deliver one feeble blow after another. "Keep it up," he growled. "Don't stop until you chop all the way through." Turning at the whinny of a horse, Abdul stepped back to the barnyard to meet, Baran, one of the hired hands riding up the road. The rider's head and neck were wrapped in a wool scarf, and only his eyes were visible through a narrow slit.

"Any sign of Kazerian?" Pasha barked when the man was within earshot.

"No, Effendi. The farm was just as we left it."

"Damn it," Abdul fumed. "I should've forced him to sell the land while I had the chance. I want you to check Kazerian's farm every single day. If the Armenian plans to return, he must plant cotton by the middle of May. Let me know immediately if you see any signs of activity at the farm. Do you understand? But don't dally there too much. We're far enough behind as it is."

"Effendi, we lost two more men yesterday. Yener and Ufuk were spotted by an army induction officer."

"Damn it! How will I ever plant the crops if we keep losing men? Didn't the lieutenant governor-general promise your brother there'd be no more men taken from my farm?"

"He did, but this was a roving detachment looking for men defying the new government decree. I was checking the Armenian's farm, or they surely would've taken me, too. At least Mohammad got your exemption papers from the governor-general."

"Yes, and for this I'm grateful, but I can't run this farm by myself. Go speak to your brother again. Get him to ask the lieutenant governor-general for orders to release Yener and Ufuk."

"I'll do my best, Effendi. See you in the morning."

Abdul Pasha watched Baran until he disappeared. He turned and walked to the woodpile. "Erol, are you making any progress?"

Erol set the head of the axe on the ground. Beads of sweat were streaking down his cheeks.

Pasha glanced at the log. "I'll be damned. You're nearly through it. Here, give me that axe."

Erol handed his father the axe and Abdul chopped the rest of the way through the log with three powerful swings. "Okay, let's go in and get some lunch. But I want you back out here as soon as we finish. No excuses."

"I will, Father," Erol muttered tiredly. He rounded the house and held his hands up to his eyes. His fingers and palms were covered with angry-looking blisters—some tense with blood. Wiping his brow on his sleeve, he went into the house to find his mother.

CHAPTER 16

April 10, 1915

The rays of the early-morning sun filtered through the curtains into the women's makeshift dining room. Kristina and Fadime sat at a wobbly wooden table strewn with fabric and spools of thread.

Kristina passed a needle through a knee patch she was sewing on a pair of pants. "This is it for these pants. Sirak needs a new pair."

"Oh, dear," Fadime muttered, with a slap to her forehead. "I forgot to ask Kemal to stop by the fabric souk in Diyarbekir. Özker's outgrown his pants, too, and all three of our girls need new dresses. I think Kemal's going into the village on Monday. Don't let me forget to ask him to look for fabric."

Kristina tied a knot in the thread. "I'll try to remember."

Fadime pushed herself up from the table. "I need another cup of tea. Would you like some?"

"I'd love a cup. As much as I miss my home, I'm so grateful for the time we've had together over the past two months. I haven't had talks like these since my sister-in-law moved to Istanbul. I couldn't have survived without your friendship and support."

"Kristina," Fadime said, her eyes soft and compassionate as she looked across the table at her friend, "it's been wonderful having you here. You're like a sister to me now, and I needed a sister. As you might have guessed, Nahid and I are not close."

"Well, now that you've mentioned it, I have noticed the strain between you. Nahid speaks respectfully of you, of course, and she's so sweet to the children. Did something happen?"

Fadime sighed. "It's a long and painful story."

"And none of my business, either. I didn't mean to pry."

"It's okay. Let me get the tea and I'll tell you my life's story. That should take about five minutes."

Fadime returned with a tray bearing two cups, a teapot and a plate of bread. "Flora wants us to try her flatbread. It just came out of the oven." Fadime set the cups on the table and poured the steaming tea. "Okay, where do I begin?

"I was raised on a farm less than three kilometers from here. My parents were poor cotton farmers, just like their parents before them, and just as we are today. Kemal and I have lived on this farm for eighteen years."

"Did you meet in school?"

"No, our marriage was arranged by my mother and father. Father was very traditional. So, I never met Kemal before our wedding day."

"You must have known who he was."

"Actually, I never laid eyes on him before the wedding."

"Really?" Kristina murmured with surprise. "I know this is common among your people, but then, I only spoke with Mourad three or four times before our engagement. So I hardly knew him, either. Were you pleased with your parents' arrangement?"

"Oh, yes." Fadime glanced back at the door to make sure it was closed. "Kemal was the handsome young man I'd always dreamed of marrying, so kind and gentle. I gave thanks to Allah every day for this blessing.

Those first eight years together were the happiest of my life. Each day seemed like springtime. "

Kristina smiled. "I know that feeling. It's how I felt about Mourad. I still do."

"I know you do. Your face lights up when he walks into the room."

"What happened between you and Kemal?"

"Sabiha was born a year and a half after our wedding, and I felt I'd found paradise here on earth. But then..." She took a deep breath.

"This is too much for you, Fadime. Please don't feel you need..."

"No," Fadime interrupted, shaking her head, "it's important to me that you understand. After I bore Sabiha, I couldn't get pregnant again. We tried, oh, we tried so hard, but somehow I knew something had changed inside my body. Sometimes I'd go six months without my menses. Finally, after six long years, Kemal expressed his desire to have more children. He wanted a son so badly. Even then, he was so considerate. He told me if I was opposed he'd never mention it again. I told him I understood, but inside, my heart was breaking. Another year passed, and I thought maybe he'd decided against it. But, then, one day out of the blue, his mother informed me they'd made the arrangements. Kemal and Nahid were married two months later. She was only fifteen years old on their wedding day—just eight years older than my daughter."

"How horrible." Kristina shifted uncomfortably in her chair. "I can't imagine such pain."

"God, forgive me, I despised Nahid at first. I tried not to, but I couldn't help myself. Kemal made every effort to keep us both content, switching bedrooms every night; but the passion left our marriage," she sobbed. "And it never returned."

Kristina reached for Fadime's hand. She rubbed fingers that were roughened and chafed from years of labor. "I'm so sorry."

"The hardest part was lying alone in my bed at night hearing Nahid whimper with bliss through these paper-thin walls. It was so painful hearing her enjoy the pleasures that'd been wrenched from my life forever.

Finally, I couldn't take it anymore. I began to sleep on the sofa and only returned to my bedroom when I was certain they'd fallen asleep. Then, when it was my night with Kemal, I'd turn to ice. I remember wondering how he could possibly want me when he'd just spent the night before making love to a fifteen year old with a perfect figure."

"I can't imagine."

"It must've been hard for Nahid, too. But, on the other hand, it was all she ever knew. It wasn't long before she got pregnant. I helped her as much as I could when Verda and Lale were born. For a while, when the twins were very young, Kemal spent most nights with me. But that lasted only a few months. Then, he began to alternate bedrooms again. Finally, in a fit of jealousy, I told Kemal I couldn't take it anymore. I told him he should sleep only with Nahid. I moved into the smaller back bedroom where I didn't have to hear them together, and we haven't shared a bed since. It's been ten long and lonely years." Fadime took a deep breath and sighed.

"I'm sorry, Fadime. Maybe you should try and talk to Kemal about how you feel. It's not too..."

"No. I'm fine now. I find my happiness in Islam, and in helping Sabiha and the other children grow up in a stable and loving home. Özker's like a son to me now—the son I could never bear."

"What a delightful child—so happy and well-mannered. Sirak loves him like a brother."

"He's a very special little boy. You've done a wonderful job with your children, too. My Sabiha never stops talking about Flora. And she'd never admit it, but she's got a crush on Stepannos, too."

"My Stepannos? Really?"

Fadime smiled. "I think so."

"Just wait until she meets Alek. I'm partial, I admit, he being my oldest and all, but Flora told me the young women at church swoon when they speak of him."

"I can't wait to meet him. What about you and Mourad?"

"What about us?"

"You're obviously very much in love. How long have you been married?"

Kristina smiled. "It'll be twenty-one years this July. He's a wonderful husband, a devoted father and my best friend. There is nothing I would change about him—except maybe his messiness."

"All men are messy," Fadime said matter-of-factly. "It comes with a penis."

Both women erupted into laughter. Fadime's jowls quivered with delight and tears flooded Kristina's eyes.

Fadime sipped at her tea and set the cup on the table. "God blessed you with six children to comfort you in your old age." She chuckled. "I tell Sabiha she must bear me ten grandchildren. Hopefully, we'll find her a suitable husband someday, but the war has made that impossible—at least for now."

"Sabiha is a beautiful and intelligent young woman. She'll have no trouble attracting a proper husband when this war is over."

"I hope you're right, and hopefully one who's too poor to afford more than one wife. Your Sirak is such a sweet young boy. His heart is gentle, but he's as brave as a lion."

Kristina sipped from her cup and smiled. "Sirak's the apple of his mama's eye. He's my little fighter."

"And so wise for his age."

"His short life has been filled with heartache. He was constantly sick when he was younger, and there was his encounter with the viper. Then this war took away his older brother, his colt and his home. But, through it all, he's been a pillar of strength. God gave him the gift of perseverance and..."

A knock at the door interrupted the conversation.

"Yes," Fadime called out.

The door cracked open. It was Sabiha.

"Father's home. He's putting away the wagon."

"Thank you, darling," Fadime replied. "Well, I'd better prepare something for him to eat. Would you like anything?"

"Not right now, thank you. I want to bathe Mourad's mother first. I'll eat a bite when I'm finished."

"Papa!" Özker squealed, jumping up and down. "Did you bring us presents?"

Kemal grinned at Mourad. He thrust his hand into his coat pocket and pulled out a small box. He handed it to Özker. "I found these fishhooks and weights in the village. You must share them with Sirak and his brothers. Okay?"

Özker grabbed the box. "Yes, Papa," he replied excitedly. "Come on, Sirak, let's show Stepannos and Mikael."

The two young boys turned and ran arm-in-arm into the house.

Mourad smiled after them, before turning back to Kemal. "How was the city?"

Kemal shook his head. "Most of the shops were closed. I was lucky to find anything. Russian forces occupied Tavriz, and now they're attacking villages around Lake Urmia. There's panic in the air. People are packing up what they can carry and fleeing west. Hamid, the governor-general of Diyarbekir Province, was fired and replaced with Doctor Mehmed Reshid. Within hours of taking office, Reshid ordered mass arrests of Armenian and Syrian Christians. Many people were killed."

"Merciful God. What should we do?"

"You must stay here. There's no way to travel to Istanbul—at least not right now. It's too dangerous."

"And so it all begins again: the disappearances, the imprisonments, the killings…" Mourad spread his arms and peered up at the clouded sky. "Lord Jesus, have you no mercy?"

Kemal wrapped his arm around Mourad's shoulders. "You'll be safe here, my friend."

Mourad nodded solemnly. "For this I'm grateful. I thank God for your friendship and loyalty."

Mourad stepped through a patch of snow in Kemal's barren field and headed for a formation of rocks along the riverbank. A few weeds were already poking up from the ground—harbingers of the approaching spring. He walked past a stand of spruce trees and spotted Stepannos and Mikael sitting on a rock tending their fishing lines.

Stepannos cast his line into the fast-flowing stream.

Mourad placed his hand on Mikael's shoulder. "Having any luck?"

"Not even a nibble. They must be sleeping."

"Where's Sirak?"

"He's fishing with Özker by the fallen tree."

"Go tell them to come here. I'll tend your line."

Mikael handed his makeshift fishing pole to his father, and pushing himself up from ground, headed upstream around a rock formation. He reappeared a few moments later with Sirak and Özker.

Mourad smiled. "Hello, Özker. Your mother wants you up at the house."

The dark-skinned Turkish youth turned and jogged away. Mourad watched him until he reached the barnyard before turning back to his sons. "Put your poles down. I want to talk to you boys about something important."

Stepannos lodged his pole in the rocks and turned to face his father. Mikael pulled in his line from the water and set the pole on the bank.

Mourad sat beside Stepannos and gathered Sirak into his lap. He glanced up at the sweltering noonday sun. "Oh, my sons, where did all the years go?"

"What do you want to talk to us about?" Stepannos asked impatiently.

"I want to tell you what happened to your grandfather's brothers, Ohan and Daniel."

Sirak turned in his father's lap. "We already know that, Papa. They went to live in Baghdad."

Mourad picked up a stone and hurled it into the rapids. "That's what I told you, but it's not what really happened."

"What happened?" Mikael asked.

"Twenty years ago—actually, exactly twenty years ago this past November—during the reign of Sultan Abdul Hamid the Second, something horrible happened here in Anatolia. A storm of hatred and evil swept through the walled city and many of the villages in the province."

Mikael glanced at Stepannos, and his brother returned a vacant stare. "Where did it come from, Papa?"

"From the Devil. It rose up from misunderstanding and distrust among the people living in Diyarbekir Province and many of the other provinces here in Anatolia. The Bloody Sultan—as we called him back then—used this misunderstanding to stir up madness."

"Misunderstanding?" Mikael queried. "What misunderstanding?"

"Misunderstanding about the beliefs and intentions of our people. Many other Christians suffered too—especially the Syrians. The Sultan stirred up a terrifying hatred among the Turks and Kurds, and as a result, many of our people, including grandfather's brothers, were killed. Grandfather and the rest of us probably would've been killed, too, if it hadn't been for Kemal's father. He hid us on this farm until the storm passed."

"You lived here before?" Mikael asked.

"Yes, Son, we lived in this same house and caught fish in this same stream. That was just before Alek was born."

Sirak crawled out of his father's lap and tossed a rock into the water. "Did Uncle Ohan and Uncle Daniel have children too, Papa?"

"Yes, they did, but we don't know what happened to them. They just disappeared."

Stepannos squinted at Mourad. "That's why we came here, isn't it?"

"Yes, that's why we came. Another terrible storm of hatred is sweeping through Anatolia, and once again, many of our people are being arrested, are disappearing, or worse. I think we'll be safe here, but just in case, I wanted you to know the truth. If something happens to me, I want you to protect your mother and sisters. Do whatever you must do. Do you understand?"

"Yes, Papa," Stepannos replied solemnly, "we understand."

"If we somehow get separated, I'll return to Kemal's farm as soon as I can. I expect you boys to stay here and take care of your mother and sisters. Keep the family together, no matter what the cost. Do you understand?"

Both of the older boys nodded somberly. Sirak stared down at the ground.

"Do you understand, Sirak?"

Sirak looked up gloomily. "Yes, Papa."

"And if the worst happens, and we get separated and it's impossible to return here, then we'll all meet in Jerusalem. Find your way to the Saint James Monastery. People in the monastery will take care of you. Okay?"

One by one, each of the boys nodded that they understood.

Mourad stood up from the rock. "Good. This is the last time we will speak of these matters. God willing, we'll be safe here and none of this madness will touch us. But I felt we should have a plan."

"Papa?" Sirak asked inquisitively.

"Yes, Son?"

"When *can* we go home?"

Mourad stared into Sirak's eyes for a long moment. "I don't know. Maybe in a year or so."

"*A year*," Stepannos said with surprise. "That's a long time."

"Yes, it is, but it's not safe there. There's something else I must tell you, and I want you boys to keep this a secret between you and me. I don't want to frighten your mother and sisters. Someone burned our house and barn. There's nothing left but ashes."

Stepannos clenched his jaw in stunned disbelief. Mikael mumbled unintelligibly.

"Do not despair. At least we're all together, and someday, when this war ends, we'll rebuild our house. It'll be even better than it was before."

"Why, Papa?" Sirak asked sadly. "Why would someone burn our house?"

"Hatred, Son. If a man lets hatred into his heart, it will control him, and then anything can be justified—no matter how terrible or how much it hurts other people. Regardless of what happens, you must put your faith in Jesus, and He will cleanse the hatred from your heart. Otherwise, the evil one will own your soul. Do you understand?"

"Yes, Papa."

"Good boy. Okay, that's all I wanted to say." Mourad picked up Mikael's pole. "Help me catch some fish for dinner. Whoever catches the biggest..."

"Mourad!" came a shout from the house. "Mourad!"

Kemal ran across the field, with Özker right behind him. "It's your mother!" he shouted. "She's not breathing!"

Mourad tossed the fishing pole on the ground and sprinted to the house.

CHAPTER 17

Abdul Pasha looked up from his plow, and spotting Baran on horseback, pulled up his mule at the end of the row.

"My eyes must be failing me, Effendi," the Turk said sarcastically. "You're plowing all by yourself?"

"Shut up, Baran. Who else will do it? My farmhands are all off fighting Russians. Besides, I'd rather plow the fields than listen to Jasmine's endless complaining."

"Why don't you get that lazy son of yours out here?"

Pasha's eyes narrowed and his face melted into a scowl. "Fuck you, Baran!"

"I meant no offense, Effendi. I've heard you say it yourself."

"Maybe I have, but you'll not mock my son."

"No offense intended. Actually, I just rode by your house, and Erol was chopping firewood. He's getting much better."

"Slowly, but surely, he's making progress. I still ride him hard to get his chores done."

"Where's Ali?"

"He and his brother decided to accept the amnesty offer."

"They reported?"

"I took them to the Army Induction Center yesterday."

"Are you mad, Effendi? Why would you do that?"

"Haven't you heard? The lieutenant governor-general issued orders revoking the *bedel* of anyone caught sheltering their workers from service. I don't want you hanging around here any more, either."

"Just pay me what you owe me." Baran glanced at the plow mule. The sickly-looking animal was mottled with matted black patches. "What the hell happened to your mule?"

"That's tar, moron. It got him a not-fit-for-service designation, so I can keep the military procurement scum from taking him."

Abdul glanced up at the sun. "Well, Baran, what do you want? I must finish this field today."

"I rode by Kazerian's farm this morning. Pay me my wages, and I'll tell you what I found. You'll be interested."

Abdul stared up at Baran for a moment. "Is he back?"

"I want my pay, Abdul. I've got a family to feed, too."

Abdul glared at the disheveled Turk for a moment. Digging into his pocket, he pulled out a handful of coins. He counted and handed them up to Baran. "That's all I've got now. I'll give you the rest next month."

Baran carefully counted the coins and stuffed them into his pocket. "Someone tilled the Armenian's field and cleared the debris from his foundation."

"Bullshit," Abdul growled. "You lie to get your money."

Baran shrugged. "Go see for yourself. There's also a fresh grave beneath the trees."

"When was the last time you rode over there?"

"A week ago, and nothing had been touched."

"Did you see anyone?"

"Not a soul. I hid in the trees for a while, but I didn't see anyone."

Abdul stared at Baran for several moments. Finally, he stepped out from behind the plow and began to unharness the mule.

"What are you doing?" Baran asked with amusement.

"I'm riding over to see for myself."

"Do you want me to come, too?"

"Hell no! Get your scrawny ass out of here before I lose my *bedel*."

"As you wish, Effendi."

Abdul grabbed the mule's reins, and leaving the plow behind, headed off across the untilled field. "I'll cut your balls off if you're still here when I get back," he shouted over his shoulder.

"Yes, Effendi," Baran replied. He watched Abdul until the Turk reached the barn. "You piece of shit," he muttered.

Baran dismounted his horse. Retrieving a hunk of bread from his saddlebags, he squatted down and took a bite. He wiped his mouth on his sleeve and mumbled angrily beneath his breath.

Abdul emerged from the barn on horseback and trotted off to the road.

Baran waited a few minutes. Finally, he remounted his horse and trotted across the field to the Pasha farmhouse.

Abdul stopped his horse at the crest of the hill overlooking the Kazerian farm. Shading his eyes from the afternoon sun, he scanned the valley from the foundation to the murky green pond. Both the cotton field and the pasture inside the fence were freshly tilled.

"Where are you, Kazerian? I'll kill you, infidel—no matter how long it takes." He jerked Timurhan's pistol out of his saddlebag and advanced a bullet into the chamber. Tucking the gun beneath his belt, he rode slowly down to the farm.

The chimney stood statue-like in the middle of the foundation littered with charred wood. To one side, however, someone had painstakingly sorted fire-tinged stones.

Abdul turned and gazed out past the tilled fields toward the rolling hills west of the farm. Gnashing his teeth, he spit on the ground. "Fuck you, Sufyan," he snarled. Finally, he spun his horse around and trotted off.

Kemal plucked a nail out of his mouth, and pressing a board into posi-tion on the wagon, started the nail with a few taps. "Özker, hand me some more nails."

Özker grabbed a handful of nails from a wooden box and handed them to his father.

Kemal started another nail, but looked up at the distant whinny of a horse. A lone rider trotted out of the trees at the bend in the river.

"Sirak," Kemal barked, "run to the house and tell your father a rider's coming. Özker, you go with him."

The two boys scampered off across the barnyard.

Kemal tucked the hammer beneath the waistband of his pants and walked out to meet the rider. The man finally got close enough for him to discern the visitor's swarthy features. "Abdul Pasha," he muttered warily.

"Good afternoon, Kemal."

"What can I do for you, Abdul?"

Pasha glanced across the field behind the barn. "I didn't realize you had such a fine-looking farm. It looks like you've gotten a good start on your planting."

"God is great. The weather was perfect this week."

"Spring is finally here. I take it you got your military exemption."

"Yes, at least for one year," Kemal lied guardedly.

"Are you available for work? All of my men were conscripted, and I need help planting my crops."

"No, I've got my hands full with my own crops."

"I'll pay you double what you earned from me last year. I'll even barter provisions for your family."

"I'm sorry, Abdul, but I just don't have time."

Pasha sighed with frustration. "Let me know if you change your mind." He glanced toward the farmhouse. "By the way, have you seen Mourad Kazerian?"

The hairs stood up on the back of Kemal's neck. "Uh…no," he stut-tered, "I haven't seen Mourad in months. The last I heard, he was moving his family to Istanbul to live with his brother. Why do you ask?"

"I thought maybe he needed some work."

"If I see him, I'll be sure to tell him you're looking for help."

"I'd appreciate that. But be careful, my friend, the governor-general's new regulations forbid dealings with Russian sympathizers. The penalty is death by hanging."

"Mourad Kazerian is not a Russian sympathizer," Kemal snapped.

"Easy, my friend. I wasn't referring to Kazerian." Abdul handed down a small piece of paper. "I picked up the *Agence* in the village. There's a story about a lot of Armenian leaders being arrested in Istanbul for plotting against the Empire. Since your farm isn't far from the north road to Bingöl, you could encounter sympathizers fleeing to the east from Istanbul. Remain vigilant."

"Thank you for the warning. I'll keep my eyes open. How's your family?"

"It's a difficult time for everyone. We barely have enough food to make it to the next harvest, but somehow we'll get by. I just wish this damned war would end." Pasha glanced toward the farmhouse. "How are your sons?"

"I have only one son. Özker is fine."

"I thought I saw two boys. Perhaps I was mistaken."

"That was Özker's cousin from Siverek."

"His cousin from Siverek," Abdul repeated with a toothy grin. "Well, I must be going now. God willing, I'll see you soon."

"Goodbye, Abdul. May God protect you and your family."

Pasha turned and rode off across the barnyard. Kemal stood watching until the Turk disappeared beyond an embankment sprinkled with yellow and white wildflowers. Finally, he turned and walked across the barnyard to the house.

CHAPTER 18

"Good morning!" Kemal called out cheerfully. The Turk was dressed in tattered work clothes. He took a seat at the table beside Mourad. "Did you hear the warblers this morning?"

"No, I missed them."

Nahid, adorned in a baggy *shalwar*, with a long-sleeved blouse and veil, set a platter of bread and cheese between the two men.

Kemal sliced off a hunk of cheese, and wrapping it with bread, stuffed it into his mouth. "It's a beautiful day outside," he said through a mouthful of food. "Özker and I went to fetch water from the river and we spotted a bear and her cubs basking on the far bank. It shouldn't take us more than a couple of hours to finish planting the cotton. How about if we ride over to your farm after we finish?"

Mourad took a sip of his tea. "No, I want to stay here today. Pasha spooked me. He knows...I feel it in my bones."

"Relax, my friend. Don't let him get to you. He's desperate, or he wouldn't come to ask me for help."

"How can you be so calm? I couldn't sleep at all last night."

Kemal patted Mourad's arm. "Relax, everything will be..."

The pounding of horses' hooves brought Mourad out of his chair. "What's that?"

"Kemal Sufyan," a gruff voice bellowed from the barnyard, "come out now!"

Kemal glanced anxiously at Mourad. He got up from the table, opened the door and stepped outside.

More than two-dozen uniformed gendarmes were scattered across the barnyard. Several had guns trained on the house. Another group was inspecting the barn.

"We already gave up our horses and mules," Kemal offered guardedly, "along with fifty percent of our supplies. I'll get the receipt."

"I'm Lieutenant Mohammad," the leader barked. "Are you Kemal Sufyan?"

"Yes, sir."

"Are you sheltering the Armenian Mourad Kazerian?"

Kemal stared back at the lieutenant in stunned silence.

"Are you?"

"Sir, Mourad and his family are close friends, and someone burned their home to the ground."

"I have a warrant for his arrest. Stand clear while my men search the house."

The officer motioned several men into the house. The first gendarme, a chubby Turk with a pistol, grabbed Mourad and forced his arm behind his back. He pushed him outside. Another gendarme led Stepannos to the barnyard. The others searched the house.

The portly gendarme bound Mourad's hands behind his back with a stretch of rope.

"Armenian dogs," the lieutenant hissed.

Mourad glanced over his shoulder at another policeman binding Stepannos' hands. "Why are you doing this? We've done nothing wrong."

"Do you deny recruiting men for the Dashnak forces in the east?"

"I absolutely deny it. My oldest son is a soldier in the Ottoman Army."

"How old are you?"

"Fifty," Mourad replied tersely.

"Why haven't you reported for army service?"

"I've got a wife and five children. They need my protection."

"Thousands of men with even larger families reported for service to the Empire. Failure to report is itself a crime punishable by death."

"I paid my *bedel*," Mourad replied defiantly. "I've done nothing wrong."

"Tell it to the magistrate. Put him on a horse," the lieutenant ordered. He turned and walked over to Stepannos. "How old are you?"

"Eighteen, sir," Stepannos whispered fearfully.

"Why didn't you report for army service?"

"I've been helping Mr. Sufyan and my papa plant the crops, sir."

"You're under arrest," the lieutenant said calmly. He motioned to the gendarme.

Stepannos hung his head submissively. The gendarme forced him up onto a horse.

"What's in the barn, Sergeant Faraz?" the lieutenant asked a wiry gendarme.

"Two scrawny work horses and a few bags of flour and rice, sir."

"Search the house for weapons. See that no harm comes to the women and children."

"Yes, sir." The gendarme jogged past Kemal and disappeared into the house.

Nearly an hour passed before the young sergeant and several other gendarmes emerged from the house. Fadime followed them out wearing a blue dress and veil.

"Did you find anything, Sergeant?" the lieutenant asked.

"Three women and several children under the age of fifteen are in the house, sir. I also found these." He pulled an ivory-handled knife from a wooden box.

The lieutenant took the knife, and turning it over in his hand, inspected the engraved blade. He glanced at Kemal. "Are these your knives?"

"No," Kemal replied uneasily.

"They belong to the Armenian?"

"I don't know. I've never seen them before."

"Sir," Mourad began, "I can explain..."

"Shut up!" the lieutenant demanded angrily.

"I found something else, sir," the sergeant said. He handed a sheet of paper up to the lieutenant.

The lieutenant scanned the page. "What is this?"

"It's some sort of code, sir."

Lieutenant Mohammad thrust the sheet of paper in front of Kemal. "What is this, Mr. Sufyan?"

Kemal glanced at the page. "I have no idea. I've never seen it before."

The lieutenant stepped over to Mourad and held the paper up. "What is this, Armenian?"

Mourad glanced at the sheet and swallowed nervously. "Sir, my brother's a member of the Ottoman Assembly. We exchanged these codes so we could communicate in case of emergency."

"In case of emergency?" the lieutenant mocked. "What emergency?"

Mourad shrugged his shoulders. "I don't know. We've never used them."

The lieutenant glared at Mourad for a moment before turning back to Kemal. "Bind his hands," he ordered a young policeman standing beside the Turk. "You're under arrest, Mr. Sufyan."

"For what?" Kemal protested.

"For providing sanctuary to enemy agents," the lieutenant replied indignantly.

"Let him be!" Fadime screamed. She angrily pushed past the gendarme. "None of these men did anything wrong."

"Get back in the house, woman!" the lieutenant shouted.

"But they're innocent."

"If they're innocent, then they've got nothing to fear."

"Where are you taking them?"

"To the Central Prison in Diyarbekir. Now get out of my way." He took the reins from one of the gendarmes and swung up onto his horse.

Suddenly, the front door burst open and Sirak dashed headlong into the barnyard. He was carrying a large spoon.

Kristina ran out of the house a step behind him. "Sirak! Get back in here!"

Fadime tried to intercept the boy, but he sidestepped her and ran straight for the lieutenant's horse.

"Don't hurt my papa!" the red-faced boy hollered. "Leave him alone!"

The lieutenant's horse spun in place, and spooked by the stick-toting assailant, reared up on his hind legs. The lieutenant, though clinging desperately to the horse's neck, tumbled off. Sirak swung the stick and landed a glancing blow on the officer's hands before a gendarme grabbed him. The gendarme dragged Sirak toward the house. Twisting and turning like a fish, Sirak struggled out of the man's grasp and ran toward the horses once again.

"Sirak!" Mourad shouted from atop the horse.

The boy stopped in his tracks.

"Get back to the house with your mother."

"Papa," Sirak cried out mournfully. Tears streamed down his face.

"I'm okay, Son." Mourad's voice trembled with emotion. "Take care of your mother and sisters."

Sirak turned and staggered back to his mother. Kristina pulled the sobbing boy to her side.

"Are you okay, sir?" one of the gendarmes asked the lieutenant.

The lieutenant didn't reply. He brushed the dirt from his uniform, and grabbing the reins, remounted his horse. He angrily turned his horse and wove through the clot of riders. "You'll pay dearly for this, Armenian!" His voice dripped hatred.

Mourad didn't reply. He turned and nodded at Stepannos in tacit support.

Stepannos' eyes betrayed terror. He stared back at his father in silence, his jaw quivering.

The company of riders trotted away from the farmhouse to the bend in the river.

Mourad turned his head and caught a glimpse of Kristina, Mikael and Sirak standing in the barnyard with Fadime. "God, have mercy," he murmured.

The hinges of the massive prison doors creaked open and the lieutenant led Mourad, Stepannos and Kemal, along with six other prisoners from the surrounding villages, into the expansive central yard. The procession marched beneath the imposing black walls and Mourad glanced up at the guard shack. One of the sentries, a dark-skinned man with a rifle, leaned out through a breach and caught his eye. Nodding smugly, the guard saluted.

The detail stopped in front of a small hut and a stout Turkish guard with a clipboard limped outside to converse with the lieutenant. Sheltering his eyes from the searing rays of the afternoon sun, the man recorded details provided by the lieutenant before several guards sorted the prisoners and led them away to cells. They led Kemal off in one direction and the other prisoners, including Mourad and Stepannos, in another.

The guards took Mourad and Stepannos down a sinuous passageway and finally stopped in front of a heavy wooden door. Fumbling with a ring of keys, the guards unlocked the door and led the captives past a long row of cells, each one overflowing with prisoners. The air was thick with the commingled stench of sweat, urine and feces.

One guard led Mourad and Stepannos to the last cell. He untied them, unlocked the door and pushed them inside.

Mourad scanned the somber faces of the two dozen men sitting on the floor. They stared back in silence. Finally, an old man rose from the floor and stepped forward.

"May the Lord's mercy be upon you," he said barely above a whisper. "My name is Farhad, from Sasun."

"I'm Mourad from Seghir, and this is my son, Stepannos."

"It's my pleasure to meet you. I regret that we've met in this godforsaken place."

Mourad glanced at a curly-haired man who erupted into a fit of coughing. "How long have you been here?" he asked the old man.

"Just over two weeks, but it seems like two years. Every male in my village over the age of sixteen was arrested and brought here. They've detained thousands of men all over the province."

Mourad wrapped his arm around Stepannos' shoulders. "Can you spare a drink of water for my son? We haven't had a sip since early this morning."

"The guards will come by later with a ration for each prisoner. If they bring food, I advise you to get your share. We're lucky to get a crust of bread or some watered-down soup. If you pass it up, there will be nothing more until tomorrow."

"Thank you," Mourad replied somberly. "I appreciate your help."

"Let an old man give you one more bit of advice. Confess your crime."

"But we've done nothing wrong."

"Then make something up. If you tell the interrogators what they want to hear, they'll move on to another prisoner. Otherwise, the devils will thrash you day and night until you confess. Then you'll end up like him." He pointed at a man lying along one side of the cell. Apparently unconscious, the man's shirt was stained with blood. "But whatever you do, don't admit you assisted Andranik or Dashnak forces. Two men from my village made that mistake and the devils hanged them in the courtyard early the next morning. Tell them you hid horses, withheld food supplies, or something else."

"We will admit nothing," Mourad countered. He glanced resolutely at Stepannos and clenched his fist. "We've done nothing. For God's sake, my oldest son serves in the army."

"Suit yourselves," Farhad replied, "but don't say you weren't warned." The old man turned away and sat along the wall.

Mourad took Stepannos by the arm and led him across the cell. A middle-aged man scooted over to make room. Mourad bade Stepannos sit down and sat down beside him. "We will not confess to anything," he whispered. He squeezed Stepannos' knee. "Do you understand?"

"Yes, Papa." The terrified young man fidgeted mindlessly.

"No matter what they do. The wicked accusers will not have the satisfaction of besmirching our family name. We will find our strength in each other, and in God."

"Yes, Papa. I understand."

Nearly an hour passed before a guard detail appeared outside the cell. The taller of the two men, a strapping, acne-ridden Turk, with a jagged scar ranging down his jaw, opened the cell door. "Mourad Kazerian!" he barked.

"Remember, Stepannos, admit nothing." Mourad patted his son on the leg, and standing up, wove past several other prisoners to the door.

"Hands behind your back," the guard growled. He spun Mourad around, clamped handcuffs on his wrists and shoved him down the cell-block.

The guards led Mourad out of the building and across the bleak central yard. The taller guard seemed to make a point of leading him past towering gallows that loomed ominously at one end of the yard. He stopped in front of worn steps that led up to a narrow platform, and smiling callously at Mourad, pressed his hand to the latter's throat.

Mourad glanced up at the three nooses swaying in the breeze above the platform. He shuddered. "Yea, though I walk through the valley of the shadow of death, I will fear no evil," he whispered.

Ducking back into the building, the guards led Mourad through a maze of offices along a dimly-lit corridor.

"Stop!" the burly guard ordered. He opened the last door and jerked Mourad to a chair in the middle of the windowless rectangular room. In the rear of the room there was a long bench and a wooden chair in front of a wall studded with wooden bludgeons, chains and other implements of torture. Unclasping Mourad's hands, the guard cuffed his wrists to the arms of the chair.

Mourad craned his neck for a glimpse at the guards.

The taller man smiled menacingly. "I'll bet one *lira* he confesses in less than five minutes," he whispered to his comrade.

"Three minutes for him and five for the son," the second guard replied.

Mourad looked away and both men erupted into boisterous laughter. A chill ran up his spine. He bowed his head in silent prayer.

After a few minutes, a rather slight man with black-rimmed glasses and a red fez stepped into the room. His bushy black mustache and eyebrows framed deep-set, cold eyes. He was dressed in a charcoal-gray officer's jacket that was trimmed in red. His pants were tucked into black knee-high boots. But it was the gleaming sword at the officer's side that caught Mourad's eye.

The man stepped in front of the chair and glared down at Mourad for several moments. Mourad's mouth went dry and his heart began to pound.

"My name is Major Tezer Akcam," the man began. He had a surprisingly deep voice. "I'm your interrogator. Two eyewitnesses confirmed you serve as an agent for the Andranik forces. Your primary responsibilities are recruitment and financial support. Do you admit it?"

"I deny it," Mourad replied determinedly. "I'm nothing more than a simple cotton farmer."

"Do you also deny your son, Stepannos, colludes with traitors who support the Andraniks from the American Missionary School in Chunkoush?"

Mourad's heart pounded. The memory of Stepannos' careless comments and Bedros' sharp rebuke came flooding back.

"My sons attended school in Chunkoush, but they had nothing to do with traitors who betrayed the Empire. How can we be accused of treason when my brother is a member of the Ottoman Assembly and my son serves loyally in the Ottoman Army?"

"Your brother, Bedros? He was arrested for conspiracy two weeks ago."

"Arrested?" Mourad exclaimed in disbelief.

"Yes, arrested and sent to the gallows."

"Bedros?" Mourad gasped.

"Yes, and your spineless son deserted at the height of the battle for Sarikamish."

Mourad shook his head vehemently at the abhorrent thought. "Alek would never desert."

"He was a gutless coward who ran like a rabbit. My patience is at an end, infidel. Who are your Andranik contacts?"

"There are no contacts. I'm only a..."

The Turk swung his gloved hand and struck Mourad full on the face. "No more lies!"

Mourad felt blood trickle from his nose. "I'm not lying," he gasped. "We are loyal..."

"Shut up, pig! Perhaps the cane will loosen your tongue." He nodded at the two guards.

The burly guard released Mourad's arms, jerked him up from the chair and forced him onto his stomach on the bench. Grabbing his shirttail, the brute yanked it over Mourad's head and lashed his outstretched arms to the boards. Fetching another rope from his pocket, the man bound Mourad's ankles and stretched him out across the bench. He stepped to the wall, chose a cane and positioned himself astride Mourad.

Straining against the bindings, Mourad glanced up at the major. Akcam stared back with an expression of indifference.

"Twenty lashes," he hissed.

The burly Turk lifted the cane high over his head with both hands and whipped it down. "Haa!" he barked.

Mourad arched his back under the force of the vicious blow and screamed in agony.

Time and again the Turk raised the cane in the air and smashed it down on Mourad's back. After the eighth blow, Mourad lapsed into a stupor.

The major held out his hand to stay the guard. "Who are your Andranik contacts, Armenian?"

Mourad—unable to speak—slowly shook his head.

"Again!" the major barked.

The guard raised the cane again. He whipped it down on Mourad's back and the rod snapped in two. The man walked to the rack and chose another. Stepping astride the bench, he resumed the beating until all twenty lashes had been delivered.

The major grabbed Mourad's hair and lifted his head off the bench. "Fucking pussy," he hissed. Take him to his cell and bring him back in the morning—this time with his son. He'll confess soon enough."

Stepannos cradled Mourad's head in his arms. He glanced down at the angry red stripes across his father's back. Sprawled against the back wall of the cell, Mourad hadn't moved since the guards carried him back.

Old man Farhad crouched beside Stepannos and squeezed the boy's shoulder. "Let him sleep."

Tears streamed down Stepannos' cheeks. He ran his fingers through his father's hair. "Why?" he whispered. "Why?"

"I can't explain it, Stepannos, except to say they're evil, unprincipled men, blindly following their false God of hate. Remember what Jesus said to His disciples: blessed are they who are persecuted for righteousness' sake, for theirs is the kingdom of heaven."

CHAPTER 19

Kristina peered through the curtain at the masked men carting bags from the barn to a wagon. "Oh, my God! They're coming this way!"

Fadime closed the curtain. "Hide yourselves in the back!" she shouted frantically to the children huddled in the hallway. "Don't make a sound until I come for you."

The children scurried down the hall into the bedrooms.

"What should we do?" Kristina cried frantically.

"We'll let them have what they want, and pray they..."

A loud rap on the door reverberated through the living room. Fadime opened the door. A man in worker's clothing, wearing a black hood over his head, pushed through the door waving a pistol.

"Please, have mercy," Fadime pleaded. She pushed Kristina back with her outstretched arm. "In the name of God, take whatever you want, but please don't harm..."

"Shut up!" the man barked. He pushed her aside. "Where's your food?"

"There's flour and rice in the cabinet next to the stove," Fadime replied. "Take what you want."

The man leaned back through the doorway. "There's more inside. Come and get it."

Another man ran through the door. He, too, was wearing a mask.

"Check the cabinets in the kitchen," the leader barked. He turned back to Fadime and Kristina. "Where are the young women?"

"There are no young women," Fadime replied calmly. "The children went to stay with relatives."

"Bullshit," the man hissed. Pushing past Fadime and Kristina, he headed for the bedrooms.

Fadime shrieked in horror. She flung herself onto the man and buried her nails into his chest. "Leave our children alone!"

"Fucking bitch!" The intruder swung his pistol and landed a powerful blow just above Fadime's temple.

Kristina crouched down and crawled to the stricken woman's side. Rolling her over, she gasped at the purple welt rising above Fadime's eye.

"I'll shoot her if she does that again," the bandit growled. He turned and headed toward the back bedrooms.

The man forced the first bedroom door open. Nahid and Sabiha, along with Nahid's twin girls, were cowering in the corner.

Nahid gathered Verda and Lale into her arms. "Please, sir, don't hurt us."

The hooded man turned, and without uttering a word, stepped from the room. He glanced through an open door into the second bedroom. It was empty, except for a mound of blankets in the back corner. He headed to the end of the hall and pushed against the last door. It didn't budge. He forced his shoulder against the door, cracked it open and peered into the room. Mikael, Sirak and Özker were leaning on a dresser pressed against the door.

"Stand back!" the intruder demanded. He pointed his gun at the door. "Stand back or I'll shoot!"

Mikael stood up and pulled Sirak away from the dresser. "Okay, don't shoot."

The masked man pushed the door open, stepped inside the room and pushed the boys to one side. "Get out of my way."

Flora and Izabella were cowering behind the bed. Paralyzed with terror, they peered up at the intruder.

"Get over here," the bandit snarled. He leaned across the bed, grabbed Flora's arm and dragged her across the bed.

Flora whimpered fearfully and struggled to pull away.

"Leave her alone!" Mikael bellowed. He lunged past Özker and grabbed the man's arm.

Sirak crouched down and bit the intruder's calf.

"Aww!" the man screamed. He bashed Mikael on the top of the head with his pistol and knocked him to the floor before Sirak bit him on the leg again.

"You little bastard!" The man jabbed the pistol barrel against Sirak's ear and pulled the trigger. A loud click echoed through the room. "Damn it!" He rapped Sirak atop the head and the boy collapsed on the floor.

"Come here," the thug snapped. He grabbed Flora's arm and dragged her from the room.

Kristina leapt to her feet. "No!" She bounded into the intruder's path.

"This is your last chance, bitch." The brute pressed his gun to Flora's head. "Get out of my way or I'll shoot her."

Kristina dropped to her knees. "Please, sir, don't take my daughter. Do what you want with me, but leave her alone."

"Get out of my way." He pushed her aside and yanked Flora out the door.

"Did you get everything?" the leader asked another bandit.

"Yes, Effendi, it's all in the wagon."

"Help me get her onto my horse."

The men grabbed Flora. The leader mounted his horse and reached down to seize her by one arm. He pulled her up and draped her across the horse's back.

"Okay, let's go!" the leader called out. He turned his horse and galloped across the barnyard.

The wagon rumbled after him, and the other bandits tailed close behind.

Kristina shrieked hysterically. Running across the barnyard, she stumbled to her knees. "Flora! Dear God, no! My Flora!"

CHAPTER 20

The band of outlaws galloped for several kilometers along the deserted rocky road. Flora's arms and legs were bound with rope, and a handkerchief was tied across her mouth.

The leader finally pulled up at a fork in the road. "Baran, store these supplies in my barn and let the men go home. I'll be back in a week or two."

"When do we get our share?" the wagon driver shouted. "My children are hungry."

"We'll divide the supplies when I return," the leader groused. "Hasan has money and four bags of flour for each of you back at the farm."

"Where are you headed, Effendi?" another man asked.

"None of your damned business."

"We all took the risk and we should all share the spoils," the man persisted. "I say we draw lots to settle on who gets to fuck the girl first."

"Screw you!" the leader barked. "I found her, and she's mine."

"Okay, then, how about drawing to see who gets her next?"

"Bullshit. Kemal Sufyan is a Turk. Don't forget that. If you've got a *cheki* of sense, you'll just forget about her."

"Okay, Effendi. You're the boss."

"Be on your way, before it gets dark. Baran, tell Hasan I'm traveling to Aleppo on urgent business. I'll be back in a week or two."

"Aleppo?" Baran asked suspiciously. "Will you sell the girl at the great auction? We should split that, too."

"Damn it, will you just do as I say? You'll see my intentions soon enough."

"Okay, Effendi. I'll tell him."

"Off with you, then."

The wagon rumbled away to the north and the riders galloped after it.

"Idiots," the leader mumbled. He glanced down at Flora and patted her back.

Flora moaned and struggled to lift her head.

"Be patient, my sweet. We'll be home soon enough." He ran his hand down her spine and cupped her buttocks.

Flora groaned loudly and struggled against her ties.

The bandit laughed heartily. He spun his horse around and trotted away down the east fork.

Eventually, he guided his horse up a muddy ravine and through a stand of brush at the top of a rocky knoll. He rode over the crest toward a rundown shack built of stone and wood. The ground around the structure was overgrown with weeds and brush.

"Rest assured, my darling, this is only temporary. You'll soon be the queen of one of the largest farms in the province."

The rider guided his horse down a short embankment, dismounted in front of the cabin and untied the bindings from Flora's legs. "You should've seen this place before I cleaned it out. It's really not that bad now. Anyway, it'll have to do for a week or two until we get better acquainted. Now, I'm going to set you on the ground, and if you're good, I'll untie your hands and give you water." He lifted Flora off the horse and set her on the ground. "That's my girl. Okay, let's go inside."

Flora stared out across the endless scrub-dotted wasteland surrounding the cabin. They were completely isolated.

Now,

He led her through a rickety door into the darkened shack. The single-room dwelling was empty except for a small rug and a stack of blankets set against one wall. Rays of sunlight beamed through cracks in the ceiling.

"How do you like our castle, my sweet?" he asked, as he removed the gag. He untied her hands and turned her slowly around. He admired her beauty in the muted light. "So very fine," he whispered. Reaching out, he brushed his fingers through a wisp of hair protruding beneath her headscarf and traced his fingertips across her cheek and down to her breasts.

"No," Flora sobbed. She pushed his hand away and sank to her knees. Her scarf dropped to the floor and her hair cascaded across her face. "Please don't hurt me."

"No one will hurt you." Pulling off his mask, he knelt before her. He lifted her tear-streaked chin and brushed her hair back from her eyes. "Look at me, little one."

Flora gasped. Her terrified expression melted into shock.

"So, you do remember me. Fool that he was, your father refused to sell me his land. Did you imagine then we'd soon be lovers? From this moment on, I'll be your protector and your provider. In due time, God willing, you'll bear me many strong sons."

Flora gawked at Pasha and clenched her jaw with rage. "Never," she gasped. "I'd rather die."

"Oh, but you are wrong, my princess. Soon enough you'll beg for my attention."

Abdul fetched a cloth from his saddlebag and wet it with water poured from a leather pouch. Squatting beside Flora, he lifted her head and dabbed dirt from her face.

Flora turned her head. "Don't!"

"I'm being patient, my sweet, because I know this is difficult for you, but my patience is coming to an end. You'll take this cloth and wash your face. Then, you'll remove your filthy dress and..."

Flora glared defiantly, her eyes flashing anger. "No!"

"Yes, and then you'll cleanse yourself and put on this new dress."

She shook her head rebelliously. "No, sir, I will not."

"Yes, you will, and then you'll willingly offer me your affection."

Flora shook her head. "I will never..."

Pasha grasped Flora's jaw to silence her. He turned her face to his and glowered into her eyes. "You will, or tonight, I'll send my men back to Kemal Sufyan's farm to kill your mother and all your brothers and sisters."

Flora's eyes widened with fear. "Please, sir," she sobbed, "don't hurt my family."

"It's up to you, princess. If you willingly give me your love, then I'll see they're all safe and provided for, including your father."

Flora's eyes opened wider. "My papa?"

Abdul nodded. "I'll do all I can for them, including your father and brother in prison. Now, I'm going to feed the horse. There'll be no more tears when I come back inside. Okay?"

Flora took a deep breath. She bowed her head and stared at the floor. Tears were streaming down her face.

Abdul reached out and tenderly caressed her cheek. "Do you agree?"

Flora sighed, wiped her eyes on her sleeve and nodded.

"That's good. You will see, we will be very happy." He turned and walked to the door. "I'll be back in ten minutes."

Abdul stepped inside the house and shut the door. "That's much better."

Flora was sitting on the rug with her knees drawn beneath her. She wore a blue and green cotton dress and her hair was rolled up in a bun. "You promise to help my family?" she asked, without looking up.

"You have my word."

"Including my papa and brother?"

"I'll do everything I can. I have some influence with the lieutenant governor-general."

Flora looked up. "Promise me."

"I promise, if you agree to accept me as your husband."

Flora took a deep breath and slowly nodded her head. "If you will help them, I will do what you ask of me."

"You must understand, my princess; it'll be many months before you can see your family again."

"Months? I can't wait..."

"You must," Pasha interrupted. "That's how it must be. It's forbidden to help an Armenian—especially one accused of treason."

Flora's eyes bulged. "Treason? My papa never committed treason."

"Listen to me. If you want me to help your father and brother, then you must accept me as your husband and they must never know. It's the only chance they have to survive. Do you agree?"

Flora stared at the floor.

"Do you agree?" Pasha prodded. "Without my help, they will surely hang."

Flora looked up at Pasha. She tearfully nodded her head.

"No more tears. I'll make you very happy." He stepped across the room and picked up the rag from the floor. He rinsed it with water from the bag. He took off his cap and scrubbed dirt from his face and hands. Finally, he peeled off his shirt and knelt before Flora.

Flora looked up. "I've never..."

"I know. I'll teach you, my beautiful princess." Abdul gathered her into his arms. He kissed the nape her neck and pulled her dress down to expose her pert breasts. He traced his hands down her hips and legs, and slowly lifted her dress. "All the virgins in paradise pale by comparison," Abdul whispered breathlessly. He tracked kisses across her ear and kissed her full on the mouth.

Flora tensed reflexively.

Abdul ran his hand across her breasts and gently squeezed one nipple. "Relax, my darling," he whispered. Running his hand between her thighs, he slid his fingertips beneath her undergarment.

Flora caught her breath. "No," she whispered.

"Yes, oh yes. It won't hurt. I promise." Abdul pushed Flora onto her back and slowly tracked kisses down her stomach.

Staring up at the rickety roof, Flora bit her lower lip and closed her eyes.

CHAPTER 21

Fadime held a crust of bread to Kristina's chafed lips. "Eat it for the sake of your children."

"I can't," Kristina whispered. She glanced at Sirak and Izabella. The two youngsters were sleeping together at the foot of the bed. "Save it for them."

"Thanks be to God, they're finally asleep." Fadime whispered. "I thought their little hearts would break."

"My God, oh my God: first Mourad and Stepannos and now my precious Flora. I can't imagine her horror."

Fadime pulled Kristina's head to her chest. "You too must sleep, my friend. God will..." She turned at the creak of the door.

Sabiha stuck her head inside. "Mother, it's Father. Thanks be to God!"

"Kemal's here?"

"Yes! He's home."

Fadime and Kristina rushed to the front room.

Kemal was disheveled and dirty and soaked to the skin. "They took everything?" he asked incredulously.

"Yes, everything," Nahid replied dejectedly. "And they took Flora, too."

Kemal stared back in shock. He buried his face in his hands. "The world's gone mad."

Kristina pushed past Fadime. "Thank God you're safe, Kemal. What happened to Mourad and Stepannos?"

"They locked them up in the Central Prison in Diyarbekir."

"Prison? Dear God, why?"

"They're charged with aiding the enemy."

"What enemy?" Kristina gasped in disbelief. "They've done nothing."

"It makes no sense whatsoever. They've charged all the Armenians with the same crime."

"Have they been hurt?"

"I don't know. I haven't seen them since they took us to the prison. I was jailed in a different building."

"Mother Mary, full of grace," Kristina whispered.

"They separated the Turkish prisoners from the Armenians, Christian Syrians and other Christians. I'm sure they'll let them out soon."

"Did they hurt you?" Fadime asked.

"No, I was well treated. They locked me up for three days and then interrogated me. The interrogator warned me not to harbor any more infidels and threatened to terminate my deferment. I told him I'd known Mourad my whole life and that he'd done absolutely nothing to undermine the Empire. I told the man Alek was serving in the army, but his ears were closed."

"But why?" Kristina asked anxiously.

Kemal sighed. "I don't know. The prison is overflowing with Armenians from all over the province, and many of them are little more than boys. We're fortunate Mikael looks so young or they would've taken him, too."

Kristina glanced at Mikael. He stared back with vacant, sorrowful eyes.

"I wish they had taken me," he said.

Kristina traced the sign of the cross across her chest. "Don't say that. God spared you for a reason. We must leave here in the morning, and I need your help with Sirak and Izabella."

"You can't leave now," Fadime protested. "Where will you go? You can't stay alone on your farm."

"We'll go to Diyarbekir to find Nurse Elizabeth and Dr. Charles. I pray they're still there. Maybe Dr. Charles can help Mourad and Stepannos. If we stay here, we'll only put you at further risk."

Kemal sighed with resignation. "Perhaps you're right. We should also report Flora's kidnapping to the authorities in Diyarbekir so someone's looking for her. I'll take you to the Missionary Hospital tomorrow. While I'm there, I'll ask for a hearing with the lieutenant governor-general to appeal for Mourad's release. Then, I must move my family somewhere safer, too."

"Where will you go?" Kristina asked.

"Fadime has a brother with a farm near Ergani. We'll go there. I'll leave a message for you and Mourad at the post office in Ergani if we must leave there for some reason."

"Thank you, Kemal. Thank you all for everything," said Kristina.

Fadime gave Kristina a lingering hug. "We'll pray for all of you unendingly. You're my sister now."

"Wait here for a minute," Kemal shouted. He turned and walked to the barn.

Kristina examined the knapsack, blanket and other items strapped to Mikael's back. Sirak stepped from the house with Izabella in tow. The young girl was cradling her precious doll in her arms.

"Goodbye, Kristina," Fadime said sadly. "Promise you'll come back as soon as you can."

Kristina gave her friend a warm embrace. "I promise. Thank you for everything you've done for us. I want to give you these." She pressed her pearl earrings into Fadime's palm. "Take whatever you're offered to help feed your family."

"I can't take these," Fadime protested. "This is Mourad's gift to you."

Kristina closed Fadime's hand around the earrings. "Please, I want you to take them."

"I'll keep them here until you return. God bless you."

Kemal jogged out of the barn. "Okay, we must leave now or we won't make it to Diyarbekir before the afternoon heat." He picked up Izabella, set her on his shoulders and headed across the barnyard with Kristina and her sons.

"Goodbye, Sirak!" Özker yelled through his cupped hands.

Sirak turned and waved. "Goodbye, Özker! Best friends forever!"

The Sufyan family stood in the barnyard and watched Kemal, Kristina and her children walk down to the river bend. Finally, they disappeared into the stand of spruce trees.

"Allah's grace be upon you, Kazerians," Fadime said. She turned, and taking Özker's hand, solemnly led the others inside the house.

CHAPTER 22

May 4, 1915

Mourad looked up at Major Akcam. His breathing was labored and perspiration was beaded on his forehead.

The major walked deliberately around the interrogation chair. "This is your last chance, infidel. Who are your Andranik contacts?"

Mourad took a deep breath. "I told you, we're just simple farmers. We never helped the Andraniks."

The major slapped Mourad across the face. "Liar! I've had enough of your lies." He turned to the guards. "Get the boy."

"Yes, sir," the guard replied.

Mourad's right eye was swollen completely shut. The left was only a slit. "Please, sir, don't hurt my son. He's only an innocent boy."

Akcam stepped across the room and chose one of the canes. He whipped the rod down on the bench with a resounding crack. "This one will do nicely," he grunted.

"In the name of God!" Mourad cried out. "We've done nothing wrong! Please, sir, have mercy."

"Let your Christ save you," the major scoffed.

The door opened and the taller guard pushed Stepannos into the room. The boy locked eyes with his father. He was trembling with terror.

Tearing off the boy's shirt, the guard forced him down on the bench and bound his arms and legs to the ends.

"This is your last chance, infidel," the major barked. "Who are your Andranik contacts?"

"Papa!" Stepannos cried out.

Tears streamed from Mourad's swollen eyes. He nodded to his son in silent support, and then bowed his head. "Yea though I walk through the valley of the shadow of death, I will fear no..."

The major drew his sword. "Look at him! Look at your son or I'll chop off his head."

Mourad looked up at Stepannos. The tall guard arched the cane over his head and whipped it down on the boy's back. A loud thwack echoed through the room and Stepannos screamed in pain. Droplets of blood trickled from the scarlet welts emblazoned across the boy's shoulder blades.

The major stepped in front of Mourad and tapped his knee with his sword. "Confess your crimes and I'll spare the boy. If you persist with this charade, I'll kill him."

Mourad dropped his head to his chest. "Lord Jesus, please have mercy."

Major Akcam punched Mourad in the face. "Shut up, infidel! Your God has no power here. Light the boy's hair on fire."

Mourad's face contorted with anguish. "No! In the name of God, no!"

The guard smiled and fetched several matches from his pocket. Striking them, he yanked Stepannos' head up off the bench and held the flaming matches in front of the boy's face.

"Stop it!" Mourad shrieked. "I confess. I'm an Andranik spy—a recruiter for the Andranik forces. Please don't hurt him anymore."

The major waved the guard away. "You confess? You recruited fighters for the Andranik forces?"

"Yes, yes," Mourad moaned. "Whatever you want."

"Untie the boy. Mohammad, go tell the clerk to prepare the confession."

The tall guard hurried from the room. His partner untied Stepannos and sat him up on the bench.

"What was you handler's name?" Major Akcam demanded.

"He called himself Gagik," Mourad muttered.

"Did you say Gagik?" the major asked.

"Yes, Gagik."

"How did you make contact with this Gagik to send him recruits?"

"He came to the farm every week or two. He always came late at night."

"Papa, why do you lie? There was no Gagik. Nobody came to our farm."

The major rushed at Stepannos "Shut up! One more word and I'll cut out your tongue. Take him to his cell. And tell that clerk to get his worthless butt in here."

"Yes, sir," the guard replied. He untied Stepannos' legs and pulled him out the door.

The major turned back to Mourad. "Okay, now, tell me what this Gagik looks like. Is he tall or short?"

"Just one more block," Kemal said encouragingly. He took a deep breath and headed down the street to the Missionary Hospital.

Sirak turned to check on his mother. Kristina—haggard and dirty—staggered under Izabella's weight. Mikael brought up the rear.

Making their way to the hospital grounds, they wove through dozens of men loitering outside the main entrance. The stench of human waste permeated the air.

Kemal turned up the walk. Taking Sirak's hand, he led him through the throng to the front door. "Pardon me. Please, let us pass."

Sirak stared at a soldier dressed in a ragged army uniform. His eyes tracked down to the muddy rags wrapped around the man's feet and then up to his matted hair and beard.

The soldier spat on the ground at Kemal's feet. "Scum! Why do you coddle these infidels?"

"Let us pass!" Kemal snapped. Glancing back at Kristina and Mikael, he pushed past the soldier to the door.

"What do you want?" asked an armed guard.

"We're here to see Dr. Charles. This woman and her children are his personal friends."

The guard stared at Kristina. "Is Dr. Charles expecting her?" he asked suspiciously.

Euphoric hope swept over Kristina. *Dr. Charles hasn't left! Maybe Nurse Barton's still here, too!*

"Yes," Kemal lied assertively, "and they're late."

"What's the woman's name?"

"Kristina Kazerian. Tell the doctor she's here with her son, Sirak."

"Wait right here."

The guard whispered something to his partner and disappeared through the door.

Kristina was too exhausted to stand a moment longer. She led her children to a vacant spot in the yard and slumped to the ground.

Kemal squatted beside them. He glanced back at the street. Several Ottoman soldiers were taking stock of the new arrivals. "I hope Dr. Charles maintains some authority here," he whispered to Kristina.

Kristina and her children passed several anxious minutes before a commotion erupted at the entrance.

"Kristina!" a woman shouted. "Kristina, where are you?" Nurse Barton pushed her way through the throng at the door. Spotting them, she rushed across the yard and flung her arms around Kristina. "Thank God you're safe. We've been so worried about you."

Kristina pressed her face against Elizabeth's shoulder and lapsed into uncontrollable weeping.

"It's okay, Kristina, you're safe now."

Sirak clutched his mother's leg and stared up sadly at the nurse. "Some bad men came and took my papa."

"Oh, dear God," Elizabeth gasped. "When?"

"Two days ago," Kristina sobbed. "The police came to Kemal's farm and arrested Mourad and Stepannos. Then a group of highwaymen raided Kemal's farm and snatched my Flora."

"Oh, Kristina, I knew something horrible happened. We sent Abraham to your farm two weeks ago. I've been so worried ever since he found your house had burned down."

Kristina looked up in wide-eyed shock. "Our house...it's burned?"

"You didn't know?"

"No, I didn't know. We've been staying with Kemal and his family for the past four months."

"Merciful God," Elizabeth breathed.

"We don't have a place to go," Kristina wept. Tears streamed down her face.

"You can stay here with us," Elizabeth reassured her. "We've got plenty of room." She took Mikael's bedding and backpack. "Poor dears, you must be starving. Ibrahim!"

"Yes, Nurse Barton," the guard replied.

Kristina handed him the belongings. "I want you to deliver Mrs. Kazerian and her children to our living quarters. They'll stay in my old bedroom. Tell Lala to prepare them something to eat and help them fill the bath."

"Yes, madam. Right away."

Kristina embraced Elizabeth again. "Thank you. Thank you so much."

She turned to Kemal and took his hand. "Where would we be without you? Thank you and Fadime and Nahid for everything. Hopefully, we'll see you again soon."

Kemal smiled sorrowfully. "We'll pray that day comes very soon." He held out a piece of paper. "These are the directions to Fadime's brother's farm. If you need help with anything—anything at all—this is where you'll find us."

Kristina kissed him on the cheek. "You are wonderful friends. God will reward you all for your compassion and generosity. We'll always honor and miss you."

"And we'll miss you. Goodbye children. Take care of your mother."

Kemal wove through the crowd to the street and headed back in the direction he'd come.

K ristina awoke with a start from a nightmare. She bolted upright in the bed and found Sirak and Izabella sound asleep beside her. Mikael was lying on a pallet across the darkened room.

Getting up quietly, she shuffled across the room and slipped out the door. Dr. Charles and Elizabeth were sitting at the table sipping tea. Neither of them sensed her presence.

"The only chance they have is for me to appeal directly to the governor-general," she heard Dr. Charles say.

"What good will it do?" Elizabeth demanded. "Reshid's a cold-blooded psychopath."

Dr. Charles turned at Kristina's footsteps. He rushed to embrace her. "Kristina, my dear woman, it's so good to see you. I'm devastated about Mourad and your children. I'll do everything in my power to help you. In the meantime, you and your children will be safe here with us."

"I'm so grateful, Dr. Charles, but we don't want to create trouble for you and Elizabeth."

"It's no trouble. I'm delighted you're here. We've been beside ourselves ever since we got word about your farm."

"Thank you. God bless you."

"What's happening is terrible. So many Armenian men have been arrested, including some of my own staff."

"I should've insisted on Mourad taking us to Istanbul when that was still possible. Now, the farm is destroyed anyway, and Mourad and my children are gone. It's my fault."

"You must not blame yourself, Kristina. Nobody foresaw what's happened here in Diyarbekir. I'll go today to make an appeal to the governor-general on Mourad's behalf."

"Thank you from the bottom of my heart, Dr. Charles."

"It's time you called me David. We're all good friends now."

"Okay, David. I thank God you're both still here. I feared you would be gone by now."

Elizabeth stepped forward and took Kristina's hands. "We have something to tell you," she said with a coy smile. "David and I were married on March fourteenth."

Kristina's eyes widened with surprise. She gave Elizabeth a hug. "May God bless you."

Elizabeth took David's arm and rested her head adoringly on his shoulder. "I'm so happy. God brought me halfway around the world to meet the man of my dreams, and to work with him to ease the suffering of the people of Anatolia."

"I'm happy for you. May God bless your marriage with many children."

Elizabeth glanced at her husband and smiled. "We've decided against children—at least for now. Maybe we'll change our minds when our work here is done. But for now, we've decided to devote our lives to God and this hospital."

The door opened and a small Turkish man dressed in white, with a red fez, stepped into the room. "Dr. Charles, dinner will be ready in fifteen minutes."

"Thank you, Hakan. Please ask Lala to set the table for six."

"As you wish, sir," Hakan replied politely.

"I'll help you get the children ready for dinner," Elizabeth said. She took Kristina's arm.

"So how's our brave little boy doing?" Dr. Charles asked.

"His leg is so much better, but I'm afraid the shock of what's happened to his papa, brothers and sister has taken a heavy toll. He's just not himself."

Dr. Charles nodded understandingly. "How could he be?" He reached out and squeezed Kristina's hand. "These are crazy times in Anatolia, but we'll do everything we can to help you."

"Thank you, David. I pray for another of your miracles."

"Let's go clean up for dinner," Elizabeth said. "I think I have the perfect dress for you."

CHAPTER 23

The phone rang and Dr. Charles glanced up at the pudgy assistant sitting behind the reception desk. Several men had waited two hours to see Governor-general Reshid, including his acquaintance from a small hospital in Silvan.

She muttered a few words and hung up the phone. "Dr. Charles, Governor-General Reshid will see you now."

Dr. Charles glanced at the man seated next to him, and suddenly feeling anxious, rose to his feet and stepped through the door into the governor-general's office.

A young army officer met him in the vestibule. "Dr. Charles?"

"Yes, sir."

"I'm Lieutenant Jalal, Doctor Reshid's assistant. I'm sorry to keep you waiting, sir, but his prior appointment ran over."

"I appreciate him seeing me on such short notice. I realize he's very busy."

"Doctor Reshid only has a few minutes. Please get right to your point."

Charles nodded and the assistant led him into the inner office.

A dour-looking man sat behind the desk shuffling through a three-inch stack of papers. He had Circassian features, a heavy black mustache and a balding crown. He took a document from the stack, scanned the page and signed it. He slipped the paper into a basket before looking up over his half-eye glasses. "Dr. Charles, I received your letter. My assistant looked into the supplies and equipment requisitioned from your hospital. Unfortunately, the military hospital is short of many resources that are critical for the care of wounded and sick soldiers. Please submit an invoice and I'll see that you are reimbursed. Have a good day, Doctor."

"Thank you, Doctor Reshid, but I've come regarding a different matter."

"What is it now, Doctor?" the governor-general replied impatiently.

Charles handed the governor-general a sheet of paper. "Five workers at my hospital, including a surgeon and two nurses, were arrested last week. The names are listed there. We're short-staffed as it is, and we won't be able to care for our patients, including more than a hundred injured soldiers, unless they're released."

Reshid glanced at the paper. "They're all Armenians."

"Yes, sir."

"Doctor, are you aware Armenian forces are fighting us in Van? Hundreds of Ottoman soldiers have been killed or wounded."

"I can assure you, sir, none of these men had anything to do with the fighting in Van."

"Maybe not directly, but they must've been supporting the enemy in some fashion or they wouldn't have been arrested. However, I'll look into it. If these men were arrested in error, I'll have them released immediately."

"Thank you, sir. I ask for your special consideration for Mourad Kazerian. He's a personal friend who's being held at Diyarbekir Central Prison, along with his son, Stepannos. Mourad's brother is an Ottoman assemblyman and his son, Alek, serves in the Ottoman Army. I personally vouch for his loyalty to the Empire."

"Jalal," the governor-general said to his assistant, "see if Mourad Kazerian is listed in this week's prison report."

"Yes, sir."

Reshid glanced at the list again. "Flora Kazerian—is she his wife?"

"No, sir, Flora is Mourad's fifteen year-old daughter. As I noted there, highwaymen operating near Seghir abducted her last week. I appeal to you to ask the police in the area to search for her."

"Dr. Charles, do you have any idea how many people go missing every week in this province? We don't have the resources to search for a missing teenager. She probably ran away from home."

"She didn't run away, sir; she was kidnapped by armed intruders."

"Whatever, Doctor. I hear similar stories every day."

"But can't you just send a..."

Reshid raised his hand to silence Dr. Charles. His assistant stepped back into the room and set an open file on the governor-general's desk. Reshid—his glasses resting precariously at the tip of his nose—read down the page. "So, Doctor, you personally vouch for Mourad Kazerian's loyal service to the Empire?"

"Yes, I do, sir. Mourad's a wonderful, God-fearing man."

"Well, according to the chief interrogator at the Central Prison, he and his son confessed to spying and recruiting for the Andranik collaborators."

"That's preposterous. They must've been forced to confess."

"Doctor, I've known Major Tezer Akcam, his interrogator at the prison, for many years. His work is beyond reproach."

"I don't care what the major says; Mourad Kazerian and his son are not Andranik collaborators."

"Dr. Charles, I advise you to forget about these men. I signed their execution orders this morning."

"Dear God! These men are innocent."

"Dr. Charles, I have six more men waiting to speak to me. Good afternoon, sir."

The doctor's anger rose to the boiling point and he glared at the governor-general. "Sir, you will be held personally responsible if these innocent men are harmed."

The governor-general jumped to his feet. "Remove this imbecile from my office."

The attendant grabbed Dr. Charles by the arm but the latter jerked out of the attendant's grasp.

"I'll find my own way out, thank you." Charles took a step toward the door, but suddenly turned. "You leave me no choice but to contact Ambassador Morgenthau and Enver Pasha about your sanctioning, if not orchestrating, the atrocities that are being committed against Armenians and Syrians in Diyarbekir Province."

"Go ahead and write your damned letters. I can assure you, Doctor, they'll meet with disdain in Istanbul. The Armenian collaborators are a threat to the Empire and I've been given explicit orders to crush them."

"Clearly, Governor-general, you diligently carry out your orders— even if it means killing totally innocent people."

"They can all go to hell for all I care. Let me give you a little advice, Dr. Charles. Get your nose out of my office before I have it cut off. Don't forget, sir, the capitulations have been abrogated, and I've now got absolute power to punish you in any way I see fit. I'll tolerate your insolence this time because the Empire needs skilled medical professionals, but my tolerance is nearly at an end. Good afternoon."

Dr. Charles stormed out of the office past the governor-general's assistant.

Reshid shook his head. "I can't believe the impudence of these foreigners. It's time to teach them a lesson they'll not soon forget."

"You have said it, sir," his assistant replied. "We're censoring all foreign correspondence, but somehow details about the measures we've taken to deal with the collaborators have leaked out. I put another letter in your basket this morning."

"From whom?"

"From Lord Gray, the British Minister of Foreign Affairs. It's a warning about what he refers to as atrocities being committed against the minorities. He specifically mentions the Armenian and Syrian Christians."

"To hell with him. I'll not suffer an inglorious dismissal like my predecessor. We must press ahead without delay. Inform Colonel Tamir he's got one week to round up the remaining infidels or I'll promote someone else to his position."

"I'll tell him. What about Dr. Charles?"

"It's a cane with shit on both ends," the governor-general replied pensively. "We need help in the hospitals, but I'll not tolerate him meddling in my affairs. Ask Colonel Tamir to keep an eye on him."

"Yes, sir. I'll see to it."

CHAPTER 24

May 11, 1915

Abdul Pasha reined his horse in at the crest of the hill overlooking his freshly plowed fields. Just as he'd hoped, the barnyard was empty. He nuzzled Flora's neck beneath her veil. "This is your castle, my princess."

Flora didn't reply. Sitting sidesaddle in front of Abdul, she felt only emptiness and sorrow.

Abdul dug his heals into the mare's flanks. Guiding it down a gentle embankment, he trotted across the barnyard to the house. "Whoa," he muttered.

Pasha helped Flora down from the horse and led her to the front door. "Remember, you are the chosen one." Opening the door, Abdul led her inside.

Erol was kneeling on the floor in front of the coffee table playing chess with his uncle.

Hasan turned and shot up from his chair. "Abdul," he stammered, "welcome home. We were worried some evil befell you in Aleppo."

"My business took longer than expected. Did Baran finish the planting?"

"Yes, he planted the north field the day after you left and the west field two days ago."

"Very good. Erol, why haven't you chopped the wood? I told you to finish those limbs before I returned."

"The boy's been with fever for several days now," Hasan said.

"He's well enough to play games. Erol, go get the women."

The boy jumped up and dashed down the hall.

Abdul removed Flora's veil. "Hasan, let me introduce you to Flora, my beautiful third wife. God willing, she'll bear me many sons."

Hasan, too shocked to reply, stared open-mouthed at the young woman. Sabriye led Jasmine and her daughters into the room. Flora stared at the floor.

"Good morning," Abdul greeted them cheerfully. "This is Flora, my new wife."

"Wife?" Sabriye gasped in disbelief. "She's Armenian."

"Flora converted to Islam, and the mullah blessed our marriage."

"But where?" Jasmine demanded incredulously. "There's no room for another wife."

"We'll make room," Abdul replied. "Henceforth, Flora will be my favored wife, and God willing, she will bear me many strong sons. She'll take the large bedroom."

"The large bedroom?" Jasmine asked incredulously. "What about the children and me?"

"You will take the room next to Sabriye's, or divorce me and live with your brother. It matters not to me."

"You know Nadir can't support us," Jasmine said bitterly. "He can't even provide for his own family."

"Then you must make do with the room I give you."

"This is outrageous! That tiny room isn't big enough for one person, let alone the four of us."

"Make it work," Abdul replied calmly. "Erol can sleep here in the front room."

Jasmine glared at Abdul. "How can you treat your own flesh and blood so callously? If you won't listen to me, then perhaps you'll consult the Holy Koran. A man may only take another wife if he can provide..."

"Enough!" Abdul bellowed. "There will be no more discussion. Sabriye, I ask you to oversee the arrangements, and I expect Flora to take her place in the large bedroom before I return."

"A small room is all I need," Flora whispered.

Everyone turned to stare at the impassive young woman. Glancing up for a brief moment, she quickly looked back down.

Abdul scowled at Jasmine. "I've made my decision. Flora will be recognized as my first wife, and she will take the large bedroom. If you cross her, or me, you do so at your own peril." He stepped outside and slammed the door shut behind him. An uncomfortable silence hung over the room.

"Well, Abdul made his decision, and we all must accept it," Sabriye finally said. She smiled at Flora. "I'm Sabriye, Abdul's oldest wife, and this is my brother, Hasan."

"I'm delighted to meet you, Flora," Hasan said sincerely. "Welcome to our family."

"Thank you for your kindness," Flora whispered timidly.

"And this is Jasmine, Abdul's second wife," Sabriye added. "These are her children, Ayse, Fairuza and Erol. We all welcome you."

Flora nodded at Jasmine and her children.

Jasmine sighed resignedly. "I bear you no malice, Flora. I'm just stunned. You must be hungry. Can I prepare you a bowl of soup?"

"No, thank you. I'd just like to lie down for a while, if you don't mind."

"Of course," Sabriye said. "You can rest in my bedroom while we sort things out."

"Thank you. You're all very kind."

Jasmine waited for Sabriye to lead Flora out of the front room before turning to Hasan. "There's no way her family consented to this marriage.

She's only a shy young girl."

Hasan shrugged his shoulders. "There is no point in arguing. Abdul will do as he pleases, and if we want to remain in his household, we must comply with his decisions. Think of your children. The Empire is at war. This is no time to be reliant on the generosity of strangers. I'll help you move your things."

CHAPTER 25

Sirak looked over Dr. Charles' shoulder and watched him incise a boil on a wounded infantryman's leg. Hyperventilating with pain, the soldier clutched the bedrails and sank his teeth into a rolled towel.

"Bite down, Corporal," Charles said. "Sirak, hold his leg still."

Sirak struggled to hold the soldier's foot. He watched intently as Dr. Charles expressed foul-smelling pus from the angry wound and inserted a drainage tube. Finally, Dr. Charles sutured the tube to the skin. "You can relax now. We're still not out of danger, but your leg looks better today. I'll do everything I can to save it."

"Thank you, Doctor," the corporal gasped. "May God bless you."

Dr. Charles ruffled Sirak's hair and smiled kindheartedly. "I think I've found a new assistant. What's your weekly fee?"

"My fee?"

"Yes, your fee. How much do you charge?"

Sirak stared up at the doctor. "Nothing, sir. But could it help my papa?"

Dr. Charles squatted eye to eye with the boy. "Sirak, I'll do everything in my power to get your papa out of that prison. I promise."

"Thank you. My mama says if anyone can get Papa out, it's you. Can I ask you a question?"

"Of course."

"Do you like being a doctor?"

Charles broke into a broad grin. "Absolutely; at least most of the time."

"What *don't* you like about it?"

"Well, I guess when people are so sick I can't help them. Unfortunately, that happens far too often since the war started."

"What do you like best?"

"That's easy. The best part is helping patients like you—someone who's hurt really bad, but then recovers to live a full and happy life."

"You know what Mama says? She says healing people is God's work."

Dr. Charles smiled and patted Sirak on the head. "Your mama's a very smart woman. We're all God's little helpers."

"Can I be a doctor when I grow up?"

"Yes, but first you must learn to read and write."

"Mama's already teaching me to read and write, but where do I learn to doctor?"

Charles smiled. "The Medical College of Istanbul would be a very good choice. Did you know the great Sultan Mehmet's doctor was Armenian?"

"The Sultan's doctor? Really?"

"Yes, his name was Shashian, and they established the medical school together. That was almost one hundred years ago, in 1817, I believe. Come now, young man, we must finish rounds before clinic. Can you fill this basin with soapy water? I'll be over there with the next patient."

Sirak took the basin and ran out the door at the end of the ward.

"How are you feeling today, Sergeant?" the doctor asked a burly Turk.

The man grimaced and held up his bandaged hand. "It hurts like hell, but I can move my fingers."

"That's a good sign." Dr. Charles sat on the edge of the bed. Unwinding gauze from the man's hand, he examined the remnants of his index finger. Only a swollen and discolored stump remained. "It looks better today, and there's no infection. How'd this happen?"

"I was cutting meat and my knife slipped."

Dr. Charles looked up amusedly. "I guess it'll be hard to shoot a gun without your index finger?"

"Truly. If you write that in my record, they'll send me home."

"I'll write it, but only if you let me throw out that filthy fez."

The soldier reluctantly pulled off his fez and handed it to the doctor. Charles stuffed it into his back pocket. "Where's your family, Sergeant?"

"In Bitlis; at least that's where we lived when the war started, but they evacuated when the Russian army attacked Van. Only God knows where they are now. They're probably dead."

"I'm sorry," Dr. Charles said solemnly. He patted the man on the shoulder. "I'll pray for them."

Sirak hustled through the door carrying the water basin. "I'm sorry," he gasped. "Nurse Barton washed the basin."

"That's okay. Set it here on the table. Sergeant, I want you to soak your hand in this soapy water for at least ten minutes." Dr. Charles looked up. The sergeant was glaring at Sirak.

"Is he Armenian?" the sergeant asked.

"Yes," Charles replied.

The soldier lunged at Sirak. "I'll cut your fucking head off!"

Charles pulled the wide-eyed boy to the door and squatted beside him. "It's alright, Sirak. You didn't do anything wrong. Go tell Nurse Barton I'll join her in clinic in a few minutes."

Sirak hurried off with his head down.

"What's wrong with you, Sergeant?" Charles snapped.

"I hate infidel scum. The Armenian dogs captured two of my men near Van. One of them was my best friend. We only found pieces after the infidels got through with them. God willing, we'll kill every last one of them."

"He's just a boy, and his older brother serves in the Ottoman Army."

"There were dozens of Armenians in my regiment, but most of them deserted during the fight for Van. We should've lined them all up and cut their..."

"That's enough! If you want my care, you'll keep your hatred to yourself. Soak your hand in this water and I'll send the nurse in to replace your bandage."

Dr. Charles turned and made his way past a line of staring patients.

A man near the door struggled up on his cot. "Don't side with the Armenians, Doctor," he warned in a hoarse whisper. "Their tricks are well known, and nobody will fall for them anymore."

Ignoring the man's comment, Charles stepped out of the ward and shut the door behind him.

"*Allahu Akbar!*" a deep voice shouted in the ward behind him. A chorus of men repeated the cry.

CHAPTER 26

May 30, 1915

"Good morning," Elizabeth murmured tiredly. She stepped to the table and affectionately squeezed Kristina's arm.

Kristina smiled. "Good morning." She tried to spoon-feed Izabella a mouthful of rice, but the young girl twisted up her face and turned away. "You must eat, Izabella. If you'll eat the rest of this, I'll play dolls with you. Okay?" She looked up at Elizabeth. "I came to your room for some aspirin early this morning. I think Izabella's coming down with a cold."

"Did you find it?"

"Lala got me some. We're feeling better now, aren't we angel?"

The little girl nodded and took another bite.

"Did you get any rest last night?" Kristina asked.

"I managed to nap for a couple of hours. They brought in several wounded soldiers, so I was lucky to get that much."

"Why didn't you wake me?"

"The orderlies had the situation under control. Besides, you had your hands full with Izabella. Did she finally sleep?"

"After I rocked her for two hours. Hopefully, she'll take a nap this afternoon. Are you going to church this morning?"

"I can't. David has an emergency amputation and he needs my help. Maybe we can go tonight."

"I'd like to go, if you can make it."

"I'll do my best. Hakan's headed to the souk today to buy provisions. Do you want anything?"

"We're out of black tea."

"Oh, yes, thanks for reminding me. David wants more coffee, too. Perhaps Lala can stay with the kids and we can finish..."

The door burst open and Dr. Charles rushed into the room. His face was drawn.

Elizabeth shot up from her chair. "What is it?"

Charles nodded at the children. "Are they finished with their breakfast?"

Kristina got up from the table. "Mikael, take Sirak and Izabella to the bedroom to play."

"I don't want to play," Mikael sulked.

"Don't argue with me." Kristina helped Izabella out of her chair and ushered the children to the bedroom. She rushed back into the kitchen a moment later.

"I just got terrible news from Reverend Hollis," David said. "They executed over a hundred prisoners at the Central Prison this morning."

Kristina clutched her hands to her face in horror. "Mourad and Stepannos?"

"He didn't know. They haven't posted the names. Reverend Hollis brought a proclamation from the governor-general's office. Reshid ordered the prison emptied of all non-Muslims. The remaining captives are to be sent down the river into exile."

"Exile?" Kristina asked fretfully. "To where?"

"I don't know anything more, but people are already gathering outside the prison. Doctor Saunders offered to do my surgeries so I can take you to the prison."

Kristina nodded her head dolefully. "Give me a few minutes to get the children ready."

"Are you sure you want to take the children?" Dr. Charles queried skeptically. "God knows what'll happen down there."

"David's right," Elizabeth agreed. "Lala will watch your children."

"No, I want to take the children. God forbid, it could be their last chance to see their father." She buried her face against Elizabeth's chest.

Dr. Charles wrapped his arm around her shoulder. "I'll tell Hakan to harness the wagon." "I'm coming, too," Elizabeth whispered. She took Kristina's arm and helped her to the bedroom.

The street outside the hospital was in chaos when the horse-drawn wagon pulled away from the hospital an hour later. Dozens of people, some carrying stretchers, were milling about the front entrance and more than a dozen wagons were lined up down the street.

One of the guards caught sight of Dr. Charles riding beside his driver. Running to the street, he jogged alongside the wagon. "Where are you going, Doctor?"

"We're going to the Central Prison. I'll be back this afternoon."

"But all these wagons are loaded with sick and wounded soldiers."

"Doctor Saunders will take care of them until I return. Let's go, Hakan."

Hakan whipped the horse, and the wagon jerked away from the hospital. Weaving through pedestrian traffic, they slowly made their way along sun-drenched streets to the access road outside the front gate of Diyarbekir Central Prison. Pulling wide-eyed Izabella to her side, Kristina covered her ears to shelter her from mournful wails echoing from the large crowd gathered in the street.

"My God, where is Thy mercy?" an old woman blubbered above the din.

"Hakan, park over there," Dr. Charles shouted. He pointed to a clearing beneath a tree. "Wait for us there. We may want to use the wagon."

Dr. Charles helped the women and children down to the ground. He swept Sirak up in his arms and led them towards the black-walled prison. Kristina grabbed Izabella and followed him into the fringes of the crowd.

"Have there been any announcements?" Charles asked an old man.

"The crier announced the prisoners would be brought out in thirty minutes. That was an hour and a half ago."

"Any word about the men they executed?"

"No, nothing; but there's a rumor that they..."

Suddenly, the murmur of the crowd intensified to a roar.

Kristina stood on her tiptoes and saw the prison gate open wide. She caught a glimpse of the large procession of men being herded out to the access road before the crowd closed around her. "I can't see!" she cried.

"We'll stay here with the children!" Elizabeth shouted. "You go ahead."

"No, we must stay together. If Mourad and Stepannos come out, I want the children to see them."

"This is insanity!" Dr. Charles shouted above a hundred jumbled cries. He picked up Sirak. "Our only hope is to race up the street ahead of the crowd."

Kristina grabbed Mikael's hand. "Should we head back to the wagon?"

"No, we'll never get the wagon through this mob. Follow me."

The group clung together and wove through the crowd. Breaking into the clear, they raced up a parallel service road. Finally, they turned up an alley and dashed back to the main street.

Dr. Charles ducked behind a cart parked at the corner. Fighting to catch his breath, he hoisted Sirak onto his shoulders and gathered the others around him. "They'll have to pass this way to get to the river."

Peering up the street from atop Dr. Charles' shoulders, Sirak watched mounted policemen clear the mob ahead of the procession. "Is my papa coming now?" he cried out hopefully.

"I don't know, Son," Charles replied distractedly. "We'll find out soon."

Several minutes passed before policemen on horseback reached their position. Whimpers, wails and shouts from distraught relatives echoed off the walls of surrounding buildings.

"Hovan! Oh, my Hovan!" a young woman screamed hysterically above the clamor.

"I love you, Vartan," an old man yelled.

The huge leading throng of relatives streamed on both sides of the cart and a phalanx of armed guards surged forward ahead of the prisoners.

"Dear God," Kristina called out frantically, "they're all bound together."

More than twenty abreast, the long column of scruffy men and boys in tattered rags stumbled past them. A fetid communal odor hung over them like a cloud. Telltale signs of torture—cuts and bruises, blackened eyes and charred heads—were visible on many of the prisoners. Some prisoners carried other men on stretchers. Clean white bandages worn by a few men seemed oddly out of place. A few prisoners searched the surrounding multitude for loved ones, but the majority stared trance-like at the ground beneath their feet. Club-toting guards shouted commands and forced the desperate crowd out of their path.

Bobbing and craning, Kristina scrutinized the vacant faces of the closest prisoners. "Mikael, climb up on this cart!"

Mikael climbed up the tailgate and jumped into the bed. His eyes darted from face to face, searching for Mourad and Stepannos. "There they are!" he shouted. "Papa! I'm up here! Stepannos! I'm up here!"

Stepannos hobbled along with his father near the end of the procession. Hunched over at the waist, Mourad looked as if he'd aged twenty years. His right eye was swollen shut.

"Papa!" Mikael yelled again.

Mourad looked up and searched the crowd. Suddenly, he spotted Mikael. He waved his hand and yelled to his son.

"I can't hear you, Papa!" Mikael called out mournfully. He held his arms extended. "Papa, I love you. Stepannos, my brother, I love you, too. May God protect you!"

"Mikael, take Sirak so he can see, too," Dr. Charles shouted. He handed the boy up. Kristina passed Izabella to Elizabeth. Climbing into the cart, she leaned down and lifted her daughter into the wagon. Mikael climbed into the driver's seat. Reaching back into the bed, he pulled Sirak in beside him.

Sirak stood in the seat and scanned the faces streaming past. "Where's Papa?"

Mikael pointed to the road behind the cart. "Right there!"

Sirak spotted them. He jumped up and down. "Papa!" he called out jubilantly. "Papa, I miss you. I love you. Stepannos, I love you, too."

"Stepannos! Mourad!" Kristina shouted. "I miss you, my darlings. We pray for you." She lifted Izabella and turned her head. "Look Izabella! There's your papa and brother."

Mourad waved his arms. He cupped his bandaged hands over his mouth and yelled up at Kristina, but the roar of the crowd muffled his shout.

"What?" Kristina shouted frantically. "We can't hear you!"

"Jerusalem!" Stepannos bellowed up to her. "Saint James in Jerusalem!"

"Yes!" Kristina shouted. "I heard you! Saint James in Jerusalem." Staring helplessly, with tears streaming down her face, she locked eyes with Mourad. She held his gaze for a moment, before the trailing throng pushed him past.

Mikael and Sirak crawled over the side of the cart and jumped to the ground. Dr. Charles plucked Izabella out of the bed. Elizabeth helped Kristina climb over the tailgate.

"They look terrible," Mikael gasped. "Did you see Papa's eye?"

"Yes," Kristina sobbed, "and there were bandages wound around both of his hands."

"At least they're alive," Charles said. "Thank God Almighty."

"Yes, they're alive," Kristina said gratefully. Looking to the heavens, she traced the sign of the cross across her head and chest. "Thank you, dear God."

Dr. Charles grabbed Sirak's hand. "Come on, let's hurry back to the wagon and follow them down to the river."

Hakan pulled the wagon to a stop at the top of an embankment overlooking the Tigris River. The blazing noonday sun hung directly overhead in a cloudless sky. Far below, at the crowded river's edge, the prisoners were being transferred onto *kelek* rafts supported by inflated animal skins. Twenty to thirty men, all bound together, were being loaded on to each raft, along with an oarsman and an armed gendarme.

Several overloaded rafts were already drifting down the slow-moving river. Distraught friends and family members scattered along the bank and many shadowed rafts bearing their loved ones. A line of jagged rocks several hundred yards downstream blocked the progress of the hordes on land. Heartbreaking wails and mournful goodbyes reverberated up and down the river.

"Wait here, Hakan!" Dr. Charles shouted. Jumping to the ground, he helped the women and children out of the wagon and led them down the riverbank and into the teeming crowd.

Sirak spotted his father immediately. He jumped up and down and waved his arms. "Papa! Papa!" he called out frantically. "Papa, I'm over here!"

A guard led Mourad and Stepannos onto a raft and tethered them to a dozen other men. Mourad slumped to his knees. He peered up at the boisterous, crowd-covered embankment and caught sight of Kristina and his children. Nudging Stepannos, he pointed to the shore and raised his shackled arm.

Panicked cries suddenly arose from downstream.

Dr. Charles gasped in horror at the sight of one raft listing precipitously to the side. "Merciful God!" he breathed.

The raft abruptly rolled over amid a chorus of terrified screams. The guard and helmsman bobbed to the surface a moment later. Glancing back toward the stricken raft, they swam for shore.

"Someone help them!" Kristina shrieked.

The gendarmes watched passively from the shore, as ripples in the water rolled gently onto the bank.

One man swam out to the capsized raft. He tried to turn the raft over, but failed. "Help me!" he bellowed.

Several men, including Dr. Charles rushed out to join him. But it was hopeless. Bound together with manacles and ropes, the prisoners sank straight to the bottom.

"Did you see that?" one of the guards asked his comrade within earshot of Dr. Charles. "They sank like cannons."

"They must have gold in their pockets," another guard snickered. "We should've searched them more carefully."

"Murderers! Child killers!" Dr. Charles bellowed, his baritone voice booming with anger. "You will all rot in hell!" He waded to shore and gazed helplessly at the overturned raft.

Two gendarmes ran down the embankment and grabbed Dr. Charles' arms.

"Let me go!" Charles exclaimed angrily. He tried to pull away, but the gendarmes twisted his arm behind his back. They kicked his feet out from beneath him and forced him to the ground.

"You're under arrest," one gendarme shouted.

"For what?" Charles asked indignantly.

"Incitement to rebellion," the man replied.

"Let him go!" Elizabeth cried out. "He did nothing!" She rushed forward and tried to pull the gendarme away from her husband, but the man shoved her to the ground.

The gendarmes led Charles up the embankment to a group of officials standing on the ridge. One of the men, a Turk wearing civilian clothes, stepped forward and punched Charles in the face.

A trickle of blood ran from Dr. Charles' nose. He glared back defiantly.

"Hell on earth awaits you, infidel," one man snarled. "Take him to the prison."

Sirak watched helplessly as the gendarmes escorted Dr. Charles away. Suddenly, he whirled back to the river and scanned the rafts floating downstream. His eyes locked onto a large raft crowded with prisoners that was abreast of the rocky peninsula jutting into the slow-moving river. "Papa," he whispered, as the raft drifted out of sight.

CHAPTER 27

June 1, 1915

L ala poked her head through the door into the gloomy bedroom. She tiptoed across the room with a tray. Grief hung in the air like the poignant dirge of a lone piper.

Nurse Barton was lying on the bed beside Kristina. She had a washcloth draped over her eyes. Izabella and Sirak were huddled against the wall on a pallet and Mikael was slumped in the chair across the room.

"Lala," Elizabeth whispered, "please bring me a glass of water."

"Right away, madam. I also brought a tray of fruit and cheese." She set the tray on the nightstand and fetched a water pitcher from the bureau.

"Did Hakan take my letter to the governor-general?"

"Yes, madam. He left two hours ago, but he's not back yet."

"Send him in as soon as he gets back, even if I'm asleep."

"Of course, madam. I'm sorry to trouble you, but there's a problem in the clinic."

"What problem?"

"Doctor Karinget's been asking for you. He's fretting about a soldier he admitted this morning. He needs surgery, but there's no scrub nurse."

"Tell him I'll be there in half an hour."

"Yes, madam. Nurse Barton, we're all heartbroken about Dr. Charles. It's shameful after everything he's done to help people here in Diyarbekir. I pray they release him soon."

"Thank you, Lala," Elizabeth said wearily. "I appreciate your prayers."

"Maybe Dr. Charles will be with Hakan when he returns. Someone must have some common sense down at that prison."

"I hope you're right."

"Miss Lala?" Sirak called out.

The old Turkish woman turned and peered at Sirak through her veil. "Yes, my little angel?"

"Would you pray for my papa, too?"

"Oh, you poor little dear. Of course—I'll say a special prayer just for him."

"His name is Mourad Kazerian."

"I know. I'll remember him in all of my prayers."

"Thank you, Miss Lala."

Lala stepped out and Nurse Barton rolled onto her back. Sobbing softly, she stared up at the ceiling.

"Have you ever been to Jerusalem?" Kristina whispered.

"No. David and I intended to go last winter, but then the war ruined our plans."

"I've heard you can worship any God you want there and nobody interferes. Can you imagine that—Muslims, Jews and Christians living together in peace?"

"I doubt the Ottoman officials in Jerusalem are all that tolerant now that there's war. In America, religious freedom is guaranteed by our Constitution."

"America," Kristina whispered. "It must be a wonderful country."

"Mama, where *is* America?" Sirak asked.

"It's far, far away, little mouse—on the other side of the great ocean."

"Is that where God lives?"

"No, God doesn't live there, but lot's of wonderful people do, like Nurse Barton and Dr. Charles. Uncle Bedros called it paradise on earth."

"Has Papa ever been there?"

"No, little mouse, he's never been there. Maybe someday, after we meet Papa and Stepannos in Jerusalem, we can all visit America together."

"How do we know Papa's in Jerusalem?" Mikael called out skeptically.

"He said he'd meet us there," Kristina replied. "We must have faith he'll find his way."

"Can we go find them tomorrow?" Sirak asked impatiently.

Kristina sighed sadly. "We can't go tomorrow, but we'll go..."

A knock at the door resounded through the room.

"Who is it?" Elizabeth called out.

Lala pushed the door ajar. "Hakan is back, madam. He's here with me now."

Elizabeth bolted up in the bed. "Have him wait in the parlor. I'll be right there." She grabbed her robe off the bedpost and hurried out.

Hakan was standing in the parlor. He looked up with a long face.

"What happened?" Nurse Barton demanded.

"They wouldn't listen to me, Nurse Barton."

"Did you ask to see the governor-general?"

"Yes, I did just what you said, but I only got to speak to his assistant. He said the governor-general was busy and couldn't be interrupted."

"Did you give him my letter?"

"Yes, I did."

"Good," she whispered. "Hopefully, he'll read it soon."

"No, madam."

"No? Why not?"

"I'm so sorry. I did the best I could."

"What happened? Tell me."

"He burned the letter."

"He *burned* it?"

"Yes, he lit a match and set fire to it right there on his desk."

"But why?"

"He told me to tell you murderers and child killers don't read letters."

"Murderers and child killers?"

"That's what he said. Those were his exact words."

"Dear God. Did he say anything else?"

Hakan shook his head "No."

Nurse Barton bit her lip and stared tearfully at a collage of photographs on the wall. One was a grainy black and white image of David Charles, along with several other white-coated doctors, standing in front of the American Missionary Hospital in Chunkoush. A snapshot from a happier day, Charles stood cheerfully, with his arm draped around a young Turkish colleague's shoulders. He stared back with his indomitable grin. Nurse Barton gazed at his image for several moments. "Leave me now," she sobbed.

CHAPTER 28

The front door opened and Erol struggled inside toting a large burlap bag. His red face was streaked with perspiration. Straining under the weight of the bulky load, he tripped and nearly fell. "Father told me to bring in these potatoes."

Flora rushed around the kitchen table. "Here, let me help you." She grabbed one end of the bag and helped him hoist it onto the counter. "This is much too big for you. You shouldn't be lifting anything this heavy."

Erol bent over and propped his arms on his knees. "Tell Father," he replied wearily. "If I don't, he whips me."

Flora grabbed a wet cloth from the kitchen and dabbed perspiration from the boy's forehead. "I'm sorry. I don't understand why he hits you. Is it my fault?"

Erol took a deep breath and sighed. "No, it's not you. It's because I'm not Timurhan."

Kristina frowned. "Timurhan?"

"Timurhan was my half-brother, born of Sabriye. Don't you remember him? He was with us that day Father offered to buy your farm."

"Oh yes, I do remember. Where is he now?"

"He got killed in the war. Father always hated me, but since Timurhan died, it's been even worse. He hates Mother, too."

"Erol, he doesn't hate you. He's just a very strict man. He's that way with me, too."

"No, he hates me. He constantly tells me I'll never amount to anything, and that I'll never be like Timurhan."

Flora smiled and brushed Erol's bangs back from his face. "You must be thirsty. Would you like some water?"

"Thank you, but then I must get back to my chores."

Flora poured a glass of water and handed it to Erol. He gulped it down and she refilled his glass. "Slow down, or you'll get a side ache."

Erol took another sip and handed her the glass. "Thank you."

"I'm sorry he forced your mother and sisters out of the large bedroom."

"He hates them, too. He wants us all to leave, but we've got no place to go."

"Well, I don't hate you. Always remember that. How old are you Erol?"

"Eight." He glanced at the door.

"My youngest brother is eight, too."

"I know."

"You know Sirak?"

"I met him when we came to your farm. Where is he now?"

"I don't know. Somewhere safe, I hope."

"You aren't really Armenian, are you?" Erol asked Flora.

"Yes, I am. Why do you doubt it?"

"The Armenian fighters killed Timurhan. If there's anyone Father hates more than me, it's the Armenians."

"I *am* Armenian, so I guess he must hate me, too."

Erol shook his head. "No, he doesn't. I see the way he treats you."

Flora took his empty glass. "How does he treat me?"

"With love—like he treated Timurhan."

Flora chuckled. "I think sometimes you let your imagination run wild."

"Are you scared to have a baby?"

Flora's eyes widened with surprise. She blushed crimson. "Please, Erol, don't ask me questions about such things."

"I'm sorry. I heard Sabriye tell Mother you're pregnant. Now you hate me, too."

Flora regained her composure. She took Erol by the shoulders. "No, I don't hate you. I'll never hate you. You and I will always be good friends. Okay?"

Erol nodded gratefully. "Okay."

"*Erol,*" a gruff voice bellowed from the barnyard, "*where the hell are you?*"

Erol's eyes filled with fear. "Don't let him hit me."

The door burst open and Abdul lunged inside. His face was flushed red with anger. "What are you doing? I told you to feed the chickens."

Erol hurried past Abdul and out the door.

Abdul slapped him on the back of the head. "Idiot," he spat out. He turned and caught Flora's disapproving glare. "What?"

"He's your own son. Why do you treat him like a dog?"

"Watch your tongue, woman. I told him to bring in the bag of rice and come right back to the barn. The boy's lazy. He uses every possible excuse to avoid work."

"I asked him to help me rearrange heavy supplies and utensils here in the kitchen, and he was kind enough to lend a hand. He did nothing wrong."

"In that case, I'll spare him the whip."

"You'd whip your own flesh and blood? It hurts when I see you abuse your own son this way. Is this how you'll treat our children?"

Abdul raised his hand. "You'll not speak to me this way."

"Go ahead, hit me."

Abdul glared at her menacingly for a moment. Finally, he dropped his hand. "Women," he huffed beneath his breath, "you're all the same."

"Yes, we're all the same. We all expect affection and kindness from our fathers and husbands. My father raised four sons and two daughters, and I never saw him raise his hand in anger—not even once."

Abdul crossed his arms and glowered at Flora. "I'm doing the best I can." Then, considering her youth and beauty, Abdul leaned his pitchfork against the wall and took her hands in his. "I have some good news. My friend met with the governor-general."

"What did he say?" Flora asked with trepidation.

"He agreed to spare your father and brother. They're to be exiled to Syria."

"Syria? Why? They've done nothing wrong."

"Your father admitted he aided the enemy, and the punishment for treason is hanging. It's the best I could do."

Flora took a deep breath. "What about my mother?"

"All Armenians in Anatolia are being relocated. She will probably be exiled to Syria, too—along with your sister and brothers."

"With my papa?"

"I asked friends with influence to spare your father and brother. That's all I can do. I'm not a miracle worker."

"Please, Abdul," Flora begged tearfully. "I kept my promises to you, and you must keep yours to me. Will you do this for me?"

"There's a war going on. I saved your father and brother. What more do you want?"

"I want my mama, papa, and my siblings to all live together in peace. That's what you promised me."

Abdul stared at Flora for several moments. She glared back with unwavering determination.

Abdul grinned. "How can I deny such beauty?" He reached for her hand, but Flora spun away.

"I don't want your flattery. I want you to honor your promise. Otherwise, I will not be bound by my promise to you."

"I can force you to stay."

"Yes, you can, but you can't force me to be happy."

Taking a deep breath, Abdul groaned frustratedly. "I'll do everything I can." He stepped outside and shut the door behind him.

CHAPTER 29

June 8, 1915

"We're leaving now," Elizabeth muttered dejectedly. She was wearing a long black dress and white gloves. Her hair was pulled back beneath a scarf.

Kristina got up from the table and gave Elizabeth a hug. "I'll pray your message finds its way to someone who will open the prison doors."

"I'm grateful for everything you've done, Kristina. Thank God you're here."

"Do they need me in clinic while you're gone?"

"No, everything's okay for now. I should be back in a couple of hours, and then we'll have Hakan take us to the market. Do you need anything?"

"No, we're fine. Be careful, Elizabeth."

"I'll see you later."

Elizabeth made her way through the throng outside the main door of the hospital.

"Good morning, madam," Hakan greeted politely. "I brought water. It's extremely hot today."

"Thank you," Elizabeth replied distractedly. "We must hurry to the telegraph office. The clinic is already overflowing with patients."

"Yes, madam; I know a route that shouldn't be very crowded."

Hakan helped Elizabeth into the wagon. He climbed into the driver's seat and flicked the reins. The wagon jerked away from the hospital and sped down a crowded boulevard for several blocks before turning into a residential neighborhood in a rundown section of the city.

It rattled past dozens of people, including many young children, gathered in front of the old basalt homes and buildings that lined the street. Here and there, small groups of haggard men stood guard over their beleaguered families and what little they had in the way of worldly possessions.

Elizabeth caught sight of an emaciated young woman clutching a half-starved toddler in her lap. "God have mercy," she muttered.

Two young boys darted into the street. Holding up their tiny little hands, they ran alongside the wagon. "Bread please!" the younger one called up to her.

Hakan cracked his whip above their heads. "Stay back!" he shouted gruffly.

"Stop that, Hakan!" Elizabeth ordered. "Stop the wagon."

"But, madam, we don't have time to..."

"Stop the wagon!"

Hakan pulled up on the reins and brought the wagon to a rolling stop.

Elizabeth fished through her purse and pulled out a handful of coins. Leaning down, she pressed coins into the eager hands of the youngsters crowding around the wagon. "God bless you," she said to each grateful child.

The throng quickly swelled. Soon other teenagers and adults gathered expectantly behind the horde of children.

Elizabeth, her face beading droplets of sweat, continued doling out coins. Finally, she held up her empty palms. "That's all I have. May God bless each one of you."

The throng melted away and Elizabeth caught sight of a slight young girl standing alone just off the road. The dark-haired child's left leg was amputated at the knee and she was leaning on a cane fashioned from a tree branch.

The wagon eased forward.

"Wait just a minute," Elizabeth said.

Hakan reined the horse to a stop.

Climbing down from the wagon, Elizabeth walked to the side of the road and crouched beside the little girl. Shading her eyes, she smiled warmly. "Hello, sweetheart. What's your name?"

The girl didn't reply. She stared back with doe-eyed innocence.

"Where is your mommy, honey?"

The little girl turned and pointed at a scruffy young woman in a worn dress. Elizabeth guessed she was seventeen or eighteen years old. She was standing beside a gaunt, middle-aged man.

"Let's go talk to them." Elizabeth took the little girl's arm and helped her hobble to the couple. "Hello, I'm Elizabeth Barton, the head nurse at the Missionary Hospital."

"Good morning," the young woman replied politely. "My name is Azra and this is my husband, Farhad."

"Where are you from?"

"We lived in the village of Tatum near Van."

"Van?" Elizabeth muttered with surprise. "That's a long way. Did you flee from the war?"

The young woman nodded solemnly. "Our village was burned to the ground. Ottoman soldiers killed my mother and father, and both of my brothers. They slaughtered over three hundred of our friends and neighbors, too. We're the only ones left, except for a neighbor boy who's asleep on the ground over there."

Elizabeth reached out and squeezed the young woman's shoulder. "God bless you."

"We lost everything, but we should be grateful to be alive—at least that's what the German doctor told me when he amputated Sima's leg."

Elizabeth reflected for a moment. Suddenly, she reached up, unfastened her earrings and handed them to the young woman. "They're gold. Trade them to buy food and clothing for your family."

Azra stared down at the shiny loops in her hand and glanced at her husband.

"And, if you come to the Missionary Hospital this afternoon, we have a room where the four of you can stay. It's in the basement, but it's a lot better than living out here. Just ask the guards for Nurse Barton."

"Thanks be to God," Azra whispered tearfully.

Nurse Barton glanced at her watch. "I must go now. Will I see you this afternoon?"

"You will see us," the young woman's husband replied. He nodded respectfully and wrapped his arm around Azra's shoulders.

"Have a good morning, and I'll see you later." Elizabeth walked into the street and climbed up into the wagon. She felt the weight of Hakan's astonished stare. "What?"

"The compassion within your heart is limitless, Nurse Barton. Please forgive my indifference."

"It was the least I could do. Let's hurry on now. I need to send my telegram and get back to the hospital."

The wagon pulled to a stop outside the telegraph office at a little before nine o'clock. Hakan tied the horse to a post. He helped Nurse Barton down and followed her inside.

A young clerk looked up from behind the desk. "May I help you?"

Elizabeth handed him a single sheet of paper. "This is an urgent message for Ambassador Henry Morgenthau at the American Embassy in Istanbul."

"I'm sorry, madam," the young man replied regretfully, "but all private communications have been suspended until further notice."

"Suspended?" Elizabeth asked incredulously. "On whose orders?"

"By order of the governor-general," a man called out from the back of the room.

Elizabeth turned and glared at the pudgy gendarme sitting in a chair.

The man got up and stepped to the desk. He grabbed the paper out of the clerk's hand. "What's your name, madam?"

"Elizabeth Barton Charles."

"Wait here until I return."

The gendarme turned and disappeared through an open door at the back of the room. A few minutes passed before he reappeared with a tall, uniformed army officer. The man wore a belted red jacket and knee-high leather boots. His coal-black eyes and bushy brows lent him a menacing air.

"That's her there," the gendarme said.

The officer held up the paper. "Did you write this telegram, madam?"

"Yes, sir, I did."

"You're Elizabeth Barton, the Missionary Hospital nurse?"

"I am she."

"And you wrote that the governor-general is a cold-blooded murderer responsible for the death of hundreds, if not thousands, of Armenians and other Christians throughout Diyarbekir Province?"

"I did, and he is."

"You are an American, madam?"

"Yes, I am. And what is your name, sir?"

"Major Akeem al-Kawukji, madam," the officer replied evenly. "Gendarme!" he barked out.

The man jumped to attention. "Yes, sir!"

"Escort Nurse Barton back to the Missionary Hospital. Madam, you are hereby confined to the hospital until further notice. You are forbidden to make any further attempts to contact individuals outside this city. Do you understand?"

"Yes, Major," Nurse Barton replied defiantly. "I understand your aim perfectly."

"I hope so, madam, for your own sake." The major turned and walked to the rear door.

"Major," Elizabeth called after him, "I'd like my telegram back, if you don't mind."

The major stopped and turned to face her. He glanced at the gendarme, and the man stared back, awaiting the major's response. "Take care, madam," al-Kawukji finally replied. "I trust you'll bear in mind that the capitulations which once protected you no longer exist." Finally, he turned and disappeared through the door.

Elizabeth was busy dispensing afternoon medications to the patients on the surgery ward when a young orderly drew her attention from the doorway. "Excuse me," Elizabeth told a wounded soldier before setting her tray on the stand at the end of the bed, "I'll be right back." She turned to the orderly. "Yes, what is it, Joseph?"

"There's someone here to see you, Nurse Barton. He says he's representing Yousouf Zia Ali, Mufti of Diyarbekir."

"Mufti Ali?" she asked with surprise. "Did he say what he wanted?"

The orderly stared back uneasily. He cleared his throat. "He's been to the prison, Nurse Barton."

Elizabeth's face lit up. She looked at the young man with hopeful anticipation. He stared back awkwardly, and then looked away.

"What is it, Ahmed?" Getting no reply, she brushed past him and rushed down the hall. "Tell Beatrice to dispense the medications," she called back anxiously.

Hakan and Lala were standing outside the administrative office with a slight Turk in cleric's robes. He was speaking to Doctor Saunders. They all turned at the sound of footsteps.

"Is something wrong?" Elizabeth asked anxiously.

The Turk swallowed uneasily. "Nurse Barton, I'm Ismael Selmin, the Mufti's personal assistant. I'm afraid I bear horrible news. Dr. Charles died early this morning."

Elizabeth's expression melted into horror. "You're mistaken." She glanced at Doctor Saunders' grim expression. "No, it's a lie. It's not true."

"I'm sorry," Selmin said sorrowfully. "His body was released to the Mufti an hour ago. I've brought him back to the hospital."

Tears streamed from Elizabeth's eyes. She gasped. "How did he die?"

"We were told he came down with the typhus and passed very quickly."

"Where is he?" she demanded.

"Nurse Barton," Hakan interjected, "I asked the guards to take the doctor's body to the morgue."

"I want to see him!" Elizabeth turned and took a step down the hall.

"Elizabeth!" Doctor Saunders exclaimed. He grabbed her arm. "I've seen David's body. You must not..."

"I want to see him!" Elizabeth yelled hysterically. She pulled away from the doctor and ran headlong down the hall.

"Come with me," Doctor Saunders said to Hakan and Lala.

The three of them rushed after Nurse Barton. Hurrying to the end of the long corridor, they turned the corner and caught a glimpse of her, ducking into the stairwell. They followed her down the stairs into the dimly lit bowels of the hospital. Doctor Saunders ran into the rank-smelling morgue.

Two bodies were lying on carts in the middle of the small room. The sheets had been pulled back to reveal dark-skinned corpses. Elizabeth stood beside a wooden box resting atop a table near the back wall.

Doctor Saunders charged to the back of the room. "Don't!" he pleaded, grabbing her hands. "For God's sake, you must not see him this way. It wasn't typhus."

Elizabeth stared into Doctor Saunders' eyes. She pushed his hands away. Grabbing the wooden top, she yanked it up and gasped in horror.

Dr. Charles' face was charred beyond recognition. All of his hair—including his beard and eyebrows—was burned completely away. His upper lip hung across his neck—attached only by a thin sliver of skin—and exposed a jagged line of broken teeth. In the center of his blackened face, all that remained of his nose was a discolored irregular gash.

Protruding from his chest was a wooden-handled knife that had been thrust through a blood-soaked sheet of paper.

Elizabeth bent down to scrutinize the paper. It was the hand-written telegram Major al-Kawukji had taken from her at the telegraph office earlier that morning. "Merciful God," she gasped. She turned to Doctor Saunders. "I killed him! My God, I killed David!" Her eyes rolled up in her head and she slumped heavily against the box.

Doctor Saunders lifted her into his arms and carried her out of the morgue.

S itting solemnly on the side of the bed, Kristina dabbed Elizabeth's forehead with a washcloth. She'd fallen into a deep sleep.

Sirak sat down beside her and patted Nurse Barton's hand. He peered up at Kristina with innocent, teary eyes. "Mama, why did the bad men hurt Dr. Charles?"

"I don't know, dear one," Kristina replied somberly. "I guess he was just too good."

"How could he be *too* good?"

"Dr. Charles made the governor-general realize how badly he was treating people. He didn't like that, so he hurt Dr. Charles."

"The governor-general will never get to heaven, will he, Mama?"

"That's for God to decide, little mouse."

The door opened behind them. Lala stepped over Izabella's toys and walked to the bedside. "Nurse Barton," she whispered. She jiggled Elizabeth's arm. "I'm sorry to disturb you, but there's a young woman asking for you at the hospital entrance—Azra from Tatum. She's got an injured daughter with her. She said you told her to bring her family to the hospital."

"Oh, dear God, I forgot. Lala, take them down to the old storage room in the basement and give them some blankets and food and water. Tell the guards they'll be living there until things settle down. Tell Azra I'll come see her later this afternoon."

"Okay, Nurse Barton. Mrs. Kazerian, can I bring you something to eat?"

"Nothing for me, thank you, but the children might eat a little bread and cheese."

"I'll bring a tray. Oh, Nurse Barton, we reached Father Martin. He's planning the funeral for the day after tomorrow."

"Did he mention where?"

"He said he'd hold the mass here in the chapel."

Elizabeth nodded approvingly. "I'm sure David would've wanted it that way. May God's peace be upon us all."

CHAPTER 30

June 11, 1915

The motley formation of pallbearers carried the wooden coffin bearing Dr. Charles' body out the door of the dilapidated main hospital building. Two men were dressed in doctor's whites, but the rest wore Turkish garments with red-tasseled tarboosh caps. They headed down the walkway to the street and passed through a gauntlet of melancholy mourners.

A handful of hospital staff, along with dozens of grateful former patients, including a few festooned in Ottoman military uniforms, stood beneath the blazing sun to pay their last respects to the beloved physician-missionary who'd given everything to ease the suffering of those he'd served in Anatolia. A pocket of veiled women at the end of the walk wailed demonstratively, but most of the mourners stood by in stunned silence.

Elizabeth and Kristina shuffled dejectedly behind the casket. Both women were dressed in long black dresses and veils. Elizabeth's shoulders were stooped with grief. Sirak, his expression at once bemused and sorrowful, trailed behind his mother clutching Mikael's hand. Father Martin, a paunchy, middle-aged German wearing purple robes, brought up the rear of the procession.

Scattered across the courtyard, several armed gendarmes monitored the funeral assembly. To the left of the walkway, a knot of Ottoman soldiers stood outside the commissary tent.

Elizabeth glanced up and froze dead in her tracks. "Bastard!" she hissed.

Kristina followed Nurse Barton's gaze across the courtyard. "What's wrong, Elizabeth?"

"Wait here," Elizabeth said. Letting go of Kristina's hand, she marched purposefully through the mourners to an officer dressed in a smart gray uniform and a red tarboosh cap. His baggy pants were tucked inside thigh-high brown leather boots. Without warning, Elizabeth slapped him full across the face. The slap echoed across the courtyard and launched the officer's cap high into the air.

The man flinched, but maintained his composure. Several soldiers grabbed Nurse Barton's arms.

"Let her go," the officer ordered.

Elizabeth jerked her arms away, and trembling with emotion, glared at the officer. "Have you no shame, Major al-Kawukji? How dare you defile my husband's funeral? I ask you to leave immediately."

"You falsely malign me, Nurse Barton," al-Kawukji protested. "I can assure you, I was also shocked and heartbroken to learn of Dr. Charles' death. His death is a staggering loss to us all. I'm here to pay my respects."

"You are a liar, sir, a vile, two-faced murderer. Your hands are stained with David's blood."

"You are mistaken, madam. I've long been an admirer of Dr. Charles, and of you, too."

"Liar!" she cried out vehemently. "The telegram you took from me was impaled on the knife they plunged into my David's heart. You are nothing but depraved savages." She bowed her head and wept inconsolably.

The major winced and glanced awkwardly at the glowering soldier standing beside him. "I assure you, madam. I had no part whatsoever in

Dr. Charles' death. I passed your telegram on to provincial officials, along with a stack of others I confiscated the past week, but I really had little choice. The gendarme in the telegraph office saw it first and he reported what you wrote to his superior. I was reprimanded by my commanding officer for not arresting you on the spot."

"Did you know David was tortured?" Elizabeth sniffled.

"I assure you, madam, I did not. I had the utmost respect for him, and everything he's done to help the wounded and ill soldiers who are brought here for treatment. I'm stunned to learn he was tortured. General al-Zifar told me he died from typhus."

Elizabeth took a deep breath and exhaled. "If I've wrongly accused you, Major, I'm truly sorry."

"I feel your sorrow. If there's anything I can do to help you—anything at all—please contact me." He handed her a slip of paper.

"Thank you, Major," Elizabeth replied solemnly. She turned and walked back across the courtyard.

The cortege shuffled into the street. Doctor Saunders helped Hakan and the other pallbearers hoist the casket into the horse-drawn caisson. Kristina helped Mikael and Sirak into a waiting coach. The pallbearers, along with several other men from the hospital, mounted their horses. A lone rider led the way, and the modest procession inched away from the hospital. It clattered down the street lined with mourners and onlookers and headed to the eastern gate of the city.

Major al-Kawukji stood at the curb watching until the caisson turned the next corner. Taking a deep breath, he turned and walked across the street to his horse. A young soldier held out the reins. "Thank you, Corporal. Let's head back to headquarters."

"Sir, do you want me to follow them out to the cemetery to make sure there's no trouble?"

Al-Kawukji mounted his horse. "That won't be necessary. I'm sure they'll be fine."

The procession followed Father Martin and the pallbearers bearing Dr. Charles' coffin up a dusty trail. Stepping through an open gate, they made their way into a small cemetery on a windswept hillside overlooking Diyarbekir. The rumble of distant thunder echoed overhead.

Sirak clutched his mother's hand. "Mama, when does Dr. Charles go to heaven?"

"He's already in heaven, little mouse. We go to heaven the moment we die."

He motioned toward the coffin. "Then what's in that box?"

"That's only Dr. Charles' earthly body. He won't need it in heaven."

Sirak glanced up at his mother and started to ask another question, but fell silent.

The priest stopped before a fresh grave. The pallbearers set the coffin on the ground and filed slowly away.

Father Martin stepped to the head of the grave and clutched a small black Bible in his hands. Standing tall, with sadness emanating from his drawn face, he cleared his throat to speak. "Dear friends," he began in a clear baritone voice, "the burial of a loved one is never easy, but it is even more difficult today. This pious man of God, Doctor David Charles, touched all of you standing here today. His impact in Anatolia over the past fifteen years—both physical and spiritual—is immeasurable. David was my best friend and closest confidant since the first month he arrived from America with a heart filled with love and compassion. When my first appointment ended, and I prepared to return home, it was David who convinced me to stay here in Anatolia. I've thanked him many times for the countless blessings I've received here during the past seven years. I saw David for the last time two weeks ago. We had lunch together at the hospital and he happily told me he'd finally decided to leave Anatolia to return to America to live with his brother on a farm outside a little town called Altus, Oklahoma. David shared something else with me that day." He gazed forlornly at Elizabeth, and sighing heavily, peered up at the sky. "He told me he'd fallen in love again."

The big man tucked his head against his chest. Squeezing his eyes shut, his head bobbed rhythmically up and down. He tried to speak again, but abandoned the attempt with a frustrated shake of his head. Several more moments passed before he took a deep breath and looked up. "I'm sorry," he whispered hoarsely. "I still can't grasp David's passing.

"This morning I spoke to Elizabeth. I asked her why they hadn't left Anatolia last month, as they'd planned, and she told me David just couldn't leave. He couldn't leave the battered and broken people who depended on him for help during this dark time of suffering and war.

"David and Elizabeth paid a terrible price for their devotion and service to God and the people of Anatolia. I know in my heart that David will receive a king's reward in heaven, but those of us who remain behind will long for his solace and goodness until the day we join him in heaven."

The priest grasped a golden cross in his hands and thrust it out before him. "Ashes to ashes, dust to dust, I commend thy fearless and unwavering servant to you, dear Lord."

Father Martin nodded and the pallbearers grasped the ropes beneath the coffin.

Stepping over the grave, they lowered it carefully to the bottom.

Doctor Saunders led Elizabeth to the grave. She bowed her head in prayer for a moment before tossing a bouquet of flowers onto the coffin.

Sirak looked up at his mother. Tears were streaming down his face. He wiped them on his sleeve.

"Here, Sirak," she whispered, handing him a single white flower. "Throw this into Dr. Charles' grave and thank him. Don't ever forget that Dr. Charles saved your life."

"Will Dr. Charles hear me, Mama?" he sobbed.

"Yes, he'll definitely hear you."

Sirak's mother led him to the grave. He stood for a moment and peered into the abyss. He dropped the flower and watched it land atop the coffin beside the bouquet. "Thank you, Dr. Charles," he whispered sadly. "God bless you."

Elizabeth shuffled to the table and sat between Kristina and Mikael. "I'm sorry; I completely lost track of time."

"That's okay. Lala told us you'd be late. Hakan found some fresh carrots and onions at the market and Lala prepared a wonderful stew. Let me serve you."

"Just a taste. I'm not hungry."

Kristina ladled stew into her bowl. "I'll be back in a few minutes. Come on, children, it's time for bed."

"I'm not tired," Mikael groaned. "Can't we play a game of checkers?"

"No, you can't; it's been a long day. You all need a good night's sleep. Are you done, Sirak?"

Sirak stared at his bowl. He didn't look up.

Kristina stepped over to the boy's chair and squatted beside him. "Sirak, are you okay?"

He looked up at her with tears in his eyes.

"Are you okay, little mouse?" she asked tenderly.

"Papa's in heaven, too. Isn't he?"

Kristina stared back at him.

"Isn't he, Mama?"

"I don't know," she finally replied. She gently squeezed Sirak's arm. "I hope Papa and Stepannos are waiting for us in Jerusalem, but only God knows where they are now."

"Can't we go and see if they're there?"

Kristina glanced mournfully at Elizabeth. "Jerusalem is a long way from here. We can't leave now. If we did, we'd be giving up any chance of finding Flora again. Alek might come to the hospital, too. Do you under-stand?"

"Maybe Flora and Alek are already in Jerusalem. Maybe they're waiting with Papa."

"If they are, then we'll meet them there later. But, for now, we need to wait a little longer. It'll be just a few more weeks. Okay?"

Sirak nodded his head. "Okay."

Kristina lifted Izabella out of her chair. "Come on, sweetheart; it's time for bed."

"Goodnight, children," Elizabeth called out after them. "I'll see you in the morning."

"Goodnight, Nurse Barton," Sirak called back.

"Goodnight," Mikael muttered wearily.

Kristina returned from the bedroom a few minutes later and sat down beside Elizabeth. "I'm worried about Sirak. When he says his prayers, he asks God to protect his papa and brothers and sister from the bad men and to help them all get to Jerusalem. Then he prays for God to protect Mikael, Izabella and me from the bad men, too. It breaks my heart."

Elizabeth took Kristina's hand. "Sirak has an inner strength far beyond his years. He'll bear some psychological scars forever, to be sure, but something tells me he'll be just fine."

"I hope you're right."

"I'm more worried about Izabella. She's gotten so quiet these past few weeks. She won't even play dolls with me anymore."

Kristina nodded. "She misses her papa. She keeps asking me to take her home to see him."

Elizabeth sighed. "I've got to leave Anatolia soon. I'll go crazy if I stay."

"I understand. There's nothing left here for you now."

"I want you to leave with me. We can travel to Jerusalem together. Then, I'll leave for America once I know you and the children are safe."

"I can't leave Diyarbekir yet. I'll lose all hope of ever seeing my Flora again. As long as we're here, there's a chance she'll find us."

"I can't begin to comprehend it. How terrible it is to lose your child, but you must also think of Mikael, Sirak and Izabella. You've already been here a month without any news about Flora. Meanwhile, the situation here grows more desperate every day."

Kristina stared at the tabletop. Finally, she looked up. "I know you're right, but I just can't leave Flora behind."

Elizabeth reached out to squeeze her hand. "There's still time. It'll take me two or three weeks to get my affairs in order."

"I guess we'd better get some rest. We've both got a lot to do tomorrow. Let me know if you need help with the patients tonight. Goodnight."

"Goodnight, Kristina."

CHAPTER 31

Jasmine slid a tray onto the nightstand. "Flora, I've brought bread and honey. You must eat something."

Flora barely opened her eyes. "I can't. I'm so sick."

Jasmine dipped a piece of bread into the honey and held it to Flora's mouth. "You must eat. You've only eaten a few bites of bread the past three days."

"No, please, I can't even stand the smell."

Jasmine sighed. "I'll leave it here on the nightstand. Try to get a few bites down. Erol's been asking for you. Would you mind if he came in for a moment?"

"No, of course not."

Jasmine dabbed perspiration from Flora's forehead with a cloth. "He's so fond of you."

A hint of a smile came to Flora's face. "I'm fond of him, too."

"I can't imagine how much you miss your family, but your coming here's the best thing that ever happened for my Erol. His spirit is alive again, and it's all because of you."

"I've done nothing but give him love and encouragement."

"You've given him so much more," Jasmine said appreciatively. "You've given him the self-confidence of knowing that someone other than his mother cares whether he lives or dies. Even his father treats him better. It's truly a miracle." She gave Flora a warm hug. "God bless you."

"He's a wonderful boy with a heart of gold. He's been just as much comfort to me as I've been to him."

Jasmine smiled. "I'll tell him he can come visit you as soon as he finishes his breakfast."

Erol looked up expectantly. "Does Flora feel better?"

"Maybe a little," Jasmine replied. "She still isn't eating, but she'd like to see you. Finish your breakfast and you can go in for a few minutes."

"Really?" he asked excitedly. "I'm already full. Can I go see her now?"

"As soon as you finish your bread."

Erol stuffed the bread into his mouth and stood up from the table. "Can I go now?" he begged.

"Yes," Jasmine replied amusedly. "Take her this glass of water, please."

Erol took the glass and hurried off to the bedroom.

"You have chores to do in the barn, Erol," Abdul called out after him. "Five minutes, and then I want you to clean the horses' stalls."

Erol didn't respond. He darted through the doorway and disappeared down the hall.

"Did you get her to eat?" Sabriye asked from the kitchen.

"Not yet, but she seems a little better today. At least she's talking."

"What the hell's wrong with her?" Abdul grumbled, his mouth full of food.

Jasmine rolled her eyes at Sabriye. "She's sick to her stomach."

"For three days? What's she got, the grippe or something? Women," he muttered beneath his breath, "they'll be the death of me."

"We think she's with child," Jasmine replied matter-of-factly.

Abdul sat back from the table and stared wide-eyed at Hasan. "With child? Did she say Flora's with child?"

Hasan didn't look up from a copy of the *Agence* he was perusing. "That's what she said," he replied disinterestedly.

Abdul bolted up from the table and held his arms to the heavens. "Thanks be to Allah! I'm having another son!"

"What if it's another daughter?" Hasan muttered.

"Hold your tongue!" Abdul demanded crossly. "God promised me in a dream. Flora's first-born will be a son. He'll be a strong and fearless warrior."

Jasmine grinned mischievously at Sabriye. "I dreamed it's a girl, a sweet, angel-faced girl—just like her mother."

Abdul's face flushed crimson. "Shut up! I will not tolerate this sacrilege. He will be a son. From this moment onward, I command all of you to pray the child is a son. Do you understand?"

"I understand, Effendi," Hasan replied deferentially.

"Good. I'm heading into Diyarbekir this afternoon for supplies. Baran is going with me. Remain vigilant, there are many deserters and vagrants about."

"Don't worry, Effendi. I'll be on my guard."

Abdul grabbed the last piece of bread and stuffed it into his mouth. "Jasmine, go tell Erol to get his butt out to the barn. Make sure he finishes all of his chores before lunch. Do you understand?"

"Yes, Abdul, I'll make sure he gets them done."

"I'll be back before dark, and I want my dinner ready." Grabbing his pistol off the fireplace mantle, the Turk stuffed it beneath his belt. He jerked the door open, stepped outside and slammed it closed behind him.

Jasmine glanced up at Sabriye and caught her frosty stare. "What?" she asked defensively.

"You'd better pray the child's a boy, for everyone's sake."

"I'll pray what I want to pray," Jasmine huffed. She slapped her dishrag down on the countertop and marched off to the bedroom.

Chapter 32

Elizabeth pulled open the bottom dresser drawer and grabbed a pair of sweaters. She handed them to Lala, who set them in an open trunk on the floor.

"That's everything," Elizabeth said.

Kristina held out a framed photograph. "Don't forget this."

It was the black and white shot of a smiling Dr. Charles standing on the steps of the American Missionary Hospital in Chunkoush, squinting at the sun. Elizabeth gazed at David's eyes for a moment and lovingly passed the photo to Lala. "Wrap it in sweaters. You're welcome to anything I left behind, Kristina. I shall not return."

Kristina nodded and smiled. "Thank you. Thank you for everything."

Elizabeth smiled warmly. "It's not too late, you know. There's plenty of room in the wagon."

"We'd only hold you up."

"That's nonsense."

"I need to stay for at least a couple more months. I want to wait for Flora."

All three women turned at a determined knock at the door.

"Just a moment," Elizabeth called out. She opened the door. "Yes, Hakan; what is it?"

"Sorry to bother you, madam, but Major al-Kawukji is here to see you."

"He's here now?"

"Yes, madam."

"Show him into the parlor and I'll be there in a minute."

Hakan nodded and hurried away.

Elizabeth tied her hair back in a bun and covered her head with a floppy black hat. "I wonder what he wants now? Kristina, perhaps you should join me."

"Yes, of course." Kristina pulled a scarf over her head and followed Nurse Barton out of the bedroom.

Elizabeth offered her hand. "Good afternoon, Major. To what do we owe the honor?"

"Good afternoon, Nurse Barton. It's a pleasure to see you again. I'm sorry to disturb you, but I'm afraid I've brought urgent news. I heard from a colleague that Governor-general Reshid is preparing orders for the arrest of all non-Muslim peoples, including Europeans and Americans. The arrests will begin in three days—on the twenty-second of the month."

"Dear God. For what purpose?"

"I don't know, but I fear the worst. There are alarming developments in the north and east of Anatolia. I've come to offer my assistance, as a friend. If you leave quickly, you can slip out of Diyarbekir Province before the orders are implemented."

"I'm leaving for Mardin in the morning. From there I plan to go on to Ras Ul-ain to meet the train to Aleppo."

"Excellent," he said with a nod. "How will you travel to Ras Ul-ain?"

"Hakan will take me in the wagon."

"It's too dangerous to travel to Ras Ul-ain without an armed escort. There are bandits and deserters everywhere—especially in the hills south of Diyarbekir. I'll return with a detachment of soldiers and accompany you to the train station early tomorrow morning. You'll be safe once you've boarded the train to Aleppo."

Elizabeth glanced at Kristina. "What about Mrs. Kazerian and her children?"

"They are Armenian?" al-Kawukji asked.

"Yes, Major," Elizabeth responded. "Her brother-in-law is a member of the Ottoman Assembly."

"How old are the children?"

"My sons are thirteen and eight, and my daughter is six," Kristina said.

The major sighed uneasily. "What I've told Nurse Barton applies all the more to you. You must leave Diyarbekir without delay."

"We can't leave. My older daughter is missing. I'm waiting for her return."

"Mrs. Kazerian," the major said sternly, "three weeks ago, all of the Armenians living in the northern villages of Erzerum Province were rounded up for deportation. Last week the deportees were forced out of Erzinjan in large caravans bound for Syria. Most of them were women and children with little more than what they could carry on their backs. My commanding officer received a telegram this morning. It appears most of them didn't even make it to Kemakh. There was a terrible massacre and only a handful survived."

"Dear God," Elizabeth gasped. "Who did this?"

"It appears they were attacked by bandits. There are rumors of many other atrocities elsewhere in the north and east. And now arrest orders have been issued for Diyarbekir. God knows what will happen next. You must leave now, madam."

Kristina stared into the major's grim, deep-set eyes. Then she glanced at Elizabeth and slowly shook her head. "I won't abandon my daughter."

The major sighed with frustration. "Think it over. It may be your last chance. I must go now, but I'll return at five in the morning. Bring only what you can pack in two bags. There won't be room on the train for more. Good evening, ladies." Al-Kawukji turned to open the door.

"Major al-Kawukji," Elizabeth called out after him.

"Yes, madam."

"I'm grateful for your concern and assistance."

"It's my privilege, Nurse Barton. I wish I could do more."

"Goodnight, Major."

"Goodnight, Nurse Barton."

Elizabeth took a deep breath and glanced up at the clock on the wall. "Eight o'clock," she said anxiously. "Only nine hours before our departure. Let me help you pack."

"Didn't you hear me?" Kristina asked. "I'm not leaving."

"You *must* leave. Can't you see what's happening? I'll not spend the rest of my life regretting having left you behind."

Kristina's eyes filled with tears. "Please, Elizabeth, try to understand. I can't abandon Flora. We'll stay for a while longer, then..."

"Flora is dead!" Elizabeth blurted out. "She's dead, and you staying here won't bring her back. I'm sorry, but I just couldn't bring myself to tell you."

Kristina face melted into a stunned look of dismay. "What are you saying?"

"I'm sorry, Kristina. I just couldn't tell you. David received word from the governor-general's office a few days after he went to ask for Mourad's release. He decided it was better not to tell you until later."

Kristina grimaced with horror. "But why?"

"David was afraid to tell you. He feared it would crush your spirit." She sighed uncomfortably. "Your other children needed you." Elizabeth reached out to her friend, but Kristina pushed her hand away.

Her mouth quivering, Kristina glared at Elizabeth. "No, it's not true. I see what you're trying to do."

"As God is my witness, I swear it's true. You and your other children will be lost, too, if you stay behind in Diyarbekir."

Kristina stared at Elizabeth for several moments. Suddenly, she turned and bolted from the room.

Elizabeth repacked her belongings into leather bags, keeping only essential items and a few priceless mementos. When she finished, she slipped into the bedroom and found Kristina lying on the bed beside Sirak and Izabella. "Kristina, are you awake?" she whispered.

"Yes," Kristina replied coldly.

"I'm sorry. I didn't mean to hurt you."

"How could you deceive me? I thought you were my friend."

"I love you like a sister. I would never lie to you."

"But you did lie."

"I *didn't* lie. What good would've come from ripping away your last shred of hope?"

Kristina began to sob hysterically and buried her face in the pillow.

Sirak rolled to his knees and hugged her back. Izabella peered up sadly at Mikael. He picked her up and cradled her in his arms.

Nearly an hour passed before Kristina's mournful wails subsided. Elizabeth sat on the edge of the bed and stroked the back of her head. "I'm so sorry."

Kristina took a deep breath and let out a sigh. "How did she die?"

"I don't know. The lieutenant governor-general's assistant brought word to David that a Turkish farmer dropped her body off at a police station in a small village east of Diyarbekir."

"What village?"

"I don't know. David didn't tell me."

"What was the farmer's name?"

"I don't know, Kristina."

"How did he know it was Flora?"

"I never learned all these details."

"What did they do with her?"

"David sent Hakan to take her body to Kemal Sufyan."

"Kemal? How did he find him?"

"Kemal left David directions to his brother-in-law's farm, and Hakan found him there. He told Hakan to tell you he'd bury Flora on your farm. So many times I wanted to tell you, but David told me to wait until everything else got better—and it never did. Please forgive me."

Kristina pulled Elizabeth into a long, heartfelt embrace. She brushed tears from her cheek. "I forgive you. At least she's not suffering."

"Will you leave with me in the morning?"

Kristina nodded. "Now we can leave."

"Thank God." She gave Kristina another hug and got up from the bed. "I'll ask Lala to pack your things."

Kristina lay in the darkness beside Sirak and Izabella. She traced the sign of the cross across her chest. "Blessed Virgin Mary, Mother of God, I beg for your intercession with Almighty God on our behalf. Help us as we begin this new journey. We pray you'll reunite us with Mourad and Stepannos in Jerusalem. Protect Alek, wherever he may be, and give Flora everlasting peace."

Elizabeth took a lingering look at the rundown hospital and climbed into the wagon. She sat beside Kristina atop the bags stacked in the bed.

"Sirak, did you remember your grandfather's Bible?" Kristina asked.

"Yes, Mama, it's here in my pack."

She gave him a reassuring pat on the head. "That's a good place for it."

Major al-Kawukji closed the tailgate. He mounted his horse, and the handle of his sword glistened in the light of torches held by the orderlies, nurses and doctors who'd arisen early to see them off.

"Goodbye, Elizabeth," Doctor Saunders called out, "we'll miss you."

Everyone crowded around the wagon and shouted their goodbyes and good wishes. Elizabeth exchanged a few last words with the doctors, the nurses and some of the hospital staff. Several people said farewell to Kristina and the children.

From his perch atop the suitcases, Sirak peered sleepily at the mounted soldiers. Suddenly, he bolted upright and he leaned over the sideboard of the wagon. "Tiran?" he exclaimed. The lean chestnut colt ridden by a young sergeant spun to face him. "Tiran!" Sirak shouted joyfully.

The horse's ears shot up. Rearing his head, he whinnied.

"Mama, it's Tiran! That soldier's riding my Tiran."

"Are you sure? He seems too old."

"It's my Tiran! I know it's him!"

Smiling munificently, the sergeant eased his mount forward so Sirak could reach out and pat him on the head. "I named him Musa after the horse I had as a boy," the soldier said proudly. "He's not that old. Musa carried me through many battles these past six months, including the great charge on Sarikamish. Fighting so many battles has taken a toll on him. Haven't they boy?" He scratched the horse behind his ears. "But Musa's strong and courageous, and without him, I wouldn't be here today. If he belonged to you, I thank you from the bottom of my heart. What's your name?"

"Sirak, sir."

Tiran whinnied again and playfully nuzzled Sirak's chest.

The sergeant laughed. "It seems Musa would like you to ride with us."

"Really?" Sirak asked excitedly. "Can I, Mama?"

Kristina smiled appreciatively. "If Major al-Kawukji says it's okay, then it's okay."

The major winked at Kristina. "It's fine with me, if it's okay with the horse."

The sergeant maneuvered the horse alongside the wagon, and lifting Sirak onto the horse, pressed the reins into the boy's hands. "Here, you take these."

Sirak patted the horse's neck and smiled at the sergeant. "What's your name, sir?"

"I'm Isa and that's my best friend Bekir," he said, pointing to the man beside him. The other soldier smiled and nodded.

"We must go now," Major al-Kawukji called out. "It's imperative that we leave the city as soon as the gates open and travel as far as possible before the sun peaks in the sky. It will be hot in the hills."

The wagon pulled away from the hospital. The soldiers trailed close behind, and the wagon rumbled on for several blocks before Hakan turned down a narrow street. They slowed near a small mosque where dozens of men were gathered for morning prayers. Hakan eased the wagon through the knot of people and they bumped through a tight turn before merging onto a wide boulevard. The imposing southern gates of Diyarbekir loomed directly ahead.

"How far is Ras ul-Ain?" Elizabeth shouted above the clatter of the wagon.

The major spurred his mount alongside. "Just over seventy kilometers."

She grimaced. "That far?"

"It's at least two days of hard travel. We'll see how it goes. Hopefully, those clouds in the distance bring us rain to ease the heat. If not, we'll need to stop at midday and continue late in the afternoon."

The plaza in front of the massive gate was swarming with people and animals of every sort—horses, mules, donkeys, oxen and even a few camels. Dozens of vendors were milling about amongst the multitude of travelers. Some people reposed on the ground, trying to catch a bit more sleep before the beginning of an arduous journey.

Hakan pulled the wagon to a stop behind a small unit of the Ottoman Army Cavalry, and the major trotted over to a lieutenant standing beside a water trough.

Isa slid to the ground and lifted Sirak off his horse. Too excited to rest, Sirak ran to the back of the wagon. He grabbed a handful of feed and held it out for the horse. The chestnut whinnied and nibbled contentedly from the boy's hand.

Mikael stroked the powerful horse's neck. "If he isn't Tiran, he sure looks a lot like him."

"It *is* Tiran," Sirak said. "I know it's him."

Mikael ran his hand down the horse's chest to a scar just above his leg. "I wonder how he got hurt."

"Where?" Sirak asked. "Oh yeah, that's a big cut. Sergeant, how did Tiran get hurt on his leg?"

"He was wounded when we charged through Russian infantry during the battle of Sarikamish," he said proudly. "Musa didn't even flinch. He charged on despite heavy gun and cannon fire. The soldier who slashed him paid with his life."

"Maybe he knows Alek," Sirak whispered to his brother.

"I'll ask him." Mikael walked over to Isa. "Sergeant, did you know my brother, Alek Kazerian? He's in the army, too."

"Kazerian? No, I don't think so, or at least not well enough to remember. There were thousands of men in the Ninth Corp."

Major al-Kawukji jogged back from the cavalry unit. "Okay, get ready to pull out. They're opening the gates."

Sirak glanced over his shoulder. Through the gathering early morning light, he watched a squad of men lift the bar securing the massive wooden gates. They marched it off to the side and another crew pulled the creaking doors wide open.

As if on command, the mass of people gathered in the plaza rose to their feet. A hubbub ran through the crowd.

"Cavalry first!" a guard barked.

"We're riding with them," Major al-Kawukji shouted. "Let's go!"

Isa mounted Tiran and pulled Sirak up on the horse. Hakan climbed up into the driver's seat, and flicking the reins, turned the wagon.

The cavalrymen wove through the unruly throng to the gate. They broke into the open and the horses kicked up a billowing cloud of dust that swept up the wall to the guard posts. The major galloped in behind them. The wagon and the other two soldiers followed close behind.

Sirak peered up at the guards atop the wall as the brigade trotted through the breach. A grinning Turk, with a full black beard, dipped his rifle in mock salute.

Isa zigzagged Tiran through the tangled knot of travelers waiting beyond the gate to enter the city.

Finally, the soldiers and wagon broke clear. They thundered south down the road to Ras ul-Ain through rocky terrain strewn with black basalt boulders and patches of yellowed grass and sagebrush. The meandering Tigris River cut a winding path through the landscape into the distance.

Sirak peered out across the expansive countryside toward a distant line of hills cloaked in angry dark clouds.

The sergeant pointed. "Sirak, do you see that gap in the hills, there in the distance?"

"Yes, sir."

"That's where we're headed. God willing, we'll make that pass by midday."

Sirak gazed out across the inhospitable panorama. "How much farther do we need to go after we reach the pass?"

"Another day, if the weather holds out."

Sirak recoiled at a rank smell that filled his nostrils. Glancing around, he tensed with fear. He pointed at a line of rotting, headless corpses just off the road. "*What's that?*"

"Traitors!" Sergeant Isa snarled disdainfully. He turned Sirak's head toward the river. "Don't look!"

Sirak covered his nose and glanced at his equally shaken brother. "What'd they do?"

"They plotted to destroy the Empire."

Sirak's eyes darted back and forth at dozens of animal carcasses lying in trenches on both sides of the road. They ranged from bare-boned skeletons to a huge ox, buzzing with flies. "Are these their animals?"

"No, Son, most of these animals were lost to thirst and hunger. This is a harsh and unforgiving land. Tell me about Musa," he said, changing the subject. "You named him Tiran?"

"Yes, sir."

"You raised him from birth?"

"My papa gave him to me when he was born. We trained him together until he was over a year old, but then the bad soldiers took him."

Isa smiled ruefully. "These things happen in war. You must not blame the soldiers. They were only following orders. I worked on a procurement detail myself right after the war started. I hated it, but it had to be done. We must all sacrifice for the Empire. How about if I make you a deal? If you feed and water Tiran all the way to Ras ul-Ain, then, when this war is over, I'll give him back to you."

"Really?" Sirak squealed excitedly.

"Absolutely." Isa gave him a kindly grin. The golden cap on his front tooth sparkled in the early morning sunlight. "Musa's earned a leisurely retirement. I can get another horse."

"But how will I find you?"

"I'll write down the directions to my family farm when we get to Ras ul-Ain. It's only an hour's ride from here. You can come get him when you return to Diyarbekir."

"Okay! Mama," Sirak yelled. "Isa promised to give Tiran back to me when the war is over!"

Kristina smiled and waved from the back of the wagon.

Major al-Kawukji guided the group south along the main road to Mardin. Half a kilometer from Diyarbekir the road skirted the Tigris, where the lazy river cut a swath of green through the otherwise barren wasteland. They passed irrigated islands of cultivation where peasant farmers grew crops of wheat and rice. They were dutifully tending their fields and paddies beneath the unforgiving sun.

Sirak and Mikael lapsed into forlorn silence when they rode past the spot on the riverbank where they'd watched their father and brother float down the river with scores of other Armenian men and boys. Now strangely serene, the bank was dotted with the makeshift tents of a band of nomadic tribesmen who were gathered around a smoky pit a few meters up from the water.

Sirak caught the icy stare of a leather-faced old man who turned to scrutinize the odd procession. Dressed in traditional garments, he was watching over a mixed herd of sheep and goats that were foraging in the tall grass along the riverbank.

Glancing ahead to the wagon, Sirak caught a glimpse of his mother and Nurse Barton peering out at the incongruous scene. He muttered pensively beneath his breath.

"What did you say?" the sergeant asked.

"Jerusalem," Sirak repeated sadly.

Isa smiled. "What about it?"

"That's where my papa is now."

"Your papa's in the Holy City?"

"Yes, he and my brother, Stepannos, are both there. Have you been there?"

"No," Isa replied thoughtfully, his forehead glistening with sweat. "*Al Kuds* is very far from here, but I hope someday to lay my eyes on the great mosque erected on the spot where the Prophet ascended into Heaven."

"We're headed there to meet my papa. How far is it?"

"It's a journey of many days—thirty or forty, depending on the weather."

"What if we travel by train?"

"Maybe twenty-five days by train, but you still must travel by horse or on foot beyond Aleppo. It is a difficult journey."

Sirak sighed sadly. *Twenty-five days*, he thought to himself. *How will I ever find my way back to Tiran?*

After more than an hour of riding, the cavalry pulled up at a fork in the road and waited for the trailing wagon.

"May God protect you, Major," the wiry leader shouted.

"Thank you, Lieutenant," al-Kawukji replied. "I'll see you back in Diyarbekir."

The soldier turned and scanned the distant hills. "God smiles on you. It looks like there's rain ahead. Take care in the pass, especially at night.

The bloodthirsty nomad tribesmen will slit your throat for the women and horses. I wish we could escort you further, but my orders are to patrol the river to the east."

"Thank you, Lieutenant. We'll be on our guard. I'll see you next week."

The cavalry trotted off in a cloud of dust and the major led the wagon down the southern fork that led directly toward the notch in the distant hills. As they rode away from the river, the terrain became an arid, inhospitable wasteland that was dotted here and there with patches of olive and emerald. These oases were invariably crowded with the makeshift shacks of lowly peasants who eked out an existence on the unforgiving, barren land.

The closer they got to the hills, the more rutted and treacherous the rocky dirt road became. From time to time, they passed travelers headed in the opposite direction, toward Diyarbekir—including entire families that carried what little they owned on their backs. In one group, Sirak spotted a dark-skinned young boy hobbling along the road holding his mother's hand. His hair was mottled with alopecia and he was dressed in filthy, ragged clothes. Staggering under his own weight, he bore the inimitable look of the incurably ill. Staring indifferently at the ground in front of him, he suddenly glanced up, and squinting through slit-like eyes, smiled at Sirak.

Sirak waved and returned his smile. He wondered where the boy had been and where he was going.

The hills grew larger and darker the further they traveled. As the tiny caravan made its way through mile after mile of monotonous wasteland, the oppressive heat and humidity soared. The sweat streamed down the faces of the travelers and saturated their garments. Then, as if sent by God, a merciful drizzle began to fall, followed a short time later by a blinding downpour that forced the wagon to the side of the road. It rained hard for nearly two hours, but ended as quickly as it had begun.

They pressed on for several more hours through insufferable heat and biting insects making slow, but steady, progress toward the hills. Along the way, they passed several dilapidated inns that had once fed and sheltered wealthier travelers on the arduous journey through southeast Anatolia. All of them were abandoned, used now only as cover for vagrants and homeless people. Several had been burned to the ground.

A little after midday, they reached the starting point of the sinuous trail into the hills. Major al-Kawukji pulled up his horse and directed Hakan into a grassy clearing beneath a stand of trees.

Al-Kawukji mopped his sweaty brow with a handkerchief. "It's too hot to go any further. We'll wait here for a few hours and rest the horses. Hakan, water the horses and tie them over there beneath the trees in the long grass. Sergeant, you and Bekir stand guard in those rocks where you can see the road in both directions. Stay alert and signal me immediately if you spot anything worrisome. I'll send the boys with food and drink."

"Yes, sir," the sergeant replied. He and Bekir trotted up the hill and climbed onto a rocky ledge overlooking the narrow curve in the road.

Kristina and Elizabeth spread blankets on the ground beneath a tree and unpacked several loaves of bread and a small block of cheese. They set the food on the blanket and prepared a portion for the soldiers.

The major plopped down on one of the blankets. "Where's Sirak?"

Hakan chuckled. "With the horse. Look at them."

Al-Kawukji glanced around and chuckled at the sight of Sirak standing with his arms wrapped around Tiran's foreleg. The horse whinnied and playfully nuzzled his head. "Let me ask you, who seeing that could say the horse didn't belong to him?"

Kristina laughed at the spectacle. "They were inseparable from the moment Tiran was born. It truly *is* a miracle."

"Isa could find another mount in Ras ul-Ain, but, unfortunately, there's no chance the horse can get on that train."

"Just let them enjoy being together while they can," Kristina said. "Sirak's a bright boy. He'll understand Tiran can't go with us."

"Sirak should eat while he has the chance," Elizabeth said. "He must keep up his strength."

Kristina passed the bread. "Don't worry, I'll take him some after we finish. So, Major, where's your home?"

"My family owns a small farm near Sinop—on the Black Sea."

"I've heard of it. How did you come to be a soldier?"

"I joined the army when I was seventeen years old. My father was a fisherman, but the sea doesn't suit me. My stomach seizes violently when I even look at swells."

"When did you come to Diyarbekir?"

"Two months before the war started, although I was stationed in the east near Erzerum for the first six months."

"My eldest son reported for service a year ago, but I haven't seen or heard from him since. Perhaps you know him—Alek Kazerian?"

Al-Kawukji stared at the blanket. "No, I don't know him."

"I just wish I knew where he was," Kristina lamented. "Major, how much longer will this war last?"

"I really don't know. But the end is written—the Empire is destined to lose."

"Really? What makes you so certain?"

The major sighed. "A blind man could see it. We joined the wrong side. The army could've held off the Russians for years, but not when they're in an alliance with the British and the French, too. Even Enver Pasha's alliance with the Germans won't make a bit of difference."

"Major, why are my people being deported?" Kristina asked thoughtfully.

"There's no simple explanation. To be sure, Pasha doesn't trust your people and he blames them for many of his own failings. He foolishly sent the army into the mountains in the dead of winter. Our troops were annihilated by weather and disease. Now he blames the Armenians for his own stupidity. Without a doubt, there were Armenians fighting with the Russians, and in the heat of the battle, some of our own Armenian soldiers went over to the other side in Sarikamish. But there were many others who fought to the bitter end."

"But why are they arresting the Americans, too?"

"Your guess is as good as mine," the major replied. He glanced up at the rocks where Isa and Bekir were standing guard.

"I'll tell you why," Elizabeth said, "to eliminate witnesses. Reshid is determined to hide his depraved acts from the rest of the world—atrocities like the torture and murder of my husband."

A long silence fell over the group. The major glanced up at the sun. He stuffed another chunk of bread into his mouth.

"Am I right, Major?" Elizabeth asked.

The major didn't reply. He broke off a chunk of cheese.

"Am I, Major?" Elizabeth persisted.

Al-Kawukji stood up. "Yes, you're right. I must relieve my men now." He walked away, cradling his rifle.

Kristina watched him until he disappeared. "He's a good man."

"Maybe," Elizabeth said warily, "but he knows a lot more than he's willing to tell."

"About what?"

"I don't know, but there's something he's not telling us. Maybe Reshid sent him to do away with us."

"That's ridiculous," Kristina scoffed. "Why travel two days across the desert to kill us? If that was his scheme, he could've done it early this morning, and nobody would've been the wiser."

"Maybe he was ordered to get us as far from Diyarbekir as possible."

"Nonsense. You're always so suspicious of people, especially when they treat you with kindness. I'm willing to accept his help as a simple act of humanity. Besides, what choice do we have?"

"None," Elizabeth replied uneasily. "None at all."

The travelers set out for Mardin again a few hours later. The narrow road wove monotonously south and their pace slowed to a crawl.

Although the sun was lower in the sky, its sweltering rays weren't blocked by the parched hilltops that rose above the road.

"How much farther, Major?" Hakan asked. "My horse isn't accustomed to such hard work."

"Two hours more. We'll stop well before dark."

Al-Kawukji turned at the sound of horses galloping up the road. Four men on horseback rounded the bend and bore down on them. They wore scruffy clothes and white turbans. The youngest was just a boy.

"Good afternoon," one of them called out. He was a swarthy man with a long beard and mustache.

"Good afternoon," the major replied. "I'm Major al-Kawukji."

The man wiped his forehead with a sleeve. "Good to meet you, Major. My name is Adem from Elbis. Could you spare us feed for our horses and a loaf of bread?"

"I'm sorry, but we're short ourselves, with a long journey ahead of us."

"I understand. Where are you headed?"

"We're taking the women and children to Mardin."

"That's where we're headed, too. Well, actually, we're riding to my uncle's farm just west of the city." He peered past the major at Kristina and Elizabeth sitting with Hakan and Izabella on a slope behind the wagon. Mikael and Sirak were standing in the rocks at the top of the slope. "We'll take them to Mardin for you."

"I appreciate your offer, but Mardin is just our first stop. We're taking them on to Ras ul-Ain to meet the train to Aleppo."

"Ras ul-Ain isn't far out of our way. We'd be happy to relieve you, if you can spare us some food for our horses."

"Dear God, no," Kristina whispered beneath her breath. She glanced worriedly at Elizabeth.

"Thank you," the major replied, "but we're meeting a detachment of cavalry in Ras ul-Ain. You can buy food and supplies from the villagers at Kabu Oasis."

"Yes, God willing, I'm sure you're right. We'll be on our way then. Good afternoon."

The man rode past the major, and his companions trotted up the trail after him. All four men ogled the women as they passed. The leader whispered something to the rider next to him, and the man laughed out loud.

Major al-Kawukji watched the riders until they disappeared around the bend in the road. "Kurdish *chetes*," he growled contemptuously. "They're probably some of the criminals who were released from the Central Prison in Mardin."

"Maybe we should stop here for the night," the sergeant suggested. He glanced over his shoulder at the women. "We could hide the wagon in the trees and sleep up there in the rocks."

The major let out a worried sigh. "No, we can't stop yet. We've got to make it to Ras ul-Ain tomorrow before the arrest orders are issued."

"What about the Armenians, sir?" Private Bekir asked pointedly.

"What about them?" the major asked brusquely.

"Well, I just thought..."

"Don't think, Private. Just do as you're told."

"Yes, sir."

"Quiet now, here they come."

"Who were those men, Major?" Elizabeth asked worriedly.

"Just some Kurdish villagers looking to buy feed for their horses."

"They're headed to Mardin?"

"That's what they said. Are you ready? We've got to ride for two more hours before we stop for the night."

"I'm ready. I'll tell Kristina."

Al-Kawukji glanced up at the westward progress of the sun. "We'll ride in five minutes."

The last leg of the day's journey proved uneventful. Late in the afternoon, they passed a few small villages and a contingent of haggard infantrymen headed north, but otherwise traffic was sparse through the desolate hills. The major considered stopping for the night at a small Kurdish village, but ultimately decided they'd be better off camping alone-

—preferring not to place their security in the hands of strangers. They finally stopped in a clearing where an L-shaped rocky enclosure created a perfect view up and down the road in both directions. The blood-red sun dropped beneath a jagged hilltop and the sweltering afternoon faded into twilight.

After another meal of bread and cheese, Elizabeth, Kristina and the children settled down on blankets in a small ravine. The soldiers secured the horses and wagon nearby.

Major al-Kawukji gazed up the road. "Two of us will stand watch while the other sleeps, and we'll switch every two hours. Who wants to sleep first? You, Isa?"

"No, sir, it's too early for me."

"I'm not tired either, Major," Bekir said. "You should rest first."

"Okay, then, I'll sleep first. Awaken me in two hours."

"Yes, sir," Isa replied.

The major fetched his bedding from the wagon and unrolled it across the ground. He checked his rifle, rolled over on his side and closed his eyes. His snore soon echoed across the clearing.

Bekir mused aloud about the war and his family for the better part of an hour.

Isa listened attentively and gazed up at the rising moon. Finally, he knelt on the ground to clean his rifle. When he finished, he reloaded and rose to his feet. Bekir had dozed against a rock. *What the hell?* Isa thought to himself. *Why should both of us lose sleep?* He sat beside the private and peered at the darkened trail below.

Staring down at the shadowy, darkened road, Isa cradled his rifle in his arms. He listened for a long while to the chirp of a cricket. He nodded off briefly, but his head jerked up with a start. Rubbing his eyes, he rose to his feet and stretched. He ate the last of his cheese and took a deep breath before crouching back down.

Isa scanned down to the bend in the road and stretched his arms into the air. He stared up through the trees at the moon and yawned loudly. He peered bleary-eyed at the dark road. Finally, yielding to the muggy night, his chin dropped to his chest.

Major al-Kawukji bolted upright on his blanket. He glanced behind him. The women and children were asleep on the ground a few meters away. Peering through the darkness, he glimpsed the silhouettes of two men scurrying across the ravine to the wagon and horses. He groped for his rifle and jumped to his feet. "Isa? Is that you?"

The high-pitched whinny of a horse echoed across the clearing.

Al-Kawukji ran toward the trees. "Isa! Bekir!" he shouted. "Bandits!"

An instant later, a blood-curdling scream echoed through the darkness.

Al-Kawukji spotted a man with a white turban climbing atop one of the horses. The horse broke for the road. The major raised his rifle and squeezed off a shot. The rider fell backwards off the horse to the ground. Running down the hill, the major caught a glimpse of two more men in turbans sprinting away from the rocks. He fired again, and the nearest man tumbled to the ground. Al-Kawukji took aim again, but lost the other intruder in the shadows. He dashed to the horses.

Tiran was galloping in circles around the clearing. Spinning to face the major, the chestnut stallion whinnied defiantly.

"Easy, boy," al-Kawukji whispered. He grabbed the reins.

Sirak and Mikael ran down the hillside. "Tiran!" Sirak shouted excitedly.

"He's okay," al-Kawukji whispered. "You boys hold him here while I secure the other horses."

Sirak pointed toward a mound on the ground. "What's that?"

Aiming his rifle, al-Kawukji stepped warily toward the motionless figure. "It's a bandit with his forehead bashed in. The horse must have kicked him."

The major ran across the clearing to the man he'd shot. Lying on his back and trembling with fear, the wide-eyed bandit raised his hand and gasped for mercy.

"Go to hell!" al-Kawukji barked. He drew his sword and slashed the thief across the neck.

Then he grabbed a knife that lay on the ground and ran back to the boys. "Stay here with the horses while I check on Isa and Bekir. Use this knife to defend yourselves and the women."

Al-Kawukji skulked warily up the hill to the rocky enclosure where he'd left his men. Stepping around a boulder, he gasped in horror. Isa and Bekir were lying on the ground in pools of blood. Their throats were slit wide open.

"Fucking murderers!" al-Kawukji bellowed in anguish. He dropped his rifle and slumped to his knees beside Isa's body. "Isa, my friend," he sobbed.

Al-Kawukji mounted his horse, and repositioning his sword, turned toward the wagon. Elizabeth, Kristina and the children were huddled in the rear. Hakan sat in the driver's seat with a rifle across his lap. Two riderless horses were tied to the tail of the wagon.

"Okay," the major called out, "we'll take the next few turns on the run. If we get ambushed, don't stop. Keep going, no matter what. Mikael, are you ready?"

"I'm ready," Mikael called back from the wagon bed. He held up a rifle.

"Okay, move!" al-Kawukji shouted. He galloped past them with his rifle clutched beneath his arm.

The wagon lurched around the first bend, and tipping onto two wheels, rumbled down a steep incline. It splashed through a muddy furrow, rattled into a narrow clearing and slid sideways through a patch of underbrush. Jostled about in the bed, the women and younger children clung desperately to the sideboards.

Al-Kawukji galloped across a dry riverbed and through a series of short switchbacks. Peeking back over his shoulder, he re-gripped the reins, galloped to the next turn and rode to the top of a ridge. Finally, he tugged on the reins and stopped in the middle of the road.

The wagon thundered through the last turn and Hakan jerked back on the reins. "Whoa!" he bellowed. The wagon clattered to a stop.

"Is everyone okay?" Major al-Kawukji called out.

"I'm okay," Elizabeth gasped.

Kristina pulled herself to her knees and clutched wide-eyed Izabella. "We're okay, too."

"Whee!" Sirak shouted. He jumped up on the tailgate and patted Tiran on the head. "Can we do it again?"

The major shook his head and grinned. "No, little fearless one, we must save the horses. We're still four or five hours from Mardin."

"Can I ride Tiran, Major?" Sirak pleaded. He smoothed back the horse's glistening mane.

"That's up to your mother."

Kristina nodded. "It's okay, if you stay beside the wagon."

Major al-Kawukji untied Tiran, and pulling him along the sideboard, held him steady. Sirak climbed onto the horse's back and grabbed the reins. Shifting his weight forward on Tiran's back, he smiled at his mother. "Don't worry, Mama, we'll protect you."

CHAPTER 33

June 22, 1915

Major al-Kawukji led his charges along the winding road deep into the windswept hills of southern Anatolia, approaching the ancient city of Mardin from the north. Sirak rode Tiran for nearly two hours, but tired of the constant jostling and returned to the wagon. Enduring a scorching sun and bothersome insects, the tiny caravan pressed on doggedly through the middle of the second morning.

At first they passed only occasional travelers and military units headed in the opposite direction. Early in the afternoon, however, the trickle of traffic headed north became a flood, and an unsettling trend developed. Many travelers ran headlong into the brush the moment they spotted the wagon and horses.

"Where are all these people from?" Elizabeth asked anxiously.

"Mardin," Major al-Kawukji replied. "Or from the railway station in Ras ul-Ain."

Elizabeth glanced up at another large group that appeared around the next curve. They, too, scattered like mice into the brush. "Look!"

"They're terrified," Kristina gasped.

Sirak and Mikael climbed into the driver's seat with Hakan. They watched with amazement as the same response played out time and again. Fleeing in panic from the road, each group hid in the brush until their wagon passed.

Finally, a rundown ox cart overloaded with household goods headed directly toward them. The driver—an old Turk wearing a fez—nodded at the major.

"What's going on up ahead?" al-Kawukji called out to him. "What are all these travelers running from?"

"The army is rounding up all the infidels in Mardin and the surrounding villages," the man yelled back. "The city is total chaos. Be on your guard."

"Thanks for the warning," Al-Kawukji replied. He glanced worriedly at Elizabeth. "We must hurry to make it to Ras ul-Ain before dark."

A few kilometers north of Mardin, an army detail herding a large group of detainees appeared in the middle of the road ahead of them. A young Turkish officer on horseback was the first to spot them. Breaking away from the others, he galloped toward the wagon.

"Damn it," al-Kawukji grumbled beneath his breath. "Don't anyone say a word. Let me do all the talking."

The brash lieutenant trotted up to the major. "Good afternoon, sir."

"Good day, Lieutenant. It looks like you've got your hands full."

"Yes, sir. We began a northern sweep this morning and I've already rounded up more than one hundred fifty infidels who escaped from the city. Where are you headed, sir?"

"To Ras Ul-ain. How's the road, Lieutenant?"

"Crowded, sir. All the roads have been choked with traffic headed to the internment centers ever since Governor-General Reshid issued his orders early this morning."

Al-Kawukji peered up the road at the prisoners. "Armenians and Syrians?"

"Not only them—Maronites, Nestorians and Europeans, too. Are those horses tied to the wagon available, sir? We could sure use them."

"The chestnut stallion belongs to me, but you can take the other one. It belonged to one of my men who was murdered by Kurdish bandits."

"Sorry to hear that, sir. Those damned *chetes* are creating havoc all over Southern Anatolia. Would you like me to take those detainees off your hands?"

"The lieutenant governor-general ordered me to personally take them to Ras ul-Ain. The brother-in-law of the dark-haired woman is a member of the Ottoman Assembly."

The lieutenant stared at the wagon. "The Ottoman Assembly, huh? What about the European woman?"

"An American nurse from Diyarbekir, and my mistress."

"Your mistress?" the young soldier blurted out. He glanced into the wagon once again.

Elizabeth's face and clothes were smeared with dirt, and her tangled hair was blowing haphazardly in the warm breeze.

"She cleans up well," al-Kawukji whispered. "She's headed to Aleppo and, unfortunately for me, then back home."

The lieutenant laughed and rode over to Major al-Kawukji. "It's your lucky day, sir," he whispered. "There's plenty of young pussy up there to go around." He chuckled. "Take any girl you like except for the slender brunette in the blue dress up front. I'm taking her home with me."

"No thanks, Lieutenant," the major replied good-humoredly. "I've already got one." He motioned toward the wagon, where Izabella was standing at the sideboard with her mother. "I've taken a fancy to the young one."

The lieutenant erupted into laughter. "I see, sir. I'm fond of the young ones myself. Well, you'd better be on your way if you plan to make Ras ul-Ain before dark. Take the direct route to the west of Mardin to avoid the heaviest traffic. You'll see a sign a kilometer up the road. I'll just take that extra horse."

"Yes, of course. Thank you for your advice, Lieutenant."

The lieutenant rode up to the wagon and untied the black horse under Sirak's watchful eyes. He rode back to the caravan and passed the horse off to one of his men.

Major al-Kawukji led the wagon through the disheveled and dejected detainees. Tied together in groups of twenty or more, the soldiers forced them off the road so the wagon could pass.

Sirak stared at the crestfallen prisoners as the wagon rumbled past them. None of them looked up. "Where are they taking them, mama?"

Kristina wrapped her arm around Sirak's shoulders. "I don't know, Son. Home, I hope."

Sirak nuzzled against Mikael, and the two boys watched in silence until the wagon rattled around a bend in the road.

The major took the lieutenant's advice and led his charges through the barren countryside via the direct road to Ras ul-Ain. That route allowed them to bypass much of the traffic created by the sudden deportation of thousands of non-Muslim citizens from Mardin and the surrounding villages. A few kilometers beyond the fork, they passed a sprawling, makeshift camp dotted with improvised tents and surrounded by dozens of armed soldiers and gendarmes.

Izabella scooted between her mother and Sirak and clutched the sideboard as they rumbled past. Sirak waved at a group of women and children standing together just inside the perimeter. A young boy waved back. A gendarme on horseback rode out and screamed obscenities. He shooed the group back to the center of the enclosure.

Sirak glanced up at his mother's angst-ridden face. "Is he going home, too, Mama?"

Kristina looked down and smiled dolefully. "I don't know, little mouse, but I hope so."

Izabella tugged at Kristina's dress. "Mama, I need to pee pee."

The major turned his horse to the wagon. "I don't want to answer any more questions. We'll stop in fifteen minutes to water the horses. Can she hold off until then?"

Kristina nodded. She gathered Izabella into her lap and whispered words of comfort into her ear.

The badly rutted road twisted and turned through parched, sun-baked wasteland for several more kilometers. Finally, they reached the crest of a precipitous descent, and a sweeping view of the Mesopotamian Plains opened up to the south. Desolate and harsh, the gently rolling, sandy-brown hills appeared completely devoid of life. Far to the east, the city of Mardin sprawled down a sloping hillside beneath majestic vertical cliffs. Constructed over the centuries from indigenous yellow-brown calcareous rock, the city seemed to sparkle invitingly in the blistering rays of the afternoon sun.

Sheltering her eyes with her hand, Kristina gazed out at the distant plains. "It's magnificent," she whispered. She handed Izabella to the major, jumped to the ground and took the little girl's hand. "Izabella, let's go behind those rocks. Mikael, don't wander off too far, and keep an eye on your brother. This is no time for another viper bite."

"Okay, mama. Can we hike to the top of the hill and come right back?"

"Ask Major al-Kawukji," she called back over her shoulder. "We'll be back in a minute."

Sirak jumped up and down beside Mikael. "Can we, sir?"

"What about your horse? Don't you think he's thirsty, too?"

Sulking disappointedly, the young boy stuck out his bottom lip and walked back to the wagon.

The major chuckled. "Hakan and I will take care of him."

Sirak grinned and turned to run after his brother.

"But you can't expect to get Tiran back if you don't take care of him."

Sirak stopped dead in his tracks and kicked dejectedly at the dirt.

Hakan glanced at al-Kawukji, and the major grinned mischievously. "I'll give him his water," the old Turk called out to Sirak.

"Be back in five minutes," al-Kawukji yelled. "We've only got three or four more hours of sunlight."

"Thank you, Hakan!" Sirak called out gleefully. He ran up the hill after Mikael.

The spiteful sun became a sliver of red beneath a line of distant clouds and set below the horizon by the time the wagon jerked to a stop outside the East Ras ul-Ain train station. The lot teemed with frenzied people, some of whom looked like they'd camped outside for days. Again, a commotion ensued when the major trotted his horse in ahead of the wagon. Dozens of people, apparently fearful of being detained, melted away into the nearby slum neighborhood.

"You're wasting your time," an old Turk called out to them from his perch atop a wall outside the station. "There aren't any tickets available— at least for a month."

"A month?" al-Kawukji asked incredulously. "Heading to Aleppo?"

"Heading anywhere. Even the Mosul trains are booked solid. If you have enough money, there's a scum clerk inside selling tickets for outrageous sum—enough to buy a farm."

"What does he look like?"

"He's the fat man wearing a black uniform. I think he's the supervisor."

"Thank you," Major al-Kawukji grumbled. Tying his horse to the tailgate, he walked around the side of the wagon. "Do you have money to pay a bribe?" he asked Nurse Barton.

"I hope so. I brought every *kurus* we had."

"I'll go bargain with the clerk. How much can you spend?"

"Whatever it takes," she replied determinedly.

The major nodded. "Mrs. Kazerian, how much money do you have for tickets?"

"I've got one hundred ten *lire* and a gold necklace and earrings. I'll pay whatever the man asks."

"Kristina, you'll need your money to travel to Jerusalem," Elizabeth interrupted. "I've got plenty for everyone. It doesn't matter how much he wants; just get us tickets on the first available train."

"We can't take your money, Elizabeth," Kristina said.

"Yes you can. Major, I've got enough money and I insist on paying for all the tickets. Kristina needs everything she has for her journey to Jerusalem."

"Okay, I'll do my best," al-Kawukji replied. He headed up the steps and disappeared into the depot.

The station was total bedlam. Several hundred adults and children were sprawled across the floor, and belongings were piled high against the walls. Dozens of people were standing in each of the four ticket lines.

The major scrutinized the clerks at the windows. He bypassed the lines and headed to the first window. A young European couple at the front was engaged in a heated discussion with the clerk.

"You, sir," the young man barked in broken Arabic, "are a shyster. Rest assured, we'll be reporting you to the German ambassador! Come on, Gretchen, let's get out of here."

"Excuse me, sir," Major al-Kawukji said, cutting in front of the next person in line—a dark-skinned old man with Kurdish features, "I'd like to have a word with this clerk." He pushed to the window.

Puffed with self-importance, the clerk scowled through the window, but cleared his throat nervously when he spied the insignias on the major's uniform. "Good evening, sir. How may I help you?"

"I'm Major al-Kawukji from Army Central Intelligence. I've brought five important travelers from Diyarbekir, and I want them on the next train to Aleppo."

"I'm sorry, sir, but that's impossible. There's not a single seat available until July 28."

"Do you mind?" the major barked gruffly at the man behind him. Pushing the startled man back, al-Kawukji leaned beneath the window. "Sir, these people must be on the next train. I understand priority seating is available if one pays a commission."

The clerk's eyes widened with surprise, but he quickly recovered his composure. Glancing warily down the counter, he leaned against the window. "How many passengers?" he whispered.

"I told you, five—two women and three children."

"Can they make the trip in three seats?"

"I should think so."

"What are the nationalities of your travelers?"

"One woman is American, and the rest are Armenian."

The clerk's eye bulged even wider. "I'm sorry, but you must be aware of the governor-general's orders. I can't sell tickets to..."

"I don't give a damn about the orders," al-Kawukji interrupted. "I want them on the next train."

"No, sir. I'm sorry, but I can't help you."

Standing back from the window, Major al-Kawukji took a deep breath. He scowled once again at the man behind him and leaned down to the window. "What's your name?" he demanded sternly.

The clerk's cheeks flushed. "My...my name?"

"Yes, what's your name?"

"Ali Atta, sir."

"Ali, do you have sons?"

"Yes, sir, I have two."

"How old are they and what are their names?"

The clerk stared back with terror-filled eyes.

"How old are they and what are their names?" the major demanded.

"Hasan is fifteen and Okan is fourteen," the clerk muttered warily.

"Well, if you don't want Hasan sent to the Russian front tomorrow, I suggest you find a way to get my charges on that next train. Do you understand me?"

The clerk gaped at the major for a long moment. Sweating profusely, he glanced at two clerks talking nearby. "Okay," he whispered beneath the window, "one hundred *lire* per person for three seats."

"One hundred *lire!*" al-Kawukji growled. "That's outrageous! I'll give you fifty *lire* total—for all five people."

The clerk stared at the counter for a moment and then closed his eyes in resignation. "Okay, bring them to the rear door of the last passenger car when the train arrives. Under no circumstances should any of them admit they're Armenian."

"I understand. What time is the train expected?"

"Twenty-one hundred hours, but it's almost always late." The clerk pushed three tickets and a white envelope beneath the window. "Put the commission in this envelope and hand it to the conductor when he asks for your tickets. Make sure his name is Sencer. He should be the first one on the car. Only one piece of luggage is allowed per seat—three total for the five of them. Everything else must be left behind."

"Very well. I'll make sure they get on that train. Good evening, sir."

The westbound train to Aleppo pulled into the station a few minutes after midnight. Elizabeth and Kristina ushered the children to the last car.

Kristina glanced back down the busy platform. "Where's Sirak?" she called out frantically.

"He's saying goodbye to his horse," al-Kawukji said. "Don't worry, Hakan's bringing him."

Elizabeth waited patiently for several other passengers to board the car ahead of them. "Row 16, A, B, and C," she said. "That must be nearly the last row."

Kristina handed her son a leather bag. "Mikael, I'm going to find Sirak. Take your sister to our seats and store this wherever you can."

Major al-Kawukji smiled at Nurse Barton. "Well, it looks like we made it. May God bless you. God willing, I hope to see you again when this wretched war ends."

Elizabeth took the major's hand. "God bless you, Major. I can't begin to express my gratitude for all you've done to help us. But I must ask you, why would you take this risk for an American and four Armenians?"

"I've long admired the selfless sacrifices you and Dr. Charles made for the people of Anatolia and especially for the care you provided to my soldiers who were wounded in battle. I'd like to leave it at that, if you don't mind."

Elizabeth smiled warmly. "Okay, take care, Major." She squeezed his hand. "May God bless you."

Kristina hurried down the platform with Sirak in tow. Hakan followed quickly behind them, lugging another bag.

"Major al-Kawukji, we'll be forever grateful to you and your men. We'll pray for God to protect you on your journey back to Diyarbekir."

"Thank you, Mrs. Kazerian. I hope you find your husband and son waiting for you in Jerusalem. Please, light a candle for me."

"I will, Major. I promise."

Sirak—tears welling in his eyes—took his mother's hand and peered up at the major. "Major al-Kawukji, can I really keep Tiran when we come back?"

The major squatted next to Sirak and patted him on the head. "Of course you can, Sirak. He'll be waiting for you. That's a promise." He folded Sirak's tiny hand over a slip of paper. "These are the directions to my farm. Keep them in a safe place."

"What if I can't come back for a long, long time?"

The major gripped Sirak's shoulders. "I will keep him, no matter how long it takes. I'll look forward to seeing you soon."

Hakan picked Sirak up and set him down at the top of the ramp.

Kristina climbed onto the car and took his hand. "Thank you for everything, Hakan."

The old Turk nodded his head and smiled with satisfaction.

The conductor blew his whistle and darted up the front stairs of the last car. The couplers between the cars clanked in cadenced succession, and the train began to inch forward.

"Come on, Elizabeth!" Kristina called out to Nurse Barton.

Elizabeth gave Hakan a final hug. Running up the steps, she turned and waved a last goodbye.

"Thank you again, Major," Kristina shouted above the screech of the wheels. "God bless you."

Major al-Kawukji waved a last goodbye. He stood on the platform beside Hakan and they watched the train clear the station and head toward central Ras Ul-ain.

"Do you think they'll make it?" Hakan asked glumly.

"No," al-Kawukji replied matter-of-factly. "It'll be a miracle if they even get past the Ras ul-Ain Central Station."

Hakan turned and glared at the major. "What? Why didn't you warn them?"

"What purpose would it serve?" al-Kawukji replied somberly. "At least, at this moment, they have hope. More importantly, I've repaid all my obligations to Abdul Pasha."

Hakan stared at the major with a bewildered scowl. "Who?"

"Nobody—just an old war buddy. You're my witness. I put the Armenian woman and her children safely on that train to Aleppo.

"Well," he continued. "it was a pleasure traveling with you, Hakan." Al-Kawukji nodded and walked away down the platform.

"Where are you going?" Hakan called after him.

The major turned and smiled. "To find a warm bath, a soft bed and a sympathetic whore."

"Aren't you heading back to Diyarbekir?"

"Someday, I'm sure, but I can't say when that might be."

"But it's not safe for me to travel alone. The *chetes* will slit my throat before I reach the pass."

"Goodbye, Hakan," the major said impatiently. "You've got a wagon and a strong horse. I advise you to sell the belongings Nurse Barton left behind and find yourself some burly guards. I should think you'll have no trouble finding travelers willing to pay you for transportation to Diyarbekir."

"What about the boy's horse?"

"What about him?"

"You promised Sirak you'd keep him on your farm."

The major smiled and shook his head amusedly. "Someday, my friend, you'll learn the value of hope. I must be on my way now." He turned and walked purposefully toward the station.

Hakan, still flabbergasted, stared after al-Kawukji for several moments. "Bastard," he muttered. He turned and peered down the empty tracks. Finally, he took a deep breath, shook his head and hobbled back to the train station.

PART TWO

This page intentionally left blank

CHAPTER 34

Keri stood up from his chair and stepped across the darkened room. He took an empty glass from his father's hand. Sirak awakened with a start and stared fearfully into his son's eyes.

"It's okay, Papa," Keri whispered. "You dozed off."

Sirak sighed with relief. "I'm sorry; I got up with the songbirds this morning. After the train pulled out of the train station in Ras Ul-ain, we..."

"Papa, that's enough for today. It's getting late. You know, I learned more today about our family than in the past fifty-nine years combined. Thank you, Papa, for telling me the story of your parents, brothers and sisters."

"I'm sorry now that I didn't tell you years ago. I should have. And, there's much more to tell you."

"And I do want to hear it all. But I think we should continue this talk next weekend. The doctor doesn't want you to get overtired."

"Okay, but Keri, I have a favor to ask."

"Anything, Papa. What is it?"

"Will you take me to St. Gregory's for next Sunday's service? It's the special requiem service for the Armenians."

"Sure, Papa. The requiem service never meant much to me because I didn't feel any connection. But now I do, and I want David and Michael to understand, too. We'll all go together and go out to lunch afterward."

"That would mean so much to me. It starts at ten in the morning."

"Your opening up about the past means a lot to me, too."

"There's something I didn't tell you about that Turkish doctor I worked with at the hospital. It's important."

"You can tell me next Sunday. I'll pick you up at nine forty-five. Goodnight, Papa."

Sirak heard Keri lock the door and rev the car engine before silence engulfed the room. He thought about his mother, brothers and sisters, and the rest of their story he had yet to tell. Suddenly, an irrepressible urge swept over him. He raised his unsteady hand and traced out the sign of the cross across his chest. "Thank you, dear God," he whispered for the first time in twenty-nine long years.

The following Sunday, Keri turned his car into the church parking lot and followed a line of cars to the rear of the lot. More than a hundred people were already gathered on the grass around the granite memorial. Glancing into the side-view mirror, he spotted David's Suburban a few vehicles back and Michael's car directly behind it.

Sirak parked and struggled out of his car into the bright springtime sunshine. He smiled at Keri. "Thank you, Son."

"You're welcome, Papa. Cathy and Sarah need to take the kids to the skating club after the service, but David and Michael plan to join us. I told them about Anatolia, and they want to hear more about those years, too."

Sirak nodded acceptingly. "That's good. It's time they knew the story of their grandparents and great-grandparents, too." Leaning on his cane, he hobbled to his waiting grandsons.

David, a tall young man with an athletic build, stepped forward, hugged his grandfather and took his hand. "Good morning, Papa Sirak. It's great to see you getting around so well. How's that cane working out?"

Sirak held up his silver-handled hardwood cane. "Great, thank you, David. It also makes a good weapon. Ask your father about that."

David chuckled. "Dad told me about that poor guy you whacked the hell out of at the coffee shop."

"George Liralian deserved it! Anyway, how's the business?"

"Pretty good, considering. Like always, the winter's been slow, but business will pick up now that spring is finally here."

"I'm sure it will; you've got a good business and work hard. You will always find a way to succeed. Where is Michael?"

"He's helping Sarah with the kids. Wait right here and I'll...oh, there he is."

Michael stepped out from between the cars with a pretty, dark-haired teenager on crutches. He was a slender man of average height, with a full head of curly black hair. He gave Sirak a toothy grin and extended his hand. "Hello, Papa Sirak, you're looking well. From Papa's reports, I expected to find you with one foot in the grave and the other on a banana peel."

"I'm well, thank you," Sirak replied amusedly. "I guess you'll have to wait a bit longer than you expected for your inheritance."

"And we had such big plans for that money," Michael joked.

Sirak smiled, turned to Michael's wife and offered his gnarled hand. "Hello, Sarah. Thank you for the beautiful flowers. I'm sure they were your doing."

Sarah kissed Sirak on the cheek. "It's good to see you up and around, Doctor Kazerian."

"Papa Sirak," David called out. He was holding his wife Cathy's arm, and their three teenage daughters were trailing behind. "We'd better hustle over to the service. It's about to start."

Sirak greeted Cathy and each of David's daughters with a warm hug, a peck on the cheek and a few kind words. Finally, the Kazerian brood—

four generations strong—walked across the freshly-mowed grass and fell in with the standing-room-only crowd facing the commemorative monument. The priest, wearing black vestments, and a teenage boy holding a golden Khatchkar Cross, stood talking with an older couple. Father Petrosian turned and spotted Sirak. He whispered something to the boy and walked over to Sirak and his family.

"Hello, Sirak. It's been a long time."

"Yes, Father, it's been a very long time."

"I see your grandsons have grown up to be fine young men with beautiful families of their own," Father Petrosian said. "To what do we owe your presence here today?"

Sirak smiled at Keri. "Well, Father, my son helped me finally realize that it was more important for me to appreciate the living than dwell on the dead. I think you'll be seeing a lot more of us all in the future."

"I'm delighted to hear that. Well, it's wonderful to see you, but it's time to begin the service. Let's have lunch sometime."

"I'd like that, Father. I'll give you a call."

Father Petrosian walked back to the monument and raised his hand to silence the crowd. "Dear friends, thank you all for coming on this solemn day of remembrance. We must thank God for blessing us with this beautiful sunny day.

"Eighty-one years ago today, in Istanbul, the Young Turks initiated several years of unspeakable atrocities against the Armenian people. They began with the execution of hundreds of our finest intellectuals—writers, teachers, doctors, attorneys, and even legislators in the Ottoman Assembly." Father Petrosian nodded somberly at Sirak. "Men like Sirak Kazerian's uncle, Bedros.

"Before the carnage ended, at least one and a half million of our people perished by hanging, beating, burning and every other imaginable act of brutality. Many innocents, including infants and children, died from hunger and thirst in the Syrian deserts. It's important for us—the sons and daughters, brothers and sisters, nephews and grandchildren of those who perished—to ensure the world never forgets what happened there. And so we gather here in front of this commemorative monument to recite the names of the loved ones of our members who suffered and died there. As Jesus said, *blessed are they that suffer for my name's sake...*"

Keri closed the car door and Sirak hobbled past him. David and Michael were waiting just outside the front door of a cozy Italian restaurant festooned with green and red bunting. David took Sirak's arm and helped him up the curb. "I hope you're hungry, Papa Sirak. A good friend of mine owns this restaurant, and they serve the largest portions you've ever seen. There's a private room in the back where we can talk."

"I'm too old to care much about what food I eat. Whatever you boys like is fine with me."

A young man in a suit and tie looked up from behind the reception desk. "Hey, David, how's the family?"

"Just great, Emilio. Did the baby finally come?"

"Yes! Julie finally had him night before last, and they're both doing fine. We named him Steven."

"Congratulations!" David exclaimed gleefully. "Better late than never. Emilio, this is Grandpapa Sirak, my father Keri, and you know my brother, Michael."

"Welcome to Mama Lucci's. It's an honor to meet more Kazerians."

"We're starving," David said. "What's the lunch special today?"

"We've got several. Let's find you a table and I'll tell you about them."

"We have some private family matters to discuss. Can we use the back room?"

"It's all yours. Right this way, please." Emilio led them back through the diminutive main dining room and into a smaller room with a table set for four. He handed each man a menu. "I recommend the antipasti salad and the four-cheese ravioli. The lasagna special is great, too."

The food and drinks came quickly and the conversation revolved around the mundane details of David and Michael's family life until the main course was done and Emilio cleared the table. It was David who finally broached the past.

"Papa Sirak, Papa told us our family was Catholic when they lived in Anatolia. I never realized that."

"Yes, all of our people were Catholic, at least back to my grandfather."

"So why aren't we Catholic now?"

"I wanted to worship with other Armenians when we moved to Cleveland, and there weren't any Armenian Catholic churches in northeast Ohio."

David nodded. "That makes sense. Did you ever find out what happened to your father and your brothers, Alek and Stepannos?"

"No, I never did. Alek probably died in the war or was executed by the Ottomans. As far as Stepannos is concerned, I searched the records at the Saint James Convent when we finally made it to Jerusalem, but there was no record of Papa and Stepannos arriving there. After learning more about the fate of the men and boys who were sent out of Anatolia, I think it's likely Papa and Stepannos perished in the Syrian Desert. But only God knows what really happened."

Sirak settled back in his seat and looked at his son. "Keri, have you told them everything I told you last week?"

"Yes, Papa, right up to the point you reached the train station in Ras Ul-ain."

"Did you make it to your destination?" David asked.

"Yes, we did, but not without several more terrifying moments, especially for Mama and Nurse Barton. We were all euphoric when that train pulled out of the Ras Ul-ain station, but after a brief glimmer of hope, our situation deteriorated from desperate to hopeless.

CHAPTER 35

June 23, 1915

The train rattled out of the station headed to central Ras ul-Ain and Sirak dozed in his mother's lap. Mikael cuddled Izabella and peered restlessly out the window at the dilapidated houses and buildings that lined the Baghdad Railway tracks.

Elizabeth sat nervously watching the Turkish conductor as he checked tickets at the front of the car.

The car was overflowing with passengers of every age and description, and at least half of the seats held two people. A smartly-dressed Turkish woman was busy tending her colicky baby in the seat directly across the aisle. Two Turkish men and a veiled woman occupied the seats directly in front of them. One of the men—a rather frail-looking gentleman with a persistent cough—glanced repeatedly back at Kristina. Each time he did, she looked away, fearful he was questioning the presence of an Armenian woman and her children on the train bound for Aleppo.

Elizabeth glanced at Kristina. "Are you okay?"

Kristina nodded. "Thanks to you. But you shouldn't have paid for our tickets."

"We can thank David. I used the money he set aside for our return trip to America. He would've done the same thing."

"I wish he were here. God rest his soul."

Elizabeth smiled sadly. "You should try to sleep. Do you want me to take Sirak?"

"I'm too anxious to sleep." She nodded toward the man in the seat ahead of them and Elizabeth nodded back knowingly.

Making his way to the rear of the car, the conductor finally reached the row ahead of them. The Turk sitting in front of Elizabeth handed the man his tickets, and glancing again at Kristina, muttered something inaudible to the conductor. The conductor looked at Elizabeth and nodded before handing back the man's tickets.

Kristina glanced anxiously at Elizabeth. Repositioning Sirak in her lap, she closed her eyes and began to pray.

"Good evening, ladies," the conductor said cheerfully. "My name is Senser. Your tickets, please."

Elizabeth handed him the envelope, along with their tickets.

He glanced at the tickets and peered up at her over the top of half-eye reading glasses. "Headed to Aleppo, are you?"

"Yes, sir," Elizabeth replied calmly.

He concealed the envelope behind the seat and pulled out the money. He thumbed through the bills, slipped the money into his pocket and handed the envelope and tickets back to Elizabeth. "Thank you, ladies; have a nice trip."

Elizabeth held up the envelope. "Do you want this?"

"You keep it," he replied sarcastically. "It'll come in handy at the Ras Ul-ain Central Station. We'll be there in ten minutes, and if I'm not mistaken, gendarmes will come on board to inspect everyone's documents. At least they did this morning."

The conductor turned and headed back to the front of the car before Elizabeth could question him further.

Shifting in her seat, Elizabeth caught Kristina's mortified stare. "It'll be fine. If they do come to speak to us, let me talk to them."

Kristina made the sign of the cross and let out an anxious sigh.

Elizabeth reached beneath the seat and fished through the bottom of her bag. Counting out several more banknotes, she stuffed them inside the envelope.

The train screeched to a stop in a dimly-lit station. Gazing out the window, Kristina spied dozens of people crowded onto the platform. Suddenly, a group of gendarmes caught her eye. Waiting for the doors to open, they hurried to the train.

"Ras Ul-ain Central Station," the conductor shouted.

Izabella and Sirak pressed their noses to the window. They peered at the commotion on the platform and several passengers got up to retrieve their belongings, including the trio in the seat in front of them.

"Mama, is this Jerusalem?" Sirak asked hopefully.

"No, Son, we're still in Ras Ul-ain." Kristina glanced warily out the window at a gendarme waiting to board the car. "I want you boys to listen to me. If a policeman comes onto the train, I don't want you to speak to him. Do you understand? Nurse Barton does the talking."

"Why, Mama?" Sirak asked innocently.

Kristina grasped his knee. "Don't ask me why; just do as I say."

Sirak nodded woundedly. Standing in the aisle, he peered toward the front of the train.

The gendarme boarded a moment later. He exchanged pleasantries with the conductor and asked the passengers in the front row for their documents.

It seemed an eternity before the gendarme reached the back of the car. He glanced at Kristina and the children while checking the documents of the couple in front of them.

Kristina's pulse raced and beads of sweat ran down her neck. She watched the passenger in the seat in front of them pull several letters and books out of his luggage and hand them to the gendarme. The policeman glanced at the books and handed them back, but placed the letters in a basket overflowing with newspapers, letters and other confiscated materials. Finally, he handed the couple back their documents and stepped back to Nurse Barton and the Kazerians.

"Documents," he said gruffly.

Elizabeth handed him hers. "Sir," she said coolly, "my name is Elizabeth Barton. I'm an American nurse. I've been working at hospitals in Anatolia for the past five years, including the Missionary Hospital in Diyarbekir. This is my sister, Kristina, and her children. They don't have their documents because of a fire that broke out in our quarters just before we left Diyarbekir."

"Sister," the man repeated skeptically. He glanced at Elizabeth's documents for a moment, and then stared at Kristina and the children. "Where were you born?" he asked Kristina.

"She was born in Syria," Elizabeth replied. "My parents adopted her when my father worked in Damascus many years ago."

"Can she speak for herself?" the gendarme asked frustratedly. "Where is your husband?"

"I, I don't know, sir," Kristina stuttered. "He joined the army at the beginning of the war and we haven't heard from him since."

"And your husband, madam?" he asked Elizabeth. "Where is he?"

"He died of typhus two weeks ago. That's why we've decided to leave Anatolia."

"Where are you headed?" he asked Elizabeth.

"To Aleppo, and then on to America."

"Well, before you can travel any further, you'll need to obtain new documents for your sister and her children. The mayor's office opens at nine tomorrow morning."

"But we'll lose our seats on the train," Elizabeth protested.

"That's not my concern. Please collect your belongings."

"Wait," Elizabeth said, holding Kristina in her seat. "I forgot; I do have documents." She reached into her pocket and pulled out the white envelope. She handed it to the gendarme.

The gendarme opened the envelope and spread the banknotes. "Do you have gold *lire?*"

"That's all I have, sir."

"Then my fee is two hundred paper *lire.*"

"Two hundred *lire,*" Elizabeth snapped. "That's outrageous!"

He handed her the envelope. "Two hundred," he repeated sternly. "That's my fee."

Elizabeth sighed. She reached beneath the seat, slipped several more banknotes from the side pocket of her bag and handed them to the gendarme.

The man counted the money and stuffed the envelope into his pocket. "Do you have any written or printed materials?"

"I have books and letters," Elizabeth replied. She glanced at Kristina.

"I've got a few letters, too," Kristina admitted.

"Give them to me."

Standing up, both women rummaged through their bags. They handed him several letters and books.

The gendarme pointed at the overhead rack. "What about this bag?"

"There are no printed materials in that bag," Kristina replied. "It contains my children's clothes."

The man tossed the letters into his basket and thumbed through the books one at a time. He handed Elizabeth each book he finished, until he came to the last book—The Holy Bible. He opened it and glanced up. "Are you Christians?"

"Yes," Elizabeth replied candidly, "we are Christians."

"How about you, young man?" he asked Sirak. "Are you a Christian?"

"Yes, sir," Sirak replied, "I'm a Christian, too."

"Does your God protect you?"

"Yes, sir," Sirak replied, with a definitive nod. "He saved me when a viper bit my foot. See, right here?"

"Your God must be a very powerful. What is your name, young man?"

"Sirak, sir."

"And your last name—what is it?"

"Kazerian, sir."

"Kazerian," the gendarme repeated with a smile. "Are you Armenian, Sirak?"

Sirak peered up at his mother. She was white as a sheet. She stared at Sirak, but did not speak.

"Yes, sir," Sirak finally replied, "I am Armenian."

"And your brother and sister, are they Armenian, too?"

Sirak glanced at Izabella and Mikael, and then looked up at the gendarme. "Yes, sir, they're Armenians, too."

Kristina closed her eyes and gripped the back of the seat in front of her. Her heart was pounding.

The gendarme stood silently regarding Sirak for several moments. Finally, he handed Elizabeth her Bible. "Such honesty is deserving of reward. But I advise all of you to adopt the surname Barton and deny your Armenian heritage until you are far away from the Ottoman Empire. Have a good night." The gendarme walked to the rear of the car and disappeared down the stairs.

Elizabeth sat back in her seat and sighed with relief.

Kristina took a deep breath and exhaled loudly. She traced the sign of the cross across her chest.

The train pulled out of the Ras Ul-ain Central Station a little after one in the morning and rumbled west through dark, featureless desert. A long delay ensued in Jerablus—an ancient city sprawled along the banks of the Euphrates River—and Elizabeth was forced to pay yet another bribe, this time to a conductor who threatened to give their seats to a French family. Elizabeth slipped him one hundred *lire*. A young couple at the front of the car was removed from the train. It was four in the morning when they finally rattled out of Jerablus.

Sirak fought to keep his eyes open. Finally, he drifted off to a restless sleep.

The train approached Aleppo a little before six the next morning. Just north of the city, on a road that paralleled the railroad tracks, Mikael spied a large caravan of people—mostly women and children—trekking south toward Aleppo. Most of the travelers were on foot, although a few had horses or donkeys.

"Look at them all," he muttered loudly enough to wake up Sirak.

Sirak wiped the sleep from his eyes and stared out through the window at the disheveled and exhausted travelers. One young woman in a tattered white dress caught his eye. Laboring with her baby behind the main body of refugees, she stumbled to her knees, then struggled to her feet and staggered after the others.

Sirak glanced at his mother. "Mama, are they going to Jerusalem, too?"

"I hope so," Kristina replied with a sad smile. She patted him on the head and hugged him to her chest.

The train screeched to a stop beside a platform teeming with passengers. Gathering their bags, Elizabeth and Kristina helped the children off the train.

Before they could reach the terminal, a young lieutenant stationed outside caught sight of them. "Are you Armenians?" he asked Kristina.

"No, sir, I'm Syrian."

"Let me see your papers."

"I'm an American and this is my adopted daughter and her children," Elizabeth interjected. "Their bag was stolen in the Ras Ul-ain station. Here are my papers."

The officer glanced through her papers and handed them back. "What's your destination?"

"America, but we're staying here in Aleppo tonight."

"Madam, your daughter and grandchildren must obtain replacement papers. The mayor's office is a few blocks north of the station."

"Thank you, sir. We'll be sure to go this afternoon, but first we need a warm bath. Can you recommend a nearby inn?"

"You'll find several just down the street from the train station. Just go left out the main entrance."

"I appreciate your help, sir."

The officer nodded and headed off to another group of passengers. One of his men—a young private—lingered behind. He waited for the officer to engage another group before approaching Kristina.

"I'm Armenian, and believe me anyone who sees you will know you're Armenian, too. Don't go anywhere near the mayor's office. You and your children will be forced into one of the detention centers outside the city. It is unspeakable what is happening to our people there."

"Where should we go?" Kristina asked.

The soldier glanced once again toward the lieutenant, then whispered. "Go to Father Leonian at the Gregorian Church. He'll help you. I must go now. May God protect you." The private hurried after his unit and disappeared into the station.

Kristina turned to Elizabeth. "Dear God, what should we do now?"

"Take his advice." She picked up her bag. "Come on, let's go."

Nurse Barton negotiated with an old Turk outside the station, and soon they were bumping along the uneven streets of Aleppo in the chaff-strewn bed of a horse-drawn cart. The driver headed directly to the Jdeide Quarter—home not only to the Gregorian Church, but also the Syrian Catholic Church and the Greek Orthodox Church.

Sirak peered out at the ancient city dominated by the massive walls of the citadel. In the distance, the dome and minaret of the Great Mosque loomed majestically atop a hill.

As he stared into the distance, he felt the weight of Izabella's stare. Sitting in Kristina's lap, she was peeking out from beneath her mother's arms. He smiled and reached out to brush her hair back from her eyes.

The cart bumped on for several blocks before turning onto a wide avenue and making a U-turn in the middle of the street. They pulled to a stop in front of a rather plain church.

Tying his horse to a post, the driver helped the women and children down from the cart. He lined up their bags along the side of the building, climbed back into the cart and drove away without uttering a word.

The street in front of the church was strangely deserted. Kristina picked up Izabella and followed Elizabeth to the main entrance.

Elizabeth tugged on the wooden door. "It's locked," she muttered with surprise. She rapped her knuckles on the frame. "I hope someone's here."

Nearly a minute passed before a small peephole in the middle of the door clinked open. The door swung wide open and a giant of a man wearing soiled worker's clothes stood before them.

"What do you want?" he asked.

"We need help," Elizabeth replied. "An Armenian soldier at the train station told us to come here. He said Father Leonian would help us."

"What was the soldier's name?" he asked suspiciously.

Elizabeth turned to Kristina. "I forgot his name. Do you remember?"

"I think it was Majarian."

"Yes, that's right," Mikael said. "It was Private Majarian."

The man picked up their bags and set them inside the door. "Come in."

The women and children stepped inside a dimly lit vestibule and the man secured the door with a heavy bar.

"I'm Vartan. Wait here and I'll tell Father Leonian."

Vartan hobbled off. Weaving his way through a clot of people, he ducked through a small door on the opposite side of the vestibule.

Taking a few steps into the main hall, Sirak gawked at the mass of people crowded into the pews of the darkened church. Bedding and other belongings were strewn haphazardly in the aisles. "Mama, do all these people live here?"

"They must." Lifting Izabella into her arms, Kristina peered at the gold and white altar adorned with an ancient painting of Jesus. Off to the side, an ornate red and gold bishop's chair was covered with an icon-studded golden cupola. "It's beautiful," she whispered.

Sirak tugged at her dress. "I can't see it, Mama."

Kristina handed Izabella to Elizabeth. She picked up Sirak and walked a short distance down the aisle.

"Is this your first visit to Gregorian?" a clear baritone voice asked.

Kristina turned. The middle-aged priest standing behind them was robed in black vestments, with paired golden crosses emblazoned across his chest. He had a rather ordinary face, with deep forehead furrows that had been fixed by incessant worry, but his pale blue eyes were filled with benevolence.

"Yes. We just arrived in Aleppo an hour ago."

Smiling warmly, the priest reached out and ruffled Sirak's hair. "Where are you from, young man?"

"Seghir, sir," Sirak said politely.

"Seghir? In Anatolia?"

"Yes," Kristina replied. "It's a small farming village east of Diyarbekir. This is our American friend, Elizabeth Barton. She's been a nurse in Anatolia for several years—most recently at the Missionary Hospital in Diyarbekir."

"I'm Father Leonian and I'm delighted to meet you. How can I be of service to you?"

"We have no place to go," Kristina said. "My husband and son were deported from Diyarbekir Province, and we're on our way to join them in Jerusalem. A soldier at the train station told us to come here."

"I'll do all I can to help you, but I have a funeral to conduct. Find a spot in the sanctuary, and I'll send Vartan to find you when I'm finished. I'd like to meet privately with you and Nurse Barton. Your children will be safe with the other families."

"Thank you," Kristina said.

Kristina and the children retrieved their bags and headed down the aisle. Several people acknowledged them when they walked past.

Kristina ducked into an open pew near the front. "Let's take this spot." She took Elizabeth's bag, slipped it beneath the pew and sat down.

"Mama, I'm hungry," Izabella whined.

Kristina gathered Izabella into her lap. "I know you are. I'm sure they'll give us something to eat a little later."

An old disheveled woman sleeping in the pew in front of them looked up. She nodded at Kristina and Elizabeth, and dropped her head back down.

Kristina pulled Sirak to her side and reached for Mikael's hand. Leaning back in the pew, she closed her eyes, nuzzled Izabella's neck and gave thanks to God for bringing them safely to the Gregorian Church.

Vartan stopped in front of a door at the end of a long hall and knocked softly.

"Come in," a voice inside called out.

Vartan opened the door and ushered the women into a dim office lit only by an oil lamp. Father Leonian was sitting at an old wooden desk covered with books and papers. He was dressed in a shirt and trousers. A faded painting of Jesus and his disciples hung on the wall behind him.

The priest looked up over the top of his reading glasses and smiled. "Please sit down. I trust the bread Vartan brought you was edible."

"Yes, thank you," Kristina replied.

"We never know what the mayor's office will send us, but at this point we're grateful for anything we get."

"It was fine."

"What's the situation in Ras Ul-ain and Mardin? We've heard rumors, but you're the first travelers to reach us from southeastern Anatolia in over a week."

"It was terrifying," Kristina replied. "We saw hundreds of Armenian people being herded like cattle on the road north of Mardin, and many more were detained in camps outside the city. I'm sure we would've been arrested, too, if we hadn't been escorted by Major al-Kawukji."

Father Leonian's eyes widened with surprise. "You had a military escort?"

"Yes, sir," Elizabeth answered. "The major knew my husband, Doctor David Charles. We worked at the Missionary Hospital in Diyarbekir."

"That explains how you made it. Where is your husband now?"

"He was murdered two weeks ago at Diyarbekir Central Prison."

The priest winced at the news. "May God rest his soul. Nurse Barton, you're in grave danger. Many foreigners have been arrested over the past few days, and we know some were sent to the prison in Mardin. You must leave Aleppo immediately."

"But where will I go?"

"There's a man I know. He'll take you to Alexandretta for a fee of fifty *lire.* You should be able to arrange safe passage out of the Empire from there."

"But what about Kristina and her children?" Elizabeth asked dubiously.

"Their best hope is to stay here with us. They'll be arrested if they're spotted on the road, and nobody—even the smugglers—will run the risk of being charged with aiding Armenians. Those who get caught defying the governor-general's proclamation are immediately executed."

"So we're prisoners here?" Kristina murmured.

"You're free to leave any time, Mrs. Kazerian, but I beg you to stay, at least until I can arrange safe passage for you and your children. Believe me, there are worse places. Thousands of Armenians arrive in Aleppo every day. These women, children and old people come in desperate caravans carrying everything they own on their backs. The survivors are crowded into khans, unoccupied houses, courtyards and even vacant lots. They die by the hundreds every day."

"Dear God," Kristina gasped.

"Our Merciful Father has guided you here to the Gregorian Church, and by His grace, you and your children are safe." Father Leonian stood up behind his desk. "Well, I must contact my friend. He's a Chechen, but you can trust him. He's guided countless Europeans and Americans to safety over the past six months. If he's in Aleppo, he'll likely come to the church around midnight, so be prepared to leave."

Elizabeth took the cleric's hand. "Thank you, Father. You're very brave to take these risks for people you've just met."

"Yes, God bless you, sir," Kristina chimed in.

"It's the least I can do to help my brothers and sisters who are persecuted simply because they're Christians. I'll let you know when I make contact with your guide."

E lizabeth slipped into the pew and awoke Kristina with a gentle tug on her arm. "It's time for me to say goodbye."

Kristina sat up and rubbed sleep from her eyes. She glanced at the children. Sirak and Izabella were sprawled across the bench and Mikael was lying on a pallet beneath them. "He found the guide?"

Elizabeth nodded. "He'll be here a little after midnight."

"What time is it now?"

Elizabeth held up her timepiece and struggled to read the dial in the dim candlelight. "It's eleven forty-five."

"I'll miss you so much," Kristina said sadly.

Elizabeth dabbed her eyes with a handkerchief. "I'll miss you, too. What will I do without you?"

"Shhh," a woman in the pew behind them whispered. "The children are sleeping."

Kristina led Elizabeth out of the pew. She wrapped her arm around her friend and walked her up the aisle. "How long will it take you to reach Alexandretta?"

"Three or four days."

"I wish we could go, too. We'll go stir crazy waiting to travel on to Jerusalem."

Elizabeth embraced Kristina. "Mourad is waiting for you there. I just know it."

"I pray you're right."

Elizabeth smiled. "Thank you for being such a good friend. Your support meant so much to me these last few months."

"It was you who supported me," Kristina said.

"We supported each other. That's what friends do."

Then Elizabeth handed Kristina a note. "This is David's brother's address in Oklahoma. Write me when you can. I'll be worried sick about you and the children."

Kristina folded up the paper and slipped it into her pocket. "Remember what we talked about in Chunkoush back in September?"

"September? Has it really been that long?"

"Do you remember?"

"Yes, of course; but I didn't listen to you."

"No, thank God. If you hadn't married David, you'd have missed the wonderful times you shared together and we wouldn't be here today. But everything else I said that day still holds true."

"I'll never love anyone the way I loved David."

"Maybe not, but David would want you to be happy. Someday there will be another man—one who wants a family. Don't miss that opportunity when it comes."

"You still feel that way after all that's happened to you and to your children?"

Kristina smiled. "Absolutely. Children bring despair and heartache, but they also bring unbridled joy and contentment."

Elizabeth didn't respond, but reached into her pocket and pulled out a small bag. She pressed it into Kristina's hand. "I want you to take this. It's five hundred *lire*."

Kristina's eyes widened with surprise. She shook her head. "I can't accept this."

"I want you to have it. You'll need transportation and supplies, and God knows what else, to reach Jerusalem. I've got more than enough money to get home. Please, take it."

Kristina gave Elizabeth a heartfelt hug. "God bless you. Someday I'll find a way to repay you."

"No you won't. It's my gift to you and the children."

"You're truly an angel. Please ask your guide to get word back to Father..."

A loud knock resounded through the vestibule. Vartan hurried out of the offices and Father Leonian followed a moment later. Vartan removed the bar from the door and pulled it open. A wiry, dark-skinned man, with a long unruly beard stepped inside.

"It's good to see you again, Movsar," the priest said. "How's travel to the Mediterranean these days?"

"Very risky, my friend. But it's still possible, if you know the right people."

Father Leonian smiled. "That's why we contacted you. This is Elizabeth Barton—an American friend who wants to go home."

Movsar bowed politely. "It's my pleasure to guide you to safety, Mrs. Barton. I trust that Father Leonian informed you about my modest fee?"

"Oh, so now you call fifty *lire* a modest fee," the priest teased.

The Chechen threw back his head, and howling with delight, revealed a line of decayed teeth beneath his unkempt mustache. "Fifty *lire* would have been unimaginable for a trip to Alexandretta before the war, but now, considering the risk, it's a pittance. I'll collect my fee before we leave."

Elizabeth handed the Chechen a roll of bills. He carefully counted the money before thrusting it into his pocket.

"I've arranged safe passage for you and two other women on a German freighter scheduled to leave for Belgium in five days. From there you can catch a ship bound for New York. The captain will expect thirty-five *lire*. Have you ever ridden a horse?" he asked skeptically.

"I was raised on a farm, Mr. Movsar," Elizabeth replied confidently.

"Excellent!" Movsar handed her a baggy black dress and veil. "Put this on."

Elizabeth slipped the dress over her clothes and Kristina helped her with the veil.

Mosvar grinned approvingly. "You are my wife, Aset. Do not speak to anyone who's not traveling in our party from now until we reach the ship in Alexandretta. I will speak for you. Do you understand?"

Elizabeth nodded.

"Then let's be on our way."

"Thank you, Movsar," the priest said solemnly. "I'll pray for your safe passage and return."

Kristina turned and embraced Elizabeth. "I'll be praying for you."

"I'll pray for you, too. Write me as soon as you're safe."

Vartan unbarred the door and pulled it open. Movsar took Elizabeth's arm and led her into the night. The door boomed closed and the patter of footsteps faded into silence.

CHAPTER 36

July 2, 1915

A bdul held a loose plank against the side of the wagon. "Erol, fetch me more nails. Hurry!"

Erol ran into the barn. He sprinted out the door a moment later, and bowing his head obsequiously, handed his father a box of nails.

Abdul seated a nail. Stepping back, he crouched to make sure the plank was level before pounding the nail home. He drove in several more nails and handed the hammer to Erol. "Put this back in the tool box."

Abdul lifted a pitchfork of hay and carried it to the corral. He tossed it over the fence and headed back for another load. Suddenly, he turned and squinted toward the main road.

Four riders on horseback trotted down the gently sloping trail and pulled up outside the barn.

"Good morning, Abdul," Baran called out. The Turk wore tattered work clothes and a red fez.

"I told you not to come back unless you got a deferment," Abdul replied gruffly. "What do you want?"

"We've come for our wages. We won't wait any longer."

"I can't pay you anything more until I sell my harvest. I told you that last week."

"That's not soon enough," Baran said angrily. "We've got hungry families to feed."

"Well, I don't have it."

"Then pay us with flour and rice," another rider bellowed. "My sons are bloated with hunger."

"I haven't got enough food for my own family."

Baran dismounted his horse. He handed his reins to another rider and walked toward the barn door.

Abdul ducked through the fence and rushed to cut him off. "Stay out of my barn, you bastard!"

Baran whirled to face him. "I just want to check your stores. If you're as short as you say, then we'll leave."

"Get the hell off my land!" Abdul shouted. "I told you, I don't have enough to feed my own family."

Baran turned to walk to the barn door. "Just let me look and we'll be on our way."

Abdul spun Baran around and knocked him to the ground with a powerful punch to the jaw.

The other riders dismounted their horses and fanned out around him.

Muhammad—the oldest of the four—held up his hands. "We only want what's owed to us, Abdul."

Baran rose to his feet and inched toward Abdul. "There are four of us, Abdul. Don't be a fool."

"Stay away!" Abdul yelled. He slowly turned in a circle and threateningly jabbed the air with his pitchfork. "I'll kill the first man who sets foot in my barn."

"Papa?" Erol called out anxiously from the barn door.

"Run, boy!" Abdul bellowed. "Tell your uncle to get the gun."

Erol ran headlong across the barnyard to the house. Baran sprinted toward the barn door, but Abdul tackled him before he got halfway across the yard and punched him in the mouth.

"You son of a whore," Baran grunted. He struggled to roll Abdul off.

Suddenly, the youngest of the men, a Kurd named Ibrahim, pulled a knife from his belt. He lunged forward and plunged the gleaming blade into Abdul's side.

Abdul's eyes bulged in surprise. He rolled onto his back and groaned with pain. "You stabbed me?" he demanded in disbelief.

Baran jumped to his feet and wiped a trickle of blood from the corner of his mouth. "We warned you." He jogged into the barn and ran back out a moment later. "You bastard! You've hoarded at least two hundred bags of flour and rice. Ibrahim, go get the wagon."

The younger man handed Baran his knife and ran to his horse. He galloped up the trail toward the main road. A minute later, a horse-drawn wagon rumbled into barnyard and pulled to a stop at the barn door. Baran stood guard over Abdul, and the other three men began loading flour and rice into the wagon.

The front door of the house creaked open. Hasan stepped tentatively outside. Erol and Sabriye came behind him.

Baran held up the knife. "Stay in the house. Nobody else needs to get hurt."

Sabriye pushed past Hasan and rushed to Abdul's side. "You stabbed him in the back?"

"I didn't do it," Baran said contritely. "Ibrahim stabbed Abdul after he punched me in the mouth and threatened to kill us."

Sabriye knelt on the ground and wiped beads of perspiration from Abdul's forehead with her veil. "Can you get up?"

Catching his breath, Abdul gurgled unintelligibly.

"Hasan, bring water! Hurry! Why did you do this, Baran?" Sabriye asked the Turk. "After Abdul supported you and your family for all these years. Why? He has a family to feed, a child on the way!"

"We just wanted what was due," Baran answered. "We have families, too. I'm sorry it came to this."

"He's bleeding to death. Can you at least help me carry him into the house?"

Baran turned to the other men. "Let's take him inside."

Tarkan tossed a bag of rice into the back of the wagon. He hustled over, peered down at Abdul and shook his head. "He's dead."

"He's not dead, you idiot," Sabriye huffed, pointing to the house. "Come on!"

Erol opened the door and Baran and Tarkan carried Abdul inside. They laid him on the sofa in the front room, and Sabriye knelt beside him. He opened his eyes, let out a long sigh, and closed them again.

"I'm sorry, Abdul," Baran said remorsefully. "I didn't mean for this to happen. Why are you so damned stubborn?"

Abdul opened his eyes again and looked up at Baran. "Fuck you," he gasped weakly.

Baran ignored his insult. "Don't worry, I'll leave plenty of flour and rice for your family."

Sabriye blotted Abdul's ashen face with a cloth. "Could you ride to the village for help?"

"Of course," Baran replied. "I'll go find the doctor." He looked up and spotted Flora and Jasmine hovering in the hall with the children. Both women were wearing veils. "Don't worry," he reassured them, "I'll take care of you until Abdul gets well."

Getting no reply, he rushed out of the house.

CHAPTER 37

Two months later, August 5, 1915

M ikael ducked into the darkened pew beside Sirak.

"Did you get any bread?" Kristina asked.

"Only one piece," he replied frustratedly. He held out a dry crust. "Most of it was covered with mold."

"Take anything you can get next time. We'll scrape it off." Kristina took the bread and carefully broke it into pieces. She handed Sirak one piece and Mikael another. "We thank Thee for this bread, Christ our God. We trust in your goodness and know you'll provide for all our needs. Glory to the Father, and to the Son, and to the Holy Spirit, now and ever and unto ages of ages, Amen." She gathered Izabella onto her lap and tore off a bite. She pressed it into the little girl's mouth. "Eat it slowly, angel."

Izabella screwed up her face. "It tastes bad, Mama."

"Eat it anyway. It's all we have."

Mikael patted Izabella's knee and offered her a bite of his bread. The emaciated little girl stared vacantly at the ceiling as she chewed. "Aren't you eating, too, Mama?"

"No, Son, you go ahead. Hopefully, there'll be more later."

Sirak held out his bread. "Mama, please take some of mine."

"Thank you. Your father would be very proud of you, of all three of you." Kristina tore off a morsel and slipped it into her mouth.

The old woman who shared their pew stumbled back empty-handed, as cries of despair echoed from the rear of the church. "God have mercy. They're starving us all to death."

Sirak held out his bread. "You can have the rest of mine, Mrs. Arulian."

"You're so precious, but you need it more than me. Vartan went to find us more."

"We should've gone with Elizabeth. Nothing's worse than starving to death," Kristina mumbled. "No food and precious little water for over a month. Help us, dear God."

Father Leonian, his expression heavy with despair, walked past the pew to the altar. He slowly mounted the steps, turned to face the crowd and raised his arms. "May I please have your attention," he called out hoarsely. "I have an announcement to make. We've distributed all the bread and rice we're likely to get today, so conserve what you've been given. I sent Vartan to look for more, but there's a severe shortage of food throughout Aleppo. Pray he finds enough for everyone."

"My baby hasn't eaten in two days," a young woman cried out frantically.

"I'm sorry," Father Leonian lamented. "Would some of you kindly share some bread with Mrs. Veorkian?"

An old woman in the pew behind the young mother leaned forward and shared a portion of hers.

"God bless you," Father Leonian called out. "As you all know by now, Aleppo has sunk into utter chaos. More and more people are arriving from the north every day, and there isn't enough food to provide for them all. And now, there's more news: The governor-general has ordered all Armenians in the city to join caravans leaving for Der-el Zor the day after tomorrow."

A murmur arose among the refugees.

"I'd rather die here than starve in the desert!" an old man shouted above the clamor. "There's nothing out there but sand!"

"And bloodthirsty bandits and child-stealing devils!" a young woman cried.

Father Leonian raised his hands. "The lieutenant governor-general promised to provide guards to protect the caravans. He also informed me that there'd be no more food brought to the church. So staying here is not an option. I've received his personal assurance that bread will be available to everyone traveling in the caravans. All of you must decide what you'll take and what you'll leave behind. Bring only what you can carry."

"We want to stay with you," a woman shouted from the back of the church.

"I'm sorry, but there's nothing more I can do to help you. I, too, have been told to join the caravans. We should all pray for God's mercy and guidance. I ask each of you to join me in an appeal to God to end the war that's brought this horrible crisis. Sunday service will be held at ten o'clock tomorrow morning. We'll have another prayer service tomorrow night in preparation for the beginning of our journey the following day. God bless us all." Father Leonian walked, head down, up the center aisle and disappeared into the vestibule.

CHAPTER 38

"Get off the road!" a gendarme shouted. "Let the wagon pass!"
Glancing up at the blazing sun, Kristina took Izabella's tiny hand and pulled her to the side of the road. Too tired and thirsty to speak, she motioned for Mikael and Sirak to wait beside her.

A wagon loaded with Ottoman soldiers rumbled past and kicked up a cloud of dust.

Sirak's hair and face were caked with dirt. He covered his nose and mouth with his hand and peered up the road. The wagon barreled past the long line of refugees and disappeared over a distant rise.

"Keep moving!" the gendarme shouted.

Kristina shepherded her children in behind another family of deportees and trudged down the center of the rutted dirt road.

Three caravans of more than a thousand people had set out early that morning from the Jdeide Quarter of Aleppo. A small contingent of gendarmes guided each group through the city. Departing from the southern gate, the long columns of women, children and elderly refugees had marched southwest through the arid countryside dotted with dry brush. Covered in dirt from head to toe and breathing air thick with dust, the refugees had bedding and precious personal effects strapped to their backs. Even the children—those old enough to walk on their own—bore pillows or other small items.

The refugees meandered for hours across an endless, scrub-covered plain. Along the way they passed through tiny villages surrounded by clusters of Turkish and Arab farms.

The refugees forged on until well after sundown. Finally, after a ten-hour march in sweltering heat, the gendarmes halted the caravan.

Kristina and her children dropped their belongings and huddled in the middle of a large group of deportees. They ate the remnants of the loaf of bread they'd received in Aleppo and fell into a deep sleep, only to be awoken by shouts from the gendarmes at the first light of morning. The refugees had half an hour to eat and repack their possessions. Then they broke camp before the sun peeked above a distant mountain range.

Traveling in eerie silence, the caravan came to a Turkish and Arab village that was surrounded by fields of late-summer wheat, barley and cotton. Desperate for water, some deportees flocked to wells and cisterns just off the road. But the gendarmes spurred them onward—even driving desperate women and children past compassionate residents who gathered along the road to offer them water.

Sirak was bone weary from the three-hour, early-morning march across the undulating Syrian plain. His spirits began to rise, however, as the once-distant foothills grew nearer. He picked up a stone from the dirt road and flung it into an adjoining field of cotton.

"Save your energy, Sirak," Kristina whispered. "Heaven only knows how far they'll force us to walk today."

Sirak glanced back at his mother and sister. Izabella's matted hair hung across her open mouth and her dress and shoes were caked with mud. She stumbled and her exhausted mother tugged her back up by the arm. Mikael struggled on a few paces behind them under the added weight of Kristina's bedroll and knapsack.

Sirak waited for his brother to catch up. "Give me Mama's blankets."

Mikael, his face streaked with perspiration and his lips chafed and cracked, bent down so Sirak could grab the bedroll. "Thank you," he gasped wearily. Adjusting the remaining load, he trudged onward up the steep grade.

The caravan turned southwest and headed toward the coastal mountains before the sun peaked in the sky. In the distance, a town, nestled at the base of a humpback hill, came gradually into view.

"Look there, Mama!" Sirak yelled excitedly. He pointed up the road ahead of the caravan. "We've made it through the desert."

"Look at the olive trees!" Mikael chimed in. "We *have* made it!"

One of the gendarmes rode back through the caravan. "Idlib ahead!" he yelled. "Stay clear of the wells. We'll stop for water at the river beyond the city."

Surrounded by olive plantations, the idyllic town was dotted with wells hewn in the rocky soil. Despite the gendarme's admonition, desperate women and children at the front of the column rushed the first wells. Gendarmes on horseback forced them away, however, before they'ed had so much as a sip. Images of cool water pervaded the thoughts of every refugee in the caravan.

The procession snaked through the town past farmers and shop-keepers who looked on impassively at the exhausted and demoralized deportees. Even those who felt pity were reluctant to meddle, fearing reprimand, or worse, from the merciless gendarmes.

One old woman rushed forward with a cup of water. She offered it to a gasping child, but a furious gendarme knocked it from her hands.

Finally, a kilometer past the town, the lead members of the caravan rounded a sweeping hillside turn and spied a small meandering spring. A group near the front, including Sirak and Mikael, broke away from the others and ran headlong to a tranquil pool.

A young woman fell to her knees. Bending down to the water, she took a drink with her cupped hand. She screwed up her face and spit the water on the ground. "It's salty!" she cried in anguish.

Sirak knelt beside her, wet his fingers and pressed them to his parched lips. The acrid water burned like fire. "It *is* salty," he muttered dejectedly.

Mikael stepped around the perimeter of the pool to the spring itself. Taking a sip from his palm, he angrily spit it out.

A cadre of gendarmes watching from the road cackled with delight. "Maybe your God can change it into wine," one guard shouted.

Mikael took his brother's arm and led him back to the road. "Don't let them know we're suffering." He looked up and froze in his tracks. "Dear God, look at Mama."

Kristina's eyes were sunken and lifeless, and her mouth hung open in despair. "I can't," she gasped. She let go of Izabella's hand. "Take her."

Mikael wrapped Kristina's arm around his shoulder. "We won't leave you, Mama. You must keep going. Sirak, you help Izabella."

The caravan continued up the road for another kilometer before the gendarme commander directed the deportees into a small pomegranate orchard. He let the deportees draw water from a cluster of small wells and everyone drank their fill. Finally, the guards herded them into a nearby grassy field.

"Find a spot to sleep for the night," one gendarme bellowed. "When you're settled, we'll pass out bread. There won't be any more for several days, so ration it carefully."

Mikael settled his mother and siblings in a small hollow. Retrieving two loaves of bread for the family, he broke one of them into pieces. He fed his mother, while Sirak tended to Izabella.

After they ate, Sirak and Mikael spread their bedding on the ground. Mikael led them in a prayer of thanks before he and Sirak fell into a deep sleep.

Kristina lay on the ground beside Izabella and cuddled the little girl to her chest. She heaved a forlorn sigh and stared up at the cloudy sky as a light rain began to fall. Rolling onto her side, she pulled the blanket over their heads, but slipped her hand out to catch the mist. She held her hand to her daughter's mouth, and Izabella sucked the moisture from her palm. Suddenly, her thoughts drifted to a happier late-summer day when she'd run laughing through the parched cotton field with Flora in a drought-ending downpour. Giddy with joy, they'd caught the rain in their hands and sipped from each other's palms before crouching gleefully to their knees among the stunted cotton plants. Kristina recalled the raindrops coursing down Flora's silky-smooth skin, and how her eyes had sparkled with delight. It was the day after her thirteenth birthday, and all had been right with the world.

"Flora, my dear Flora..." she whispered tearfully. "Why, my God? Why have you abandoned us? What have we done to deserve this hell?"

She sobbed despairingly, buried her face against Izabella's neck and drifted off to sleep.

CHAPTER 39

The gendarmes roused the deportees before dawn the next morning. Within an hour, the pitiable caravan was once again streaming along a road that meandered south through stands of olive trees.

The column descended into an uneven fertile plain dotted with hamlets and small towns. The Turks, Kurds and Arabs who populated these agricultural enclaves seemed little interested in the lowly, dejected exiles who passed silently through their remote world. The scattered remains of numerous victims from caravans that had passed before them into the heart of Syria compounded the terror of the refugees. Black and rank, and ripped to pieces by animals, these vestiges were horrifying reminders of the scope of the calamity befalling the Armenian deportees from the Ottoman Empire.

A pleasantly cool morning gave way to humidity and stifling heat. Sirak and Mikael carried the bedding and knapsacks, while Kristina and Izabella struggled to keep pace.

The caravan crossed an old bridge a little before noon. On the far side, a narrow trail wound down a rocky embankment to the river. The gendarmes at the front of the column led the deportees down to the river-bank and dismounted their horses.

"One *lira* per person!" the leader shouted. "You must pay to drink and bathe in the river."

One group of gendarmes walked their horses down to the slow-moving river, while the rest fanned out along the bank to collect the payments. Hundreds of people lined up to begrudgingly pay the fee.

"Anyone who gives water to someone who didn't pay will be whipped and left behind," the leader yelled.

Kristina thrust her hand into her dress and retrieved the roll of currency Elizabeth had given her. Furtively counting out four *lire*, she handed them to a paunchy gendarme. The man's unkempt beard was caked with road dust, and the brim of his fez was stained with sweat.

"Thank you, princess," he mocked effusively. He smiled and swept his brawny hand to allow Kristina and her children to pass.

Kristina gathered Izabella into her arms. Taking Sirak's hand, she walked down to the water.

"We don't have any money!" a woman cried out behind her. "Please, sir, just allow my children to drink. I beg you."

"If you don't pay, you can't drink," the gendarme growled. "No exceptions."

"But my children are dying of thirst!"

"That's not my concern," the man replied heartlessly.

"Mikael, take your brother and sister down to the water," Kristina whispered. She counted out three *lire* and walked back up the bank. "This is for her."

The gendarme turned with surprise. "You're as generous as you are beautiful. Okay, they can drink."

The woman nodded gratefully at Kristina and ushered her daughters down to the edge of the stream.

Kristina kicked off her shoes and set them on the bank. She helped Sirak and Mikael untie their bedrolls and knapsacks. Then, she clutched her dress and waded into the stream.

"Thank you," the woman she'd sponsored said gratefully. "I'm Anoush from Mus. How will we ever repay you?"

"It's a pleasure to meet you," Kristina replied warmly. "I'm Kristina from Seghir. I don't want repayment. It's a gift to you from God."

"May He bless you and your family."

Kristina glanced back at Sirak and Mikael frolicking in the water. Stooping down, she cleansed Izabella's hands and face and let her sip from her cupped hands, before taking a drink herself. She removed her headscarf, smoothed her long black hair behind her shoulders, and washed two-day's worth of sweat and filth from her face and arms. She opened her eyes and spotted the gendarme who'd collected the money watching her from the bank.

He grinned and scooped up water in his hands to rinse his beard. "What's your name?" he asked brashly.

"Mrs. Kazerian," Kristina replied demurely. She glanced back at Sirak and Mikael and hurriedly replaced her headscarf.

"Your *first* name?"

"Kristina."

"That's a beautiful name, befitting you. I'm Onan from Diyarbekir."

Feeling self-conscious under his lingering stare, Kristina asked, "How long before we reach Der-el Zor?"

"We're not headed to Der-el Zor."

Kristina's eyes widened with surprise. "Then where?"

"To Kahdem."

"Kahdem? Where's that?"

"A day's travel south of Damascus."

"Damascus," she repeated, letting the familiar word roll slowly over her tongue. "How long will it take?"

"Two more weeks, I'd guess, but it depends how quickly we can make it through the mountains."

"Two weeks?"

"Could be longer. Our orders are to arrive in Kahdem by the first of September, but we're already behind schedule."

"How far is Kahdem from Jerusalem?"

"Maybe a week or ten days."

"Is it a hard journey from Kahdem?" Kristina asked.

The gendarme didn't reply. Staring at her lasciviously, he imagined her with her hair clean and brushed and her features softened by healthy food.

Kristina turned and walked away from Onan. "Sirak," she called out, "stay with your brother!"

"Yes, Mama," he yelled back.

Kristina watched him wade to Mikael. They dove under the water together and headed back to the bank.

"I never imagined such a muddy little river could feel so wonderful," a woman said cheerfully.

Kristina turned to find Anoush standing behind her. Slender, with reddish-brown hair, the woman's fair complexion was marred by a large black mole on her cheek. Her preteen daughter—a strikingly pretty girl with long wavy hair and high cheekbones—was standing beside her with a younger girl. "This is my older daughter, Sima, and my younger, Alis."

Kristina smiled. "It's nice to meet you both. I love your hair, Sima. I've always wished my hair had more curl."

"Thank you," the girl replied shyly. She turned and bounded off with deer-like strides to a group of teenage girls gathered along the bank.

"Stay close, Sima," Anoush called after her.

"Yes, Mama."

Anoush watched her daughter for a few moments before turning back. "The guard favors you," she whispered.

Kristina glanced up the bank at the gendarme. He'd walked downstream to the horses and was talking with another guard. "If he does, he's wasting his time. I'm a married woman."

Anoush smiled. "So am I. But you can still be nice to him. It is a long and difficult journey."

"I'm nice to everyone," Kristina replied curtly. "But I'm not a whore."

"That's not what I meant," the woman retorted defensively. "But there's no harm in talking to him."

"Forgive me. I'm very tired and I've lost my civility. I wonder how much farther we'll travel today."

"I heard a gendarme say something about making it to the hills before we stop for the night."

Kristina looked up at the line of hills in the distance. "That far? My youngest is already struggling."

"My girls are exhausted, too, and my shoes are falling apart." She glanced at her shoes on the bank. One shoe top was separated from its sole and the other was split along the side. She gazed down the river at a cluster of tents arrayed along the opposite bank. "Maybe tonight we can sneak off and join them."

Kristina peered at the group of men standing outside one of the tents. "They're Bedouins," she whispered.

"So what? I'd rather take my chances with them than these Turkish and Kurdish gendarmes."

"No," Kristina replied, shaking her head, "the sooner we reach Kahdem, the sooner I can take my children on to Jerusalem."

"Why Jerusalem?" Anoush asked with surprise.

"My husband and son are waiting for us there."

"You're a good person, Kristina. I'll pray almighty God guides you safely to the Holy City."

"Thank you. I'll pray for you, too." Kristina turned to look at a commotion up the river. "Let's gather our children. It looks like we're leaving."

Scattered along a shallow ravine at the foot of a line of rolling foothills, the refugees lay, too tired to speak. Izabella was fast asleep beside Kristina, and her brothers were curled up on their blankets a few feet away. The gendarmes had gathered around a crackling campfire atop a narrow plateau overlooking the ravine. Their intermittent laughter echoed above the chirping crickets.

Suddenly, at the far end of the ravine, the pounding of horses' hooves reverberated above the conversations of the gendarmes. A chorus of screams tore through the darkness.

"No! Get away, devil!" a woman screamed above the din.

"Help! Gendarme! Gendarme!" yelled another. "They snatched my Lara! Help, dear God, help me!"

Kristina grabbed Izabella, clutched her to her chest and ran to Mikael and Sirak. "Run!" she screamed above the clamor.

Scampering headlong up the embankment toward the gendarme encampment, they made it nearly to the top before a rider on horseback overtook them. Leaping from his horse, the lean, mustachioed man grabbed Izabella's arm and tried to wrench her free.

"No!" Kristina screamed. She clung desperately to her daughter's waist as the fierce-eyed bandit struggled to tear her away.

"Let go of my sister!" Sirak shouted. He ran at the raider and hurled a rock that glanced off the intruder's black turban.

Mikael jumped on the man's back, but the bandit twirled him off to the ground. Then, a single gunshot rang out.

The gendarme, Onan, was standing behind them holding his smoking pistol. He pointed the gun at the bandit. "Let her go."

The bandit stepped away, but held up his knife and glared at Onan.

"Choose another!" Onan barked in Arabic.

The bandit sprinted to his horse and rode off at a gallop into the ravine.

Sirak watched him ride toward another group on the bank of the stream. Shrieking with terror, the refugees scattered in all directions. The bandit rode after a hysterical young woman and wrenched a young child from her arms. He galloped out the mouth of the ravine and disappeared into the night.

"Why didn't you stop them?" Kristina demanded incredulously.

"We can't stop them. There are too many."

"You have a gun," she persisted angrily. "You could've shot him."

"You're right, I could've shot him, but then five hundred, or even five thousand, Kurdish tribesmen would've returned in the night to kill us all."

Kristina shook her head in frustration. She picked up Izabella and walked away. "Come on, Mikael, bring your brother."

"Not even a thank you?" Onan called out.

Kristina turned back to the gendarme and a gust of wind rippled her headscarf. "I'm sorry," she said sincerely. "Thank you for helping us."

Onan smiled indulgently. "You're welcome."

"Will they return?"

"Yes, almost certainly—maybe tonight or maybe tomorrow. There are many Kurdish villages in these hills. I'll try to watch out for you and your children, but you must sleep nearer to the campfires."

"We are grateful." Kristina took Sirak's hand and headed back down the ravine.

The crowd was abuzz with terror. Weaving their way through dozens of women and children, they found their belongings scattered across the ground.

"Get your things," Kristina called out to her sons. "Let's go up there by the gendarmes." Kristina turned and spotted a woman crouched on the ground. "Anoush? Are you okay?"

Crying hysterically, her head bobbing up and down, Anoush hugged her younger daughter to her chest. "They took her!" she gasped. "They took my Sima!"

Kristina squatted beside the woman and comforted her. Then, she helped her to her feet. "Come with us. It'll be safer by the guards' camp."

Kristina, Anoush and their children picked their way silently through the crowd of refugees. Several women were wailing demonstratively over the body of a woman who'd been killed fending off an attacker.

Sirak's thoughts turned to his older sister. "God, please help Flora wherever she is," he whispered.

Mikael took Sirak's arm. "Are you okay?"

Sirak nodded his head. "Yes."

"It's okay to be frightened," Mikael whispered.

Sirak looked up. Mikael's deep-set black eyes were nearly invisible in the pitch-black night. "I'm not frightened. If that bandit comes back, I'll find an even bigger rock and bash him in the head. But I miss Flora and I miss Papa and Alek and I miss Stepannos and Uncle Bedros. I miss all of our family members and I miss the farm. I miss the way we lived before."

"I miss them, too. We all do. But we still have Mama, Izabella and each other. Let's stay with Mama and Izabella."

The boys trudged up the rocky incline beneath the gendarme encampment. The campfires flickered in the gusting breeze and the guards' unaffected laughter echoed down the ravine.

CHAPTER 40

The gendarmes woke the refugees at sunrise the next morning. They guided the caravan south toward Kahdem, along hilly trails that gradually turned into high desert. The road baked in sweltering heat. The caravan was strung out over a kilometer as it wound along the windswept road and crossed an ancient bridge. A short time later, they skirted the ruins of a city that dated back to the Roman Empire.

Mikael mopped his brow and pressed a handkerchief over his mouth to filter the dust. He reached for Izabella. "Mama, let me carry her."

Izabella stared vacantly at her brother. Her matted hair tumbled across sunken eyes and a blistered red mouth.

Kristina passed him the dazed little girl. She glanced over her shoulder as Sirak trudged out of the switchback a dozen yards behind them. Kristina held out her hand.

"I'm so thirsty, Mama."

"We all are, Son. Hopefully we'll reach the next stream soon."

"When will that be?"

"I don't know. Soon, I hope."

Sirak plodded along beside his mother and stared at the uneven road beneath his feet. He looked up at the sound of a chorus of screams from refugees ahead of them and spotted a band of men streaking down the hillside on horseback.

"Bedouins!" a woman screamed.

Kristina grabbed Izabella and ran into brush in a dry riverbed beside the road. Sirak and Mikael ducked in behind her. Sirak peeked out at the bedlam on the road ahead of them.

A pair of riders chased a large group of terrified women and children into the riverbed. Leaping to the ground, one Bedouin grabbed a cowering teenager, forced her onto his horse and trotted away.

Sirak spun around in horror at the echo of horses' hooves behind them.

Red-faced Onan pulled up his horse and drew his pistol. "Don't be afraid! I'll protect you!" He pointed his pistol in the air and spun toward the road as the last remnants of the raiders raced up the hillside and disappeared over the summit. He shoved the pistol into his holster. "They're gone now. Get back to the road. The sooner we make the hills, the safer we'll be."

As the day wore on, the caravan was raided several more times—mostly by Bedouins, but also by Kurds. The bandits sought out the youngest and the prettiest to spirit away. One band shadowed the wary refugees for hours and waited for the opportunity to swoop down on harried stragglers. Even meager resistance was met with overwhelming brutality.

Onan rode close to Kristina and her children. At one point, he galloped off to sort out a problem, but he returned a short time later. Kristina welcomed his presence, but worried silently about his intentions.

Sirak and Mikael spun around at the report of a pistol but relaxed at the sight of one of the gendarmes retrieving a plover he'd shot in the field beside the road. The man whooped with delight and swung the bird in a circle above his head, as another gendarme rode out to congratulate him.

Sirak glanced at Mikael and cringed. His brother's chest was heaving and he was whimpering unintelligibly. "Sit down on the rock, Mikael. You can rest here until they make us go on."

"I can't take anymore," Mikael muttered. "I'm losing my mind."

"Sit down. You just need rest."

Sirak understood his brother's angst. He too felt the sense of foreboding arising from the unremitting attacks and relentless prodding of the gendarmes. He too suffered the hunger pangs and the searing thirst and exhaustion from the seemingly endless trudge through the incessant heat and humidity. He too fought the disconcerting feeling that somehow death might offer a welcome respite from this march of despair. Sirak sat beside his brother and mopped the perspiration from his brow. "We can make it, Mikael. Don't give up. Mama and Izabella need us. Another hour at the most, and then we can rest. I'll carry Mama's bedding the rest of the way."

Mikael looked up from the ground and nodded. "Papa was right about you," he gasped. "You are a rock."

Sirak gave Mikael a wry smile. "He said that about you, too. Come on, let's go."

Kristina limped through a broad turn clutching Izabella to her side. Both of them were nearly delirious from exhaustion. Sirak and Mikael, a few paces ahead, struggled under the weight of the bedrolls and knapsacks. Suddenly, Izabella collapsed.

Kristina tried to pull her to her feet, but the little girl refused to budge. "Izabella, you must get up. Mama can't carry you."

Izabella was covered head to toe in dirt and her dress was tattered and torn. Her shoes were disintegrated slips of leather. She was a pitiful shadow of the little girl who'd left Diyarbekir two months earlier. "No, Mama, my legs hurt. I can't."

Kristina stooped over her. "Get up, Izabella!" she demanded. " I won't leave you behind. Come on, get up."

"No, Mama," the little girl whined.

Sirak glanced back. He tugged at Mikael's sleeve and the two of them turned back.

"Mama," Mikael said, "I can carry her, but not with the blankets, too."

Kristina nodded her head and Mikael dropped the bedrolls on the ground.

"What's wrong with her?" an ill-tempered voice called out. It was the gendarme, Onan.

"She can't go any farther," Kristina replied tearfully. "We just need a few minutes to rest."

"We can't stop! Leave her."

"No!" Kristina screamed. "We will stay here with her."

Onan peered back at the empty stretch of road behind them. He handed Kristina his leather water flask. "Let her drink."

Kristina pressed the vessel to Izabella's lips and the little girl took several sips.

"Not too much at once," Onan cautioned. "She'll get a bellyache."

Kristina returned the flask. "Thank you."

"You and your sons can drink, too. Quickly!"

Kristina handed the flask to Sirak and Mikael. Each of them took a few sips and passed the flask back to Kristina. She hurriedly took a drink and held the flask up to Onan.

"Please, sir, can't she ride with you?" Kristina pleaded.

"It's forbidden. Let me have your bedding and I'll strap it to my horse. Take turns carrying her, and we'll stop for the night at a river two kilometers ahead."

"Thank you, thank you," Kristina said gratefully. She passed him Mikael's bundle and the gendarme tied it to his own.

Mikael lifted Izabella and twirled her onto his back. He walked slowly up the road after Sirak.

About an hour later, the caravan came to the rivulet Onan had mentioned. Kristina led her children down to the bottom of a shallow gorge, and they drank and bathed in the slow-moving river before choosing a grassy hollow within a stand of poplar trees beneath the gendarme's camp to spend the night. Mikael and Sirak unrolled their blankets on the ground, and Kristina prepared a nest of foliage for herself and Izabella. Many other exhausted women and children staked out plots on the gentle slope beneath the gendarmes' campfires.

The children fell asleep immediately, but Kristina found herself restlessly apprehensive about the challenges that would test them come the new day. She lay on her back gazing at the glittering stars through the branches of a tree.

Before too long, the rhythmic music of stringed instruments and tambourines, accompanied by the clapping and laughter of gypsy women festooned in colorful costumes, filtered down from the gendarmes' camp. Kristina watched them dance with abandon around the campfire. Several gypsy children peddled food and handmade wares to gendarmes standing nearby.

The lively music and laughter wafted on the breeze for hours before the revelry faded into the chirps of crickets and the trickle of water in the nearby stream. Kristina was just dozing off when a tug at her arm roused her. Bolting upright, she found Onan bending down over her. His eyes were narrow slits and his breath reeked of cheap wine.

"Come help me with the horses," he slurred.

"The horses?" Kristina asked dubiously. "Why?"

Onan grabbed her wrist and yanked her up from the blanket. "Come help me!"

Kristina realized Onan's intentions at once. She tried to pull away but he jerked her against his chest.

"You or your daughter," he whispered. "Do you understand?"

Kristina nodded submissively.

Onan grabbed the back of Kristina's neck and marched her through the mass of deportees asleep on the ground. She locked eyes with an old woman lying by herself on the ground, who then closed her eyes and pretended not to see what was happening.

The Turk forced Kristina down an embankment and into a stand of brush on the riverbank. He eagerly groped her breasts and ground his pelvis against her backside. He pushed her to the ground and jerked up her dress. "Finally," he moaned.

Kristina tried to push him off. "No, please!"

"Stop fighting me!" Onan pressed his forearm to her throat and she dropped her arms to the ground. Pushing down his pants, he rolled between her legs and tore away her undergarments. He grasped her shoulders and forced himself inside her. "Yes," he moaned drunkenly.

Kristina emitted a muffled cry, and tears streaked down her face.

CHAPTER 41

August 17, 1915
Hamah, Syria

S irak struggled through a steep switchback and kicked a rock over a narrow ledge at the side of the road. Stopping beside his brother, he gazed out over a lush, meandering river that coursed through the valley far below. Ancient, rock-walled ruins on the cliff below them stood as silent vestiges of a bygone era.

Mikael lifted Izabella off his shoulders and peered back at the line of deportees laboring up the hill. "Where's Mama?" he asked. Kristina stumbled out of the switchback a moment later.

"Wait here," Sirak said to Mikael. He dropped his bedroll on the ground, shuffled down the uneven incline and reached for her hand.

Tears were streaming down Kristina's face. She looked up and turned away.

"Mama, what's wrong?"

"It's nothing, my son. I'm just very tired. Go help your brother and Izabella, and I'll catch up with you after I relieve myself."

"Mama, you're nearly to the top. We'll wait for you in those rocks up there. We're all going to make it, mama. The gendarme told me we'd reach Hamah soon. From there it is only a week to Kahdem."

"Which gendarme?" she asked suspiciously.

"Onan, the Turk."

Kristina clenched her jaw. She glanced behind her and squeezed his arm. "Stay away from Onan. He's evil."

"Why, Mama? He gave us water and helped when Izabella was too tired to go on."

"Listen to me! Onan is a wicked devil. If anything happens to me, you must protect Izabella from him and the other gendarmes. Those fiends will steal her virtue. Do you understand?"

Sirak stared at her confusedly.

"Do whatever you can to protect her from them. Slip her away in the night or hide along the road until someone else comes along. Do not trust them. Do you understand me?"

Sirak swallowed. "Yes, mama."

"Okay, then, go back to Izabella and Mikael. I'll catch up soon."

The caravan wound down the mountain along a narrow, dusty road under a blistering sky. Kristina walked alone behind a large group of deportees. She lowered her head to her chest and stared at the ground when a rider overtook her from behind.

"This is the hottest day yet," Onan muttered with a sigh. "Tonight, God willing, we'll sleep along the banks of the Orontes in Hamah."

"Leave me alone," Kristina blurted out angrily. She darted ahead fretfully, but stumbled in a rut and fell to her knees. Gathering herself, she rushed after the others.

Onan trotted up beside her. "I've been thinking about you. Bathe with me in the river tonight. It will be a beautiful evening."

"Leave me alone!"

"Trust me, Kristina. Nobody will know we are lovers. You can rely on me to defend your honor. I swear to it."

Kristina whirled to face him. "We are not lovers! You forced me!"

Onan dismounted his horse and slapped her face. "Shut up! You've all survived this journey only because you interest me. How many others have lost their children to thirst or bandits?" He grabbed Kristina's hair and pulled her close. "You will submit willingly the next time I come for you. Otherwise, I'll shoot your sons and spoil your daughter. Do you hear me?"

Kristina glared at Onan as he held her tightly by her hair. "I hear you."

Onan shoved her away. "You see? Before long you will ask for me."

The precipitous trek down the winding trail to the valley floor suddenly took a turn for the worse as the caravan plodded through a series of mud flats and marshes that paralleled the river. Beset by swarms of gnats and flies, the women and children labored along the road toward Hamah. The gendarmes protected themselves from the biting insects with netted head covers. Several refugees were overcome by the oppressive heat and humidity and were left behind.

Late that afternoon, the caravan made its way into cultivated lands just to the south of Hamah. The gendarmes allowed the deportees to purchase bread and cheese from traders who ventured out of the city to meet them. They bathed and rested along the picturesque, tree-lined banks of the Orontes River by an ancient water wheel that churned in the current.

The women and children had just settled down to sleep when a band of Bedouins on horseback sent them fleeing for their lives into the river and the neighboring field. One gendarme made a halfhearted effort to stop the assault by firing his weapon into the air, but the rest were content to watch amusedly as the raiders assaulted the hapless refugees.

Kristina clutched Izabella to her chest and ran for the water. "Run this way, Mikael and Sirak!" She struggled into the waist-deep river and one of the raiders rode in after her. She screamed in terror and stooped low in the water to duck his grasp.

The Bedouin turned his horse to make another pass but a rock hit him flush in the side of the head. He spun his horse around.

Sirak and Mikael were hurling a barrage of rocks from the bank. One struck the raider's leg and another glanced off his horse. He drew his sword to charge, then, suddenly, spotted an easier mark. He galloped downstream, swept up a frantic young woman and rode off across a wheat field.

The attack ended as quickly as it had begun. The mother who'd been forced to abandon one twin had her remaining infant torn from her arms. Several more women and children were also abducted. The gendarmes rounded up the dispersed deportees who now numbered fewer than half the original number.

Kristina and her children filed past Onan a few minutes later. He stared smugly down from his horse. "This time you were lucky," he called out.

Sirak and Mikael glanced up warily at the gendarme. Kristina grasped Izabella's hand and quickly walked away. This time, she didn't look for a spot near the gendarme's encampment. Instead, she led her children, along with Anoush and her daughter, Alis, down the riverbank to a small clearing.

"Mama, the flies are biting me," Izabella sobbed.

"Keep your face covered with the blanket."

"But I can't breathe."

"Do the best you can," Kristina whispered. Kristina tossed the end of the blanket over the little girl's ankles. Brushing a swarm of flies from her own face, she glanced over her shoulder at Sirak and Mikael. The boys were lying side by side along the riverbank covered head to toe with bedding. She peered through the darkness at a silhouette that passed in front of the flickering gendarme campfire in the distance. Lying back on the cold ground, she pulled the top of the blanket over her face and clutched Izabella to her side.

Kristina lay beneath her blanket listening to the trickling water of a nearby eddy for the better part of an hour. The sound of footsteps splashing through the water set her heart pounding. She peeked out from beneath her blanket and spotted two men creeping along the embankment. One of the men bent down and peeled the bedding off a sleeping refugee. He grabbed the woman by the arm and yanked her up from the ground. The gendarme smothered her cries with a hand across her mouth and forced her up river along the bank.

Kristina cringed when the second gendarme turned in her direction.

Slowly making his way though a cowering group of women and children, he glanced back and forth as he walked.

Kristina recognized his profile in the moonlight.

Onan walked directly toward them. Kristina's heart pounded, but she knew what she must do. She got up and, pushing Izabella into Mikael's lap, whispered, "Take care of your sister."

"Where are you going, Mama?" Sirak asked.

"The gendarme wants to talk to me. Stay here. I'll be back in a little while."

Onan glared at Kristina through the darkness, then bent down and grabbed Anoush by the arm. He yanked her up from the ground, but she clung to her daughter's hand. "Let go of her!" he growled.

Anoush's eyes bulged with terror. She dropped Alis' hand and Onan marched her away up the riverbank.

"Mama!" Alis called out hysterically. "Come back, Mama!"

Kristina took hold of Alis' arm. "Stay here with us and your mama will be back soon," she said, holding her close.

Nearly an hour passed before Anoush tiptoed back down the riverbank. Her hair was disheveled and her already tattered dress was torn. She hung her head in shame.

Kristina took the diminutive young woman into her arms. Anoush pressed her face against Kristina's shoulder. "He hurt me," she sobbed.

Kristina patted her back. "Come cleanse yourself in the river, and I'll sew your dress."

CHAPTER 42

Early the next morning, the weakened caravan resumed its wretched southerly journey through Syria. Day after day, the gendarmes drove the women, children and elderly along the seemingly endless road. They traveled beyond Hims through shrub and woodlands fed by the Orontes River, and then back into the unforgiving Mesopotamian desert, before heading west of Damascus along an ancient Roman road.

Depleted by starvation, thirst and ongoing attacks by tribesmen, the deportee numbers had dwindled. Kristina focused on the everyday task of finding sufficient food and water for her children. Driven by devotion to their families, she and Anoush forged a bond of mutual support and friendship. Their hours were filled with despair and the ongoing struggle to complete the day's journey in safety. At night they were gripped with apprehension and terror as the gendarmes forced the women and children to satisfy their whims and desires. Each gendarme had his favorites, a forced harem of sorts, to fulfill his perversions. Some men favored the younger women or girls, while others fancied the boys.

Kristina and Anoush, along with an older teenage girl named Lucine, came to depend on Onan for provisions and protection out of necessity born of fear. He supplied water and scraps of food, and protected them and their children from the other gendarmes and the marauding tribes they encountered along the journey. An unspoken pact—a contract of sorts—developed between them. Onan always rode nearby to protect "his women and children," and they served him at his beck and call.

All three women detested the loathsome Turk. They hated his fetid breath and repulsive body odor. They despised his callousness and disrespectfulness, and the way he took pleasure in humiliating them. But each woman realized that the brute's contentment was the key to her survival and, in the case of Kristina and Anoush, their children's survival, too.

On a hot and muggy night in late August, the caravan camped on the outskirts of a desert town three kilometers southwest of Damascus. The caravan leader announced that they were less than a two-day journey from Kahdem. Just after dark, once the gendarmes finished a supper prepared by several deportee women, a band of gypsies rode into camp. Peddling supplies and crafts, most of them left a short time later, but a troupe of musicians and dancers stayed behind to entertain the gendarmes. The encampment, positioned on the sloping edge of a broad desert plateau, was soon reverberating with rhythmic Roma music and the shouts and laughter of the performers and the guards.

Anoush looked up from her blanket. "Are you okay?" she whispered.

"I'm fine," Kristina replied with a sigh, "but the gypsies brought wine. Do you remember the last time?"

"Yes," Anoush replied solemnly. "That was the night Alis' young friend, Zagiri, was raped."

Kristina glanced over her shoulder. Sirak and Mikael were asleep on their blanket a short distance away. "That was the first time Onan forced himself on me, too."

A chorus of cheers echoed from the encampment.

Anoush peered up at the sky. "I wonder what our lives will be like in this place called Kahdem? Maybe there will be good people there—decent people who care about the suffering of children."

"I pray for that every minute of every day. Surely God has kept us all alive for something besides unbearable misery and heartbreak."

"Maybe there isn't a God after all, or at least not a God who cares about us."

"There is a God," Kristina whispered. "I feel him here with us now. I believe that passage in Romans: *All things God works for the good of those who love Him, who have been called according to His purpose.* Some day we'll understand all of this. It may not be in this life, but someday we'll all understand why we've had to suffer."

"I wish I had your faith," Anoush whispered admiringly.

"My husband, Mourad, gave me this gift. He taught me to have the faith to accept whatever life brings us, knowing, without question, that the best is yet to come for our children and us. Someday we'll all be together again in heaven, with Jesus."

Anoush stared into Kristina's eyes and smiled. "I pray you're right. In my heart I do know that God brought you and me together. Regardless of what may happen in Kahdem, I'll always be thankful for your friendship."

"And I yours," Kristina whispered. She glanced back at Sirak, Mikael and Izabella sleeping peacefully on the ground. "Today, here, we are all blessed."

Music reverberated from the gendarmes' encampment for several hours before the lutes and tambourines finally fell silent. Drunken laughter filtered down from the plateau for a while longer before the night grew eerily quiet, except for a sporadic gust of wind that whistled through the dwarf shrubs dotting the desert floor.

Kristina lay awake anticipating Onan's drunken arrival, but oddly, neither he nor any of the other gendarmes so much as showed their faces among the scattered deportees. Finally, she drifted off to sleep.

Three hours later, the pounding of hooves jarred Kristina awake. She bolted upright on her blanket. More than a hundred Bedouin warriors came galloping from the west across the sandy plateau. They charged into the encampment brandishing swords and erupted into a chilling chorus of cries and shouts. *"Allahu Akbar! Allahu Akbar!"* Swinging their swords at the hapless gendarmes who ran from their tents, they rode swiftly through the camp slaughtering everyone in their path, except for a bevy of terrified gypsy courtesans who were swept up by trailing riders. A gunshot rang out, but it was only a fleeting sign of gendarme resistance.

"Oh, my God!" Kristina gasped. She jumped to her feet and rushed to her children. "Mikael and Sirak, run!" She grabbed Izabella and stumbled headlong into the darkness.

Sirak threw his knapsack over his shoulder and stumbled after Mikael and his mother through ankle-deep sand.

A large group of Bedouin tribesmen galloped down the sandy slope toward the refugees. Pleas for mercy filled the night. Killing everyone in their path, the Arabs galloped off in all directions to chase down the scattered refugees.

Kristina turned her ankle in loose sand and stumbled to her knees. Getting back to her feet, she hoisted Izabella on her shoulders and ran to a stand of brush. Mikael and Sirak ducked in behind her.

She peered through the darkness at the Bedouins attacking the refugees. Two Bedouins broke away from the others and galloped directly toward them. "Oh, my God, they've spotted us. Sirak, stay here with your sister while Mikael and I try to draw them away. Don't move from this spot until they're all gone. Do you understand?"

Sirak nodded. His eyes were transfixed in terror.

"Mikael, run with me to those rocks!" Kristina whispered.

Kristina and Mikael dashed into the open and made a beeline for a dry riverbed. They only made it half way before the riders swooped down on them. One of the Bedouins flashed his sword and Mikael crumbled to the ground. The other rider jumped down and grabbed Kristina.

"Murderer!" Kristina screamed. She scratched fiercely at the Bedouin's face.

The warrior subdued her with a powerful slap to the face. He forced her onto his horse and rode off into the night.

Izabella peered out from the brush. "Mama," she whimpered.

Sirak drew his sister to his chest. Averting his eyes from the carnage, he brushed tears from her cheek. "Christ our God, help Mama and Mikael. Help me to take care of Izabella. Amen."

The early rays of the sun rose over the western horizon and a bone-chilling wind gusted through the brush. In the muted light, Sirak watched in fear as three black-clad men with gleaming white turbans rode through the erstwhile gendarme camp.

Sirak glanced at his sister. Izabella was lying on her back staring up at the sky. She'd been that way for hours—trance-like, not uttering so much as a sigh. He squeezed her hand. "I'm here, Sister," he whispered.

One of the riders, a younger man with a bushy mustache and beard, rode toward them from the campsite. Pausing beside the body of one of the deportees, he headed out to Mikael's corpse.

Sirak watched the rider dismount and kneel beside his brother's body. The man remounted his horse and gazed to the west. After a moment, he trotted directly toward the stand of brush concealing Sirak and Izabella.

"Izabella," Sirak whispered, "the bad men are coming!" He pulled her up to her knees.

The rider spotted their movement in the brush and dismounted his horse. He was on them in an instant.

"Hello, little ones," he called out in Arabic. His voice was melodious and gentle. "Don't be afraid. I won't hurt you. I'm Ammar of the *Muwah-hidun*. What's your name?"

Sirak stood up in the rocks. The man's smile was warm and gentle. In an instant, Sirak knew he could trust the swarthy stranger. "I'm Sirak. This is my sister, Izabella."

"Are you hurt?"

Sirak pointed at Mikael's body. "No, but the bad men killed my brother, and they took our mama."

The man stared back sadly. "You can't stay out here alone. How about if I take you back to my house and ask my wife to make you something to eat? Then we'll try to find your mama."

Sirak contemplated the offer for several moments. Then he glanced at Izabella. "I can't leave my sister."

"There's room on my horse for both of you."

Sirak peered up at the man. He glanced at his sister. "Okay, as long as she can come, too."

Ammar stepped into the brush. He patted Sirak on the shoulder reassuringly and picked up Izabella. Carrying her in his arms, he set her astride his horse and remounted. He pulled Sirak up behind him and trotted back to the other riders.

Ammar and the children rode west for nearly an hour before beginning a slow ascent into the mountains along a narrow winding road. Their route paralleled pictorial hillsides blanketed with olive and apple trees heavy with immature fruit. Nearby fields were ablaze with golden wheat swaying in the gusting breeze.

The tribesmen parted ways at a fork in the road and Ammar trotted up a weedy trail to a modest farmhouse nestled in a stand of olive trees. Izabella was sitting astride the horse in front of Ammar. Sirak rode behind the Druze, clutching his waist with one arm and the knapsack with the other.

Three girls wearing long black dresses and white scarves hurried out the front door. A middle-aged woman in similar dress followed them outside a moment later. They all crowded around the horse.

"Who are these children, Papa?" the oldest girl yelled.

"This is Sirak and his sister, Izabella. I found them stranded in the desert and they've had a terrible shock. They're Armenian refugees who escaped a murderous attack on their caravan. The Bedouins killed their brother and rode off with their mother."

"Poor little dears," the woman cooed. She lifted Izabella down from the horse and cradled her in her arms. "Fatima, go heat water on the stove. Nazira and Layla, go find her some clothes in the shed behind the house."

"Yes, Mama." Nazira replied. She hurried off around the side of the house.

The woman carried Izabella to the front door of the house.

"Azusa," Ammar called after his wife, "what about the boy?"

Azusa rolled her eyes. "Why don't you find him something to eat? I'll bathe this one first, and then her brother. Ali's wife probably has some of her sons' old clothing. Make yourself useful and go find something that fits him." She disappeared through the door cradling Izabella.

It didn't take long for Fatima to heat a large pot of water. Using olive oil and water, Azusa washed encrusted dirt and grime from Izabella's tangled hair. She held the little girl in her lap and scrubbed filth off her face, meticulously dabbing at her eyes and around the base of her nose.

Izabella was expressionless and somber. She stared up at Azusa's benevolent face, but made nary a sound.

Azusa wrung out the washcloth and scrubbed at Izabella's hands. "Oh, my precious child, what have your sad little eyes seen? It was God's will Ammar found you and you're safe now. One day, God willing, you'll smile again."

Izabella and Sirak did smile again. For fourteen years Ammar and Azusa cared for them as if for their own children. Sirak labored beside Ammar in the olive groves, apple orchards and wheat fields. In the dormant months, Sirak attended the Druze school in the village.

Azusa and her daughters doted on Izabella, but the little girl never recovered fully.

Ammar and Azusa called themselves *Muwahhidun*. One is not able to convert to Druzism; one must be born into it. Since Sirak and Izabella would never be accepted into their adoptive parents' religion, Azusa encouraged them to read the Bible Kristina had given to Sirak. It was difficult, however, as their understanding of the Armenian language was limited.

When Sirak was on the verge of passing from boyhood into adulthood, a life-altering event thrust him from his adoptive home. This experience, like the others before it, took him to a place he never expected to go....

CHAPTER 43

June 16, 1996
Richmond Heights, Ohio

Keri rapped on the door and glanced back at David and Michael. His sons were gathering up half a dozen old newspapers scattered across the yard.

David set his stack on the top step. "Maybe Papa Sirak should cancel the newspaper if he's not going to read it."

"He loves the paper. He must not be feeling well." Keri knocked on the door again. Standing on his tiptoes, he peered over the curtains into the darkened kitchen.

Michael set his newspapers on top of David's. "Maybe he forgot."

"I just reminded him on Thursday. Let's go around back."

They walked around the side of the house and headed down the weed-studded brick driveway. Rounding a twisted dogwood tree, they spied a lone figure slumped in a lounge chair in the shade of a massive oak tree.

Keri rushed across the yard and gently gripped his father's arm. "Papa," he whispered.

Sirak awoke with a start. "What is it?" he gasped.

"Happy Father's Day, Papa. The boys and I are here to take you to lunch."

"It's Sunday already?" Sirak wiped the sleep from his eyes and turned in his seat. "Hello, Michael. Hello, David."

"Happy Father's Day, Papa Sirak," David replied. "You don't look well."

"I've had a fever the last few days, but I'm a little better today. I don't think I should go out, though."

"That's fine, Papa," Keri said. "We'll stay here. Do you have anything to eat?"

"I've got *Choereg* bread in the freezer and a couple cans of beef stew."

"That's perfect. Let me help you into the house."

Keri helped his father up from the chair and led him to the back porch. David and Michael followed them into the malodorous summer room. Several garbage bags were strewn across the floor.

"Open some windows, David," Keri said. "Michael, could you take those trash bags out to the curb?" He led Sirak through the living room and into the kitchen and seated him at the table. Then he opened a window and set about preparing the stew.

Keri ladled out four bowls of beef stew and David helped him carry them to the table.

Michael was chattering about the upcoming sixth game of the NBA finals between the Chicago Bulls and Seattle Supersonics.

Keri sat down beside Sirak. "There you go. Be careful: it's hot."

Sirak slurped from his spoon. "It's good. I haven't eaten much these last few days."

"Why didn't you call me, Papa? You call me from now on if you get sick. Okay?"

"You're busy, Son. I hate to bother you."

"It's no bother. I want to know...or do we need to think about other living arrangements?"

"Okay," Sirak groaned, "I'll call next time."

"Should I cancel the paper for you? All the issues from the last week are out on the porch."

"No, I'll go through them once I get better."

Conversation was subdued at lunch. David and Michael didn't know what to talk about in the face of their grandfather's obvious infirmity. Keri talked mostly about the summer activities of his grandchildren. Sirak listened attentively and asked several questions. Finally, a hush fell over the table.

Michael glanced questioningly at his father. Keri nodded.

"Papa Sirak," Michael began, "I've been thinking about everything you told us about Anatolia and Syria. I can't get it out of my mind. I have lots of questions. Do you feel like talking?"

Sirak smiled at his grandson. "I think I can manage. What do you want to know?"

"Why did you leave Syria?"

Sirak folded his hands on the table and let out a long sigh. "I fell in love."

Michael glanced at his father. "You fell in love? You told us that you'd betrayed Ammar's trust."

"Yes, I did. You see, I fell in love with a Druze girl. It was forbidden."

Michael frowned. "Did you get her pregnant?"

"Michael!" his father scolded.

Sirak patted Keri's hand. "It's okay; it's a valid question, but no, that is not what happened. I noticed her for the first time at a community gathering when she was fourteen years old. I was sixteen and couldn't stop looking at her. We exchanged glances for months after that before I finally got up enough nerve to speak. Even then, all we managed was a self-conscious hello." Sirak smiled. "She had eyes that sparkled with joy and the sweetest temperament. My Druze sisters thought she was rather plain, but, to me, she was a vision of loveliness.

"As the years passed, pining glances and brief conversations budded into forbidden romance. We shared our first kiss when she was seventeen, and when she was eighteen—aided by her favorite brother, Umar—we began to meet every few weeks at a secluded oasis in the desert. We held hands and exchanged a kiss or two, nothing more than that. After a while, we fell helplessly in love and began making foolish plans to elope to Damascus."

"How old were you when you made those plans?" Keri asked.

Sirak's smile faded into sadness. "I was twenty. But then, in the summer of 1928, when I turned twenty-one and she was eighteen, my life shattered to pieces…"

CHAPTER 44

September 3, 1928
Just outside of Rashayya, Syria

Sirak's muscles bulged under the weight of an oversized bundle of wheat. He leaned over the tailgate of the wagon, tossed the bundle atop a stack, and brushed the chaff from his cloak. Looking up, his eyes scanned the hillside to the grassy plain of Rashayya Al Wadi and followed the meandering river to the south toward far-off Mount Hermon.

Standing erect and wiry, with broad shoulders that tapered to a narrow waist, Sirak's sun-bronzed face was framed with a neatly-trimmed mustache and beard. His head was covered with a white turban and the ends wrapped loosely around his neck. His face wasn't particularly handsome, at least by *Muwahhidun* standards, but he'd nonetheless grown into a vigorous and self-confident young man. His maturity was attributable in large measure to the nurturing and love he received from the man and woman he'd affectionately called *Abee* and *Ummee* for over fourteen years.

Ammar walked from the house wearing a baggy white *shirwal* pants that were tight at the ankles above his sandals. He wore a traditional red and white-checkered *kufiya* on his head. "Are you ready, Sirak?"

"Yes, *Abee.*"

"You can drive."

Sirak untied the horse and scampered up the side of the wagon. Sitting atop a stack of wheat, he turned the wagon in a tight circle and pulled to a stop beside Ammar.

The front door of the house burst open and Azusa rushed outside wearing a traditional dark blue dress with a white headscarf and shawl. "Where are you going? The wedding starts in less than two hours."

"We'll be home in plenty of time," Ammar called back to her. "I promised Mohamed a wagonload of wheat by Saturday, and I can't do it tomorrow."

"Be back in an hour," she huffed. "Sirak must change his clothes, even if you don't."

Ammar laughed and waved his arm. "Don't worry. If we're late, I'll ask Ali and his wife to pick you up."

"Don't *be* late!" she barked.

Sirak drove the wagon down a steep switchbacked grade and skirted a beautifully terraced hillside olive grove. Comfortable in their silence, neither man spoke over the clatter of the wheels until they reached the dry riverbed that formed the southern boundary of Ammar's farm. Sirak, his eyes squeezed to slits, reveled in the warmth of the noonday sun.

"How does the Rashayya School suit you?" Ammar hollered above the clatter of the wagon.

"Just fine. Why do you ask?"

"No reason in particular; but I heard talk from the men in the village that Abdullah Mousa's son and some of his friends had harsh words for you. What's the boy's name?"

"Barek, the green-eyed fool. That idiot's jealousy knows no bounds."

"Have you given him a reason for jealousy?"

Sirak glanced at Ammar. "Of course not. I've known his betrothed for many years, but I haven't spoken to her since their engagement was announced four months ago."

"What's the girl's name?"

"Yasmin; she's Ezekiel Jumblatt's daughter."

"Oh, Umar's sister. Do you gaze at her?"

"No, not at her in particular. I might look at a group she happens to be standing with, but when did that become a sin?"

Ammar stared amusedly at Sirak for several moments.

Sirak held the reins tightly through a sharp turn and then glanced at Ammar. "What?"

"What does this Yasmin look like?"

"Like a girl," Sirak replied curtly. He turned his eyes to the trail and ignored Ammar's persistent stare.

"Is she pretty?"

"I guess some might think so, but Nazira says there are many prettier girls in the village."

"I'm sure I've seen her. Describe her to me."

"I can't describe her. She just looks like a girl."

"Is her skin light or dark?"

"Light."

"And her eyes?"

Sirak sighed exasperatedly. "They're green."

"How about her hair?"

"Brown."

"Light or dark, short or long?"

"She has long, light-brown hair, but she usually wears it tied up."

"Is she fat?"

"No, if anything, she's on the thin side."

"Let me ask you this. If you haven't looked at her in particular, how is it you can describe her so thoroughly?"

"Whoa!" Sirak barked. He reined the horses to a stop in the middle of the trail and turned to face Ammar. "Yasmin is friendly with Layla and Izabella, and when they were younger, they played together after the meetings on Thursday nights. So, naturally, I know the color of her hair and eyes, but that doesn't mean I gave Barek any cause for jealousy. Everyone in the village knows her father forced the engagement with Barek, and initially she wasn't happy with the choice, but so far as I know, it had nothing to do with me. Layla can give you more details, if you're truly interested. Any more questions?"

"No," Ammar replied with a grin. He patted Sirak on the knee. "Let's go. We mustn't be late."

Sirak spurred the horses and the two men rode in silence until the wagon bumped over a bridge past two Druze riding in the opposite direction. Recognizing them, Ammar waved affably and both men waved back.

Ammar wrapped his arm around Sirak's shoulders. "Sirak, I know we've spoken of it before, but it's been a long time. The ways of the *Muwahhidun* are very strict, and we must all abide by the tenets of the *Tawhid* faith."

"I know, *Abee*. I've understood since I was ten that Izabella and I can never be part of the *Muwahhidun* community. There's no need to repeat it."

"You're like a son to me—my *only* son—and nothing pains me more than the fact that I cannot fully share my life with you—most of all, my faith in God. Countless times I've lain awake at night agonizing about this unbendable truth. I even petitioned the *Uqqāl* and asked if there couldn't be some exception laid out in the *hikmah*, especially considering your service during the revolution against the French oppressors, but they were unbending. No special considerations are possible."

Staring up the road, Sirak nodded in comprehension.

"You've come of age, and it's to be expected that your thoughts would turn to marriage and family. I have cordial relations with Stephen, the Christian baker in Rashayya. Would you like me to make inquiries regarding available Christian girls?"

"No, *Abee*," Sirak whispered sadly, "perhaps one day, but not right now."

"As you wish, Son, but at least you might consider a switch to the Christian school."

Sirak peered solemnly at Ammar. "Okay, I'll consider it."

Riding on in silence, the frustration of both men was palpable. One yearned desperately to lend assistance; the other felt trapped by an unbreakable web of tradition; while both were unwilling prisoners to the past.

Sirak climbed down from the wagon and tied the horse to a rail. He helped Azusa, Layla and Izabella out of the bed. All the women wore customary dark-blue dresses and white head coverings.

Fatima and Nazira rushed across the lot to greet them. "Wasn't it the loveliest wedding you've ever seen?" Fatima asked excitedly. "Nadia was so beautiful."

Azusa kissed them both. "It was a stunning ceremony."

Fatima and Nazira kissed Sirak on the cheek. "How's school?" Fatima asked.

"It's great. I'm studying with Qaseem Jumblatt this month."

Nazira gave Izabella a hug. "I missed you."

"Then why don't you come visit me anymore?" Izabella replied timidly.

Nazira took Izabella's hands. "I'm sorry, but I've been so busy helping Umar's parents with their new house. Sit with me at the reception and I'll tell you all about it."

"You women will have plenty of time to gossip later," Ammar said. "Let's go join the others."

The family walked across a grassy plaza and past a gathering of *Uqqāl* leaders sitting in a large circle. Several hundred Druze villagers from throughout the Rashayya area had already gathered for the reception. The men crowded around tables piled extravagantly high with food and drink, while the women congregated in a nearby courtyard. Many adults, both male and female, had outlined their eyes with dark kohl.

Sirak stuck close to Ammar. They served themselves and sat on the ground beside a roaring fire pit where several men engaged in a spirited conversation about ongoing French intrusions into Druze affairs.

Sirak listened for the better part of an hour before wandering off to the yard outside the *khalwa* building. He loathed weddings and funerals, for it was these events, so steeped in Druze tradition, when he was most painfully aware of being an outcast from both his adopted family and the community.

Ammar took a sip of wine. "It's excellent, Kamil. I haven't had wine since my daughter's wedding last summer. If you don't mind, I'll take Sirak a glass."

The portly farmer nodded. "Of course, what's a wedding without wine?"

Ammar spotted Sirak sitting by himself in a grassy yard next to the *Khalwa* temple. He was gazing up at the nearly full moon.

Ammar wove his way through the throng of men and cheerfully greeted everyone he passed. When he broke clear of the crowd, he looked up and stopped dead in his tracks.

A slender young woman, who was standing apart from others beneath a tree, peered out toward the temple. Sirak looked up and they locked eyes for a long moment. Finally, Sirak looked down and the young woman turned back to her friends.

Ammar retreated to the gathering of men. He sat alone beside the fire pit, and looking up, caught sight of Abdullah Mousa headed his way. Abdullah was rather tall for a Druze and his long beard was generously sprinkled with gray.

"Greetings, Ammar. God has blessed us with a glorious evening."

"Yes, He has, Abdullah. It's been a wonderful day for a wedding."

"Truly. How's your family?"

"Growing," Ammar replied with a chuckle. "Fatima is expecting another child."

"Congratulations to you all! And how was your harvest?"

"We've never harvested more apples and olives, and the wheat crop was exceptional, too."

"I'm happy to hear it. I want to talk with you about Sirak."

"What about him?"

"How old is the boy now?"

"He'll be twenty-one in February."

"Twenty-one already. Where does the time go? The mischievous boy has become a strapping young man."

"Yes, he has, with a loyal heart of gold."

"I'd expect nothing less since you and Azusa raised him. There's something difficult I must ask you, my friend. Does Sirak know of the *Tawhid* doctrines concerning outsiders?"

Ammar's smile faded to a frown. "What do you mean?"

"He knows he can never be counted among the *Muwahhidun*?"

"Yes, he's painfully aware of his circumstance. In fact, we spoke about it just today."

"Having three sons myself, I can't begin to imagine how painful this must be for both of you," Abdullah said ruefully. "Has he made a decision about his future?"

"He's preoccupied with school. He wants to be a doctor."

"A doctor," Abdullah exclaimed. "That's certainly a lofty ambition. Have you encouraged this choice?"

"I've had nothing to do with it. When Sirak was a young boy, there was an American missionary doctor in Anatolia who cared for him after a viper bite. He encouraged Sirak to pursue medical training, and the boy's never forgotten."

"It's a worthy choice, indeed; but if Sirak's to fulfill this dream, he must leave Rashayya to receive proper training. Either Damascus or Cairo would be a good choice."

"Someday, perhaps, unless he changes his mind. As you know, young men often dither about their chosen vocation."

"Yes, that's certainly true. Ammar, let me be frank with you, we *Ajaweed* discussed Sirak's situation last Thursday night. You and Azusa are to be commended for your noble efforts to rescue these orphans.

You've raised them to be trustworthy and responsible citizens, but the *Ajaweed* have decided they'll both be further harmed psychologically if they continue to reside among us. It's time for him to return to his people. His sister must go with him."

"The *Ajaweed* decided this?" Ammar asked guardedly. "Would this decision have anything to do with Ezekiel Jumblatt's daughter?"

"Yasmin? No, not in the least. Why would it? The girl is betrothed."

"Yes, I know—the girl is engaged to your son. Perhaps someone is concerned about feelings lingering in the girl's heart?"

Abdullah's black eyes revealed nothing of his thoughts. He peered at Ammar for a moment and took a deep breath. "I've come to you as a friend, Ammar, and I hope to leave as a friend. The girl is *Muwahhidun*, and she must marry *Muwahhidun*. Would you destroy her relationship with her family and her community? You know what her family's response would be to infidelity, or even the hint of infidelity. You must consider the girl's well-being, too."

Ammar glanced past Abdullah. Sirak was still sitting by himself next to the *khalwa* building. "You're right," he whispered despondently. "I'll talk to Azusa and the children."

"It's the right thing to do. You can rest assured the community will provide whatever financial assistance is needed to resettle them."

"Thank you for your candor. I'll let you know what we decide."

"Good evening, my friend. May God grant you the wisdom of *al-Hakim*." Abdullah turned and walked slowly back to the *Uqqāl* gathering.

Ammar watched two of the *Ajaweed* get up from their seats to talk to him. He downed the rest of his wine, rose to his feet, and ducked beneath a low-hanging branch. Then he walked across the grassy clearing to the temple. "Sirak."

Sirak looked up dejectedly. "Yes, *Abee*?"

"It's time to go home."

Sirak nodded. He stood up and walked with Ammar to fetch the women for the journey back to the farm.

CHAPTER 45

A week later

A zusa rested her head on Ammar's shoulder and wiped tears away with her fingertips. "Why do the Ajaweed have such callous hearts?" she asked dejectedly. "They know Izabella's completely dependent on us for her physical and emotional support. Who'll mind her while Sirak attends school?"

"I don't know. Perhaps the church in Jerusalem will help them or maybe Sirak will find a wife. As hard as this will be, we must consider his future, too. His prospects will be limited if he stays here. There'll be a better chance for him to pursue his dreams in Jerusalem."

"Who'll see that they get there safely?" Azusa asked fretfully. "The journey to Jerusalem is long and perilous."

"Mustafa, the basket-weaver, knows a merchant who travels here from Jerusalem to buy merchandise twice a year. He's dealt with him for many years and he assures me the man is trustworthy. Mustafa expects him soon. I'll ask him to take Sirak and Izabella to Saint James Cathedral when he arrives. We must trust that they'll care for their own. Dry your tears now and I'll go find Sirak."

Ammar got up from the bench and headed outside. After a few minutes, he stepped back inside with Sirak.

"Please sit down," Ammar said. "Azusa and I have something important to talk with you about."

Azusa grasped Sirak's hand mournfully.

Sirak glanced at Azusa and frowned worriedly. "What's wrong, *Abee*?"

Ammar stared at his hands. Looking up at Sirak, he opened his mouth to speak, but then turned away.

"*Abee*, what's wrong? Is it Izabella?"

Ammar took a deep breath. "No, my son, Izabella's fine, but I have something difficult to discuss with you. It's the hardest thing I've ever done in my life."

Sirak's shoulders drooped with apprehension.

"Azusa and I want to tell you how much we love you, and how proud we are of you. The past fourteen years have flown by and you and Izabella have enriched all our lives beyond comprehension. We thank God He entrusted us with your lives."

"You're sending me away," Sirak whispered.

"It's not our decision," Ammar muttered. "It's the last thing Azusa and I wanted." He looked up at the ceiling and took a deep breath. "We'll always love you, both of you. But the *Ajaweed* decided you and Izabella must leave the community, for your own good." Ammar took another deep breath and shook his head. "Dear God, help me," he whispered. He clenched his fists. "It's the last thing we wanted. The last thing…" Overcome with grief, the proud Druze lapsed into tortured silence.

Sirak wrapped his arm around Ammar and hugged him. "I understand, *Abee*. We all knew this day would come someday, and now it's here. I thank you both with all my heart for everything you've done for Izabella and me." He turned and smiled lovingly at Azusa. "May God bless you both."

"Oh, Sirak," Azusa sobbed. "Our hearts will surely break."

"Have you told Izabella?"

Ammar shook his head. "No, we wanted to tell you first."

"Let me tell her. Where should we go?"

"That's your decision," Ammar replied. "Perhaps Jerusalem would be the best choice. Many Armenians live in the Holy City, and the medical school is highly regarded."

Sirak nodded pensively. "Finally, we go to Jerusalem. Perhaps, at long last, we'll find my papa and brother there."

Ammar nodded. "It's decided, then. Mustafa, the weaver, knows a merchant who travels regularly between Rashayya and Jerusalem. He's expecting him in a week or two. Say your goodbyes and prepare to leave. We must break the news to Izabella soon so she'll have time to accept it."

Sirak nodded. "Where is she?"

"She's in sewing with Nazira," Azusa replied. "Tell her now, before someone else does."

Sirak got up from the bench.

Azusa rose to give him a warm hug. "Go easy with Izabella, Sirak. She needs to know you'll always stay with her."

"I know."

Sirak headed back through the kitchen. He stopped in front of a heavy drape hanging over the doorway. He heard Nazira giggle. "Izabella, can I come in? I need to talk to you."

"Just a moment," Nazira replied. "I'm trying on a dress."

The drapes opened a few moments later. "You can come in now," Nazira said. "We're making a dress for Fatima."

Sirak ducked inside the windowless room lit by an olive oil lamp. The small table in the center was strewn with fabric and spools of thread.

Izabella was seated at the table with her hair pulled back beneath a white scarf. "Are you looking for your Bible?" she asked timidly. She set the worn, leather-bound volume on the table. "I was reading it before Nazira got here."

"You can read it whenever you like," Sirak replied soothingly. "I want to talk to you."

"You can talk here," Nazira offered politely. "It's time to go home. Umar wants his supper early."

"No, please stay, Nazira. You are Izabella's friend. You should hear this, too."

Nazira searched Sirak's eyes. She stepped around the table and sat beside Izabella.

Sirak reached across the table and took Izabella's hands. "Do you trust me, my sister?"

Izabella stared restlessly at the tabletop. "Why do you ask me?"

"There's something important I must tell you. Please, look at me."

Izabella looked up at Sirak. "Yes, of course, my brother—you know I trust you."

"The *Ajaweed* have decided we must leave Rashayya. We will travel to Jerusalem to find Papa and Steppanos."

Izabella's mouth dropped open. "With *Abee* and *Ummee*?"

"No, just you and me."

"No! I don't want to leave our home!"

"I'm afraid we have no choice, Izabella. It's been decided for us. At least we will be together, and I will look out for you and take care of you, always."

Bursting into tears, Izabella collapsed into Nazira's arms.

Nazira cradled Izabella against her chest. Frowning at Sirak, she shook her head. "That's enough for now."

"She needs to know," Sirak said pointedly.

"Okay, you've told her. Now leave us alone."

"There is one more thing.… I need your help, Nazira. I want to say goodbye to Yasmin before we leave."

Nazira's eyes opened wide. "Are you crazy? She's betrothed."

"I must say goodbye. Tarak will bring her to the river if you ask him to. Will you help me?"

"No, I won't. None of this would've happened in the first place if Yasmin's parents hadn't found out about you meeting her."

"Shhh!" Sirak turned and peered at the curtain. "*Abee* and *Ummee* will hear you."

"Sirak, it's too risky. Don't think about yourself, think about Yasmin. Think about her future!"

"I am thinking about her. All I do is think about her. It's your fault, you know. It was your idea for me to come with you."

"Only as my escort. You weren't supposed to fall in love with Umar's sister. You knew it was forbidden."

"Your meeting Umar before marriage was forbidden, too. Please, Nazira, I just want to say goodbye."

"I'll discuss it with Umar. He'll probably say no, but I'll ask him."

Sirak reached across the table and squeezed Nazira's hand. "You're my angel."

Nazira kissed Izabella on the forehead and wiped tears from her cheeks. "Let's take you to *Ummee*." She helped the anguished young woman to her feet and guided her out through the curtain.

Azusa looked up and dropped her paring knife. She rushed around the counter and gathered Izabella into her arms.

"I don't want to leave, *Ummee*," Izabella sobbed.

"I know you don't, and it's not what we want either, but God will watch over you and your brother will protect you. Come and lie down; this has been a big shock to all of us," she said, leading Izabella out of the kitchen.

Nazira waited until they were out of earshot. "How can they do this to her?" she asked Sirak.

"They don't care. We don't exist to the *Ajaweed*."

Nazira kissed him on the cheek. "I've got to go. Umar's going to be furious."

"Don't forget to ask him about Yasmin."

"I won't. I'll see you Thursday."

CHAPTER 46

Sirak gazed down at the familiar river bend. At the water's edge, Umar was squatting in a formation of rocks at the top of the bank. Sirak watched the young Druze select a stone. He tossed it into the slow-moving water. He spotted Sirak and turned to face him.

Sirak spurred his horse and trotted down the steep trail. "Where is she?"

"It's impossible," Umar replied. "My mother knows you're leaving tomorrow. She's watching Yasmin like a hawk. My brother, Tarak, is suspicious, too. God knows what he'd do if he ever found out."

"So that's how it all ends? I never see her again…even to say goodbye?"

"Yes, that's how it ends. But I brought you a note. It's the best she could do."

Sirak dismounted and grabbed the paper from Umar. He stuffed it into his pocket and walked his horse back up the hill.

Umar squinted up at him through the bright midday sun. "Forget her, Sirak. It can never be."

"Why? Why do men let the decrees of a ruler who lived ten centuries ago dictate their lives? You *Juhhāl* know precious little about these doctrines yourselves. Doesn't that frustrate you?"

"Sometimes," Umar replied solemnly. "But Rashayya is our home, and it's always been our home. If Nazira and I want to remain part of this community, and have our children part of this community, then we must obey the *Uqqāl* decrees and so must Yasmin."

Sirak remounted his horse. "Goodbye, Umar."

"Goodbye, Sirak. May God be with you and Izabella."

Sirak rode down the hill. Sensing they were headed home, the horse broke into a trot. Sirak jerked back on the reins. "Are you anxious for me to go, too, Talon?"

Sirak turned off the main trail and rode deep into a rocky, brush-covered gorge. He dismounted his horse, sat on a boulder and pulled Yasmin's note from his pocket. It was unsigned, but he recognized the graceful Arabic script.

> *My darling Sirak, I know I've disappointed you yet again. You once said I was weak, and now you know it's really true. May God be with you and Izabella. I will never forget your kindness and the friendship we shared together. You will remain in my memory forever.*

Sirak folded the letter and slipped it back into his pocket. He gazed out over the featureless, barren desert. In the far-off distance, a line of dark clouds poured rain down on the foothills. "Why, God?" he muttered. "Why do you give me love and then take it away? Papa, Alek, Stepannos, Flora, Mikael, Mama, and now Yasmin, too."

Remounting his horse, Sirak rode back to the main road. He paralleled the river for several kilometers and ascended into the foothills through the carefully-manicured orchards and groves where he'd toiled beside Ammar since he was a boy. In the fleeting afternoon light, his shadow leapt from one tree to the next. He rounded a bend and the familiar farmhouse welcomed him home for the last time.

Sirak climbed hand over foot to the top of a rock pile at the edge of a terraced grove where two-year-old olive seedlings were taking hold. He stared out over the pitch-black valley far below and scanned the sky filled with twinkling stars and constellations. Fixing his eyes on the Big Dipper, he traced its pointers down to the North Star. He gazed at the star, closed his eyes and said a short prayer of atonement. He turned at the rustling of leaves and found Ammar climbing up the formation behind him. "Hello, Abee," he said solemnly.

"Are you okay?"

"Yes. I love to sit here at night and gaze at the heavens."

Ammar smiled up at the stars. "It's very beautiful. I'll come to this place and think of you. And I will miss you every day as I work in our groves and orchards."

Sirak got up and stood before Ammar with his hands on the older man's shoulders. "I'll miss you, too. Most men are fortunate to have one good father to teach them what's important in life and to show them how to be a man. God blessed me with two, and both are as steady as the Northern Star."

Ammar collapsed into Sirak's arms and wept unashamedly. "God, have mercy," he gasped; "it's you who taught me, my son, it's you who taught me."

The two men clung to each other in silence for a time and then sat down on the rocks.

"There's something I want to discuss with you," Ammar said. "God willing, you'll be accepted to the medical school and find a wife in Jerusalem. After you marry, the concerns of the *Uqqāl* will be mollified. I want you to come back to live with us here in Rashayya. We need another doctor and there's plenty of room to build a new house on this land—one large enough for the big family you've always wanted."

Sirak smiled gratefully. "Thank you, *Abee*."

"Put your faith in God and He'll show you the way. Take special care of Izabella. She can't survive alone. Your sister is the sweetest person I've ever known, but also the most fragile."

"I will. You mustn't worry."

"I'm not worried. She'll be a wonderful wife and devoted mother. You must help her find the right man."

Sirak stared at Ammar in the muted light of the half-moon. The patches of white in his full beard shimmered like glass wool and his sunken eyes were outlined with concentric wrinkles. Seemingly overnight, he'd aged two decades. "Don't worry, *Abee*, we'll be fine. We'll send back letters with the merchant."

Ammar smiled sadly and nodded his head. He reached out and patted Sirak's arm. "I know you'll be fine. Well, we'd better go inside. *Ummee* wants to say goodbye, too."

Sirak took Ammar's hand and the two of them walked slowly to the house.

The wagon came to a stop on the main street in Rashayya. Another wagon, pulled by an old mare, was parked alongside the building. It was half-filled with carpets and other goods.

Ammar climbed down to the ground. "Stay here with the women, Sirak. I'll be right back." He headed through the open door.

Sirak turned in the driver's seat. Asuza and Layla stared back solemnly from the bed of the wagon. Izabella was sitting between them with her face buried against Azusa's chest.

Sirak peered up the street at an approaching one-horse carriage. "Yasmin," he whispered.

Sitting between her older brother, Tarak, and her father, Ezekiel, Yasmin stared dejectedly at Sirak. Their eyes locked in silent misery. Tarak stared at Sirak, too, but Ezekiel looked straight ahead.

Ezekiel flicked the reins and the carriage sped past. Sirak stared after the buggy until it disappeared behind a building at the end of the street.

Ammar emerged from the shop a few minutes later. The weaver and a pudgy man with a long white beard were with him. All three men were carrying rolled rugs. They walked to the trader's wagon and stacked the bolts in the bed.

"Sirak, this is Jeremiah Levite," Ammar said. "He's agreed to take you and Izabella to Saint James Monastery in Jerusalem."

"Thank you, sir," Sirak replied politely.

The old Jew nodded respectfully. "I'm honored, young man. Ammar told me you're interested in medicine."

"Yes, sir. I've wanted to become a physician since I was a young boy."

"My younger brother, Eli, is a surgeon in Bethlehem. I'm sure he'll help you."

Sirak glanced at Ammar and smiled at the memory of their conversation the previous night.

"Would you prefer to ride up front with me or in the back with your sister?" the old Jew asked.

Sirak glanced at Izabella. She was clinging to Azusa and trembling with trepidation. "I'd better ride with my sister for now, but maybe later I can ride up front. I want to ask you about Jerusalem...if it's no trouble."

"It's no trouble at all. I've lived in the Holy City most of my life; I've got many customers who live in the Armenian Quarter. I can tell you everything there is to know."

"How long is our journey?"

"Nine or ten days, depending on the weather and how the old mare holds up. We'd better be on our way." Jeremiah took Sirak's bag and tossed it into his wagon.

The men turned at the clatter of an approaching wagon. Fatima, Nazira and their husbands rumbled up the street and rattled to a stop.

"Thank God," Naziria called out in relief. "I thought we'd missed you."

Azusa and her daughters shared a tearful goodbye with Izabella before showering Sirak with farewell hugs and kisses. Finally, Ammar wrapped his arm around Sirak's shoulders and walked him to Jeremiah's wagon. He slipped a pouch into Sirak's hand. "I've already paid Jeremiah. Use this gold to help you get settled in Jerusalem."

"But *Abee*," Sirak protested.

"Please take it. You've surely earned it." He gave Sirak a long hug. "Goodbye, my son."

Sirak kissed Ammar on the cheeks. "Goodbye, *Abee*. Thank you for everything."

Ammar sighed restively. "I asked Jeremiah to bring us back your letters. Please let us know how you're getting along."

"I promise, *Abee*. We'll be fine. Please don't worry." Sirak jumped up into the bed and leaned out to help Izabella.

"*Ummee!*" Izabella sobbed. She clutched at Azusa's dress and twisted her face in despair.

Azusa pulled gently away and Ammar hoisted Izabella up to Sirak in the wagon. Her whimpers became frantic wails. Sirak sat her down on a stack of carpets and held her in his arms.

The wagon jerked forward and rumbled down the dusty street. Ammar, Azusa and their children shouted goodbyes.

Sirak waved one last time. "It is finished," he muttered.

CHAPTER 47

Sirak consoled Izabella throughout the trip to Damascus, and beyond to Kahdem. The irony of finally riding into Kahdem—the city where their ill-fated Armenian refugee caravan was headed—did not escape Sirak. He dared not mention it to Izabella.

Three more days of arduous travel in the Syrian Desert took them through a bleak wasteland dotted with small villages that were sparsely populated by Arabs, Turks and Kurds. They stopped each night to rest with merchants or innkeepers Jeremiah had patronized for decades.

On the fourth night they stayed at an austere outpost dwelling owned by a crusty old Jew named Elijah with whom Jeremiah had traded for more than thirty years. The man's wife doted on Izabella, and even managed to engage her in feeding their animals—including a pair of cats that vied unremittingly for the girl's attention. It gave Sirak his first respite from his sister's incessant fretting since the wagon departed Rashayya.

They set out early the next morning and headed for the city of Amman. Sheer mental and physical exhaustion, brought on by unrelenting angst, finally brought merciful sleep to Izabella. Sirak seized the opportunity to move up to the driver's seat beside Jeremiah. The young man rode in silence for nearly an hour. This suited the taciturn Jew just fine. He'd made the trip alone hundreds of times over the preceding four decades and had come to delight in solitude.

Finally, however, after a brief stop to water the horse, Sirak steeled himself to ask the burning question that had lingered on his lips since *Abee* introduced them in Rashayya. "Can I ask you a question?" Sirak suddenly blurted out.

The trader shifted in his seat. "Yes, of course."

"You have Armenian customers in Jerusalem?"

Jeremiah nodded. "Yes, many."

"Do you know a man named Mourad Kazerian?"

"Mourad Kazerian?" Jeremiah repeated. "No, I don't recall anyone with that name."

"How about Stepannos Kazerian?" Sirak asked hopefully.

"No, I don't recall anyone named Kazerian. But there are several thousand Armenian residents in Jerusalem, and three times that number scattered throughout Palestine, so that doesn't mean they don't live there. Are these men relations of yours?"

Sirak nodded disappointedly. "My papa and brother. The last time I saw them, they were on a raft floating out of Diyarbekir. Papa yelled for us to meet them in Jerusalem. That was in 1915, and I was seven years old."

"Fourteen years is a long time."

"It's a very long time. They could be anywhere by now. I never realized there were so many Armenians living in Jerusalem. How will we ever find them, even if they are somewhere in Palestine?"

"Your best bet is to start with the leaders at Saint James Convent. The Patriarch has taken in hundreds of Armenian refugees over the years and his subordinates may know them, or at least know if they've been there. I'm sure the convent keeps records of all the refugees who reached Jerusalem during and after the Great War."

Sirak glanced up the road as the wagon jostled through a sharp turn. It emptied into a clearing offering a spectacular view of a stark, foreboding desert plain ahead of them. The road ahead twisted and turned through the wasteland like a snake. "Unbelievable," he mumbled in awe. "What is this place?"

"This desert plateau extends for more than twenty-five kilometers to the north of Amman. It's beautiful country this time of year, but don't venture here in the summer."

"Beautiful wasn't the word that came to mind. Frightening seems more appropriate to me. How long will it take us to make it through that?"

"It'll take us three more days to reach Amman, if the weather holds up."

Sirak frowned. "Where will we stay tonight?"

"At an inn just two kilometers beyond that rise in the distance. We should arrive there just before sundown."

Sirak sighed restively and lapsed into a brooding silence. Jeremiah left him to his thoughts for nearly an hour before offering him the canteen.

"Go on, drink the rest," Jeremiah said, with a yellowed, toothy grin. "There's plenty of water in the back and more where we're stopping tonight."

Sirak took a long drink. He tied the water bag and set it beside Jeremiah on the seat.

Jeremiah shook the empty bag and tossed it into the bed. "I'm curious, why do you want to be a physician? My brother likes medicine well enough, but it took him years of training and hard work to get established. Even today, he nearly works himself to death caring for his patients."

Sirak glanced at the old Jew. He leaned against the wooden seat and peered out at the expansive desert.

"I'm sorry," Jeremiah said. "You don't need to tell me if it's an uncomfortable subject. It's really none of my business."

"I'm not uncomfortable. I was just thinking about what you said about your brother. It reminded me of the man who introduced me to medicine. His name was Dr. Charles; he was an American missionary doctor. I was playing with a friend when a viper bit my foot—I was just seven years old then. Dr. Charles saved my life. Then, after the situation in Anatolia deteriorated, we fled our neighbor's farm and went to live in Diyarbekir with the doctor and his wife; she was a nurse. Dr. Charles let me follow him around the wards and he nearly worked himself to death caring for his patients, but he loved doing it. Most of the patients were wounded and sick Ottoman soldiers. I'll never forget how much those men appreciated what Dr. Charles did for them. He was a great man. Unfortunately, he was killed."

Jeremiah nodded understandingly. "After everything you've been through, I guess medical training doesn't seem like it'd be too difficult."

"I'm looking forward to it. Working hard is good for me. And helping sick people is the best way for me to repay Dr. Charles and everyone else who helped me." Sirak reached into his pocket and retrieved the old leather-bound Bible he'd carried since his mother gave it to him in Anatolia. "I started reading my Bible again before we left Rashayya. I've decided to devote my life to God and medicine, just like Dr. Charles."

"What about family? Won't there be time for that, too?"

Sirak shook his head. "No, no family, except for Izabella."

Jeremiah smiled and patted Sirak on the knee. "Young man, you're young. I'll pray God sends you the right woman and gives you the wisdom to recognize her. Only family and God can bring the happiness and contentment you deserve."

Sirak stared at the old man's face. The skin around his eyes was a roadmap of lines and creases. The eyes themselves had fleshy vascular bumps in the corners and the pupils were clouded with cataracts.

The old man coughed and cleared his throat. "That's all the advice I can offer you about love and family. God knows I myself have been an abject failure in this regard."

"Where is your family?" Sirak asked.

"I only have my brother. There was a woman I cared for many years ago, but I lost her to another man. I was too busy with my business to keep her or find another. I constantly travel to buy and sell these stupid rugs and baskets." He sighed melancholily. "So you can see, I'm not the one to advise you about women and marriage.

"There's one piece of counsel I can offer you. Search for your family in the Holy City, and then leave it as soon as you can. If you stay, Jerusalem will only bring you misery and sorrow. Fighting will undoubtedly flare between the Zionists and the Arabs, and when it does, the city and everyone in it will be consumed by war."

"Sirak!" Izabella cried out from the wagon bed. "Sirak, where are you?"

Jeremiah slowed the wagon to a stop.

Sirak jumped down and ran to the rear of the wagon. He climbed into the bed. Izabella was sitting with her back against the sidewall and her eyes were glazed with terror.

"I'm here, Izabella."

"Don't leave me alone. Is there any water?"

Sirak jumped down and ran to the front of the wagon. Jeremiah tossed him a full water bag.

"I need to ride with my sister now. Thank you for your advice."

"It was my pleasure. I'll stop to rest and water the horse in about an hour. If you fall asleep, I'll wake you."

Sirak smiled. "Thank you for everything."

"You're most welcome. Don't forget to pray for a kind and understanding wife."

Sirak chuckled. He turned and ran to the rear of the wagon and climbed into the bed. "Okay!" he shouted.

The wagon kicked up a cloud of dust and rumbled away down the road.

CHAPTER 48

September 19, 1928

The wagon bumped into the bustling city of Amman, and the travelers took lodging at a small inn. They enjoyed a leisurely rest day, with plenty to eat and drink, before they set out on the last leg of their journey. After three grueling days, they entered rocky Palestine and crossed the River Jordan on a mule-drawn ferry. They climbed into the hills to the east of the Holy City and skirted the Mount of Olives before Jerusalem sprang into full view. In the ebbing afternoon light, Sirak stared out at the golden Dome of the Rock and the imposing stone walls surrounding the city.

"Oh Jerusalem, we heed thy call," Jeremiah muttered pensively.

Sirak's eyes tracked from one guard tower to the next around the perimeter of the ancient city. "The walls are enormous. I didn't realize Jerusalem was a walled city."

"These walls were re-built by Suleiman the Magnificent in the early sixteenth century."

"It's magnificent, even more beautiful than I'd imagined."

"Don't let its splendor deceive you."

Sirak turned and gazed into the older man's eyes. "What has this city done to you?"

"My younger sister and her twin boys were killed by the typhus fifteen years ago. Then, two years ago, an uprising spread to the Jewish District and a band of Arabs killed my brother's wife and daughter. A day doesn't go by without my feeling the heartbreak of losing them."

"I'd heard there was a lot of fighting here the last few years."

"And it's getting worse. For centuries, Arab, Christian and Jew lived side by side here in Palestine, but now the British have sown the seeds of unremitting rioting, sabotage and murder."

"Why do you stay?"

"Where would I go?"

"Well, I doubt Jerusalem could be any worse than what we survived in Diyarbekir and Aleppo. We'll stay here until, God willing, we find Papa and my brother, Stepannos." He turned back to the city. "Where's Saint James Convent?"

Jeremiah pointed. "It's inside the walls in the southwest corner of the Old City—see there, beyond the golden dome. We'll enter through the Jaffa Gate and travel a short distance to the convent. I must stop to deliver carpets to a friend who manages a fleet of carriages outside the Jaffa Gate, but we'll arrive at the convent well before dark."

The wagon rumbled along the ancient Jericho Road and through a series of rutted switchbacks before bumping down a rocky hillside toward the city. Beyond Suleiman's stone walls, bathed by the last rays of the afternoon sun and reflecting pink beneath the clouded sky, Sirak's eyes wandered across the spires, towers, domes and minarets scattered throughout the Holy City.

Jeremiah pointed out the Church of Saint Mary Magdalene and the hilly area of Gethsemane. Then the wagon turned south along a road that ran parallel to the great walls. They skirted Mount Ophel and lurched through a mass of travelers clad in every sort of traditional garment.

The wagon wove along the great wall past the Dung and Zion Gates, and turned at the southwest corner of the city. Pandemonium reigned outside the Jaffa Gate, as countless worshipers, merchants and beggars converged on the fabled western entrance to the city.

Jeremiah pulled the wagon to a stop near a line of horse-drawn carriages and a heavily- bearded man leapt up from the ground to greet him.

"Jeremiah, my friend, you've returned safely."

Jeremiah gave the man a warm hug. "Yes, Eli, and I found the rugs you wanted." Jeremiah led the man to the back of the wagon. "These are my new Armenian friends, Sirak and Izabella. I'm taking them to the convent."

"Welcome to Jerusalem!" Eli said boisterously. "May God grant you peace and happiness."

"Sirak, hand down those rugs that are lying along the sideboard," Jeremiah said.

Sirak passed him the rugs and Eli helped him unroll them on the ground.

"They're magnificent. How much do I owe you?"

"Nothing, my friend. They're a gift to repay you for all the deliveries you've made for me."

Eli's face lit up with surprise. "Thank you! What a surprise. Please join us for dinner."

Jeremiah patted Eli on the back. "Thank you for the invitation, but we must go. I have to get Sirak and Izabella to Saint James before the offices close for the evening."

"We're having a celebration in honor of Rabbi Stein at our home next Saturday. Please come and join us."

"I'll be there, and I'll see you at the synagogue on Friday."

Jeremiah climbed up on the wagon and made a sharp turn through the open Jaffa Gate. Just beyond the gate, the towering Citadel and Anglican Christ Church came into view. They rattled along the narrow Patriarchate Road for a short distance and finally slowed to a stop outside the main gate of the Saint James Convent.

"Stay here with the wagon," Jeremiah said. "I'll go inside to present you." He hurried away and disappeared through the gate into the Armenian Quarter.

Sirak smiled at Izabella and gave her hand a squeeze. Looking up, he peered toward the end of the street. A few people were milling about, but otherwise the street was surprisingly quiet.

A few minutes passed before Jeremiah and a smiling, white-bearded man emerged from the building.

"Sirak and Izabella, this is Abu Apraham, Patriarch Tourian's assistant. He'll take care of you from here."

"Welcome to Saint James Convent!" Abu Apraham called up to Izabella and Sirak. "Brother Levite told me about your long journey. By the grace of God, you've at long last found refuge among your people."

A young man pulled a handcart through the Saint James Gate and stopped beside the wagon.

"Transfer your things into the cart," Abu Apraham said. "I'll take you to your new home."

Jeremiah helped Izabella down from the wagon. He helped Sirak transfer their belongings into the handcart. Finally, he patted Sirak on the back. "Good luck finding your father and brother."

Sirak grasped Jeremiah's arm. "We're grateful for everything you've done for us. May God bless you."

Jeremiah pulled Sirak into a bear hug. "This isn't goodbye. Take good care of your sister and I'll bring you back details from my brother about your best options for medical training. Goodbye, Izabella. I hope you'll soon feel at home here in Saint James."

Izabella waved timidly. "Goodbye, Jeremiah."

"Abu Apraham knows where to find me," Jeremiah said to Sirak. "Goodbye for now."

"Goodbye, Jeremiah," Sirak said.

Jeremiah climbed into the driver's seat of the wagon. He waved one last time and drove slowly away.

Abu Apraham watched Jeremiah until he rounded the corner. He turned back, and his kindly eyes sparkled with satisfaction. "Well, Son, let me show you your new home. I think you'll enjoy your new neighbors."

Abu Apraham led Sirak and Izabella down a long hall that coursed past Saint James Cathedral and into a large courtyard. They walked down a cobblestone footpath past curious residents whom he greeted by name. He stopped several times to introduce Sirak and Izabella as the newest refugees. A few more turns and a short flight of stairs brought them to a narrow walkway.

"Your apartment is owned by the Patriarch," Abu Apraham explained. "No rent will be charged, but you are required to tithe ten percent of your earnings. You're also expected to obey the convent rules—including attending the liturgy at the Church of the Holy Sepulcher on Saturdays. We want you to be good neighbors to the families who share your court-yard—which shouldn't be too difficult, since the Simouians are among the dearest *Kaghakatsi* living in the quarter."

"*Kaghakatsi?*" Sirak queried.

"*Kaghakatsi* is the term used for the Armenian families who've lived in Jerusalem for generations, and in some cases centuries. You and your sister are *Kaghtagan*, or the refugees. Perhaps unfairly, this distinction holds great weight with some people. But you're fluent in Arabic, unlike most refugees who came to this city these last few years. This will make your acclimation much easier. You're fortunate to be living side by side with *Kaghakatsi* people. It's a rare opportunity attributable to the fact that the previous occupant died without heirs. Gather your things. The cart can't follow us the rest of the way."

Abu Apraham helped Sirak and Izabella carry their belongings. He led them up a flight of stairs to a narrow passageway. "I must warn you. The Simouian woman, Mariam, is prone to fits of mania and profound depression. You should address her as Umm Krikor—after her eldest son, who died of typhus during the Great War. She lost her two daughters to the fever, too, and there's no telling how you'll find her on a particular day. Some days you'll find her cheerfully working in the courtyard garden. But then, without any warning, she'll be gripped with a profound sadness. Often the depression forces her to bed for days on end. Her elderly husband, Hovsep, dotes over her, even though he himself is in poor health. Let's see how we find her today."

Abu Apraham led them into an open courtyard. Sirak and Izabella were bedazzled by the unexpected beauty and sweet fragrance wafting through the magnificent garden. The surrounding walls were adorned with potted wisteria and rose bushes, and every nook and cranny of the yard was crammed with tins, pots and urns that bore basil, freesias and lilies. Two half-barrels overgrown with jasmine were positioned beside a wooden table and chairs at the far end of the courtyard. A matronly woman in a long dress stood atop a stool pruning a small tree.

"Mariam," Abu Apraham called out to her cheerfully, "how are you this fine afternoon?"

The woman broke into a broad grin. She climbed down from the stool and hobbled toward them with a pronounced limp. "Abu Apraham, what a wonderful surprise! How is Sara?"

"She's just fine, thank you. She's away visiting her sister in Bethlehem, but I'm expecting her home tomorrow. As usual, your garden is magnificent."

"I wish you'd come to visit when the jasmine were in bloom. They've never been so glorious. Who are your young friends?"

"This is Sirak Kazerian and his sister, Izabella. They just arrived from Syria and I've assigned them to Yeghia's old apartment."

Mariam smiled blissfully. "Welcome! I am Umm Krikor," she said, spreading her arms and embracing Izabella. "I'm delighted to meet you. I just know we'll be good friends. Do you like to garden?"

Izabella glanced over Umm Krikor's shoulder. "I've never seen such a splendid garden."

"It belongs to you, too, now," Umm Krikor said. "I'm sure you'll come to love these plants as much as I do."

"Well, you're both in good hands," Apraham said to Sirak. "Allow me to show you your new apartment."

Mariam smiled at Sirak. "You must be starving. We insist you join us for dinner."

"We don't want to trouble you," Sirak replied politely.

"I insist on it. It won't be anything extravagant, just soup and bread with olives and figs. I've also got coffee and baklava for desert. Oh, please join us. Hovsep will want to meet you, too."

Sirak smiled appreciatively. "Okay, then, we'll get settled and clean up."

"Wonderful! I'll let you know when it's ready."

Apraham led Sirak and Izabella to a door in the middle of the courtyard. He lit a paraffin lamp and ushered them inside. The single room was dank and musty, and totally devoid of furnishings—except for a tiny wooden table with a single chair at the side of the room.

"This is one of the nicest refugee apartments in the quarter. Here in the back of the room you have direct access to the cistern beneath the courtyard. You can draw as much water as you need with this bucket. Three meals a day are provided for all the refugees at the dining halls. The closest one is back down the stairs and around the corner. I hope you'll both be very happy here."

"Thank you, Abu Abraham," Sirak said. "We're very grateful the Patriarch has provided us with this apartment."

"You're welcome, my children. After everything you've lived through, it gives us all great pleasure to have you here. I'll be your contact for any matters related to Saint James Convent or the Patriarch. Enjoy your dinner and I'll see you at mass this weekend." He stepped outside, walked across the courtyard and disappeared down the stairwell.

Izabella and Sirak barely had enough time to spread a blanket on the floor before Mariam came to fetch them for dinner. She led them through the darkened courtyard and introduced her frail husband, Hovsep. The old man was seated at a small wooden table illuminated by two paraffin lamps. The table bore a soup pot, a basket of bread and several dishes of food. Mariam seated Sirak beside Hovsep and Izabella next to herself.

"Hovsep, will you lead us in prayer?" Mariam asked.

Hovsep bowed his head, and in a halting, throaty voice, recited the Lord's Prayer.

Izabella opened her eyes and caught Sirak's stare. She smiled forlornly.

Sirak took the basket offered by Mariam. He tore off a piece of bread and passed the basket to Hovsep.

Mariam served soup to Izabella and Hovsep and passed the pot to Sirak.

Sirak helped herself to an ample serving, along with portions of olives and figs. He sipped the soup. "This is delicious," he exclaimed.

Mariam smiled appreciatively. "I'm glad you like it. It's Hovsep's favorite."

The old woman rambled incessantly throughout the entire meal. Mostly, she talked about her garden, but also about the affairs of Saint James Convent and their old friend who'd lived in Sirak and Izabella's apartment for twenty-four years, before she died.

Umm Krikor brought in the coffee and desert, and the conversation turned to Sirak and Izabella's trip from Syria and details about what they could expect in the Armenian Quarter and Jerusalem. The old woman showed surprising discretion in not asking them about their past. She seemed to sense it was better left alone, at least for the time being.

Finally, they said their goodbyes and Sirak led Izabella through the darkened courtyard to their apartment. He lit a paraffin lamp on the table and filled an old basin with water from the cistern. Izabella washed herself, while Sirak retreated to the back of the room to unpack his bag. Once Izabella was done bathing, Sirak emptied the basin in the courtyard, refilled it from the cistern and cleaned himself from head to toe.

Sirak knelt beside his sister's blanket. "Goodnight, Izabella," he whispered.

"Goodnight," she replied tiredly. "Thank you for taking care of me."

Sirak kissed her tenderly on the forehead. "You're welcome. Thank you for being here. I love you; sweet dreams." Blowing out the lamps, he lay on his blanket and stared up into the darkness.

"Sirak, will you say a prayer for us?"

"Of course. Dear God, thank you for watching over Izabella and me, and bringing us safely to Jerusalem. Thank you for providing us this place to live with good neighbors. Thank you for the food we shared tonight. Please guide us in our search to find Stepannos and Papa, and show us..."

A tremendous explosion shook the ground beneath them. Sirak bolted up on his blanket. A succession of pops echoed from the distance.

"What's that?" Izabella called out through the darkness.

"It was a bomb, and that's gunfire. But it's not close."

Sirak lay back. Taking a deep breath, he exhaled anxiously. His thoughts drifted to the last time he'd heard gunfire. It was on a dark night two years earlier, when he'd joined a group of young Druze fighters in a surprise attack on a French army outpost a few kilometers from Rashayya. A tremendous firefight ensued, and several French soldiers and Druze fighters were killed—including his best friend, Joseph, who'd died when a bullet shattered his skull. The memory of his friend staring up lifelessly from the ground had haunted Sirak ever since.

"Sirak?" Izabella whispered.

"Yes, what is it?"

"Are you asleep?"

"No."

"Do you remember tonight when Abu Krikor said the Lord's Prayer?"

"Yes."

"When we were young, Papa said it on special occasions like Christmas."

"Yes, I remembered that, too."

A long silence was broken by the distant bark of a dog. Izabella sobbed quietly.

Sirak rolled onto his side and reached for her hand. "Are you okay?"

"I miss my mama and papa."

"I miss them, too."

She sniffled. "And I miss *Abee* and *Ummee*."

"Me, too."

"Goodnight, my brother. I love you."

"I love you, too."

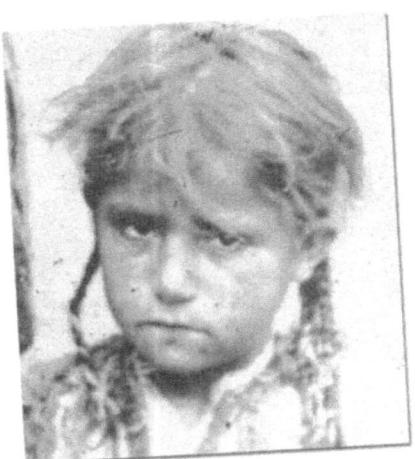

PART THREE

This page intentionally left blank

CHAPTER 49

September 13, 1996
Bedford, Ohio

A slight woman with mousy hair looked up from her computer as a wiry man in paint-spattered overalls stepped through the office door. He limped inside carrying rusty bolt cutters.

"What are you doing, Bob?" she queried with surprise. "Weren't you supposed to meet Jason for lunch?"

"I am, but Juan wants the lock cut off that past-due unit so he can clean it out. What's the number?"

Barbara opened a file on the computer and scrolled down the page. "J-2."

"If Jason calls, I'll be there in fifteen minutes." Bob, the owner of the self-storage business, walked down the alley past several one-story buildings filled with storage lockers. Heading up the last access road, he walked nearly to the end. He glanced at a pickup truck that zipped around the corner before heading up the last walk to unit J-2.

"Would you look at that?" he mumbled to himself. The keyhole on the padlock was corroded. "The damned thing hasn't been opened in decades." He jerked down hard on the padlock, but it held secure. He inserted the oxidized hasp into the teeth of the bolt cutters and forced the handles together. Suddenly, they snapped. "Shit!" Clutching his fingers, he grimaced with pain and raised his hand to his bifocals. He shook his head disgustedly and wiped the blood on his pants.

The rusted bolt resisted his dogged back-and-forth efforts to retract it out of the doorframe. He pounded the pin with the bolt cutters until it edged clear of the frame. Finally, he jerked the door open.

Stale air wafted out of the darkened locker. He reached inside the pitch-black room and flipped on the wall switch. The bulb was burned out. He fetched a flashlight from his pocket. Taking a step inside the locker, he stopped dead in his tracks when the beam fell on a stack of machine guns, rifles and shotguns piled against the back wall. "What the hell?" he muttered incredulously.

He stepped forward and crouched down for a closer look. The rusty old guns were caked with dust. Bob pointed the beam at the other side of the storage locker and it fell on a stack of cardboard boxes. He stepped across the room, opened the top box and shined the light inside. "Oh my God," he gasped, "fuckin' dynamite!" He gently set the top down and backed warily out of the unit.

The attendant jogged up the access road to the office and barged through the side door, then bent over to catch his breath.

Barbara bolted up from her computer. "What's wrong?"

Red-faced, with beads of perspiration running down his face, Bob clutched at his chest. "Call the police."

"Why?"

"Just call them, damn it!"

Bob peered up the access road at unit J-2. A portly police sergeant carrying a radio ducked beneath the yellow crime scene tape and hurried towards him.

"Are you the one who called this in?" he asked.

"I'm Bob Johnson, an attendant here; I opened the unit, and Barbara called it in."

"Mr. Johnson, the bomb squad will be here in five minutes and agents from the ATF and FBI are also on their way. There's enough dynamite in that locker to level this block. We've evacuated the day-care center, elementary school and gas station, too. I'm afraid you're closed until at least tomorrow."

"No problem, Sergeant, just get that crap out of our building."

"The feds will want anything you've got on the people who rented that unit. Why don't you go get your records together?"

"Okay, I'll be back in a few minutes."

"Wait up at the office, and I'll send the feds to find you."

Bob rounded the end of the building just as a white sedan with the blue-and-gold ATF insignia on the door panel pulled through the police blockade. He pointed up the access road and the car sped past him and stopped near the sergeant. An athletic-looking man wearing a coat and tie stepped from the car. Sergeant Vickers lifted the crime scene tape and led him to the building.

Bob watched the two men pull on gloves and disappear into the storage unit before he turned and hobbled back into the office. "Barbara, the police need the records on J-2."

She smiled and held up a file. "Got them! I knew they'd come looking for them."

"They'd have to get up early in the morning to put one over on you. All those episodes of *Hollywood Crime Story* you watch are finally paying off."

"Ha!" she chuckled. "It's a helluva lot better than those Texas Hold 'em tournaments you're married to."

Bob sat down at the desk and opened the file. He looked up at a heavily-armored truck that lumbered past the building. CPD BOMB SQUAD was stenciled on the door. "What's the tenant's name?"

"The most recent one was named Louise Corona. But look at the past few renters' names. Does anything strike you as strange?"

Bob perused the file. He shuffled back and forth through several papers. "I'll be damned—just three tenants since 1980—Louise Corona, Louise Buschel and Louise Cazian. They're all named Louise."

Barbara laughed. "No shit, Sherlock. What else?"

He shuffled through the file and looked up again. "They always paid in cash?"

"Every time."

"Is this everything?"

"That's it. I looked in the old file cabinet, but there's nothing else for that unit."

"Okay, why don't you lock up and head home? We're closed for the rest of the day. I'll call you later."

"No need to ask me twice." Barbara got up from her desk and fished a ring of keys from her purse. "If you've got any brains, you'll take them that file and get the hell out of here, too."

"What? And miss all the excitement?"

"Well, then, I just hope you left me this place in your will."

"What will?" Bob chuckled. "I'm living forever."

The ATF agent looked up from the file. "Is this everything you have, Mr. Johnson?"

"Yes, as far as I know." Bob turned, and glancing down the access road, spotted two men dressed in protective suits wheeling a cart to their truck. "Barbara searched all of our records. She's very thorough and has worked here for twenty years."

"Three women named Louise in sixteen years," the agent muttered. "What a coincidence. Do you remember what any of these women looked like?"

"No, can't say that I do, but Barbara might. She handles all the payments. She's gone home for the day, though."

"Thanks for your help, Mr. Johnson. Now, I want you to leave the area until the explosives are removed. Here's my card. Please leave your home phone number with the policeman at the gate."

"James Butler, Special Agent," Bob read aloud from the card. "Yes, of course, sir."

"I'll be in touch. Thank you."

Bob hobbled away to the office. As he walked past the units in the J building, he couldn't help but wonder what else lay hidden behind the dozens of monotonous orange doors.

CHAPTER 50

October 5, 1996
Richmond Heights, Ohio

Keri turned into the driveway and pulled forward to his father's darkened house. His truck squealed to a stop and he got out.

It was a surprisingly warm fall morning that belied the yellow, orange and brown leaves fluttering across the yard. The first rays of the sun danced through the colorful oak and maple trees that lined the narrow residential street.

He climbed the steps and rapped twice on the front door. The light snapped on above the porch and the door creaked open. Sirak was dressed in a flannel shirt and trousers with a floppy fishing hat pushed back on his balding head.

"Ready, Papa?"

"I've been ready, but I can't find my rod and reel."

"I have everything we need, including bait. Let's hurry before it gets too late. We can pick up coffee and donuts on the way."

"Okay, just let me turn off the lights."

Keri got back in the truck and started the engine. Sirak stepped outside a moment later. He locked the door and hobbled down the walk.

Keri waited patiently for his father to struggle into the seat and slam the door.

"The boys aren't coming?" Sirak asked.

"They couldn't make it after all. Troy and Kevin have a hockey tournament in Ann Arbor this weekend and both of the families drove up to cheer them on."

"You should've gone with them."

"And miss a chance to go fishing? No way. Besides, I've got tons of work to do tomorrow and they'll be home late."

"Well, next time you call and reschedule. It's important to spend as much time with your children and grandchildren as you can. Take it from your papa. I didn't, and now I regret it." Sirak smiled happily. "Better yet, next time take me with you."

"It's a long drive and a long weekend, Papa. They usually play four or five games. I'm not sure you're up to it."

"Nonsense. I'm in better shape now than I was twenty years ago."

Keri smiled and turned into the Bedford Coffeehouse. "Okay, we'll all go to the next tournament together."

Keri exited the freeway just west of downtown Cleveland. He drove to the Whiskey Island Marina and parked in a gravel lot next to the indoor boat-storage facility. They gathered their tackle and chairs and walked out to the breakwater. Finally, as the sun's rays hit the tops of the sailboat masts in the marina, they baited their hooks and cast into Lake Erie.

"Any word on your promotion?" Sirak whispered.

"Unfortunately, the central office just announced several layoffs of senior executives. I doubt I'll get promoted any time soon."

"That's too bad."

Keri felt a nibble on his line. He jerked his rod. "I missed him…"

"Papa, I was wondering, did you ever find out what happened to Nurse Barton after she left Aleppo?"

Sirak nodded. "I tried to contact her after we moved to the United States. I eventually found out that she had made it back to Oklahoma and lived with her brother on his farm. She married a banker from Altus, Oklahoma, and they had three sons. But she and her husband died in a car accident in the late thirties."

"So she never knew what happened to your mother and you?"

"No, at least not as far as I know. I wish I'd contacted her before she died."

"Maybe it was better for her to hold onto the hope that your mother and you kids made it to Jerusalem."

"Maybe, but she must've suspected the worst. Mama would've contacted her if she'd reached safety. They were like sisters."

"Yeah, I guess so. Papa, do you feel like telling me about the years you spent in Jerusalem before we kids were born? How did you meet Mama?"

Sirak didn't look up. He stared at the water rippling circles out from his line.

Keri glanced up at his father. The old man's haggard face was sallow in the rays of the early morning sun.

"We got a lot of help from the Armenian community and the old woman, Umm Krikor. I'm sure Izabella would have gone crazy without her. After all the years of support she'd gotten from Asuza and Ammar, there's no way she could've kept her sanity without Umm Krikor's mothering. I owed her a lot. Medical school would've remained little more than a dream, if it hadn't been for her."

"What was it like living in the Armenian Quarter?"

"We settled into the community as lowly Kaghtagan, as the long-term residents of the Holy City referred to us. Izabella spent her days in the courtyard gardening with Umm Krikor; while I began an arduous search through the Patriarch's records for any sign that Papa and Stepannos had reached Jerusalem. I spent many long and lonely and futile weeks in those offices. I searched refugee lists, baptismal records, and birth and death records, along with many other Patriarchal records Abu Apraham made available to me. I never found even a scrap of evidence Papa or Stepannos reached Jerusalem. All the while, I longed to return to Rashayya, to the only peace I'd ever known and the pretty young woman I left behind."

"You were still in love with her?"

"Yes, hopelessly. I never stopped thinking about her, not for a single day. I met a few young Armenian women in Jerusalem. One father even talked with me about marrying his daughter. But my heart was still in Syria.

"I enrolled at the St. George's School in Jerusalem. I studied the Bible, Arabic, geography and other topics, until Jeremiah and his brother made arrangements for me to enroll in the medical school at the American University in Beirut. That began just over a year after we arrived in Jerusalem. At first I declined the opportunity because I was sure Izabella would not be able to function if I left Jerusalem. But several of the church elders, along with Umm Krikor, encouraged me to go."

"How could you afford it? It must've been very expensive."

"It was, but I entered into an agreement with the Patriarch to provide three years medical care to the poor Armenians of Jerusalem for each year of support I received to attend school. And so, in 1929, just before the Palestine riots erupted, I began my medical training in Beirut. During that time, I returned to Jerusalem only two or three times a year, and then only for a few days at a time. It took several days to travel by boat from Beirut to Jaffa, and then by train from Jaffa to Jerusalem, but the biggest problem was that growing Arab resistance made the trip increasingly more dangerous. I earned my degree in five years. Then I returned to Jerusalem and the ongoing strife between the Arabs and Jews that tore the city apart."

"You went back to live in the Armenian Quarter?"

"Yes, in that same tiny apartment. I could've afforded to move, but I feared what might happen to Izabella without Umm Krikor's love and attention. I took a position in a hospital in the Jewish section of the city and honed my surgical skills on the battered bodies of the victims of the ongoing embittered struggle between the Arabs and Jews. There was little joy in our lives during those years—only the daily struggle to survive amidst the constant echoes of gunfire and bomb blasts. I came to feel like my only reason for living was to nurture and protect Izabella, since I was the only family she had left. In retrospect, I realized that I was severely depressed and didn't even know it."

"But we were born in the Katamon. When did you move?"

"One day, out of the blue, everything suddenly changed. It was a few months after my twenty-ninth birthday, and I remember that day like it was yesterday. It was a beautiful Saturday afternoon in June, just a few months before the Arab revolt exploded into open warfare. Izabella and Umm Krikor were tending vines in the courtyard, while I sat at the outside table sipping coffee with old man Abu Krikor. We heard voices on the stairs leading to the courtyard and the old Jew, Jeremiah, suddenly appeared. Unbelievably, Ammar was right behind him. And yet again, my life abruptly changed.

CHAPTER 51

June 20, 1936
The Armenian Quarter in Jerusalem

"*Abee!*" Izabella screamed from atop her stepladder. Jumping down, she tossed her clippers on the ground and ran headlong into Ammar's arms. "Oh, *Abee,* I missed you so!"

"I missed you, too," Ammar whispered. He smiled over the top of her head at Sirak.

Sirak stood in dumbfounded silence. It was as if he'd seen a ghost.

"Is *Ummee* here?" Izabella asked hopefully.

"No, little one, *Ummee* wasn't strong enough to make the long journey. She sends you her love and devotion. Here's a letter she wrote."

Ammar spread his arms and stepped to Sirak. "My son," he blurted out, his voice cracking with emotion.

Sirak buried his face against Ammar's chest. "*Abee,* I missed you so much."

"I missed you, too. It's been painful for us all. Thank you for all the letters you wrote."

"Is *Ummee* ill?"

"She's recovering from a bout of the grippe. She wanted to come anyway, but I thought the long journey was too much for her. I brought someone else to see you though."

Sirak looked at Ammar, and then glanced at Jeremiah. "Who?"

Jeremiah walked back to the steps and reappeared a moment later with a young woman. She wore a dark blue dress and headscarf, and her eyes were riveted on the ground.

At first Sirak didn't recognize her. Then, she looked up, and his mouth dropped open. "Yasmin?" he gasped in disbelief.

The young woman, her curly brown hair cascading across her shoulders, nodded apprehensively.

"Well, Umm Krikor," Jeremiah said, "how about some coffee for the weary travelers?"

The old woman laughed. "Of course. How about something to eat, too?"

"I was hoping," Jeremiah chuckled. He glanced at Sirak, who was standing trancelike at arm's length from Yasmin. Jeremiah winked at Ammar. "Izabella, Papa Ammar and I would like to wash up before we eat. Could you draw our water?"

"Of course," Izabella replied excitedly, "come inside with me."

Sirak and Yasmin stood alone in the courtyard. They sat down opposite each other at the table. The sweet scent of jasmine wafted in the air.

"Yasmin, what are you doing here?" Sirak finally asked.

"Ammar brought me to live in Jerusalem."

"*You're moving to Jerusalem?* Where's you husband?"

"Barek abandoned me six months ago."

"He abandoned you? Why?"

"Because I committed the greatest sin of all for a Druze wife. I didn't bear him children." Yasmin smiled timidly and stared at the tabletop. "Sirak," she whispered, "did you ever think of me?"

Sirak stepped around the table and lifted Yasmin up from the bench. He grasped her tiny shoulders and drew her to his chest. "Every single day."

"Oh, Sirak, I never stopped loving you. God forgive me, I never did."

Sirak kissed her tenderly on the forehead and brushed tears from her cheeks. "I love you."

"Sirak, do you have a woman?"

"No, *Habibi*, there's never been anyone but you."

"Oh, Sirak, God answered my prayers."

Sirak smiled reassuringly and sat Yasmin down at the table. He spotted Umm Krikor standing outside with a tray. "Umm Krikor, hurry before the coffee gets cold."

They all gathered around the courtyard table to share vegetable stew, olives and dried figs. Jeremiah and Ammar ate and drank ravenously, but Sirak and Yasmin couldn't take their eyes off each other. They groped each other's hands beneath the table.

"Well," Ammar said, "under the circumstances, I guess we should all speak openly. Sirak, you appear pleased to see Yasmin."

Sirak smiled at Yasmin. "Yes, *Abee*—she is a gift from God. The happiness that fled my heart eight long years ago has returned."

"I'm happy for you, for both of you. God is great."

"How long will you stay, *Abee*?" Sirak asked.

"I can stay for a week, but then I must return to Rashayya. I'll help Yasmin find a place to live before I go."

"Yasmin is welcome to stay with us until she finds her own place," Umm Krikor offered.

They all enjoyed Turkish coffee before Jeremiah finally left for home. The stunningly bright afternoon faded into a warm evening. Umm Krikor and her husband retired to their apartment and Izabella helped Ammar get settled in theirs.

Yasmin and Sirak found themselves alone again in the courtyard. Sitting beneath a jasmine bush, they talked about the years they were apart. Sirak told her about his training in Beirut and the challenges of living in increasingly dangerous Jerusalem. He also told her about Izabella's progressive psychological infirmity. Yasmin bemoaned the unhappy years with her husband and his demanding family—who'd become more belligerent and abusive the longer she remained barren. She told Sirak how she learned to weave baskets to sell to Jeremiah, giving her the opportunity to secretly query the noble-minded Jew about Sirak's life and well-being in Jerusalem.

"He never told me."

She smiled happily and folded her hand in his. "I asked him not to."

"What about your family?"

"My father renounced me. I shamed him by deciding to leave Rashayya. I can never return, but there's nothing there for me now."

Sirak glanced back to his darkened apartment. He leaned forward and pecked her on the lips. "Yasmin, I love you. I've always loved you. If you'll have me, I want to marry you."

Yasmin smiled adoringly. "But I'm Druze, my love, and you are Armenian."

"What difference does that make? We love each other."

"It makes a difference to your people...and to your sister."

"Izabella will accept and love you. Her mind may be weak, but her heart is gold."

"What about your church? Jeremiah told me intermarriage is not condoned by the Armenian leaders here in Jerusalem."

"I'll ask for dispensation from the Patriarch. Surely he'll understand the suffering we've both endured and that God, Himself, has brought us back together."

"Oh, my darling, you're sweeter than honey, but your love for me will fade like these blossoms. Think about yourself for once. I can never bear you children."

"That doesn't matter now. It only matters that you are happy and I am happy. There are many orphans here in Palestine. We can give some of them what *Abee* and *Ummee* gave me—hope and love."

"I want you to think about it. Then, if you really..."

They both jerked around at a resounding boom that echoed through the courtyard.

"What's that?" Yasmin gasped.

"A bomb," Sirak replied matter-of-factly.

"It sounded very close."

"It exploded in the Jewish neighborhood just beyond the wall. The gunfire and bombings have become more and more frequent since the Arab strike began in April, but we're safe here. Well, you must be very tired. I'm sure Umm Krikor is waiting up for you."

Sirak took Yasmin's hand and led her through the darkened courtyard to the Krikor front door. He kissed her full on the lips.

"Forgive me for forsaking you," she whispered. "I was afraid."

Sirak kissed her forehead. "That doesn't matter now." He rapped softly on the door and it creaked open.

Umm Krikor smiled and took the young woman's arm.

"Good night, Sirak," Yasmin whispered.

"Good night. I'll see you in the morning."

Two weeks later

Sirak sat patiently outside Patriarch Torkom Koushagian's office for nearly thirty minutes before the door opened and Abu Apraham stepped into the hall. He closed the door behind him.

"I'm sorry it took so long. There were many matters for the Patriarch to consider."

"Did he approve my dispensation request?"

"Come to my office and we'll discuss his decision in detail."

Abu Apraham led Sirak down two flights of stairs to a dimly lit hallway. He opened a door at the end of the hall and showed him into a simple office furnished with a small desk and three chairs. "Please sit down."

Abu Apraham sat behind his desk. The old cleric put on a pair of reading glasses and opened Sirak's file. "How long have you been with us in Jerusalem?"

"Eight years, sir, including the five years I spent mostly in Beirut during my medical training."

"God has blessed you, my son. What you've accomplished since you left Syria is an inspiration to us all, especially when you've cared for your sister at the same time. We appreciate your hard work."

Sirak's apprehension was growing by the second. "Thank you, sir. What's his decision?"

Abu Apraham folded his hands on the desk. "The Patriarch decided not to give his dispensation for you to marry the young Druze woman."

Sirak's mouth dropped open. "Why?"

"He doesn't believe it's in either one of your best interests, or your future children's best interest. The woman is Druze, and she'll always be Druze. *Be ye not unequally yoked together.*"

Sirak stared at the old man for several moments. "I will marry Yasmin, no matter what the Patriarch or anyone else decides," he said defiantly. "I love her and she loves me. That's all that matters."

"Then you will leave the convent, and your sister will leave with you. You must also repay the Patriarch the debt you owe him for the four years of medical school that have yet to be satisfied by service to the poor."

Sirak gawked in disbelief. "But my sister needs the love and support of Umm Krikor."

"That's your decision, my son. The Patriarch will not reconsider."

Sirak sat for a few moments staring at his hands. Finally, he looked up at Abu Apraham. "I will marry Yasmin. That is *my* decision. Please provide me with an accounting of the debt I owe the Patriarch and I'll repay him. We'll need two weeks to find a place to live." He stood up and opened the door.

"Sirak," Abu Apraham called after him, "think about what you're doing. Don't make this decision in haste, my son."

"I've thought about it, sir. I've done nothing but think about Yasmin for eight long years. I'm marrying her, and I know in my heart God understands, even if the Patriarch doesn't." Sirak stepped into the hall and shut the door quietly behind him.

CHAPTER 52

Cleveland, Ohio, October 26, 1996

irak stared at the float bobbing on his line. He looked up at Keri. "So now you know the truth. Your mother wasn't Armenian; she was Druze."

"Is that why we only attended church on Christmas and Easter?"

"That's one reason. I also resented the Patriarch's decision. Then, we couldn't travel to the Armenian Quarter for twenty years after the 1948 Arab-Israeli War. We lived on the Israeli side, and the Old City was occupied by the Arabs."

"I remember. Did you tell Ara about Mother?"

Sirak let out a weighty sigh. "Yes, I told him two years before he died."

"Why didn't you tell me, Papa?"

"Ara was five years older than you. Then, after I told him, we lost him. I wasn't willing to take that risk with you. You're older now and the situation has changed. I've changed, too."

Keri nodded acceptingly. "Did you ever see Ammar and Azusa again?"

"No, I never did. I got a letter from them now and then, and we sent them letters. Then, a year or so before we left Jerusalem, I got a letter from their daughter, Nazira. Ammar and Azusa died a few days apart from some sickness that swept the town. Ammar told Nazira to tell me he loved me just before he died. I always regretted not going back to see them before they died."

Keri nodded thoughtfully. "Did you repay the Patriarch?"

"Eventually, but it took me many years. Your mother and I were married in a civil ceremony, and we moved into the house where you grew up in Katamon. I was fortunate to be appointed to the surgical staff at nearby Hadassah Hospital. It was a tough time for us all. Your Aunt Izabella sank into profound depression despite your mama's loving care for her. I worked twelve or more hours a day treating the battered and broken victims of one uprising or another. We took Izabella to visit Umm Krikor every week, until that became impossible, but nothing would dispel the gloom that consumed her. Then, the Arab revolt exploded into violent conflict and hundreds more Arabs, Jews and British soldiers were maimed and killed. Bombs exploded around us every single day. But through it all, your mama and I remained happy as lovebirds." Sirak looked up from the water. "Your mama was a very special woman."

Keri smiled. "I know, Papa. How long were you and Mama married before Ara was born?"

"Eleven years."

"*Eleven years?*" Keri blurted out with surprise.

Sirak nodded. "We didn't think your mama could have children. We looked at adoption, but with all the turmoil in Jerusalem, and the entire world going to war, we decided the orphaned children were better off leaving Palestine. Then, in the summer of 1947, when your mama was thirty-seven years old and I was forty, she became pregnant. Ara was born in January of 1948, just as the Arab-Israeli conflict raged into all-out war. Snipers killed two of our neighbors when they ventured out to buy supplies. Then thirty of my colleagues from the hospital, including one of my best friends, Doctor Chaim Yassky, the director of the hospital, were killed when Arab fighters attacked a medical convoy transporting supplies and injured patients to the hospital. The fighting finally tapered off near the end of 1948, but our neighborhood ended up in the Israeli-occupied territory, cut off from the Arab-dominated Old City—including the Armenian Quarter and St. James Cathedral. We never saw Umm Krikor or her husband again. For a time, we at least had telephone contact, but then the wires were cut, and that ended, too."

"That must've been terrible for Aunt Izabella."

"It was, when it first happened, but somehow—after the birth of your brother—she got much better. She immersed herself in helping your mama take care of the baby. Then, five years later, you were born, and your sister came a year after that. God truly blessed us and we were blissfully happy." He smiled nostalgically. "You kids did well in school and the neighbors were good to us. Most of them were Jewish, since our Arab neighbors either fled or were forced out of their homes when Palestine was partitioned. It's ironic. Both your mama and I were outcasts from our own peoples, but the Jews we lived and worked with accepted us unconditionally as friends and colleagues.

"The Arabs and Jews battled on, but for the most part, we lived in peace during those years. I poured myself into my work at the hospital, and after a few years I got promoted to senior staff surgeon. But then the world came crashing down around us. The fighting intensified again and your mama pleaded with me to take the family out of Jerusalem. But I didn't want to lose the power and prestige of my position at the hospital, and for this, we all paid dearly."

"Papa, it was war. It wasn't your fault."

"It *was* my fault. In early 1967, rumors began to circulate that Syria and Israel would soon go to war. Your mama pleaded with me to take the family to Beirut or Amman, or even America. Ara was nineteen at the time, which means you were fourteen and Mina was thirteen. Every day we risked being shot by snipers or wandering into some no-man's-land peppered with mines and being blown to pieces. But I valued the trappings of my position at the hospital more than my family, and because of this, your mama, sister, and Aunt Izabella were killed."

"Papa, it was war."

"I've had to live with my failure ever since that horrible day."

"Where were you that day? I've forgotten."

"I was at work. I remember that the day before I heard on the wireless at the hospital that the Egyptian Air Force had been destroyed on the ground and I rushed home to be with you kids and your mama. Shortly thereafter, we learned the Iraqi, Jordanian and Syrian air forces had also been destroyed. That night we heard distant gunfire, and a deafening artillery barrage shook the house. Most of the shells seemed to be directed to the west, but a couple fell nearby. There was a lull in the fighting the next morning, and I was called back to the hospital to care for wounded soldiers and private citizens. I'd just finished operating on a soldier who'd had both of his legs blown off, when Doctor Levin rushed into the operating room to find me…"

June 6, 1967, Jerusalem

The door outside the surgery control desk burst open and a doctor dressed in blue surgical scrubs and cap rushed through the door.

Sirak glanced up from his paperwork. "Hello, Joseph," he said tiredly.

Doctor Levin stared back sorrowfully.

"What's wrong?" Sirak asked.

"It's your family."

Sirak dropped his pen. "My family? What about my family?"

"My dear friend, something horrible happened. An artillery shell hit your house."

"Who told you this?"

"Your neighbor, Adam Bluestone. He's waiting downstairs. I'm so sorry."

Sirak rushed past Doctor Levin, and running to the stairwell, took the stairs two at a time down to the ground floor. He burst through the door into the lobby and spotted Bluestone standing at the main entrance. "Adam!" he called out.

Tears in Bluestone's red eyes were daggers to his heart.

Sirak collapsed to his knees. "Oh, my God, no! Please, God, no!"

"Your sons are alive," Bluestone whispered compassionately. "I'll take you to them."

Sirak followed the old man out to the curb and climbed into his dusty old Renault sedan. The boom of artillery and crackle of gunfire echoed from the distance. Too numb to speak, Sirak slumped into the front passenger's seat and slammed the door. Bluestone made a U-turn in front of the hospital and accelerated up a nearly-deserted access road that wound to the east toward the Old City walls.

They came across a dozen dead Arab fighters sprawled across the road half a mile from the hospital.

"Dear, God, the fighting is everywhere," Bluestone muttered. "Should we stop?"

"No, they're dead. Keep going."

Bluestone wove through the grisly scene and raced toward the Katamon neighborhood. The rat-a-tat-tat of machine gun fire and the boom of artillery and mortars grew louder as they got closer. Finally, they reached the main Katamon road and the old Jew turned into their residential neighborhood.

Bam, bam, bam, resounded three shots to the rear passenger's door and window.

"Keep going!" Sirak shouted. "Don't stop!"

Bluestone accelerated down the street and swerved around a pickup truck sitting cockeyed in the middle of the street. Sirak glanced out Bluestone's window at a body slumped against the steering wheel of the vehicle. He spotted two Arabs firing on the car from atop a wall surrounding the neighborhood.

"Bastards!" Bluestone bellowed angrily. "They fire at anything that moves."

Two more shots hit the rear of the car before Bluestone turned the next corner. He eased the car to the curb halfway down the street and pulled to a stop in front of a one-story house.

Steven E. Wilson

Sirak gaped at the collapsed wall on one side of his house. "Oh, my God." He leapt from the car and bounded up the walkway and through the open door. The entry side of the house hadn't been touched, but it smelled of explosives and was blanketed in eerie silence.

Sirak rushed into the shattered kitchen. Looking up, he peered at the sky through a gaping hole in the roof. He darted through the open door into the back yard.

Three sheet-draped bodies were arranged side-by-side in the middle of the sandy, weed-choked yard. Ara and Keri were huddled beside two neighborhood women.

Sirak felt he would vomit. He stumbled down from the porch and spread his arms. "My sons."

Both boys whirled around and lunged into their father's embrace.

Ara peered up at Sirak. "Papa, they're dead. Mama, Mina and Aunt Izabella—they're all dead."

Sirak hugged the boys to his chest. After a moment, he knelt beside the first body. He pulled the sheet back and bit down on his lip in horror. Mina's pale countenance was framed by her dark, curly hair. Her expression was peaceful, with a hint of surprise.

"My precious baby," Sirak cried. "Oh, my darling, please forgive me." He buried his face against his little girl's chest and sobbed.

Sirak crawled on his knees to the next shrouded body and pulled back the sheet. Yasmin's pasty-white face was heavily pocked with shrapnel. "*Habibi! Habibi,* I failed you!" Cupping the back of her head in his trembling hands, he kissed her tenderly on the forehead. "How can I live without you?" Sobbing, he beat his fists on the ground.

Keri knelt beside his father and comforted him. Sirak crumbled face-down to the ground beside his wife. Howling with grief, he clutched Yasmin's dress, as mortar blasts and rifle fire echoed in the distance.

After a long while, Sirak crawled to the last body. He pulled down the sheet and Izabella's half-opened eyes stared up at him. He traced his fingertips across two deep puncture wounds on her left cheek and a gash across her chin. "My precious sister," he sobbed, "you've finally found peace. I pray you're with Jesus now, with Mama, Papa and our brothers and sister." He closed her eyes and kissed her forehead before replacing the shroud.

Struggling to his feet, Sirak hugged Ara and Keri to his chest. "Thank God you boys are safe. Why didn't I heed old man Jeremiah's warnings? How many times did he tell me this city would break my heart?" Sirak gasped despondently. "And your mama told me, too. My sons, forgive me."

"What should we do now, Papa?" Ara asked.

Sirak turned and looked over the rooftops at the distant, pink-tinged walls of Jerusalem and the great golden Dome of the Rock shrouded in smoky haze. "We'll bury them properly, and then we'll leave this place forever. We'll leave for America as soon as possible."

Ara nodded and wrapped his arm around Keri's shoulders.

Adam Bluestone stepped around the bodies. "I'm deeply sorry, my friend. Come with me and I'll help you make funeral arrangements."

Sirak nodded. He glanced down once more at the shrouded bodies and led his sons into the house.

"For years after that, I saw your mother's sunken, lifeless eyes everywhere I went. I saw them at the market, in the church and at the hospital. I thought nothing could ever be worse than losing her—until we lost your brother."

Keri looked up at a sailboat easing out of a slip. "What did you do with our house in Jerusalem?"

"I sold it for a pittance. The Israeli Army secured all of Jerusalem and we buried your mama, Mira and Izabella in the Armenian Cemetery just outside the Old City walls."

"I remember that, Papa. Did you ever feel like you wanted to go back to Jerusalem—you know, to visit their graves?"

Sirak sighed deeply and looked up at Keri. "Only once, when your brother died. But I knew no good would come of it."

Both men sat staring at the rippling water beyond the breakwater. Each was lost in his own thoughts—transported to another place and another time.

CHAPTER 53

November 11, 1996

Agent Jim Butler leaned back from his desk and stared out the window. He watched yellow, orange and red leaves flutter across the grass at the front of the building. He stood up, stretched his frame to its full height, and stepped over to the window to watch a pretty young woman secure a package on the back of her motor scooter. A brisk knock at the door snapped him out of his trance. "Come in!" Butler called out.

The door opened and a young, clean-cut Asian in a dark blue suit stepped through the door. "Good morning, Jim."

"Welcome back, Leo. How was your vacation?"

"Awesome. Have you ever been to Colombia?"

"No, never."

"It's incredible, man. I've never seen such amazing fishing, wonderful beaches and awesome women."

Listen, do you have time to go over the analysis performed on the explosives from the Bedford storage locker case?"

"Sure," Butler replied. "I just reviewed my notes yesterday. What've you got?"

The young agent handed Butler several sheets of paper. "Take a look at this. The composition of the dynamite from Bedford matches the 1976 theft at a Michigan drilling site."

Butler perused the first page and turned to the next. "So what's the numerical correlation?"

"Ninety-nine point eight percent. It doesn't get much better than that, buddy."

"It sure doesn't."

"It also matches the dynamite the FBI found at an Armenian youth camp in Massachusetts back in the eighties. Did you get the traces back on the firearms?"

"All the guns were untraceable, except for that Winchester rifle with carving on the stock. It belonged to a woman from West Virginia, but she lived in Cleveland until ten years ago. I interviewed her last Friday. Her son sold the gun to his boss at an Open Pantry convenience store in Euclid."

Leo's mouth dropped open. "You're full of shit. Open Pantry?"

Butler nodded. "The same one on the storage locker rental agreement."

"Bingo! Who was the boss at Open Pantry?"

"He was an Armenian guy in his thirties named Moose. I pulled up the tax records on the store. An outfit named Zakian Enterprises owned it."

Leo clapped his hands. "So it was owned by Armenians, too?"

"Yeah, then I really got lucky. On a hunch, I had Donna run 'Zakian' and all the last names the woman, Louise, used when she rented the Bedford storage locker—Corona, Buschel and Cazian. She found a couple named Gevork Zakian and Michelle Cazian who lived in a house in Mayfield Heights. They live in Florida now. We pulled up Michelle Cazian's driver's license photo. Unfortunately, she doesn't look anything like the composite drawing of the woman who rented the locker."

"When are you going to talk to them?"

"Maybe next week. I'm driving out this afternoon to visit another Zakian who lives in Euclid—a Lucy Zakian."

Leo smirked. "You're kidding. Louise Zakian?"

"No, Lucy—but that's pretty close. She doesn't have a driver's license, but she's forty-nine years old according to tax records."

"Perfect."

"Do you want to drive over with me? We can grab some lunch on the way."

"Just give me fifteen minutes to sort through my mail." Leo glanced at his watch. "How about if I meet you downstairs at eleven-thirty?"

"See you then."

B utler merged onto I-71 headed north and, squinting through the bright afternoon sun, eased into the left lane. He popped on his sunglasses. "What's up with your love life? Are you and Suzie still dating?"

"Nope," Leo said emphatically. "She dumped me for some weasel music producer with a Mercedes."

"That figures. Didn't I tell you she was a gold-digger?"

"Yeah, you did. I was getting tired of her bitching and moaning anyway. She did me a favor doing it just before my vacation. That Colombian girl, Caro, was unbelievable. Too bad you weren't there to meet her sister. What a hottie she was." Leo pounded out a drum roll on the dash with his fingertips. "Are you gettin' any?"

Jim shook his head. "Ha! Teri and I go out every once in a while, but she's busy most of the time with her kids. I had a blind date last weekend. She was nice, but there was no chemistry."

"Have you visited FBI headquarters lately?" Leo asked.

"Last week."

"Did you meet the new receptionist?"

"You mean the one with the long curly hair?"

"Yeah, that's her. Now that's what I mean by chemistry."

"She's hot, but too tall for me. Besides, she's married."

"She's not married, dumbass. She wears that ring to ward off lowlife."

"Are you serious?"

"That's what she told me. She broke off her engagement to a fireman a couple of months ago when he decided he didn't want children."

"Really?"

"I asked her out myself, but she said I wasn't her type. She was nice about it though. She seems like an old-fashioned girl—a real sweetheart. You'd better hurry before those vultures at the Bureau start circling."

Butler rolled his eyes. "What's her name?"

"Hailey—Hailey Stevens."

"Hailey," Butler muttered. "I've always loved that name. Let's drive by there this afternoon. There're a couple of details related to this case I need to pull up on their computer."

"Sounds good to me."

The two agents sped along in silence for a few minutes.

"Did you ever hear about the Armenian Holocaust during World War I?" Butler finally asked.

The young agent nodded his head. "A little, but history wasn't my strongest subject."

"My dad was a history professor, so I got interested in it early on. This past week, I did some research on the Internet. From 1915 to 1919 more than a million Armenians died in the Ottoman Empire, mostly in the area of Turkey called Anatolia and in Syria. There's a huge controversy about what really happened, but books and documents written during that time by American missionaries and German Army officers documented the outright slaughter of thousands of Armenian men. After that, hundreds of caravans of women, children and old people were driven into the Syrian desert. Most of them either starved to death or were pillaged by local tribes. The accounts I read were shocking."

"I think I read somewhere that the Turks deny it even happened."

"They do. The Turkish government claims anyone who died during that time was swept away in the fighting and starvation brought on by the First World War. They say millions of Turks died, too. Anyway, the ongoing Turkish denials, and the failure to return lost land and other belongings, really pissed off some of the surviving descendants. Beginning in 1973, several militant Armenian groups carried out bombings and assassinations all around the world, including in some major U.S. cities. A lot of the hostility was aimed at Turkish diplomats—like Kemal Arikan, the Turkish consul general in LA. He was assassinated in 1982 by a nineteen-year-old Armenian youth who was caught and sentenced to twenty-some years in prison."

"I'll be damned. Why haven't I heard more about this?"

Jim changed lanes and accelerated around a dump truck. "Probably because the attacks suddenly ended in 1986, when you and I were in grade school."

"What was the name of the terrorist group that carried out the attacks?"

"There were several. The Armenian Secret Army for the Liberation of Armenia, or ASALA, is the best known, but there were several other mysterious groups who took responsibility for one or more attacks, including the Justice Commandos for the Armenian Genocide, or JCAG, the Commandos of Armenian Militants Against Genocide and the Armenian Revolutionary Army. They called themselves the ARA."

"Why did the attacks stop?"

"I'm not sure. There was infighting between the groups and some of their leaders were killed, but it's not clear what really happened. Maybe the fall of the Soviet Union and the independence of Armenia had something to do with it."

Leo shook his head. "You sure get all the winners, Butler," he wisecracked. "Talk about a cold case."

"You know I like history—it's damned fascinating, if you ask me. All these years and dozens of unsolved crimes around the world, and suddenly the big break may come from a storage locker in Bedford, Ohio."

"So you believe the guns and dynamite belonged to the terrorists?"

"It's possible." Butler fished a paper from his briefcase. "Take a good look at this drawing. It's a composite of the woman who paid for the storage locker all those years."

Leo studied the sketch for a few moments. "How old did the witness say she was?"

"In her forties."

"She looks a lot older than that."

"Just memorize it, knucklehead."

Butler took I-90 east and got off the highway in Euclid. Weaving through a neighborhood just off the freeway, he pulled to a stop across the street from a small sixties-vintage stucco house with an overgrown yard. "That's the one," he muttered.

The two agents got out of the car and crossed the street. Ambling up the sidewalk to the porch, Butler knocked briskly on the screen door. After a few moments, a peephole in the door opened.

"Who is it?" a weary-sounding female voice called out.

Butler held up his identification. "Good morning, ma'am; I'm Federal Agent Jim Butler and this is Agent Leo Wang from the Bureau of Alcohol, Tobacco, Firearms and Explosives. We're here to speak with Lucy Zakian."

The front door creaked open and a middle-aged woman with gray-streaked brown hair peeked out through the screen. "I'm Lucy. Is something wrong?"

"We'd like to ask you a few questions. May we come inside?"

The woman stared at the two men for several moments.

"Ma'am?" Butler finally asked.

"Okay," she replied, with a tremor in her voice, "just let me put my dog in the bedroom."

Wang glanced at Butler. "It's her," he whispered.

Butler nodded and signaled for silence.

Lucy reappeared a moment later. Visibly shaken, she opened the screen door. The front room was neat but crowded with shabby furniture and a heap of woven carpets. The musty odor of old books wafted through the air. She motioned the visitors toward the couch. "Can I get you anything to drink?"

"Nothing for me, thanks," Butler replied.

"No, thank you." Wang opened up his notebook and fished a pen out of his coat pocket.

The woman sat facing them and anxiously clasped her hands in her lap. "How can I help you, officers?"

"Mrs. Zakian," Butler began, "have you ever heard of Louise Corona?"

The woman shifted nervously in her chair. "Louise Corona? No, I've never heard of her."

"That name doesn't ring a bell? How about Louise Buschel?"

"I've never heard of her, either. What is this about?"

"How about an Armenian woman named Louise Cazian?"

Mrs. Zakian shook her head and brushed a strand of hair back from her forehead. "No," she stammered, before erupting into a coughing fit. "Ex...excuse me."

Butler made a note on his pad and glared menacingly at the shaken woman. "But you have been to the Bedford Self-Serve Mini Storage Facility just off the freeway in Bedford Heights. Isn't that right?"

She looked down at her hands. "No, I've never been there."

Butler held up the composite sketch. "Mrs. Zakian, I think you've visited that storage facility. Perhaps you've forgotten? Take a look at this drawing our artist made with help from the manager."

Lucy Zakian stared at the drawing. She looked at Agent Butler and wiped her hands on her dress.

"This is your handwriting on this rental agreement, isn't it, Mrs. Zakian?"

The woman peered at the photocopy for several moments and then looked back down. "It may be, but I don't remember."

"Mrs. Zakian, Agent Wang and I are investigating a storage locker in the Bedford Self-Serve Mini Storage Facility that was filled with guns, ammunition, blasting caps and dynamite. It's located across the street from a day-care center and school that care for over a hundred small kids.

We're certain that dynamite was stolen from a drill operator in Michigan. So several felonies have been committed and someone will likely spend a very long time in prison. We'd prefer not to add obstruction of justice to the other charges, so let me ask you this question one more time. Have you ever been to the Bedford Self-Serve Mini Storage Facility?"

Lucy Zakian stared fearfully into Agent Butler's blue eyes. She glanced at Agent Wang, and then looked at her hands. "I've been there."

Butler reached out and rested his hand reassuringly on the woman's arm. "Mrs. Zakian, are you the woman who paid the rent for that storage locker all those years?"

Mrs. Zakian sat pensively for several moments and then nodded. "I rented a storage unit for my former husband, but I didn't know anything about what was stored there."

"I understand, ma'am. What's your former husband's name?"

"Gevork Zakian."

"Do you know why he had the dynamite and guns?"

"I have no idea what he'd be doing with guns and explosives. I'm shocked."

"Where is he now?"

"In Miami."

"Did your husband have a nickname, ma'am?"

"Some people call him Moose."

Butler glanced at Wang and smiled ever so slightly. "Did Mr. Zakian own an Open Pantry convenience store in Cleveland?"

"Yes, many years ago."

"What does your ex-husband do now, Mrs. Zakian?" Agent Wang interjected.

"He's the chairman of ANCA."

"ANCA?" Butler repeated. "What's that?"

"The Armenian National Committee of America."

Butler jotted the moniker on his pad and underlined it twice. He looked up. "Do you have your ex-husband's phone number and address?"

"Yes, but I haven't spoken to him in years—ever since he remarried."

"He's remarried?" Butler asked. "Is that why you stopped paying the rent on the storage locker?"

Lucy took a deep breath and dabbed at her eyes. "Well, he stopped sending me money and I got tired of spending my settlement. I'm not rich, you know."

"I understand. Mrs. Zakian, we'd like you to call your husband and ask him about the storage locker and its contents while we record the conversation. It's the only way to prove you knew nothing about what he stored there. Will you do that for us?"

Lucy stared at the agent.

"Mrs. Zakian?"

"I'll get his number." The beleaguered woman got up from her chair and shuffled into the kitchen. Returning with a small phone book, she sat down and lifted the phone receiver to dial.

"Just a moment, ma'am," Wang said. He retrieved a small recorder from his pocket and attached a microphone to the phone receiver. "Okay, go ahead."

The woman dialed, and the sound of the phone ringing reverberated from the recorder.

"Hello," a woman answered.

"This is Lucy. Is Gevork there?"

"Yeah. Hold on and I'll get him."

"Okay, thank you."

"Lucy," a deep male voice said a moment later. "What's up?"

"Listen, Gevork, the police were here earlier today. Like, they were asking me questions about that storage locker in Bedford. Why didn't you tell me what was in there?"

"Oh, Lucy."

"What? I'm scared to death."

"Oh, man."

"There were enough explosives in that room to blow up the whole damned block. Jesus...I mean, this is insane. You have five kids..."

"Lucy, please, please, please. Not over the phone… I'll fly there in the morning. Okay?"

"Okay. You'd better not let me down."

"I'll be there. Don't say anything to anyone. I'll call you when I get to the airport."

The phone line clicked to a dial tone and Lucy hung up the phone.

"You did great," Butler reassured her. He got up from his chair. "When he gets here tomorrow, I'd like you to meet him here. We'll set up a listening device. Okay?"

Lucy didn't look up. She stared at the floor and nodded submissively.

"Thank you. We'll be back at seven in the morning. Don't speak to anyone about our being here, especially to your former husband. The best thing to do is just not answer the phone if it rings." He handed her a card. "You call me if you need to talk to someone. Okay?"

Lucy nodded and the agents slipped out the door.

The next day, Butler and Wang were set up in a surveillance van in front of Lucy Zakian's house. Around the time Lucy had told them to expect Gevork's arrival, a taxi slowed to a stop and a slender, middle-aged man, dressed in a dark suit and tie, emerged and hustled up the walk to the front door.

The sound of the doorbell resounded from the digital recorder. Butler glanced at the technician and nodded approvingly.

"Lucy," a husky voice said a moment later.

"Did you hear from the police?"

"Not yet. Have they spoken to you since yesterday?"

"No."

"Why are you so upset?"

"Because I'm the one that's going to get shafted."

"Listen, Lucy, I didn't know what was in that storage locker."

"Then who put it in there? You have to know that."

"Yeah, yeah. Somebody asked me to rent that locker. They were some of the guys from overseas. And they told me to forget about it."

"You didn't know they stored dynamite and guns?"

Gevork sighed. "I didn't know any of that."

"Remember those FBI agents that came here many, many years ago?"

"Listen, I had FBI guys come in so many different times to talk to me. It never came to anything. Lucy, whatever happens, just keep your cool. They're going to go after you, and they'll try to use you to get to me. Do you hear me?"

"You're paranoid. Why would they want to get to you?"

"Why do you think? Because I'm the head of the Armenian National Committee."

"Well, at least you've got important friends to protect you."

"All you did was rent a storage locker. That's all you did. Now, here's the money I owe you for the past few months. Does that cover it?"

"Yes, I guess it does."

"Well, I've got to go now. I have a reception back in Washington this evening. Take care of yourself, Lucy. Let me know if you need anything. Okay?"

"Yeah, sure."

"I'll call you next week."

Zakian rushed down the walk to the waiting taxi. He ducked inside the car and it pulled away a moment later. Turning the corner at the end of the street, it disappeared behind a line of shrubs.

Wang waited ten minutes before he drove up the street and parked in front of the house. The agents jumped out of the van and walked up the sidewalk. Butler knocked on the door and Lucy opened it.

"Did you hear?" she asked. "He said he didn't know, either."

"We heard," Butler replied. "You did very well and we appreciate your cooperation. Before I forget, do you have anything here that belongs to your husband, like boxes, photographs, papers, or letters?"

"Yes, now that you mention it, there are two boxes of old clothes, papers and such in the basement."

"How long have these things been here?"

"At least ten or fifteen years. He left them when we split up."

"Is that all you have?"

"That's it. After twenty years of marriage to that bastard all I have is two cardboard boxes of rubbish." She dabbed her eyes with a handkerchief, and retreating into the living room, sat in a chair.

"Please don't touch any of his stuff, okay?" Butler said. "We'll get a warrant, but it's important for you not to move the boxes or even look inside them until I get back. Do you understand?"

"Yes, sir, I understand."

"It's also important for you not to tell anyone we've spoken today. Okay?"

"Yes, yes. I just hope you don't think I had anything to do with this. I swear, I didn't know what was in the storage unit; I just paid the bill like Moose told me to."

Butler patted the angst-ridden woman on the shoulder. "Mrs. Zakian, thank you for your help. If you really didn't know about the contents of the storage locker, or how they were used, then you haven't committed any crimes."

Lucy looked up. "I've told you everything I know."

"Then there's nothing to worry about. I'll be back later today. I'd appreciate it if you could stay home until I get here."

"I'm not going anywhere."

"Thank you." Butler motioned to Wang and the two men stepped outside.

Wang slammed his door and started the car. "Do you think she knew?" he asked Butler.

"No, I don't think so. Why would she protect him and risk going to prison after he dumped her for another woman?"

"Good point. Let's go. I've got a basketball game tonight."

CHAPTER 54

Jim Butler stood at a table strewn with old pamphlets, maps, books and folders. Faded jeans, tee shirts and other articles of clothing that'd already been catalogued by the clerk were stacked on a nearby table. Butler, his hands covered with latex gloves, paged slowly through a small spiral notebook. He glanced over his shoulder when the door opened behind him and Wang stepped into the evidence room.

"Leo, take a look at this," Butler said, holding up a dog-eared notebook. "There must be eighty names, addresses and phone numbers written in here. All but a couple of them end in 'ian' or 'yan.' "

Wang peered over Butler's shoulder. "See any names you recognize?"

"No, and after all these years, most of the addresses and phone numbers are likely to be dead ends, but at least they provide us with some leads to follow up."

"Did you find Zakian's name on anything?"

"Hell yes, in at least a dozen places. It's his stuff all right. Once the analyst is finished with it, I'm driving back over to Lucy Zakian's house. I want to see if she remembers any of these people."

The next morning Agent Butler was on the phone when Leo Wang knocked softly and slipped inside the office.

Butler took the telephone receiver away from his ear. "Just a minute. I'm on hold with the FBI."

Wang frowned and slumped into a chair.

Several moments passed before Butler bolted to attention. "Yes, I'm still here." He hurriedly jotted a note. "Buenos Aires?" he whispered with surprise. "Do you have an address?" He scribbled a bit more on his pad. "Okay, I guess that's plenty for now. Can you e-mail me his photo and copies of those documents?" Butler sat back in his seat. "Thanks a lot, Rich. I appreciate your help." He nodded at Leo. "Don't worry, I'll keep you posted. Have a great day."

Butler hung up the phone and swiveled around to face Wang. "The chief put me in touch with the head of the FBI Counterterrorism Division in Washington—a guy named Rich Fox— and I just spent the last two hours on the phone with him."

"What's up?"

"I took those names and addresses to Lucy Zakian last night. She'd never heard of most of them, but there were a couple she thought she recognized from the late seventies and early eighties." Butler shuffled through his notes. "One in particular, a man named Lazar Sarkesian, spent a lot of time around their house and the convenience store where her husband worked. I faxed the list to Fox this morning. He came back with information on several of them, including Sarkesian. It turns out he was chief lieutenant to one of the founders of ASALA, an Armenian named Hagop Hagopian, who was aligned early on with the PLO. Sarkesian worked as a recruiter for ASALA, and he was apparently damned good at it. One of his recruits, a chap from California named Monte Melkonian, eventually became the leader of one of the offshoots of ASALA when the organization split following the Israeli invasion of Lebanon in 1983. Anyway, Fox and his predecessors at the FBI have been tracking Sarkesian for years, and they suspect he was a major player in the Armenian terror organizations here. Sarkesian moved from Beirut to Paris, but spent a lot of time in major cities throughout the U.S. Eventually he settled in

Buenos Aires, and apparently he's lived there quietly since '93. Fox gave me his last-known address."

"Do you plan to question him?"

"Absolutely. I'm flying to Buenos Aires tonight. There's no rest for the weary. I want to get on top of these new leads. I can't take the chance that Lucy Zakian has second thoughts about cooperating and sends Sarkesian and the others into hiding."

"Good luck. Call me when you get back."

"I will. See you next week."

CHAPTER 55

Butler stepped through the doors outside of baggage claim at the Buenos Aires International Airport and scanned more than a dozen signs behind the barrier. He spotted the one he was looking for, and made his way through the crowd of waiting people toward a dark-haired young man.

"Hello, I'm Jim Butler."

"Welcome to Buenos Aires, Mr. Butler," the man replied in heavily-accented English. "How was your flight, sir?"

"Long," Butler replied. "The guy in the seat next to me was snoring like a chainsaw."

"Sorry to hear that. It'll take about a half hour to drive to the hotel, and then you can get some rest. May I take your bag?"

"Thank you." Butler handed the young man his suitcase and followed him out of the terminal.

Within minutes, the small sedan was weaving in and out of traffic on the expressway. Butler squinted out the window through dazzling sunlight at the aging high-rise residential buildings that were so close to the freeway he could see birds roosting on the balcony clotheslines.

The driver exited the freeway and drove along a wide, traffic-congested boulevard. Finally, he turned into a commercial district lined with boutiques, galleries, cafés and bars, where the sidewalks were crowded with affluent Porteños—including alluring young women adorned in chic clothes that ranged from designer jeans to elegant dresses.

"What's this area called?" Butler asked the driver.

"It's the Recoleta District, sir. We're only two blocks from your hotel."

"There's a lot going on here. Is it always this busy?"

The driver smiled at him in the rearview mirror. "Wait until tonight. It'll be impossible to move."

"Where would you recommend I have dinner tonight?"

"Is this your first visit to Buenos Aires, sir?"

"Yes."

"Then, I recommend you walk along Junin Street across from the Recoleta Cemetery. You'll find anything you like at the restaurants there, from Argentinean steak to pasta." He pulled to a stop in front of a small hotel. "Here we are, sir. Junin Street is just two blocks down. I suggest you try a tango club after dinner. They're all over the city."

The driver grabbed Butler's bag from the trunk and led him inside. An efficient young man at the reception desk checked him in. The doorman led him to a small, but pleasant, room.

Butler checked his watch. It was ten thirty in the morning. He took a quick shower, set his alarm for three in the afternoon and stretched out on the bed to nap.

Butler stepped out of the lobby and headed down the busy street. Just as the concierge told him, he found Avenida Callao four blocks south of the hotel. He turned the corner onto a narrow, tree-lined thoroughfare lined with shops, restaurants, apartments and condominiums. He scanned the numbers on the buildings until he found 257. It was a rather unattractive, but modern, three-story building, with a gated driveway that led to a first-floor parking garage.

Butler glanced up at the building and scrutinized the sliding glass windows overlooking the street before jogging up the steps. He opened the door, approached the mailboxes lining the back wall of the foyer and found the name he wanted. Taking the stairs to the third floor, he followed the numbers to the end of the hall. He paused for a moment to gather his thoughts and knocked purposefully on the last door. There was no response, so he knocked again. The door cracked open a moment later.

"*Quién esta aquí?*" a youthful woman's voice called out.

"My name is Jim Butler, ma'am. I'm an investigator from the United States. I'm here to speak with Mr. Sarkesian for a few minutes. Here's my card."

"*Un momento, por favor,*" the woman said politely. She closed the door.

Feeling rather foolish, Butler stood in the hall for five minutes before the door inched opened again.

"*Tiene documentos?*" the woman queried.

"Documents? Yes, I have documents."

"Give them, please."

Butler fished his I.D. out of his pocket and slipped it through the gap.

The door slammed shut again. Several more minutes passed before the chain slid back and the door swung open.

A ravishing, dark-haired beauty dressed in a tee shirt and blue jeans stood in the doorway. She held out his I.D. "Mr. Sarkesian see you. He sick, so only few questions." She turned and walked away.

"Thank you," Butler replied awkwardly.

He followed the shapely young woman through a brightly-lit living room and down a short hall that ended in French doors. She stepped through the doors, and led Butler into a dim bedroom. A pallid, elderly man, with an oxygen mask covering his mouth and nose, was lying in the center of a large bed that dominated the rather small room. A sheet was pulled up to his neck, and his head was propped on a stack of pillows. The air in the room was stagnant and smelled faintly of bile.

The young woman sat in a chair in the corner of the room. She glared at Butler and folded her arms across her chest.

The old man held out his feeble hand. "I'm Lazar Sarkesian," he said breathily. "How can I help you, young man?"

"Mr. Sarkesian, I'm Jim Butler, an investigator with the United States Bureau of Alcohol, Tobacco, Firearms and Explosives. I'd like to ask you a few questions, sir."

Sarkesian gazed at Butler for several moments. His eyes were a dull pitch-black and the whites were tinged with yellow. His gray beard was unkempt. He took a deep breath and cleared his throat. "Are you here to arrest me?"

"No, Mr. Sarkesian, I'm only here to ask you some questions."

"Okay, then, please sit down."

Butler sat in a chair beside the bed and retrieved a notebook from his pocket. He looked up at the young woman and smiled cheerfully. She glared back with distrustful indifference.

Butler looked down at his notebook. "Mr. Sarkesian, did you know a man named Hagop Hagopian?"

Sarkesian pulled up his mask and cleared his throat. "Yes, I knew him. That was a long time ago. Hagop has been dead for many years."

"How long ago did you know him?"

"For nearly two decades—mostly in the seventies and eighties."

"Did you know Monte Melkonian?"

It seemed that a hint of a smile came to Sarkesian's face. He reached toward the bed stand. "Could you hand me my water?"

Butler handed it to him. The old man took several sips and handed it back.

"Yes," he gasped, "Monte was one of the greatest men I ever knew. He was a natural leader and the bravest fighter of his day. What's all this about, Mr. Butler?"

"Did you recruit Melkonian to ASALA?"

Sarkesian laughed heartily. "ASALA! I haven't heard that name for years. I introduced Monte to Hagopian in San Francisco. He was a brash young Berkeley student at the time. But I'm not sure *recruit* is the right way to describe my role in bringing them together."

The young woman stood up with her arms folded. "You ask many questions, Mr. Butler. Lazar is sick."

"It's okay, Maria," Sarkesian said. "An old man like me doesn't get many opportunities to reminisce about his youth."

Maria sighed and sat back down in the chair.

"And you all ended up in Beirut?"

Sarkesian smiled weakly. "Yes, I lived there for six years. Those were heady times for all of us."

"And then, later, you moved away?"

"I lived in Paris for fifteen years. It's my favorite city in the world. Have you been there?"

Butler smiled. "Yes, sir, it's one of my favorites, too." He wrote something down on his notepad and looked up again. "Mr. Sarkesian, have you ever been to Cleveland, Ohio?"

The old man's eyes widened with surprise. "Yes, I've been to Cleveland a few times. That was a long time ago, too."

"Did you know a Gevork Zakian?"

"Gevork Zakian…" the old man repeated. "No, I don't recall that name."

"Are you sure? Gevork Zakian's the head of ANCA, the Armenian National Committee of America. I found your name in his notebook, and his former wife, Lucy, recalled you visiting their home and business."

Sarkesian stared back with the steely determination of a Samurai warrior. "I'm certain, young man, that I've never heard his name in my life."

Butler stared at Sarkesian. "Did you know weapons and dynamite linked to the Armenian terrorist movement were kept in a storage locker in Bedford, Ohio? Bedford's a small town just outside of Cleveland."

"No, I know nothing about any weapons or dynamite, but I hope that they were put to good use. Young man, let me tell you what I know about what you refer to as the 'Armenian terrorist movement.' Like the men you've mentioned, and tens of thousands of Armenians just like us, we suffered when the Ottomans butchered our parents and stole our land when we were children. If the ancestral homeland your people lived on for thousands of years were taken from you, wouldn't you do everything in your power to reclaim it? Of course you would. I can see it in your eyes. This was our purpose—our glorious dream. Shortly after Hagop Hagopian founded ASALA, I joined the organization in Beirut. I came to know many men in cities throughout the United States through my work, including a few in Cleveland, and I introduced some of them to Hagop. These young men shared our viewpoints about the plight of our people. Yes, we made mistakes, some that I deeply regret, and a few innocent people died unnecessarily, but our actions raised awareness in the world. Finally, others came to understand the scope of the atrocities committed against my people. For this, I have no misgivings. I'm an old man now, and my remaining days are few, but when my time on this earth is finished, I'll greet my maker with the satisfaction of knowing I made a difference for my people."

Agent Butler stopped writing and pondered the best way to approach his next question. "Sir, can you tell me the names of the men you recruited to ASALA from Cleveland?"

"There were only a few—Alek Topouzian, Ara Kazerian and George Liralian."

Butler handed the old man a sheet of paper and a pen. "Would you mind writing them down for me?"

Sarkesian scribbled down the names and handed the paper back to Butler.

"Where are these men now?" Butler asked.

"Topouzian and Kazerian were killed in Damascus in 1983. I'm not sure what happened to Liralian. He may be dead, too."

"I notice you only want to talk about dead men."

"Young man, when you get to be my age, most of the people you knew are dead."

Butler nodded contemplatively. "What role did these three men play in ASALA?"

"Topouzian participated in the assassinations of Turkish Ambassador Danis Tunaligil, in Vienna and Turkish Embassy Secretary Oktar Cirit, in Beirut, and one of the simultaneous bombings in Frankfurt, Essen and Cologne—I forget which one he led. Later he became a bodyguard to Hagopian. He was killed during infighting in Beirut. Kazerian was killed in the midst of his training in Damascus. Liralian fled Damascus after he realized he'd also been targeted."

"What do you mean, targeted?"

"A life-and-death struggle broke out among the leaders of ASALA shortly before they fled Beirut in the face of the 1982 Israeli invasion. Many men were lost…"

Sarkesian spent the next half-hour detailing the events that unfolded in Beirut and Damascus in 1982 and 1983. Tears filled his eyes more than once, as he recounted the events that tore ASALA apart. Finally, he reclined on his pillows and closed his eyes. "I must rest now. Maria, water, please."

The young woman got up and left the room. She returned a moment later carrying a glass of water.

Butler shuffled back through his notes. He shook his head and sighed frustratedly. "Are you sure you didn't know Gevork Zakian, sir?"

"I'm too tired to answer any more questions today. Maybe tomorrow."

Butler nodded. "Okay, I'll come back tomorrow."

"Maria, please show our guest out," Sarkesian said. "Good evening, Mr. Butler."

"Good evening, sir."

Butler followed Maria back through the living room to the front door. She unbolted the lock and let him out without a word.

CHAPTER 56

March 12, 1997
Richmond Heights, Ohio

Keri moved his black pawn diagonally one space to Sirak's king. "Check," he said confidently.

Sirak looked up from the board, smiled at his son and moved his king away from the threat.

"Damned rook," Keri huffed. He moved a second pawn to protect the first.

Sirak scanned the board for several moments and moved his queen diagonally across the board. "Checkmate!"

"Checkmate?" Keri muttered doubtfully. "Are you sure?" He scanned the board. "Damn!" He looked up sheepishly at his father and grinned. "I thought I had you."

"You did. All you had to do was move your knight—right here."

"Ahh, I totally missed it. I was concentrating on getting another queen."

"That's one of life's important lessons, Son. Never focus so completely on one goal that you miss an even better opportunity."

"You taught me that, Papa, and it's served me well."

"Your game has improved these past few months."

"I didn't play for years after Ara died. It's starting to come back since we've been playing regularly." He smiled. "I'll beat you one of these days."

Sirak laughed. "I'm sure you will."

Sirak and Keri were putting the chess pieces away when the doorbell rang twice in rapid succession. Sirak limped to the foyer, unlocked the deadbolt and opened the door.

Both men held up identification. "Are you Sirak Kazerian?" the taller man asked.

"Yes, I'm Dr. Kazerian, what can I do for you?"

"I'm Jim Butler and this is Leo Wang. We're agents with the Bureau of Alcohol, Tobacco, Firearms and Explosives, and we'd like to ask you a few questions."

Sirak blinked in surprise and glanced at his son. He opened the screen door to let the men inside. "Please, come in. We can talk here in the living room. This is my son, Keri. Would you care for something to drink?"

"No, thank you, sir," Butler replied.

Keri and Sirak sat on the sofa and the two agents took chairs across from them. Butler fetched a pen from his pocket and shuffled through several pages of his legal pad.

"Dr. Kazerian," Butler began, "how many children do you have?"

"Keri is my only living child, but I had another son and a daughter. They both died many years ago."

"May I ask their names?"

"My brother's name was Ara and our sister was Mina," Keri offered. "What is this about, anyway?"

"As we said, we're conducting an investigation. Your father's name came up on some paperwork and we're just making sure we do our research," Butler said.

Keri sat back with a frown on his face.

"How did they die, sir?" Wang asked, in a softer tone.

"Mina was killed in Jerusalem during the 1967 Israeli-Arab war. Ara died in Beirut in 1983, but I don't know anything about the circumstances surrounding his death."

"Was Ara a member of ASALA, sir?" Butler inquired.

Sirak's jaw dropped. He glanced at Keri and sighed deeply. "I don't know."

Butler scribbled a note and sat back in his chair. "You don't sound convinced."

"I'm not certain if he was or wasn't. I guess there's a chance he might have been; I suspected it after he died."

"Dr. Kazerian," Butler asked, "I need to ask the names of your other family members, dead or living?"

"Keri has two sons, Michael and David, and they both have children. My father, Mourad, and my mother, Kristina, were lost during the Great War, as were my brothers Stepannos, Alek, and Mikael. My older sister, Flora, was abducted in 1915. My younger sister, Izabella, was also killed during the Israeli-Arab conflict in 1967, along with my wife and daughter. I also had an uncle, Bedros—my father's older brother. Bedros was killed in Istanbul at the start of the Great War. I don't know what happened to his children—my cousins, Garo, Aren, Alis and Mairan. My mother had some brothers and sisters, but I don't know what happened to them either. I lost track of them after I left Anatolia with my mother in 1915."

"I'm sorry, sir. You've certainly suffered more than your share of tragedy. Do you know a man named Lazar Sarkesian?"

"Lazar Sarkesian?" Sirak repeated. "I've never met anyone by that name."

"How about Gevork Zakian?"

"I recognize the name. Isn't he the leader of one of the Armenian groups in Washington? I think I remember his name from some literature they handed out at church a few months back."

"Did you know Mr. Zakian when he lived in Cleveland?"

"He lived in Cleveland? No; I've never met him—at least not that I remember."

Butler wrote down Sirak's response and turned to the next page. "Sir, you mentioned that after your son's death, you suspected he might have been a member of ASALA. What made you think that?"

Sirak glanced at Keri.

Keri patted him on the knee. "It's okay, Papa."

"Mr. Butler, please bear with me," Sirak said. "I'll tell you what I know about Ara and ASALA, but I've never spoken about these things with Keri."

"Do you want me to leave, Papa?"

"No, I want you to hear what I've got to say. I began to see changes in Ara when he was in his early thirties and he moved home after he lost his job. At first these changes were subtle, but with time they became unmistakable. One fall day, I think it was in 1981, I was looking for my radio in Ara's room." Sirak pointed back toward the hall. "Ara had a habit of taking the radio out of the kitchen to listen to ballgames. God knows where he picked that up—school, I guess. Anyway, while searching for the radio, I found some political literature about Armenia and the killings that occurred in the Ottoman Empire. I was shocked by the hatred in those pamphlets, and I confronted him about them when he got home that afternoon. We argued. I ended up telling him the history of my family, of our experiences during the war—but to him that justified a militant attitude. He said there were good people working to return our ancestral lands, to right the wrongs that had been done to us."

Sirak looked up at Keri. Then he glanced at agent Butler. "Ara lost his smile that day, after I told him about our family. He turned into an angry young man filled with bitterness. He started hanging around men I suspected were associated with the Armenian nationalist movement. We fought about it constantly, but nothing I said made the slightest bit of difference. The hatred was like a cancer growing in Ara's brain, and I was helpless to do anything about it. I considered moving my sons out of Cleveland, somewhere far away from the insidious spell Ara had fallen under. But, for the second time in my life, I feared losing my position and privilege. The first time, in Jerusalem, it cost me my wife and daughter and sister. The second time, it cost me my son."

Tears welled in Sirak's aged eyes. He wiped them away with his palms. "Six months later, I lost him forever. Ara told me he needed to take a three-month computer design program in France so he could get a job. I know he arrived in Paris, because I received a postcard from him shortly after he left Cleveland. But three months became six months, and then a year; and then, on a snowy winter morning in February 1983, I got a phone call from a man named Abbas. That two-minute conversation tore my heart to pieces once and for all. Abbas told me he regretted to inform me that Ara had been killed. Actually, he said Ara had been murdered. He said he'd been with Ara in Beirut, and that my son had given him my phone number. Ara asked him to call me if anything ever happened."

Butler looked up from his notepad and solemnly nodded his understanding.

"I'm sorry, Dr. Kazerian," Agent Butler said. "Perhaps I can fill in details that'll bring you some closure about your son. A month ago, as a part of an ongoing investigation, I traveled to Buenos Aires to interview a man named Lazar Sarkesian."

"Yes, you said his name before, but I've never heard of him," Sirak muttered.

"Mr. Sarkesian told me about the formation of the Armenian Secret Army for the Liberation of Armenia, also called ASALA, in Beirut. ASALA was responsible for many of the attacks on Turkish diplomats and others in the late 1970s and early 1980s. Hagop Hagopian founded the organization. He became increasingly arrogant and cavalier in carrying out these attacks, which, in the eyes of some members, began to turn world opinion against the cause." Butler glanced back through his notes. "At some point, some of the other leaders of the organization, including a man named Monte Melkonian, plotted to rid ASALA of Hagopian and his henchmen."

"I've heard of Monte Melkonian," Sirak said. "He's a hero to my people."

"Anyway, they set their plot in motion after the Israeli invasion forced them to flee Lebanon for Syria. Several men in this faction killed some of Hagopian's close colleagues while the leader was away in Greece. Hagopian returned to Syria a short time later. He and his henchmen rounded up as many of the conspirators as they could. Your son, Ara, was one of them. They executed him in Damascus, not Beirut."

"Executed!" Sirak said, his face draining of color.

"We are sorry to tell you this, sir, but perhaps it will help knowing once and for all what happened to your son," Wang said.

"Sir, did Lazar Sarkesian say how my brother was killed?" Keri asked.

"He did, but I'm not sure it'll serve any purpose to get into the details."

"We want to know," Sirak insisted, looking at Keri and then back at the agents.

"I'm sorry to tell you that your son was tortured in a plan to force Monte Melkonian out of hiding. When that plan failed, Hagopian shot him."

Sirak stared open-mouthed at Agent Butler for a moment before burying his face in his hands. "My God, have you no mercy?" he muttered. "I bring my sons halfway around the world to America to escape the brutality and perils I was forced to endure, and my Ara is tortured and murdered back in Damascus?"

Agent Butler stood up and motioned to Agent Wang. "I think this is enough information for one day. Thank you for answering our questions; we'll be in touch later if we need to ask you anything more."

Sirak stood up and followed the agents to the door. "Mr. Butler, can I ask what you're investigating?"

"I'm sorry, sir, but I can't discuss that right now. I'll be happy to give you a call later."

Sirak nodded. "I understand. Can you at least tell me if George Liralian was involved in my son's torture and death?"

"George Liralian," Butler repeated. He glanced at Agent Wang. "How do you know George Liralian?"

"George Liralian was one of the men Ara hung around with here in Cleveland in the months before he left for Lebanon."

Butler glanced at Wang. "George Liralian hung around with your son? Do you know what happened to him?"

"He still lives here. Keri ran into him right here in Richmond Heights about a year ago. Right, Keri?"

"Yes, at the coffee shop down the street."

"Do you know his phone number or where he lives?" Butler asked.

"No, it was a chance encounter."

"Well, assuming it's the same man, I can tell you George Liralian was also a trainee with ASALA in Beirut. I don't think he had anything to do with killing your son, or anyone else for that matter. In fact, if it's the same man, he barely escaped with his own life. We'd really like to speak with him." Butler reached into his coat pocket. "Here's my card. Please call me if you see him again. Meanwhile, we'll try to track him down. Do you know if he goes by any other names?"

Keri shrugged his shoulders. "Not that I know about. He told me he was taking classes at the community college. You might check there."

"Thank you. We'll be in touch."

Keri and Sirak watched the two agents walk out to the street and get into their car.

Sirak wrapped his arm around Keri's shoulders. "I think I was better off not knowing. Poor Ara; he was so much like my brother Stepannos. He was full of idealism and fire, ready to right all the wrongs in the world. Expecting life to be fair and men to be just. He didn't deserve what happened to him, and I wasn't there to protect him."

"Papa, you did your best, which is all any of us can do for those we love. Ara knew that you loved him. He knew he came from a strong, good family. He made his own choices, and we must leave the rest in God's hands."

CHAPTER 57

April 16, 1997, a month later

The door opened and Leo Wang glanced up from a report on his desk. "How was your weekend?"

"Super. My cousin launched his boat and we spent most of our time at his cottage in Vermillion," Jim Butler said.

"Vermillion, huh? Did you have dinner at *Chez Francois?*"

"No, not this time. It was opening day on Saturday and we spent most of the weekend at the yacht club. Guess who else was there?"

"Chuck Noble? He's got a boat down there."

Butler laughed. "No, Hailey Stevens, that FBI receptionist you told me about. She was with some banker who owns a sixty-foot yacht. They were all over each other."

"That figures. So what's going on with the Bedford explosives case?"

"I flew to Boston and New York the past two days to interview four of the men listed in Zakian's notebook. It was maddening as hell. None of them were willing to tell me anything. Every one of them has become a respectable citizen with a decent job and a family."

"Just a waste of time, huh?"

"Yeah, and it's damned frustrating. I know that cache belonged to Gevork Zakian, but I don't have enough evidence to get a warrant. If I could just search his office.."

"At least you found Lazar Sarkesian before he died."

Butler's eyes widened with surprise. "Sarkesian died?"

"Yeah, he passed away last Thursday. Didn't you see the Argentine Federal Police report?"

"Hell no! I haven't had time to go through my mail." Butler contemplated the news for a moment. Suddenly, he turned and headed out the door. "I'll see you later, Leo."

"I thought we were driving to Columbus to interview Zakian's old associate."

Butler stepped into the hall. "We'll talk to him when I get back."

"Where are you going?"

"Buenos Aires. I'll be back in a few days."

CHAPTER 58

Buenos Aires

J im Butler wasn't sure what he would find in Buenos Aires, but he suspected there were clues yet uncovered in Sarkesian's condominium. Using his considerable charms, which would have been a surprise to Leo Wang, Butler ingratiated himself with Lazar Sarkesian's companion, Maria, and, after a few hours of sympathetic listening, dinner in an expensive restaurant, and the prospect of an American boyfriend, Maria invited the federal agent to help her pack up the last of her benefactor's belongings—yes, Sarkesian had left her everything he had, but Butler hoped there would be some surprises for the U.S. government as well.

Jim tossed a pair of socks into a cardboard box and grabbed several of the shirts that were hanging in the closet. "I'll be damned," he muttered, face-to-face with a small wall safe. He jiggled the dial. "Maria! Look at this."

Maria hurried into the bedroom. "What is it?"

"Did you know about the safe in the back wall of this closet?"

"No," she muttered in surprise. "Is it open?"

"It's locked. Okay with you if I force it open?"

"Yes! Oh, how exciting. I love surprise."

"Did Lazar have any tools?"

"Check the closet off the kitchen. He kept some things in there."

Butler found what he needed in the closet. He knelt on the floor and pressed the drill bit against the safe. With Maria peering over his shoulder, he drilled slowly into the lock. After fifteen minutes of ear-splitting screeches, the door clanked open.

Jim peered inside.

"What is it?" Maria asked excitedly.

"Just some envelopes. Let's open them on the bed."

Jim pulled on a pair of latex gloves, and tearing open the first envelope, pulled out a stack of yellowed papers. He opened the two remaining envelopes. Each contained a jumble of documents of different sizes. Some were printed, but most were handwritten. A few were written in English, but most were in other languages—including one that was written in Arabic.

"Just a lot of old papers?" Maria fumed. Getting up from the bed, she clomped out of the room. The television blared on in the living room a moment later.

Jim chuckled to himself. Keeping the piles separate, he shuffled slowly through the papers, taking time to read the documents written in English. One three-page letter, addressed to "Commander Sarkesian," detailed plans for a bomb attack on the Turkish Consulate in Los Angeles. The plan called for three men to hide a timed explosive device near the front entrance on the evening of April 23, 1981, with the bomb set to explode at ten the following morning. But it was the closing and signature at the bottom of the page that caught his eye. "In the name of our lost fathers, mothers, sons and daughters, Gevork Zakian."

Butler took two hours to go through the remaining documents. Finally, he slid them back in the folders in exactly the same order he'd discovered them. He found Maria lying on the couch in the living room.

He held up the envelopes. "Mind if I take these papers back to America?"

She smiled. "Did you find a treasure map?"

"Nope. These are just some notes, written in Armenian or Arabic."

"Take what you want, I don't need it."

CHAPTER 59

Three weeks later

Agent Wang looked up from a transcript and sighed. "It's amazing how little information we got out of all those documents from Buenos Aires."

Butler nodded. "Yeah, I was damned disappointed when I got these transcripts back. There's nothing linked to the Bedford case, but at least they tie Gevork Zakian to ASALA."

"Maybe it's time to pay him a visit."

"I think you're right. How about a trip later this week?"

"Sure. Thursday would work best for me."

"Okay, let's do it." Butler reached across the table and grabbed one of the files. "Did you see this? Look at that underlined name."

"Hovsep Kazerian," Wang read aloud. "I don't think that name came up when the old man was giving us the list of his relatives. Was he holding out on us?"

"It looks that way. I think we should pay him another visit, too."

Wang glanced at his watch. "How about if we go now? I'm free until three."

"I'll meet you in the lobby in fifteen minutes."

"See you downstairs."

Keri raked mulch around the base of the maple tree in the center of the yard and walked back to the porch. Sirak was sitting on the steps with a cup of coffee.

"Thank you, Son."

"No problem, Papa. Do you want me to mulch the trees in the back-yard, too?"

"No, just leave them. I'll pay the boy next door to do them next week."

Keri turned at the squeal of brakes. A white sedan pulled to a stop in front of the house. Agents Butler and Wang climbed out of the car and walked up the driveway.

"Good morning," Butler greeted them cordially. He shook Sirak's hand. "How've you been, Dr. Kazerian?"

"Good morning, Agent Butler. I've been a bit under the weather, but this warm-up has been a big help."

Butler smiled. "Yes, indeed, it looks like winter is finally over. I hate to bother you, sir, but Agent Wang and I want to ask you and your son a few more questions."

"Of course. Let's go inside where we can all sit down." He hobbled up the steps and opened the door for Keri and the two agents. The four men sat in the living room.

"Well, Mr. Butler," Sirak said, "how can we help you?"

Butler dated the first page on his legal pad. "Mr. Kazerian," he asked Keri, "where do you work?"

"At Third National Bank in Cleveland. I'm a loan officer."

"And you have two sons?"

"Yes, Michael and David."

"What do they do?"

"Michael is a stockbroker at Lehman, and David owns a SeaRay boat dealership in Cleveland."

Butler nodded and wrote down the information. He looked up at Sirak. "Dr. Kazerian, the last time we talked, I believe you told me you didn't know a man named Lazar Sarkesian."

"That's right, I don't know him."

"You never heard that name before?"

Sirak shook his head. "No, not that I remember."

"Well, sir, Lazar Sarkesian was a prominent member of ASALA. I think I told you I met with him in Buenos Aires."

Sirak glanced at Keri. "And he said he knew me?"

"No, sir, but he had lots of documents, and two of those documents referred to your son, Ara."

"I'd be interested to learn more about those documents, but I don't understand the point you're trying to make."

"Sir, those same documents indicated that Hovsep Kazerian had a prominent role in several ASALA terrorist attacks in Europe and the United States."

"Hovsep Kazerian?" Sirak asked with frown.

"Yes, sir."

"I never heard of him."

"You're sure."

"I'm positive. I've never heard of Hovsep Kazerian." Sirak glanced at Keri. "The Kazerian surname is very common among our people, Agent Butler. I never heard of him. You have my word."

Butler glanced at Agent Wang. Wang shrugged his shoulders.

Butler rubbed his forehead thoughtfully. "Dr. Kazerian, this is important. Do you have any other relatives—living or dead—you haven't told me about? I know about your two sons, your two grandsons and their families, and I'm not referring to your wife, your parents or your brothers and sisters you already told me about. Are there any others?"

Sirak sighed. "I told you about my Uncle Bedros and his family."

"That's right. I mean besides them."

Sirak stared into Agent Butler's probing blue eyes. He glanced again at Keri and sighed uncomfortably. "There is one more," he said in a near whisper.

Butler sat back in his chair. "Okay, what's his name?"

"Mr. Butler," Sirak replied anxiously, "this is something I've never discussed with anyone, even my son."

Keri reached out and rested his hand on his father's knee. "It's okay, Papa. Whatever it is, it's okay."

Sirak closed his eyes. His tongue flicked across his suddenly parched lips. "I have a nephew living in Los Angeles. His name is Faruk Pasha."

"Faruk Pasha?" Butler asked with surprise.

Sirak nodded. "Yes, Faruk Pasha."

Agent Butler leaned forward in his chair. "Dr. Kazerian, I'm confused; isn't Faruk Pasha a Turkish or Arabic name?"

"Yes," Sirak whispered. "It's Turkish."

Butler jotted the name on his pad and looked up. "Can you explain, sir?"

"It's a very long story."

"We've got plenty of time."

Sirak shifted in his chair and folded his hands across his knee. "I may have told you I moved my sons to Cleveland in 1971 to take a position at Euclid Community Hospital. I was appointed to the medical board after four years on the staff at the hospital. Seven of my colleagues and I oversaw the professional affairs of the medical staff. We board members, along with the executive director, Mr. Anderson, were involved in the recruitment of new staff, reviewing staff privileges, and occasionally, in disciplining other staff doctors."

"How long did you hold that position, sir?" Butler asked.

"Almost six years. After I was on the board for three years, we received an application for the head of the department of rehabilitative medicine from a senior internist who'd held a similar position in Buffalo, New York. That physician's name was Faruk Pasha."

Butler glanced up from his pad. "Did you say Buffalo?"

"Yes. The chief of staff at that time was a man named Preston Miller— a well-respected, but exceedingly arrogant, cardiologist. Well, Dr. Miller brought Dr. Pasha's appointment before the board, and I hit the ceiling."

Butler frowned. "You opposed your own nephew's appointment?"

"I steadfastly opposed the appointment of any Turk to the hospital staff. I had successfully blocked an applicant for a radiology position three years earlier, even before I joined the board. They probably offered me the board position to try to temper my cantankerousness, but I was adamant about that issue."

"Even though he was your nephew?" Butler asked confusedly.

"I had no idea about Dr. Pasha's background, except that he was a Turk, and that was enough for me. But, despite my vehement objections, Dr. Miller insisted on going forward with the appointment. The position had been open for four years without any other qualified applicants. I argued, I cajoled, I even threatened to resign from the staff, but to no avail. Dr. Pasha was hired when the majority of other medical board members supported his appointment."

"Okay," Butler said, "so what happened then?"

"After Dr. Pasha arrived at the hospital, my response was to completely deny his very existence. I never spoke to him; I never even looked at him. If he came into a room where I was sitting, I got up and left immediately. Fortunately, he wasn't a surgeon, so our contact was somewhat limited, or I shudder to think what might've happened. He didn't harbor any affection for me, either. We were two physicians working on the same hospital staff who never so much as nodded to one another when we passed in the hall. Dr. Pasha turned out to be a highly competent physician, who got high marks from colleagues and patients alike. Irony of ironies, he had actually preceded me by about five years at the American University Medical School in Beirut. But nothing could temper my feelings about a Turk being appointed to the medical staff at my beloved hospital."

"So Dr. Pasha came to Euclid in 1978?"

"Yes, or was it 1979? I can't remember. It was sometime in the late 1970s. Anyway, within a year of his arrival, Dr. Pasha and Dr. Miller had a major disagreement about how the Rehabilitative Medicine Department should be run, and especially about departmental support Dr. Pasha claimed he'd been promised during his recruitment. Dr. Pasha, like many of the Turks I've known, was the argumentative sort. He was prone to loud outbursts that offended Dr. Miller's old-school gentlemanly nature. Within weeks of Pasha's one-year anniversary at the hospital, their disagreement deteriorated into open hostility, culminating in Dr. Pasha mailing a letter to all the members of the medical board and the board of directors of the hospital. In that letter, Dr. Pasha claimed Dr. Miller was dishonest and, therefore, unfit to serve as the chief of medical staff at the hospital."

Agent Wang piped up, "That must've gone over well."

"You can't even imagine. Well, less than two months after the letter was sent, Dr. Pasha was suddenly accused of stealing morphine that he reported as wasted."

"What do you mean, wasted?"

"Not infrequently, when a patient is being treated with narcotics for pain, there would be excess drug remaining in the vial. The residual was discarded according to a strict protocol and was recorded as wasted. Anyway, Dr. Pasha's accuser was another doctor in his department—a Dr. Leonard Morgan. An investigation into Dr. Pasha's purported theft and drug abuse was launched at the hospital. Since it was well established that Dr. Pasha and Dr. Miller were at odds, and I opposed Dr. Pasha's appointment from the beginning, another board member, a neurologist named Chet Phillips, was appointed by the executive director of the hospital to head the investigating committee."

Sirak stared at the floor and continued. "The inquiry proceeded rather slowly, with many physicians, nurses, and clerks being called before the committee to give testimony. Then, several months after the inquiry began, after a long day of surgery, I happened into the physician's lounge late one evening." He looked up. "I remember opening the door and hearing loud laughter echoing from the back of the room. It was a cackle that, unbeknownst to me, would trigger the greatest professional ordeal of my life. It still comes to me in my dreams occasionally, but in the beginning, it visited itself upon me nearly every night."

Thursday, March 6, 1980, Euclid, Ohio

Dr. Miller glanced toward the door and abruptly stifled his laugher. The portly chief of staff was slouched on a sofa in the back of the room beside Doctor Phillips.

Miller recognized Sirak. "Dr. Kazerian, you must be exhausted. My God, man, how many operations did you do today?"

"Eleven," Sirak replied with a sigh. "It would've been twelve, but one gall bladder got cancelled."

Phillips stood up and slapped Sirak on the back. "What are you trying to do, single-handedly stamp out the budget deficit?"

"I was on vacation the last two weeks," Sirak replied.

Miller laughed. "That'll teach you to take time away. Listen, Kazerian, I've been meaning to have a word with you."

"Oh really. What about?"

He offered his hand. "I owe you an apology. You were right from the beginning about that low-life scoundrel, Pasha. I should've listened to you."

Sirak shook his hand. "Thank you, Preston," he replied sincerely. "I accept your apology."

"That son of a bitch is about to get what's coming to him. He'll be damned lucky to ever practice medicine in this country again once we're through with him. We've already got enough evidence to hang him. I suggest you lay low until it's all over."

"I planned on it," Sirak replied bewilderedly.

"I hope you've learned a lesson about following through on your commitments to future appointees," Phillips quipped.

"What can I do if we don't have the money?" Miller replied. "But once this is over, Leonard Morgan will be the new chief of rehabilitative medicine. I won't have to give him a damned thing."

"Leonard Morgan?" Sirak gasped. "You've got to be kidding? That slacker's not competent to be chief dog catcher."

"Listen, Kazerian," Miller whispered, with a glance at the closed door, "Morgan's done us all a big favor. You'd be well advised to support his appointment when it comes before the board. Do you understand?"

"I'm not sure I do understand. What are you saying?"

"Shut the fuck up!" Phillips whispered. "Somebody's coming."

The door opened and a crusty old custodian in overalls slipped his cleaning cart through the door.

"Oh, I'm sorry, doctors," the man called out with surprise. "I'll come back later."

"That's okay, Juan," Miller said. "We were just leaving. See you later, Sirak. Have a great evening."

Too stunned to move, Sirak watched Miller and Phillips disappear out the door. He wiped his sweaty palms on his pant legs and sat down at a dictation machine.

Sirak glanced up at Butler and Wang. "That brief conversation, and the implications of what'd been said, haunted me for the next two weeks. Then, early one morning, before most of the staff had arrived at the hospital, I went down to the medical library to read some journal articles and happened to run into Leonard Morgan. I scarcely knew the man, but after an exchange of pleasantries, I couldn't hold back any longer."

"Doctor Miller tells me you'll be nominated to succeed Faruk Pasha as chief of the department of rehabilitative medicine after this messy affair is over," Sirak baited.

Morgan smiled smugly. "Miller told you, huh. So I'll have your support?"

"Absolutely. This is important to the hospital, but even more so to me personally, as I'm sure you know. I'm very grateful."

"It's my pleasure. I hate that bastard with a passion. Did you know Pasha suspended me for a week last summer just because I fell behind on my dictation?"

"You've got to be kidding me. I told Miller not to hire him."

"You were right. That arrogant prick's been a problem from the first day he showed up."

Sirak's heart rate raced out of control. Turning to make sure no one was behind him, he leaned across the table. "How'd you set him up?"

"It was a duck shoot in a bathtub. One of the pharmacy technicians is a hunting buddy of mine. He slipped a couple of open morphine vials into that backpack Pasha carts around after the Turk had ordered morphine for a trauma patient's CAT scan. Then I went and told the head of security I saw Pasha sneak some medicine. Security searched his backpack, and bingo, *hasta la vista* Dr. Pasha."

"That's brilliant. Parker's a real Einstein."

"Parker didn't do shit. Miller masterminded the whole thing. Don't ever get on his shit list."

"Don't worry, I won't." Sirak glanced at his watch. "Oh gosh, I'm late for clinic. I'll see you later."

"Yeah, see you around."

Sirak looked up at Butler and let out a heavy sigh. "I agonized about what I'd uncovered for the next three weeks. I couldn't eat and I couldn't sleep and my guts were churning inside me. When I did manage to fall asleep, I'd wake up in a cold sweat—traumatized by the recurring nightmare of Dr. Miller's sinister laugh. All the while, I struggled with what I should do."

"Let me get this straight," Butler said. "You didn't know Dr. Pasha was your nephew?"

"I had no idea. I'm getting to that."

"Why didn't you go to the police?"

Sirak glanced at Keri, and his son took his hand.

"I was torn in opposite directions. One minute, I felt like Dr. Pasha had it coming, and the next minute, I knew I couldn't live with myself if I didn't do something. Then, one night before bed, I happened to read a verse in the Bible that kicked me right in the solar plexus. You probably know it. It's in the fourth chapter of Ephesians.

> *Get rid of all bitterness, rage, anger, harsh words, and slander, as well as all types of evil behavior. Instead, be kind to each other, tenderhearted, forgiving one another, just as God through Christ has forgiven you.*

"Suddenly, I knew what I had to do. That was a Friday night and the final hearing on Doctor Pasha's case was scheduled for the following Monday morning. It's funny, once I made my decision, the tension lifted like a fog and I slept like a baby the rest of that weekend. Bright and early Monday morning, I drove down to the hospital and made my way to the conference room in the administrative suite. When I walked into the room, Dr. Pasha and his lawyer were already seated at the table with Dr. Phillips, the executive director of the hospital, Mr. Anderson, and the rest of the committee members. Several men I didn't recognize were seated at a side table. I found out later they were attorneys for the hospital. Dr. Phillips was summarizing the findings in the case, and I remember the look of surprise and confusion on his face when I stepped into the room."

"Hello, Dr. Kazerian," Doctor Phillips said. "Can we help you with something, sir?"

Sirak cleared his throat. "Yes, I've come to address this committee. I have information critical to these deliberations."

Phillips stared at Sirak for a moment before motioning to one of the hospital attorneys. The young man approached the table and Phillips engaged him in a whispered conversation. During their tête-à-tête, both men glanced at Sirak, as though he was an apparition they hoped would disappear. Finally, the attorney took his seat beside the others.

"Dr. Kazerian," Phillips finally said, "this committee is no longer hearing testimony. Therefore, I am declining to..."

"This man is innocent of the charges leveled against him!" Sirak barked. "All of the evidence was fabricated to discredit Dr. Pasha. Unless you hear me out, I'll go directly to the police."

"Fabricated by whom?" Executive Director Anderson asked skeptically.

"By Dr. Preston Miller, Doctor Leonard Morgan and Edward Parker, a pharmacy technician here at the hospital."

"This is preposterous!" Phillips shouted. "Dr. Kazerian, I hope you can substantiate these egregious charges against the chief of staff of this hospital and several other respected employees."

"You know Dr. Phillips as well as I do that what I say is true. If you persist in this charade, you have only yourself to blame for the criminal charges that will undoubtedly be brought against you, too."

Phillips lapsed into silence and the weight of every eye in the room fell upon him.

Suddenly, Mr. Anderson jumped up from his chair and headed to the door.

"Where are you going, Mr. Anderson?" one of the committee members called out after him.

"To call the police. This meeting is over."

Executive Director Anderson disappeared into the hall and bedlam erupted in the conference room.

Sirak leaned back in his chair. "The prosecutor offered Ed Parker immunity from prosecution in exchange for his cooperation with the investigation. Parker subsequently detailed the plot to discredit Dr. Pasha. Both Dr. Miller and Dr. Morgan pleaded guilty to conspiracy charges ahead of the trial and served five-year sentences in the penitentiary. Dr. Phillips was fired for allowing Dr. Pasha's inquisition to continue when he knew the charges were false.

"Meanwhile, Dr. Pasha was cleared of all charges and received a settlement from the hospital. He resigned from the staff and began to look at opportunities outside of Cleveland. I tried to continue on with my career, but found my interactions with the hospital administration and other long-term employees increasingly difficult. Many of my former friends at the hospital shunned me. So, in June of 1980, when I was sixty-six years old, I decided to retire. I continued to do some *locum tenens* work to help local physicians during vacations and the like, but soon, even that dried up. It seems I got too old."

"You're an honorable man, sir," Butler said admiringly. "Given how you felt about the Turks, I doubt there are many men who would've done what you did to help that doctor."

"God himself led me to that fourth chapter of Ephesians and I couldn't have lived with myself if I'd allowed an innocent man to be destroyed."

"So, at this point, you knew Dr. Pasha was your nephew?" Wong asked confusedly.

Sirak shook his head. "No, I still had no idea whatsoever."

"When did you find out?"

"About a month after I retired, and about three months after the incident at the hospital, I got a thank you letter from Dr. Pasha inviting me to his home for dinner. I thought about it for a few days, and finally, with great hesitancy, I accepted his invitation. That meeting unexpectedly solved one of the great mysteries of my life."

June 21, 1980, Pepper Pike, Ohio

Sirak scanned the addresses on the mailboxes along the street and pulled his car to a stop on the grassy shoulder. Sitting for a moment to gather his thoughts, he stepped out of the car and hobbled down the long driveway. A single-story brick house was nestled beneath majestic maple and oak trees.

The door opened before Sirak reached the porch, and Faruk Pasha, smiling from ear to ear, rushed out to greet him. He bowed graciously. "Dr. Kazerian, I'm honored to welcome you to my home. Please, sir, come inside and meet my family."

Pasha opened the screen door and Sirak stepped past him into the house. An attractive-looking woman and a younger man were waiting in the foyer.

"Please allow me to introduce you to my wife, Dilara, and my grandson, Bahar," Pasha said.

"It's an honor to meet you, Dr. Kazerian," the woman said effusively. "Welcome to our home."

The younger man offered his hand. "It's a pleasure to meet you, sir. You're my hero."

Sirak shook the young man's hand. "Thank you, Bahar, and thank you, Mrs. Pasha."

"Bahar's mother, my youngest daughter, Ferah, lives in Rocky River," Faruk said. "She's coming to join us after she picks up her daughter from school."

"How many children do you have?" Sirak asked.

"Three," Faruk replied. "My son, Musa, is a heart surgeon in Seattle and my older daughter, Kamile, lives in Boston with her family. Please, we'll be more comfortable in the living room." Faruk led Sirak into a stylishly-adorned living room. "Please sit here in my favorite chair."

Sirak sat in the chair next to the fireplace and Faruk's grandson sat across from him in a recliner.

"Can I bring you wine or a soft drink?" Faruk asked politely.

"I'd enjoy a glass of wine, thank you."

Mrs. Pasha brought in a tray and handed each man a glass of wine.

Faruk raised his glass. "Respected Dr. Kazerian, my family members and I thank you from the bottom of our hearts for your courage and integrity. Thank you, sir, for restoring my honor and saving my career."

"Any man with a thread of decency would have done the same," Sirak replied graciously. He raised his glass. "It's an honor to be invited to your beautiful home."

All three men sipped from their glasses and set them down on the end tables.

"Dr. Kazerian," Faruk asked, "how long have you lived in Cleveland?"

"For almost ten years. I moved my sons here from New York in 1971."

"New York," Faruk repeated, with a nod. "What a coincidence. We lived in Buffalo for fifteen years before I took the position here in Cleveland. Were you born in New York?"

"No, I was actually born in Anatolia, but I left when I was very young."

"You don't say. Where in Anatolia?"

"Just outside a small village called Seghir. It's near Diyarbekir."

"*Really*? I was born near Seghir and I lived there until I was twelve years old."

"It's a small world, indeed," Sirak said. He sipped his wine. "Was your father a physician?"

"No, my father was a farmer, but he was killed before I was born."

"My father was a farmer, too. It seems we have a lot in common."

Faruk smiled. "There's something else we have in common, Dr. Kazerian."

"Oh, what's that?"

"My mother was Armenian."

Sirak's eyes widened with surprise. "Is that so?"

"Yes. Mama was my father's third wife. Papa took her in when her parents were lost during the Great War. And there's another thing we have in common. We both took our medical training at American University in Beirut. I noticed in the Euclid Hospital staff directory that you studied there from 1929 to 1934. I attended American University from 1924 to 1928."

"I didn't know that either."

"My stepmother arranged a position for me there after I finished undergraduate studies at Ankara University. Those were truly wonderful years. Don't you agree?"

"AUB was a great school, but that was a difficult time for me because my sister lived in Jerusalem and she often needed my help. Several times

I left Beirut for weeks, or even months, to care for her. That's why it took me five years to finish."

"Even then you were a man of principle, Dr. Kazerian. I've never gotten a chance to visit Jerusalem. Is it as wonderful as they say?"

"Some people think so, but I'm not among them. I lost my wife, daughter and sister there in the 1967 Arab-Israeli War."

"I'm sorry, I didn't know," Faruk replied awkwardly. He glanced into the dining room where his wife was setting a large platter of food in the center of the table. "I think dinner is about ready."

The group dined on tender lamb chops, rice and green beans, along with tasty flat bread Sirak remembered from his youth. Dilara queried Sirak about his sons and their families and she told him about their children and grandchildren. Faruk and Sirak talked about the conspiracy that implicated Faruk at the hospital and the pending trial of Dr. Miller.

"So, Dr. Kazerian, were you living in Anatolia at the time of the Great War?" Bahar asked when the conversation lagged.

"Yes, I lived there as a boy," Sirak replied curtly. "These lamb chops are superb."

Dilara smiled appreciatively. "I'm glad you enjoy them. They looked so wonderful I couldn't pass them up."

"They're spectacular. Could I trouble you for a bit more wine?"

"My pleasure." Dilara fetched a fresh bottle from the kitchen and refilled the glasses.

Sirak lifted his glass and smiled. "Thank you again for inviting me to your beautiful home."

"Thank you for coming," Faruk said.

Bahar took a sip of his wine and sighed impatiently. "Dr. Kazerian, I know you were very young, but do you remember the First World War? I mean, do you remember what the situation was like in Anatolia?"

Sirak set down his glass and sighed with resignation. He glanced at Bahar's grandfather. "Yes, I remember it like it was yesterday, but I don't care to talk about what happened to me in Anatolia. I'm sorry."

"Please, Dr. Kazerian," Bahar persisted. "I'm writing an article for the Turkish magazine *Kurtulus Cephesi*. I'd really appreciate your insights."

"You're a writer?"

"Yes, or at least I'm an aspiring writer. I specialize in Ottoman art history, but I was invited to contribute this article for a special issue. I've been working on it for several months. As you know, it's a highly controversial topic in Turkey. Please tell me about your experiences in Anatolia. I've never had the opportunity to discuss this with someone who actually lived there before and during the Great War."

"I have only painful memories of that time, Bahar. I can assure you they wouldn't interest your readers."

"Can I just ask you one question? Do you agree tens of thousands of Muslims died in Anatolia during those years? I know many of your people died, but didn't many Turks and Kurds die, too, not only from the fighting, but from starvation and disease?"

"I'm sure many Turks died during the war, but most of the Armenians who died were murdered."

"Did you see them murdered?"

"I saw my brother, Mikael, murdered. And one of our best friends, an American physician named David Charles, was brutally murdered in the prison in Diyarbekir. I saw my older brother and my father sent down the river from Diyarbekir on rafts with hundreds of other Armenian men. One raft overturned and nobody lifted a finger to help. At least twenty men drowned. I also saw my mother and sister abducted, and I never saw either one of them again."

"I'm sorry that happened to your family. "But isn't it true that many Turks died in the inter-ethnic conflict that engulfed the Ottoman Empire during its collapse?"

Sirak downed the last of his wine and set his glass down. "Bahar, I understand you've been taught a Turkish perspective of what happened during those years in Anatolia, but I lived through those terrible years, and I lost most my family to the hatred that swept the Empire and led to the annihilation of my people. My brother, Mikael, was brutally murdered, and my father and brother, Stepannos, vanished forever. My younger sister and I would've died, too, if a Druze family hadn't saved us. What happened was genocide. It's as simple as that."

"I'm sure there were murders, just like there are here in Cleveland, but don't you think most of what happened in Anatolia occurred in the context of the war and the resultant fear and angst of the Turkish rulers that the empire was being attacked from within by Armenian traitors collaborating with the Russians? After all, the Empire lost more than eighty thousand men during the first battle with Russia. Before the terrible war ended, many Turks died, too, including hundreds of thousands of women and children."

"Bahar, nothing could ever excuse what happened to my family. They were mercilessly obliterated. We were treated like dogs, starved, and forced from our homes to walk mile after mile in sweltering heat until we dropped from exhaustion. Many others were left for dead or, like my mother, snatched by tribesmen and never seen again. I was only seven years old when I saw this with my own eyes. It is too horrible to think about. May we change the subject please?"

Faruk cleared his throat and gazed sympathetically at Sirak. "Bahar, you have enough information for your article. Unimaginably terrible things happen in war. It has always been so, and will always be, for only during the desperate and uncertain times of war can the depraved killers living amongst us bring their distorted and zealous cruelty and terror into the mainstream of human existence. We're truly sorry about what happened to your family, Dr. Kazerian."

"Thank you," Sirak whispered sincerely.

An awkward silence engulfed the table and the patter of raindrops echoed from the patio outside.

Dilara stood up to clear the table. "How about coffee and dessert? I baked my mother's favorite baklava recipe."

Sirak smiled graciously. "Thank you. I'd love some. My mother baked baklava, too, and I haven't had any in years."

Faruk and Bahar gathered the dishes and followed Dilara into the kitchen. Sirak got up from the table and wandered to the back of the dining room where a melange of old photographs adorned the wall. As his eyes wandered from one image to the next, he lingered on a photo of Faruk and Dilara standing with their arms around their four young children. Then he examined a graduation photo of Faruk standing with several American University of Beirut professors he'd admired many years earlier. Finally, his eyes wandered to a grainy black and white photograph of three women sitting on a sofa with half a dozen children. His eyes fell on one woman in the photo and a powerful sensation of recognition swept over him. "No, it couldn't be," he whispered. "Faruk, who is this woman in the photograph?"

The Turk set down the dessert platter and walked around the table to see what Sirak was pointing at. "That's my mother."

"Your *mother*?"

Faruk pointed. "Yes, and that's me beside her. I was ten or eleven years old at the time. That's my twin sister and that's my stepbrother. This is my father's first wife, Sabriye, this is his second wife, Jasmine, and these other younger women are my half-sisters."

Sirak swallowed hard and continued to stare at the photograph. His mouth was bone-dry. "What was your mother's name?"

"Her name was Flora," Faruk replied with a smile. "She was a wonderful woman."

Sirak caught his breath and a chill ran up his spine. "What happened to her?"

"She died of typhus a few years after this photograph was taken. I was devastated. After Mama died, Jasmine and her second husband raised Kristina and me as their own."

Sirak stared at the young girl in the photograph. "Your sister's name was Kristina?"

"Yes. She lives in Istanbul with her husband and seven children."

Sirak continued to stare at the photograph. "Kristina was my mother's name."

"Well, that's something else we have in common."

Sirak took a deep breath and exhaled contemplatively. He glanced at his watch. "My gosh, look how late it's gotten. I must be getting home."

Faruk's mouth dropped open. "But what about coffee and dessert?"

"I'm sorry, but I've got to get home. Thank you for a wonderful evening." Sirak retreated through the living room to the front door.

Faruk wrung his hands in despair. "Did Bahar offend you? I'm truly sorry if he did."

"I'm not offended. I'm just very tired. Thank you for a spectacular dinner, Mrs. Pasha. It was nice to meet you, too, Bahar."

Sirak reached for the doorknob, but the door suddenly opened. A middle-aged woman and a teenage girl stepped inside.

"Oh, hello," the woman exclaimed with surprise. "You must be Dr. Kazerian. I'm Ferah and this is my youngest daughter, Flora."

"It's a pleasure to meet you, Dr. Kazerian," the girl said politely. "Thank you for helping Grandpapa Pasha."

Sirak caught his breath. Young Flora had almond-shaped brown eyes and full lips. "My God," he whispered.

"Is something wrong?" Ferah asked.

"No, I'm sorry," Sirak replied. "Flora just reminds me of someone I knew a long time ago."

Ferah set her purse on the table in the foyer. "I'm sorry we're so late. The meeting took longer than we expected. You're not leaving already... Are you okay, Dr. Kazerian?" she asked upon spotting tears pooling in Sirak's eyes.

"I'm just tired. It's been a long day. Faruk," Sirak asked, looking back at his host. "I forgot to ask, what was your father's name?"

"My birth father or the father who raised me?"

"Your birth father."

"His name was Abdul Pasha."

Sirak swallowed hard. "Abdul Pasha," he repeated in a near whisper. "Well, goodnight. I'm glad I got a chance to meet you all."

"We'll be happy to drive you home," Faruk said. "Bahar can drive your car and I'll follow in ours."

"No, I'm fine, thank you. My son is coming early in the morning to take me fishing, and I must get to bed. Thank you all for a wonderful evening." Sirak stepped outside and limped up the driveway to the street.

At long last Sirak knew what had happened to his sister, Flora, and that their malevolent neighbor Abdul Pasha had kidnapped her those many years ago. Sirak was not surprised. Even as a young boy he had known the animosity between the Kazerian and Pasha families. It had never occurred to him that Dr. Faruk Pasha was in any way related to those Pashas of long ago, who longed to own Mourad Kazerian's land. After all, Pasha was a common name in Anatolia. Sirak felt the grief of his sister's abduction all over again, and as he lay in bed that night, he tried to find some comfort in the fact that Flora bore two children who loved her and must have brought her happiness.

"So you never told him that he's your nephew?" Butler asked Sirak incredulously.

"No, I never did."

"Why not?"

"What would it accomplish to tell Dr. Pasha he owes his very existence and that of his children and grandchildren to abduction and forced marriage? Should a man be held accountable for the sins of his father?"

"How do you know it was an abduction?"

"I was there, sir. I saw the masked man drag Flora kicking and screaming out of our neighbor's house. This was not uncommon back then. Men would enter houses and take whatever girls and women they wanted. After Flora was taken, it happened again, to my mother."

Sirak glanced at his son. "I didn't tell you about it for the same reason. No good could've possibly come from your knowing this sad part of our family history. But that night I drove away from dinner at Dr. Pasha's knowing one of the longest chapters of my life had finally been closed. The burning hatred I'd harbored in my heart was extinguished once and for all by the timid innocence in my beautiful Turkish greatgrandniece's eyes, or should I say my sister Flora's eyes?"

"And now they live in Los Angeles?"

"I think so. Dr. Pasha accepted a job in Santa Monica a few weeks after I visited his home. He called to say goodbye and that was the last time we spoke to each other. He's still there as far as I know, although he's probably retired by now."

Agent Butler shut his legal pad. "Thank you, Dr. Kazerian, that's all I have for now."

"By the way, Agent Butler," Keri said, "I ran into George Liralian a few days ago. I meant to call you, but I got busy and forgot."

Butler stared blankly at Keri for a moment. Suddenly, his face lit up with recognition. "George Liralian? Here in Richmond Heights?"

"No, we saw him at the Cleveland Skating Club in Shaker Heights. My grandsons had a hockey game there last Wednesday, and he was working at the bar."

Butler wrote a note on the back of his pad. "The Cleveland Skating Club? Did you mention anything to him about me or this investigation?"

"No, we were only there an hour, and I didn't even speak to him. As soon as he saw me with Papa, he ducked into the back."

"He hid from you?"

Keri glanced at Sirak and smiled. "I think so. He and Papa don't get along very well."

Butler nodded. "Thanks for the tip. Please let me know if you hear from him."

Sirak showed the agents out. He returned to the living room and found Keri jotting down a note. "Why didn't you tell me you saw George Liralian?" he asked irritably.

Keri tucked the notepad into his shirt pocket. "Why? So you could peg him with your cane again? Papa, is there anything else you should tell me about? I can't believe you kept the truth about Faruk Pasha to yourself."

"Like I told Agent Butler, I agonized over telling you about your aunt Flora and Dr. Pasha, but I decided nothing good would come of it. But now you know our darkest family secret. If there are anymore, I don't know about them."

"Papa, I'd like to meet Dr. Pasha and his family someday."

"Maybe we'll go together someday. I haven't talked to him since he left Cleveland, so I'm not sure the phone number he gave me is still correct. I'm sure we could reach him through the hospital where he worked. Son, I realize now I should've told you and Ara everything about Anatolia and Syria, and what happened to our family, including my discovery about your aunt Flora and Faruk Pasha. I convinced myself that hiding the truth would somehow insulate you and your brother from the hatred and extremism that grew out of the events that transpired all those years ago, but in the end I guess I really only protected myself."

"Protected yourself from what, Papa?"

"Protected myself from having to relive all that in my thoughts and words. Make sure you and the boys share what happened with your grandchildren while they're still young. Don't leave it for someone else to come along and use Anatolia to stir hatred in their hearts."

Keri patted his father's knee. "We already talked to them. The children know what happened, and they understand that the evil men who were responsible died a long time ago."

"Tell them about Dr. Pasha and his family, too."

"I will."

"Are we still going fishing next Sunday?"

"I'm planning on it."

"I'll pick you up around ten-thirty Saturday morning. I've got to go now."

Sirak hugged Keri to his chest. "I love you, Son."

"I love you, too, Papa. We'll see you Saturday."

CHAPTER 60

May 15, 1998
Washington DC

The jet touched down gently on the tarmac. Butler glanced out the window at the airplanes lined up outside the Washington National Airport terminal. "Well, this should be interesting."

"Damned interesting," Wang agreed. "I'm sure Zakian's been expecting us to show up ever since he heard from his wife."

"Yeah, and now he's had six months to work on his story. At least we can turn up the heat a bit. Maybe he'll make a mistake."

The agents disembarked and wove through the crowded terminal. Walking out into bright sunshine, Butler made a beeline for a man sitting on the hood of a Town Car bearing the ATF insignia.

"Are you waiting for Butler and Wang?"

"Yes, sir!" the clean-cut, young black man replied. "The name is Jefferson, sir. Let me help you with your bag."

"I'll keep it with me, if you don't mind. We've got a few things to review during the drive."

Jefferson opened the rear door. "No problem, sir."

Wang and Butler climbed into the car and slammed the door. Jefferson jogged around the back end and ducked into the driver's seat.

"We're headed to 1711 N Street, Northwest," Butler called out. "But could you drive past the Lincoln Memorial on the way?"

"Absolutely, sir, would you like me to take a little drive around the city, too?"

"No, thank you, just the Lincoln Memorial. I make a point of seeing it whenever I'm in Washington."

Jefferson smiled at Butler in the rearview mirror. "It's my favorite, too. We sure could use old Abe in the White House right now."

"You can say that again."

Wang and Butler were lost in their own thoughts as they passed the Lincoln Memorial; then Wang said, "We still don't have anything to tie Gevork Zakian directly to the dynamite and guns, and we probably never will."

"Yeah, one step forward and two steps back. It's so damned frustrating. The FBI isn't even working the case anymore. We should've talked to this joker a year ago."

"What for?" Wang replied frustratedly. "He won't give us a damned thing."

"Maybe not, but at least he'll know we haven't forgotten him."

"He hasn't forgotten. You can bet he's been in contact with at least half of the witnesses we've interviewed."

"I'm sure. We need to find George Liralian. There's a reason he's been dodging us for the past year and a half. Why else would he move from one apartment to the next and not use credit cards or bank accounts? I wonder where he gets the money to live."

"Probably from Zakian," Wang quipped. "Maybe we should check all the registered guests staying at hotels near ANCA headquarters."

Butler laughed. "Why don't you do that when you have a few extra weeks to waste?

Ten minutes later, Jefferson pulled the car to a stop in front of an office building on N Street.

The two agents checked the directory in the ornate marble foyer and took the elevator to the third floor. They found Suite 301, and Wang followed Butler inside.

A middle-aged woman sitting at the reception desk looked up from her monitor. "May I help you, gentlemen?"

Butler held out his ID. "I'm agent Jim Butler from the Bureau of Alcohol, Tobacco, Firearms and Explosives. This is agent Leo Wang. We're here to see Gevork Zakian."

The woman perused the ID and then looked up. "What's this about?"

"It's official business," Butler replied. "It won't take long."

"Wait here, please. He's very busy today, but I'll see if he has time to speak to you."

The woman stepped through a door behind the desk and reappeared a minute later. "Mr. Zakian will see you, but only for a few minutes. He's having lunch with Congressman White in forty-five minutes."

The woman led them into an imposing corner office. Zakian was sitting behind a large mahogany desk. He was an intense-looking man, with black hair and gold-framed glasses. He stared down at a letter he was reading.

Butler glanced past him at the collection of photographs on the wall behind the desk. He recognized Bill Clinton and Newt Gingrich, along with dozens of other luminaries.

"Ridiculous," Zakian muttered. He folded the letter, slid it into his desk drawer and leaned back in his chair. "How can I help you, gentlemen?" he asked calmly.

Butler held out his ID. "Mr. Zakian, I'm Jim Butler, special agent with the ATF, and this is agent Leo Wang. We'd like to ask you a few questions, sir."

"Ask away, but all I can spare is fifteen minutes." Zakian stood up and walked to four oversized chairs arranged in a circle around a hexagonal coffee table. "Have a seat, gentlemen."

Butler retrieved a legal pad from his briefcase. "Mr. Zakian, we're here to ask you about dynamite and weapons that were found on September 13, 1996, in a storage locker in Bedford Heights, a locker you rented for the past twenty years."

"I didn't rent any locker in Ohio," Zakian replied.

"Not directly, but you had your ex-wife, Lucy, pay the rent with money you sent to her. We've done our homework, Mr. Zakian, and it brought us right here to you. You're a busy man, so let's just cut through the semantics and get to the crux of the issue. You were an ASALA member, right?"

"No, I was not."

Butler bent down and withdrew several papers from his briefcase. He handed them to Zakian. "Take a look at these documents. They were found in Lazar Sarkesian's condominium in Buenos Aires after he died."

Butler studied Zakian's face as the latter read through the top document—a photocopy of the three-page memorandum he'd written to Commander Sarkesian decades earlier. It detailed the plan to bomb the Turkish Consulate in Los Angeles, and was signed Gevork Zakian. The director remained expressionless as he stoically read the letter.

Zakian looked up. "These are forgeries. I never even met Lazar Sarkesian."

"But you knew who he was?" Butler asked.

"I may have heard of him, but I've never spoken to him, and certainly never wrote him this letter."

"In that case, you wouldn't have a problem with me asking your secretary for a few notes you wrote? I want to give them to our handwriting experts."

"Ask all you want, but I never write anything." He held up a handheld recorder. "I dictate all my notes and letters. You're squandering taxpayer money, gentlemen."

"Let me tell you what I think, sir," Butler retorted heatedly. "I think you *are* responsible for the Michigan dynamite heist and that you hid the explosives along with those guns found in that storage locker. I also think those weapons were used to kill Kemal Arikan in Los Angeles and Orhan Gündüz in Boston in 1982."

"Nonsense," Zakian huffed.

"What about that Winchester rifle with carving on the stock that was found in the storage locker? You bought it from your employee, Brad Stout."

"It was stolen from my store a few months later."

"What a coincidence. I think all of those guns belonged to you, sir."

Zakian stood up. "Sounds like you've worked up quite a tale of fiction there, gentlemen—right out of a made-for-TV movie. Look, I can't be late for my luncheon with Congressman White. So, help yourself out, and have a good day." He walked to his desk and shuffled through a stack of papers on the bookshelf.

Wang stood up and headed to the door, but Butler stepped over to the desk.

"Mr. Zakian, why was Ara Kazerian murdered in Damascus?"

Zakian scowled up at Butler. "Who?"

"Ara Kazerian. He lived in Richmond Heights before he was sent to Beirut for training."

"I have no idea what you're talking about. I don't know anyone named Ara Kazerian."

"He never came to your Open Pantry store?"

"Thousands of people came into my store, Agent Butler."

"Including George Liralian?"

Zakian shook his head. "Never heard of him, either."

"You haven't talked to him in the past two years?"

"Listen carefully, Mr. Butler; I never heard of him."

Butler stared down into Zakian's eyes for several moments. "You never called him?"

Zakian shook his head. "No, I never even heard of him."

Butler turned and walked to the door. "Thank you, Mr. Zakian. We'll be in touch."

Butler turned his car into the ATF parking lot and parked along the side of the building.

"Let's have another look at those guns from the Bedford storage locker," he said as they walked into the building. "We're missing something."

Wang patted Butler on the back. "Wouldn't be the first time."

They took the elevator down to the basement. The evidence room clerk retrieved several boxes and carted them to an inspection table in a side room. Butler and Wang opened the boxes and pulled out the rifles, machine guns and a shotgun.

Methodically examining an Uzi machine gun, Butler handed it to Wang.

Wang ran his fingers down the barrel. "Maybe he's telling the truth."

"About what?"

"Maybe Zakian's role really was merely to rent the storage locker."

Butler picked up the intricately-carved rifle. "What about this? He buys the rifle, it gets stolen and just happens to end up in the storage locker with all these other weapons? And what about the letter to Lazar Sarkesian? No, he not only built this cache, he planned some of the killings. Hell, that arrogant bastard probably carried out attacks himself."

"Maybe, but how do we prove it?"

"I don't have a clue." Butler opened a smaller box and pulled out a plastic bag. "What's this?"

"That's the old trench coat that was in the locker with everything else."

"Did we send for evidence processing?"

"Absolutely. I gave it to Nick Kennedy myself."

"Let's take it back to the lab and ask Dave Saunders to look it over. He's top notch."

"For what?" Wang asked skeptically.

"Just to make sure Kennedy didn't miss anything."

"Whatever," Wang muttered with frustration.

"You go on home. I'll take it down."

"Okay, have a great weekend."

"I'll see you Monday."

CHAPTER 61

May 30, 1998
Westlake, Ohio

When Jim Butler returned to his home in Westlake, Ohio, he walked past the answering machine a few times before noticing the light was on. Sighing in anticipation of a solicitation call, he punched the button.

"You have one message," said the mechanical female voice. "Butler," a husky voice hissed, "listen carefully, bastard. Unless you want to screw up that promotion you've got coming or even get your ass fired, stop harassing Gevork Zakian. You hear me? You don't know who you're messing with, asshole. I'm talking about some of the most powerful men in this country jumping down your fucking throat. Your family could get hurt, too. Do you understand? No more bullshit." A brief silence was followed by three blasts from a gun fired in rapid succession.

Butler stared at the answering machine for a moment, then called his partner.

"ATF, Leo Wang."

"Hey, Leo, it's Jim."

"Miss me already?"

"Yeah, right… Listen, when I got home there was a threatening message on my answering machine."

"What kind of threat?"

"Some jerk threatened to hurt my family if we didn't lay off of Zakian. He ended the message with gunshots."

"Son of a bitch. You'd better call the chief."

"Could you check to see if the jerk-off phoned from a traceable number? It came in between nine and eleven this morning."

"Okay, I'll take care of it. Should I call Zakian? He must be feeling some heat after all."

"No, I want him to wonder if I even got the message. Maybe he'll have the guy call me again. Have the department trace all incoming calls to my house. I'm going to get that bastard good."

"I do have news that'll make your day."

"What's that?"

"George Liralian walked into the Pittsburgh FBI headquarters this morning."

"Really?"

"Absolutely. He said he was tired of running."

"That's wonderful news! I want to interview him as soon as I get back."

"I guess you haven't checked your e-mail. How about even better news?"

"What could be better than that?"

"Dave Saunders from the lab found several hairs inside the old coat from the storage locker, *and* he got a clear DNA profile."

"I'll be damned," Butler muttered. "The worm has turned. Do me a favor: ask the prosecutor to subpoena a mouth smear from Zakian so we can get his DNA profile. Also, ask him if we can offer Liralian immunity in return for his cooperation. Oh, man, you've made my day!"

"I'll call you back after I call the prosecutor."

"Thanks. I'll have my cell."

"When are you coming back to work?"

"A week from Monday. I'm going sailing in Vermillion tomorrow, and then I'm driving up to Niagara Falls to visit my old roommate. I'll be there until Saturday."

"Take your gun. Those ASALA guys are freakin' crazy."

"Don't worry, I will."

"Hey, have a good time."

"Thanks, Leo, talk to you later."

CHAPTER 62

Sirak smiled happily at the cheery faces gathered around the dining room table. Keri sat at the end of the table beside David and his wife. Michael was seated on the opposite side of the table next to his wife. Sirak's great-grandchildren were intermingled with the others.

Keri glanced out the picture window at a man in a hooded parka trudging through the wind-driven snow. He stood up and tapped his wine glass with a spoon. "I'd like to toast Sarah and Cathy for preparing this delicious feast for Papa. Thank you both."

Everyone lifted their glasses in salute and shouted a chorus of appreciation.

Keri raised his glass again. "Papa, thank you for spending your ninety-first birthday with us. I know you don't care for large gatherings, but we all wanted to celebrate with you this year. Let's sing *Happy Birthday* and then we'll move into the living room to open your presents."

Everyone joined in saluting the patriarch of the family with a rousing song, as Sirak nodded and smiled cheerfully.

After they'd finished, Sirak struggled up from his chair and steadied himself with a hand on the table. "Thank you all for this wonderful birthday celebration. While you were singing, I felt a powerful sense of déjà vu and I realized it came from when I was a young boy in Anatolia and my mama and papa and all my brothers and sisters celebrated my birthday around our dinner table. If my memory serves me correctly, that was the last time we were all together before the Great War erupted and my brother, Alek, left for service in the army.

"Being here today with my son, my grandsons, and all my great-grandchildren is the greatest gift I could ever receive. My biggest regret in life is that we didn't have more celebrations over the years. I'm solely to blame for that. But I want you all to know that I love you all with all my heart." Teary eyed, Sirak scanned across the adoring faces. "We must also thank God, for He alone made it possible for us all to be here together today. I praise Him for his goodness and mercy."

"Hey, Papa Sirak," young Troy blurted out, "thank you for having Papa Keri, too, or none of us would be here today."

The group erupted into laughter and David punched him on the shoulder.

"Okay, everyone," Keri said, "let's move into the living room. You boys bring in some firewood from the back porch. David, you're in charge of gathering the gifts while I help Papa Sirak."

The family gathered in the living room around the crackling fire. Cathy helped Sirak open his gifts, while Sarah brought in drinks and cake. Sirak got a new television, a cane, a clock radio, and several smaller gifts. Once the gifts were opened, most of the children and adults filed outside to play in the snow, while Keri sat beside the fire with his father.

"Can I get you anything, Papa?"

"No thank you, Son. Perhaps a glass of port later, but I'm fine right now."

Keri took a sip of wine and set his glass on the end table. He grabbed a couple of logs and stoked the fire. "Papa, Agent Butler called me yesterday."

"Who?" Sirak asked with a vacant expression.

"The investigator who came to your house last year to ask questions about Ara. Remember? He's from the Bureau of Alcohol, Tobacco, Firearms and Explosives."

"Oh, yes, I remember now. How's he doing?"

"He's fine. He finally found George Liralian." Keri braced himself for an eruption of anger, but Sirak, his weary old eyes drooping nearly shut, merely waited for Keri's explanation. "George has agreed to testify for the government at Gevork Zakian's trial. He told Agent Butler that Zakian recruited Ara and him to ASALA, along with several other young men and then sent them to Beirut for training. Some of them carried out attacks on Turks here in the United States."

"I told you George Liralian knew what happened to Ara."

"Yes, you did, Papa. Agent Butler said that with George's testimony and DNA evidence they found in that storage locker in Bedford, he was confident Zakian would be convicted. He expects him to be sent to prison for a long time."

"What are the charges?"

"They charged him with a whole slew of things. The ones I remember are trafficking in firearms and explosives, committing acts of terrorism and sending followers to Beirut for weapons training to participate in acts of terror. He's also charged with directing several of the attacks himself. Butler thinks he'll get at least twenty years in prison."

Sirak pondered the news in silence. Glancing out the window, he watched Kevin hit Troy with a snowball at point-blank range. Kevin scampered off, with his brother in hot pursuit. "I hope the bastard rots in that prison," he muttered.

"What, Papa?"

"I hope Zakian rots in that prison for what he did to Ara and our family."

"Do you want to attend the trial? Mr. Butler said we could."

Sirak shook his head. "No," he whispered sullenly, "I don't ever want to hear that bastard's name again."

"Okay, Papa."

Sirak sighed forlornly. "Will you drive me home now?"

"Now?" Keri asked with surprise.

"Yes, I'm very tired."

"Why don't you stay here tonight and I'll take you home tomorrow?"

"No, I want to go home."

"Sure, Papa. Give me a minute to load your presents in the car. I'll ask David to drive his Suburban."

Sirak grasped Keri's arm. "I love you, Son. Thank you for a wonderful day."

"I love you, too. You stay right here by the fire and I'll go warm up the car."

CHAPTER 63

March 16, 1999
Cleveland, Ohio

The long, black hearse slowed to make a sharp left turn and skirted a uniformed motorcycle patrolman who was holding back traffic in front of the main gate of historic Lakeview Cemetery. A pair of Lincoln Town cars and a long line of other vehicles tailed closely behind. The procession snaked along a narrow road past scores of monuments, obelisks, crypts and grave markers that were nestled in the trees in the famed Cleveland graveyard.

The hearse braked to a stop beneath a magnificent sugar maple and the procession of cars parked along both sides of the access road. In the distance, the pointed pinnacle of the watchtower of U.S. President Garfield's tomb was barely visible beyond a pair of mammoth spruce trees.

Keri, David and Michael, along with a half dozen other men, gathered at the rear of the hearse beneath a dreary, cloud-covered sky. Carefully lifting the bronze casket, they proceeded across the grass and up a hill.

An elderly bearded clergyman dressed in black vestments walked ahead of the casket clutching a gold Khatchkar cross. Reciting verses from the Bible, he led the pallbearers up the grassy slope to a freshly-dug grave before a monument emblazoned with the surname 'Kazerian' and topped with a larger Khatchkar cross.

The clergyman stood in front of the open grave, raised the cross in both hands and began to recite a familiar Psalm. "The Lord is my Shepherd, I shall not want. He maketh me to lie down in green pastures. He leadeth me beside the still waters. He restoreth my soul. He leadeth me in the paths of righteousness for His name's sake. Yea, though I walk through the valley of the shadow of death, I will fear no evil; for thou art with me."

The pallbearers set the coffin on a bier atop the grave and joined the throng gathered on the hillside.

Keri glanced at the stone marker at the foot of the open grave that read "Sirak Kazerian, February 6, 1907 to February 13, 1999." His eyes tracked to the adjacent marker engraved, "Ara Kazerian, January 4, 1948 to October 3, 1983." Taking a deep breath, he peered up through the branches of a massive oak at the threatening sky.

"Dear Lord," the clergyman called out in a resonant baritone voice, "we, the friends and family of Sirak Kazerian, are gathered here to bury your loyal servant's earthly body in this final resting place. We are content in the knowledge that all is well with his soul, and that he will dwell with you in heaven forever. Sirak's son, Keri, would like to say a few words about his father's life."

Keri, looking pale and haggard, stepped in front of the grave and turned to face the gathered mourners. His face was drawn with grief. He took a deep breath and sighed despairingly. "Thank you all for coming today," he said in a near whisper. "Those of you who attended the Last Unction ceremony heard the moving eulogy delivered by Father Vasken Demirjian. He told you about Papa's service to God, the Armenian people, his family and his patients, and how, in the end, he died peacefully in his sleep. I'd just like to say a few words about what Papa meant to me. Most of you know we weren't always close. You see, for many years Papa's thoughts were dominated by the events that befell our family and him in

Anatolia, Jerusalem and here in Cleveland—including the death of my brother, Ara. But, by the grace of God, a miracle occurred and during the last few years Papa grew close to his grandsons, great-grandchildren, and me. In the end, Papa and I became very close, and for this I thank God.

"When I was young, Papa taught me the difference between right and wrong and the value of hard work and perseverance. Later in life, he taught me the importance of family and respect for the history of our people. He also taught me to love this great country that sheltered and provided for us after Mama and my sister were killed in Jerusalem. We moved here with little more than we could carry on our backs, but that didn't stop Papa from establishing a successful medical practice and helping thousands of injured and sick people. He always credited God and America for that achievement. But most importantly, Papa taught me the lesson of forgiveness he himself learned over the last few years of his life.

"I can't begin to find the words to express how important this lesson has been to my sons and me, but suffice it to say, it brought serenity and contentment to each of our lives. I'd like to invite a special guest to say a few words. What he has to say will bring perspective to Papa's incredible life. Doctor Pasha," he said with a nod.

Faruk Pasha stepped out from beneath the oak tree, gave Keri a hug and turned to the throng. Peppered with gray, and wearing a black suit, he stooped at the waist. He smiled at the crowd with heavy-lidded eyes and brushed an errant strand of hair back from his glistening forehead. "Good morning, friends. My name is Faruk Pasha. For many years, Dr. Kazerian and I were colleagues at Euclid Community Hospital, and together we took an improbable journey to forgiveness. You see, Sirak Kazerian was not only my friend; he was also my uncle, and the brother of my mother, Flora."

A murmur ran through the mourners. David looked up with surprise and glanced at an equally shocked Michael.

"Since I'm a Turk, I believe most of you understand that truly *is* a miracle. But Sirak and I weren't always friends; in fact, even though we were both born near the same small village in Anatolia, attended the same medical school in Beirut and, by chance, worked in the same medical facility, ate in the same cafeteria, and served on the same hospital committees, we never uttered a single word to each other for over two years. Then, in 1980, something truly miraculous happened here in Cleveland. This great man, Sirak Kazerian, without regard for his own career or the security of his family, rescued me from circumstances that surely would've destroyed my career. Dr. Kazerian risked *everything* for me, a Turk, even though he never imagined in his wildest dreams he was my uncle." Pasha smiled munificently.

"He learned the truth about our common ancestry a short time later when he came to my house for dinner and discovered a photograph of his sister, Flora, my mother, hanging on the wall in our dining room. But even then, he never told me. I only learned the truth three days ago when Keri Kazerian telephoned me after his father's death.

"When I arrived in Cleveland, Keri shared with me the details of his father's past, and what had happened to Dr. Kazerian as a child, and to his parents and brothers and sisters. What a remarkable life this great man lived! It was a life filled with horrible tragedy, but also enormous courage, sacrifice, faith and hope. After Keri talked with me, I kept wondering why Dr. Kazerian never told me he was my uncle, why he didn't tell me about my mother, his sister. As I thought about his life, and everything that had happened to him, I finally understood.

"He thought the truth about my father and the abduction and forced marriage of my mother would shake not only my world, but my children's world, too. And that, in a nutshell, is who Sirak Kazerian was—a man who *always* put the feelings of others ahead of his own. I'm sure it'll take a long time for me to come to grips with all that's happened. But this information also brought a new sense of compassion and understanding to my life, and for that I am grateful.

"As I stand here today, it is my hope that Sirak Kazerian's life can foster healing and understanding and build a bridge between two great peoples, the Armenians and the Turks, in the same way his death built a bridge between two unlikely families." Pasha lapsed into silence.

He turned slightly, stared at the casket for a moment, and then looked up at the mourners. "It will, of course, be difficult to achieve this reconciliation, but it's not impossible. It must begin one person at a time, and grow through understanding and compassion for the suffering of others. Sirak came to understand this, and now I understand this, too. May God bless His great servant Sirak Kazerian and bring peace to his soul."

Faruk nodded to Keri. "Thank you," he muttered. Glancing once more at Sirak's coffin, he bowed his head and walked over to David and Michael.

David smiled warmly and took Faruk's hand. In that instant, the sun broke through the clouds and shone brightly on Sirak's grave.

GLOSSARY

Abee, Arabic, term for father

Ajaweed, Arabic, the very religious people among the Druze

Al-Hakim, Arabic, worshiped by the Druze (al-Hakim, 985–1021, an Ismaili caliph) as the embodiment of God

Bedel or bedel-i askeri, Arabic, a tax paid for exemption from military service in the Ottoman Empire

Cheki, Ottoman, a unit of weight, 1 cheki = 175–195 okka = 225–250 kilograms

Chetes, Turkish, paramilitary bands often formed of criminals and bandits taken from prison

Choereg bread, Armenian, a slightly sweet bread popular with Armenians

Effendi, Turkish, Used as a title of respect for men in Turkey, equivalent to *sir.*

Habibi, Arabic, word that literally means my beloved. It is commonly also used for friend, darling and similar endearments.

Hikmah, Arabic, the Druze religious laws

Juhhāl Arabic, in the Druze religion, the "ignorant" Druze people who do not know Druze doctrine. The majority of Druze who are not *Uqqāl.*

Kelek raft, Turkish, raft made of inflated animal skins tied together and floored over with reeds.

Khalwa, Arabic, a Druze house of worship

Khan, Turkish, a lodge or crude shelter used by travelers for rest

Kufiya, Arabic, traditional headdress typically worn by men that is made of a square of cloth, usually cotton, folded and wrapped in various styles around the head

Kurus, Ottoman Turkish, a standard unit of currency in the Ottoman Empire

Lira, Turkish, Turkish gold lira was equal to 100 kurus

Muwahhidun, Arabic, term the Druze use to refer to their religion and people

Porteños, Spanish, a term used to refer to residents of Buenos Aires, Argentina

Shalwar, Hindi, loose, pajama like full-length garment worn by both men and women in India and Southeast Asia

Shirwal, Arabic, baggy traditional pants

Uqqāl, Arabic, in the Druze religion, an elite of initiates who alone know Druze doctrine

Ummee, Arabic, term for mother

ALSO BY STEVEN E. WILSON

Winter in Kandahar

Kandahar, Afghanistan, al-Qaida, the Taliban, and the Northern Alliance—history recorded forever. These names conjure images of rugged mountains, ancient cities, hardened Mujaheddin, a country rife with regional rivalries, and the eternal struggle between Tajik and Pashtun. They are indelibly recorded in history. Afghanistan comes to life in this epic adventure of love, betrayal, and war. Young Tajik Ahmed Jan's heroic journey begins in the Northern Alliance stronghold near Taloqan just a month prior to the al-Qaida 9/11 conspiracy. He is swept away by the chaos that soon engulfs the country before a chance discovery propels him to the forefront of the clash between civilizations. Pursued by both the CIA and al-Qaida, he struggles to save his people from obliteration and find the true meaning of life in a land where all seems lost.

Benjamin Franklin Award Finalist, Best New Voice in Fiction, 2004
Bowker's Recommended List, September, 2003

Ascent from Darkness

An international thriller of espionage, war, and love, interwoven with profound, world-changing current events. Reluctant CIA operative Stone Waverly is sent to hunt down weapons-grade plutonium stolen from a Ukrainian nuclear plant. The shadowy trail leads from Odessa to Cologne to Amsterdam to Damascus, as agents with terror links manage to evade an international dragnet. Tormented by his past and the betrayals of a fellow operative and those he loves most, Waverly is plunged into a mysterious and perilous world of intrigue and evil in Syria and war-torn Iraq. Everyone is suspect and nothing is as it seems, in a land where Islamic extremists determined to plunge civilization into darkness battle Special Forces, Kurds, and Arabs intent on restoring sanity, dignity, and hope to a world gone mad.

2008 Next Generation Indie Book Award Finalist, Action-Adventure
"An intense, action-packed thriller from cover to cover. Also highly recommended is Wilson's previous novel."-Midwest Book Review

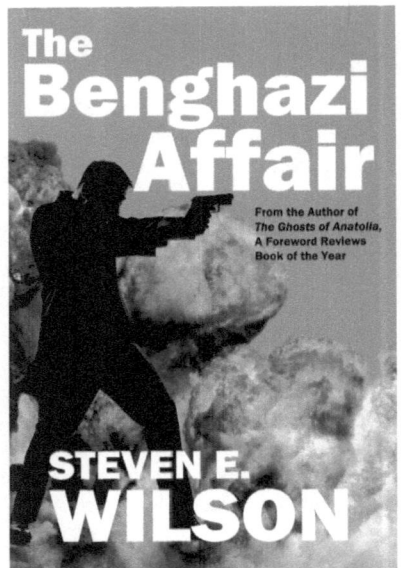

From the Author of
The Ghosts of Anatolia,
A Foreword Reviews
Book of the Year

The Benghazi Affair

Retired CIA case officer extraordinaire, Stone Waverly, is contentedly caring for his motherless children and teaching precocious middle schoolers, when out of the blue, duty calls once again. Within hours, he finds himself leading a team of covert operators in treacherous revolutionary Benghazi during the Arab Spring. Battling Gaddafi loyalists, and purportedly allied jihadists, he surreptitiously hunts for a terrifying weapon before it can be unleashed on the US homeland. Can he prevail where nothing is as it seems, despite severe injury, unsettling events at home, captivity in a chamber of horrors, and betrayal by a compatriot? The odds are stacked against him and time is running out.